THE TURNING OF OUR BONES

DI ROB MARSHALL

BOOK ONE

ED JAMES

OTHER BOOKS BY ED JAMES

DI ROB MARSHALL SCOTT BORDERS MYSTERIES

Ed's first new police procedural series in six years, focusing on DI Rob Marshall, a criminal profiler turned detective. London-based, an old case brings him back home to the Scottish Borders and the dark past he fled as a teenager.

1. THE TURNING OF OUR BONES
2. WHERE THE BODIES LIE (May 2023)

Also available is FALSE START, a prequel novella starring DS Rakesh Siyal, is available for **free** to subscribers of Ed's newsletter or on Amazon. Sign up at https://geni.us/EJF9FS

SCOTT CULLEN MYSTERIES

Eight novels featuring a detective eager to climb the career ladder, covering Edinburgh and its surrounding counties, and further across Scotland.

1. GHOST IN THE MACHINE
2. DEVIL IN THE DETAIL
3. FIRE IN THE BLOOD
4. STAB IN THE DARK
5. COPS & ROBBERS
6. LIARS & THIEVES
7. COWBOYS & INDIANS
8. HEROES & VILLAINS

CULLEN & BAIN SERIES

Six novellas spinning off from the main Cullen series covering the events of the global pandemic in 2020.

1. CITY OF THE DEAD
2. WORLD'S END
3. HELL'S KITCHEN
4. GORE GLEN
5. DEAD IN THE WATER
6. THE LAST DROP

CRAIG HUNTER SERIES

A spin-off series from the Cullen series, with Hunter first featuring in the fifth book, starring an ex-squaddie cop struggling with PTSD, investigating crimes in Scotland and further afield.

1. MISSING
2. HUNTED
3. THE BLACK ISLE

DS VICKY DODDS SERIES

Gritty crime novels set in Dundee and Tayside, featuring a DS juggling being a cop and a single mother.

1. BLOOD & GUTS
2. TOOTH & CLAW
3. FLESH & BLOOD
4. SKIN & BONE
5. GUILT TRIP

DI SIMON FENCHURCH SERIES

Set in East London, will Fenchurch ever find what happened to his daughter, missing for the last ten years?

1. THE HOPE THAT KILLS
2. WORTH KILLING FOR
3. WHAT DOESN'T KILL YOU
4. IN FOR THE KILL
5. KILL WITH KINDNESS
6. KILL THE MESSENGER
7. DEAD MAN'S SHOES
8. A HILL TO DIE ON
9. THE LAST THING TO DIE

Other Books

Other crime novels, with Lost Cause set in Scotland and Senseless set in southern England, and the other three set in Seattle, Washington.

- LOST CAUSE
- SENSELESS
- TELL ME LIES
- GONE IN SECONDS
- BEFORE SHE WAKES

CHAPTER ONE
KATE
TWO YEARS AGO

Middle of summer and Kate Pierce finally felt cool air on her skin. The temperature had dipped to almost warm, rather than melting your bones.

She walked away from the hospital, yawning into her fist. Half past four and the sun was still asleep, like the rest of London. She needed her bed and it'd be a while until she got there. She halted at the bus stop and a second yawn engulfed her.

She opened her eyes again and the bus was waiting there.

Hadn't heard it arrive. She stepped onboard and swiped her Oyster card. The machine beeped and flashed red.

The driver was a big guy, strong and lean. Pencil-line beard. Ice-cold eyes. 'Swipe it again, darling.' The guy was looking her up and down.

Perv.

Kate swiped again and it beeped. Green. She smiled at the guy – just because he was a perv didn't mean he didn't deserve to be treated with respect – then walked upstairs.

Just one guy up there, sitting at the back. Phone blasting out music. Stinking of ganja.

Kate sat right at the front and nudged her earbuds in. Billie Eilish picked up where she'd left her earlier. She shut her eyes, drifting away into the null space where—

Someone prodded her shoulder.

Kate jerked forward, music still blaring in her ears.

Donny. Smiling at her. Baseball cap low.

Where the hell had he come from?

She paused the music and eased the earbuds out. 'Sorry, I was half asleep there.'

'Looked fully asleep, Katie.' He laughed. 'How you doing?'

'Knackered. Long shift. Tough times we live in.'

'Tell me about it.'

'How are you, Donny? Things getting any better?'

He sat on the seat over the aisle from her, clutching his own phone, staring out at the passing city. 'Not so great, but thanks for asking. Just been to see Mum. They're great at the hospice, you know, letting me in after hours and all that. Because of my shifts.' He looked out of the side window. 'Not long left, they say.'

'I'm so sorry to hear that.'

'Is what it is, eh?' Donny turned back around. 'Enough about me and my travails. You just off work?'

'Yeah. Tough shift today. Covering A&E. Thursday nights are almost as bad as Fridays now.'

'Know what you mean. Coke's so cheap these days, all the nut jobs are doing so many lines their hearts explode. Or they're kicking lumps out of each other.'

'That. Exactly that.'

'Tough one.'

Kate looked out the front. The art deco curves of Willesden

Green Station lurked in the shadows up ahead. 'Sorry, Donny, this is my stop.'

'Oh, yeah. Sorry. See you around, Katie.' He nodded at her then slid over to the window side of his seat.

'You too.' She got to her feet but she was so dog tired. Took all she had to traipse back to the stairs. The bus brakes hissed and she scurried down as fast as she could go, yawning all the way.

Felt a lot more tired tonight than in ages.

She stepped out into the cool air and eased her earbuds back in and let Billie guide her home. One foot in front of the other. That was all she needed to do. Soon she'd be curled up in bed, ready to start all over again tomorrow.

A run, definitely. Ten miles too. Sod her shift, she needed to get fit for the marathon. If she wasn't up to fifteen by September, she should pull out.

She was so tired and her shoulder hurt now. Must've caught it at work.

There it was. Home. Her poky little flat, stuck on the top floor of a block. Two rooms, but *her* two rooms. Hers and the bank's.

Some absolute twat had parked a work van outside, bumped onto the pavement.

If it wasn't gone in the morning, she'd call the number on the side. Hang on, there wasn't one.

Sod it – Brent council would be getting that call. Tow the bloody thing away.

She squeezed past it, brushing her arm against the wall, and got onto her drive.

Someone grabbed her from behind, wrapping an arm around her throat. A hand covered her mouth. She tried kicking out, tried punching, but she was off her feet now. Her left earbud dropped out and she tried screaming for help.

'MMMMF!'

She was dropped onto a hard metal floor. A strong hand pinned her down by her mouth. Something went in her mouth, tasted burnt like ash.

The van.

She was inside the van.

The door slid shut.

Too dark to see now.

She tried screaming again, but nothing came out.

CHAPTER TWO
MARSHALL

Not even ten o'clock and the office was hot and dry like a kiln. DI Rob Marshall felt like he was being fired in one. Still, lumps of clay didn't sweat like this. He brushed the latest bead off his forehead, but it had nowhere to go – his hair was soaked already. His thick Scottish blood just couldn't cope with the heat of London. The windows were wide open, letting in a toxic blend of curry, half-baked pizza dough and traffic fumes, without letting out any heat or creating much of a through draught.

London in summer. Got to love it.

'How can I work in this temperature?'

'Stop complaining, Rob.' DCI Tina Rickards stood next to the whiteboard, hands in the pockets of her navy suit. Cream blouse open to the neck. Greying hair hauled back in a brutal ponytail that smoothed out her forehead. Up close, Marshall realised he was inside her reality distortion field – those big brown eyes made you forget what the hell you were doing and just believe everything she said. Listen to her and only her. She took her hand out of her pocket and ran her finger across three sheets of A3 Marshall had taped together and stuck on the wall.

A map of Greater London, with red and blue pins stuck in Acton, Brent, Hendon, Harlesden, Willesden and Cricklewood.

All inside their patch of West London.

Where their victims had been abducted.

Where their victims' bodies had been found.

She stepped away from the board like it might bite, then glanced over at Marshall. 'I don't see it, Rob.'

Wear your bloody glasses, then...

Marshall swallowed it down instead of saying it out loud. He moved towards the board and tapped the map, his damp finger blurring the printer ink. 'You asked me to do a geographic profile, boss, so please do me the courtesy of considering what I'm trying to tell you.'

She grinned at him. 'Maybe try a bit harder, then.' The grin was fleeting. 'Seriously, though. A geographic profile has to be more than sticking pins on a board.'

'And it is. But sometimes we miss the obvious.'

'Explain this to me like I'm five.'

Marshall clamped his jaw and let his swallowed sigh fizz out through his nostrils. 'Each of these red pins represents a victim's abduction site. These blue pins are the drop sites where we found the bodies.'

'Rob, I don't see the pattern.'

'Right. Ignore the blues.' Marshall swept his hand around the map, spraying dots of sweat as he drew a line from memory. 'Those red dots are all within five streets of a night bus stop on the N266 route.'

She looked over at him, head tilted to the side. 'Seriously?'

'No, I'm just making it up to look clever.' Marshall walked over to the victim board. Names and faces. Lives all laid out. 'Our guy's MO is abducting women during the night, raping and torturing them for a *week*, then murdering them and dumping their bodies. With all five victims there's evidence of repeated sexual assault, either bodily or with an object, if he was impotent.' He felt that wave of nausea, the realisation that the data was people's lives. 'Previously, we had a match in victim age, gender and time-delay. And the complete lack of forensics on the bodies. Now, we've got one in geography, which solidifies the theory of there being a connection between them all.'

'And that's supposed to make me feel more positive, is it?'

Marshall could see the stress in her eyes. Crow's feet around both. Grey hairs that hadn't been there at the start of this case. Hours of sleep that had been replaced with strong coffee. He wanted to give her some hope. 'Here's the thing. I noticed in the file that the last victim, Deanna Casey, worked at Charing Cross Hospital.'

The best photo they had of Deanna was from a friend's Instagram. Pulling rap star poses in some West End nightclub, clutching a bottle of champagne.

In the weeks between lockdowns last year.

Killed during one this year.

'Her mother told us Deanna would get that bus home after her shift.' Marshall pointed at the map way below their focus. 'Caught it from the station near Hammersmith Tube. And that got me thinking. Victim two, Angela Warburton.'

A demure passport photo, no expression on her face, blown up to A4 for their murder board.

'Angela worked as a cleaner in the City.' Marshall waved over to the east, past the end of his map. 'Every night, she'd catch the District line from Cannon Street to Hammersmith. But then she caught the night bus up to Brent.' Marshall tapped the Tube station on the map. 'Both of them did the same commute every night. Repeatable patterns. And repeatable patterns give an assailant an opportunity to observe and then strike.'

Rickards was frowning, her forehead all creased now. 'You think our guy saw these women on the bus home from work?'

'It's a theory. And it seems to fit.'

'And does it fit the other victims?'

'I don't know yet. I've—'

'You don't *know*?'

'I only spotted this ten minutes ago and have only just now requested the Oyster and bank card payment data from Transport for London. We'll hopefully be able to tie it all together, but it'll take time and some persuasion.'

'Okay, but the interviews should—'

'I've been through the files, several times. We don't have the data.'

'We haven't asked about their *jobs*?'

'No, we have. We just haven't got any detail on their commutes. Unless you live with someone, the exact minutiae of how you get to and from work are likely to be entirely private matters.'

That seemed to pacify her a bit. Saved half the team from an arse-kicking.

'Listen, boss, what I'm doing here is trying to find gaps in *our* thinking. That could be where we get leads to allow us to catch this guy.'

She gave him a nod, but someone was going to get into trouble. 'Go on.'

'Okay. We know that all five victims were single women, who lived on their own and worked evenings and nights. My thinking is that nobody was expecting them home at a certain time, so nobody knew their routes. Except maybe our killer.'

'So you think we have a connection?'

'I'm beginning to think we might.' Marshall uncapped the

pen and started writing on the blank whiteboard: 'STREET TEAM'. 'We need to get these guys asking the victims' families about their commutes.'

Her jaw was clenched tight. 'Obviously.'

The pen squeaked as Marshall wrote 'SURVEILLANCE'. 'We need to get these guys prioritising night bus footage, matching it with Oyster card data. See if this holds water.'

Rickards coughed out a sigh, then clicked her tongue. 'Rob, when we hired you, I expected you to give me solutions, but all you're giving me is more and more problems.'

'If I show you where the problems are, we can *all* find solutions. Criminal profiling and analysis provides common threads and directions. In my old job as a profiler, I had to inspect the data, in whatever form that took, and pull together testable theories. Handing them off to the police to do was pretty frustrating, but now I get to do the testing myself. See how the data stacks up against reality.'

'Okay, so does this change your profile?'

Marshall stared at the map, but didn't focus on it. 'I don't think so. Our guy is a... All we know from months of work is...' He ran a hand through his damp hair. 'It's not a lot. But. That guy we spoke to, the friend of Erin Nash...'

Her name was first on the board. Victim one. Up in Brent, near the infamous shopping centre. Her photo was culled from Instagram, a pouting selfie with wild corkscrews of hair that could've been anyone's daughter. Pen lines led out of her shot, connecting friends and family, with small photos of them all. Even at that size and on crap inkjet paper, Derek Cameron's bright blue eyes glowed.

'Mr Cameron here went to school with Erin. Mates all their lives. He said Erin was in the very early stages of a relationship with someone. Didn't know who.' Marshall stepped back from the board, like he was zooming out on the story. 'These women were all in that situation. Told friends they're seeing someone.'

'Right. And?'

'My profile says our guy's a loner. I'm guessing he sits on the bus, watching the women getting on. Doesn't chat them up, but just notices them. Say one night our guy spots a young woman on the bus he's taking home. Likes the look of her. Then he sees her the next night. And the next. Soon he's getting the bus from the next stop and only gets off if she's there. And he's building up a pattern of her life from this parasocial relationship.'

'Parasocial?'

'One-way. Like someone who listens to the radio or watches a TV show. They build up this relationship with the presenters, they feel like they know them, even though they can't.'

'And you think our guy's doing that?'

'More and more. He follows them home, develops a picture of them. Knows which ones are single and who live alone. Knows their lives better than they do. So one day he can be there when they drop their purse in the street. Knight in shining armour. He's got an in.'

'We don't know any of that, Rob. That's a lot of extrapolation.'

'I don't disagree, but I think we can at least agree that the guy our victims have all been seeing is the same man.'

'If that's right, Rob, we've got names for them, apart from Erin Nash.'

Marshall scanned the board, picking out the named boxes in each woman's section. 'Names we can't track down. I'm thinking aliases for the same man.'

'So he's running several pseudonyms at once?'

Marshall looked at the dates of the abductions, starting

three months apart but now narrowing to three weeks. 'I don't know that yet. It's going to take a lot of work correlating the victims' travel data with CCTV.'

'Hundreds of hours...' Rickards took the pen and jotted something down that Marshall couldn't read. 'We should still dig down deeper into the names, maybe find out his roots. In my experience, where I walked the streets as a cop instead of messing about with profiles—' She gave him some side eye. '—anytime someone does this level of lying, they have to embroider their own life into it, build lies around that central truth. Meaning we might already have where he's originally from, who he really is.'

Marshall disagreed with that, but then they were very different cops, with very different backgrounds.

She recapped the pen. 'What's your plan, Rob?'

'Until we've got the CCTV footage and know the commutes of the other victims, I want a team staking out Hammersmith Tube. Seeing who gets on the bus. If anyone's acting suspiciously, we tail the bus until they get off.'

'So you're just hoping to spot an abduction vehicle? You think we could strike lucky?'

'Not at all. Luck has nothing to do with it. If I'm right and he's been on the same bus with these women every night, he'll probably be on that bus tonight. Meaning he's there tonight, staking out victim six.'

Rickards shut her eyes.

'It might seem like a waste of time, boss, but I think it could lead to a face, to a name, to a suspect. Someone we already know.'

She shook her head. 'You should've stayed as a criminal profiler.'

And you should try being a cop.

Marshall raised his hands. 'I've got issues with your attitude here, but I'll park them.' He walked back to the map. 'I think there's something in this. He's got a cooldown period of three months between murders, but I'm thinking it's closer to a month, with two months of detailed and painstaking observation. I think he's already doing it again, and if he is, we can find our guy.'

The hairs on Rickards's arm rose. 'God damn you, Rob.' She winced. 'You're giving me hope.'

'Hope's important. It's what keeps us all alive.'

'Fine. I'll okay this operation.' She pointed a finger at him. 'But you're doing the first shift tonight.'

Shite.

He was going to have to let her down, big time.

CHAPTER THREE

The Tube station swelled, letting out another wave of commuters. Men and women in suits, most carrying briefcases and wearing trainers, spreading out. A couple strolled over to that new hipster café, another into the craft beer place next door that was all upturned crates and broken chairs, but most went home.

Marshall drummed his thumbs off the steering wheel. Parked on the corner, so he could keep an eye on both exits. If anyone was going to come out of the wrong one, it was her.

Still no sign.

Wait.

There she was. Dark hair scraped back into a long ponytail. Too much makeup. Typical Scottish woman on holiday, dressed for a Spanish beach rather than West London. Hot, sure, but not *that* hot.

Wheeling her suitcase behind her, lips moving, moaning about something. Anything.

Marshall got out of the car and waved. 'Jen!'

She leaned over to point at him.

Thea looked up, frowning. She was a lot taller than when Marshall last saw her, all willowy now and on that cusp of child and adult. Her torso-length blonde hair was now a smart bob. Jeans and long-sleeved Ms Marvel T-shirt. Aye, she was a teenager.

Marshall met them halfway across the road and reached for their luggage.

Jen slapped his hand away, then charged over to his car. Standing there, shaking her head.

Marshall walked over and opened the boot. 'Will you let me at least put them in here for you?'

Jen tried lifting her case, then scowled at him. 'On you go then.' She walked around to the front of the car and got in.

'Your mum's in a smashing mood.'

Thea was standing there, arms folded, rolling her eyes. 'Been like that all the way from Berwick. Almost killed someone outside King's Cross.'

'Sounds about right.' Marshall slammed the boot, then let Thea into the back. He shut the door then took a second to suck in a deep breath, filled with diesel and cigarette smoke. He covered his face in a smile and got in. 'Next stop, home.' He gunned the engine and pulled out as a bus pulled in, giving him a clear run at it. 'Listen, I've got to work tonight.'

He caught Jen sneering at him. 'Are you serious?'

'Sorry. It's later on. We can still go out first.'

She snorted.

'This case is killing me, Jen. Great to see you both, though.'

'Jesus Christ, Rob. That's it?'

'What do you want me to say?'

'A lot more than that.'

'Mum, simmer down.'

Jen twisted to look behind at her daughter. 'Less of that cheek, young lady.' She looked at Marshall. 'We're getting the

Eurostar in the morning. Would've just flown from Edinburgh if I'd known you were bumping us.'

'You say that like I have any control over my life these days.'

'Still doesn't mean I'm happy about it.' Jen folded her arms. 'Your mother was as fun as ever.'

'Sorry I wasn't there with you.'

'Are you? Because she—'

'*Mum*, you're being a bitch.'

Jen leaned around again. 'Thea, I told you to never use that word.'

'Sorry, Mum. But you are.'

Marshall parked outside his flat. Actually managed to claim the golden space. Aside from everything falling to shit today, having this one stroke of luck made it all feel almost okay.

Thea got out onto the street first and walked around to the boot.

Marshall let his seatbelt go and turned around. 'You okay, Jen?'

'I'm totally fine, *Rob*.'

'So why are you acting like that?'

'I'm fine.'

But he could tell the smile was plastered on. 'What's happened? Is everything okay with Paul?'

'Oh, it's just peachy.'

'You can talk to me.'

'You're my brother, not my shrink.' She got out and slammed the door.

Aye, something was going down, but she'd never tell him. Not that he could talk...

He let out a sigh and got out.

Jen was simpering at someone, acting like a flirtatious teenager.

Marshall saw why.

DS John Hulse was leaning against his front door, foot pressed back. Thick beard that just elongated his pointed chin rather than softening it. Dead eyes scanning the street, then flicking over to Marshall, showing that scar that ran from his left earlobe up to his hairline. 'Jen, isn't it?' Gruff accent without the usual Northumbrian lilt or cheer. 'Can see the family resemblance.'

'You must be John. Rob's told me a lot about you.'

'Bet he has. With some fiction thrown in for good measure. Down for long?'

'Just an overnighter. Rob's promised us dinner and a show.'

'Sounds good. Shame, though.'

'Eh?' Marshall frowned at him. 'What are you talking about?'

Hulse tilted his head to the side. 'Sorry, boss is calling us back in now to run through tonight's obbo.'

Marshall took a deep breath. 'There's a reason I turned my phone off.'

'Aye, she knows. Hence me being here.'

Bollocks.

First time he was going to see his sister and niece in bloody ages and it all got screwed up.

'Catch.' Marshall tossed his house keys to Jen. 'I've made up the spare beds for you both. There's food in the fridge. Please, can you feed Zlatan for me? He goes a bit feral if he doesn't eat.'

'You're expecting us to feed your cat for you?'

Marshall looked up at the blue sky. 'Unfortunately, duty calls. And you don't want to know what it's about.'

CHAPTER FOUR

They were parked by a stop on the main road, watching Hammersmith bus station. The name made it seem grander than it was – two stances facing each other at angles. At least, that's what Marshall thought they were called.

The night bus rested there, ready to ferry those Tuesday-night drunks who couldn't take a cab, along with the night-shift workers who kept the whole city ticking.

Offices overlooked them on both sides, though most seemed to be empty, save for the occasional glimpse of a cleaner in a solitary bank of activated lights.

Five minutes past midnight and Marshall let out one of those yawns that kept on going, vibrating down into his ribcage. He snapped it off and tried to blink himself awake. 'Got time for a coffee?'

Hulse was behind the wheel, hands clamped around it. 'Nope.'

'Fair enough.' Marshall wound down the window but it didn't seem to let out any heat. Even at this time. Felt like it let some in, if anything. Charcoal flavoured the air, making Marshall's stomach rumble. 'Sure we haven't got time?'

'Sure.' Hulse tapped the clock on the middle of the dashboard. 'Nine minutes now.'

'Even if I order you to get one, Sergeant?'

Hulse huffed out a sigh. 'Especially if.'

'I'll get them. Flat white?'

'Please.'

Marshall sprang out of the car into the bright night and walked towards the shops nestled around the Tube station. Nobody else, so he got straight up to the counter. 'Two flat whites, please.'

'On it.' The bearded hipster set about his espresso machine with gusto, ba-baing along with the Sixties music playing. The deep, caramel tang of grinding coffee beans.

Marshall walked up to the window and scanned the area around the bus again. Two nurses walked up to it, yawning. Too old for the profile. Maybe.

A drunk staggered along the street, constantly checking his watch.

Marshall leaned forward – could be an act.

Nope, he threw up all over a bin. Then staggered on up the road, away from the bus.

Leaving two possible victims.

No. They were travelling together. That was too much risk for their guy.

A woman got on, nervously paying for her ticket.

DS Arya Patel, dressed like she was cleaning offices.

Good.

Then another followed her onto the bus. A woman with shiny blonde hair. She matched the victimology perfectly.

A man hopped on behind her, then waited as the woman paid, scanning the street.

She went upstairs, claiming the seat at the front.

The man got off the bus, shaking his head at something. Maybe too drunk to get on. He wandered over to a kebab shop and slipped inside.

A possible.

Marshall jotted down his appearance in his notebook. Baseball cap, heavy bomber jacket, black trousers, rucksack. Didn't get a good look at his face, though.

His phone chimed. A text from Arya:

One possible. Didn't have a fare. Oyster card didn't work. Told to get off.

Thanks.

'Here you go, man.' The barista had two coffees in a cardboard tray. Plain cups with black lids. The sort of cool that hipsters the world over loved. 'Six quid.' He pointed at the card machine like a magician's assistant.

Marshall paid with his mobile. 'Thanks.' He grabbed the coffees and set off back to the car. No change at the bus, as far as he could see. He got back into the passenger seat. 'Not cheap.'

'Nothing ever is with you. But you were quick, so it was worth it. Three minutes to go.'

Marshall tore open the lid and sucked in the aroma. Dark and smoky. 'Smells good. Anything?'

'Nope. Well, maybe.' Hulse rested the coffee in the holder and showed his notebook – he'd noted down the same four passengers.

Worst case, they'd see the same people the next night. If the drunk was one of them, well – he was getting spoken to.

And the kebab shop guy...

Buzz. Another text from his sister:

Good luck with the case. Say hi to John for me.

She'd forgiven him at least.

Marshall looked over at Hulse. 'Jen says hi.'

Hulse stared hard at him, slurping his coffee like it wasn't at boiling point. 'Jen?'

Coy sod...

'My sister. It was her at my flat this evening when you picked me up.'

Hulse was blinking hard now. 'Your *little* sister.'

'Twin.'

Hulse frowned at him. 'How does that work? You look nothing alike.'

'We're fraternal twins. Two separate eggs fertilised around the same time. Identical twins are where one fertilised egg splits.'

'Right.'

'She's married, dude.'

Hulse was still scanning the area. 'Who is?'

'Jen.'

'Spoke to her for a couple of minutes while you were in the shower. That's it. Thought she was someone you were seeing.'

Marshall had that stabbing in his heart. 'I'm not seeing anyone, John. I told you that.'

Hulse sniffed. 'Anyway, the bus is leaving. We following?'

'Who's on board?'

'Two women downstairs, one up. DS Patel's at the back. No masked serial killers.'

'I didn't expect him to get on at the same spot every night. This is going to take a lot of manpower, John. Besides, are you saying women can't kill?'

'Nope. Your profile does. Says our guy is a guy. Meaning they haven't killed our victims.'

'Fair enough.' Marshall got that flush of heat up his neck. 'This is why I requested someone else to do the profiling, but Rickards hasn't got the budget. I tell you, John, the pressure that comes from pulling together a criminal profile, where everyone's looking at you, expecting you to have all the answers. To know who killed them and why. No surprise why I gave all that up to become a cop, is it?'

'Nope. We following?'

Marshall took a sip of strong coffee. 'I was thinking the killer got on the bus at the station. Here. But what if it's the second stop? Or the third? What if it's in Acton or any stops up that way?'

'Police work, mate.' Hulse drank some coffee like that explained his comment. 'Besides, Arya Patel's on that bus. She'll keep a note of who's coming on and getting off.'

This was a much bigger operation than Marshall had expected. And it was also a total punt. He was desperate to catch the killer, but this wasn't so much clutching at straws as...

Where did that phrase come from?

He pictured someone drawing the short straw from a bundle of longer ones. That felt like that was his life. Always going first, always dared to do something, always coming up short.

'Where does "clutching at straws" come from?'

'Reeds.'

'Reeds?'

'Drowning man clutching at the reeds on the riverside. Call them straws.'

'Huh.' Marshall could see it. It fit even more. And he *was* drowning. The weight of those five women who'd been killed.

The weight of the future victims who were being targeted right now. And maybe the past ones they'd missed. Maybe Erin Nash wasn't the first. Maybe there were ten like her before. Maybe he hadn't escalated to murder.

'We following the bus or not?'

Marshall sat back and sipped hot coffee. 'No.'

'Sure?'

Marshall nodded, but didn't want to. Nodding meant admitting defeat, that his theory was wrong. For the first bus anyway. 'According to the street team, our third victim, Keisha Holloway, got the third bus of the night.' He could see her profile photo in his mind's eye – head tilted forward, left eyebrow raised. 'So let's sit here for the first three buses and see if anyone tickles our fancy. We've got three cops on each of those buses. Pool car following, on high alert.'

'Then?'

'Then we get back to the station and savour the burn of the coals we're being dragged over.'

'You're the boss.'

A man walked up to Marshall's open window and peered in. 'Hello, John. Hello, Robert.'

Baseball cap. Bomber jacket. Backpack.

Thin to the point of gaunt. The pale skin and dark eye shadows of someone who worked late and didn't sleep much. Buzzing with energy. His bright blue eyes were like lasers.

Marshall recognised him.

Derek Cameron, the friend of Erin Nash from her high school class. The one who'd told them about her new boyfriend.

It all fitted together.

In Marshall's profile, their guy was someone who knew the first victim. Then carried on from there. Cameron had an alibi, though. They'd checked it.

And Marshall had thought he'd gleaned some precious insight, but in reality they'd fallen into Derek Cameron's trap. They were flies stuck in his web.

Their first night? He'd expected weeks of this. But Derek Cameron was the man getting on the bus, the one Arya saw get chucked off. He must've seen Marshall or Hulse. Spooked him.

Why not run?

Marshall stayed perfectly still. 'What do you want, Derek?' Use his name, let him know you know.

Derek put a gun to Marshall's cheek. 'I'm going to kill you.'

Everything in Marshall's body clenched. He didn't stare at the gun. Didn't even glance at Derek. Just looked right ahead. 'Not playing that game, Derek.'

'So you know who I am?'

'You picked them out on the night bus, didn't you?'

'Shut up.'

'That where you saw Erin? Your old schoolfriend. Got chatting to her one night. Then started following her, learned everything about her new life. Then you took her off the street in a van. Kept her somewhere. Raped her. Tortured her. Then dumped her body in a river.'

'I said, shut up.'

Marshall knew he needed to keep him talking. 'And then one night, you were on the night bus, maybe a bit drunk, but maybe not. Those voices were speaking again. Telling you how hungry they were. And you spotted Deanna Casey. She looks a bit like Erin, but she was wearing a nurse's uniform under her clothes. So you knew she worked at a hospital. You got the bus the next night and there she was. You kept getting that bus, then you followed her, and you knew you could do what you wanted to because of what you did to Erin.'

'About the size of it, yeah.' Derek snorted, then rubbed at his nostrils. Coke habit. Stuff was so cheap now and it got you wrecked much quicker than booze, and beer prices were shooting up. 'So, who lives, who dies?'

Marshall did a quick check of the street. Wing mirrors too. Nothing. No sign of their uniform backup.

Hulse looked over. 'Give yourself up, Derek.'

Derek shrugged. He shifted the gun away from Marshall's skin and fired.

Hulse screamed.

Derek moved the gun back to Marshall. His finger started squeezing the trigger.

Marshall popped his seat's recline lever.

The round missed Marshall.

The glass smashed.

Hulse grunted. Screamed.

Derek pointed the gun at Marshall. 'Cheeky bastard.'

Marshall was reclining. Stuck. Hardly the best way to be killed.

The gun clicked. Then again. Again. Again.

For all of Cameron's bravado, he only had two bullets.

Derek ran off, away from the bus station.

Marshall could get out, chase after him. Catch the Chameleon.

Hulse was gurgling. His chest was already a red mess. His leg was even worse. 'Go... after... him!'

Not an option.

Marshall reached for his radio. 'This is Serial Bravo requesting urgent medical attention to Hammersmith bus station.' He got out into the warm air and swung around.

No sign of Derek Cameron anywhere.

'Officer shot. Repeat, officer shot.' He got back into the car and gunned the engine, tugging on his seatbelt as he shot off towards Charing Cross Hospital. 'Stay with me, John!'

CHAPTER FIVE

WENDY

TWO YEARS LATER

Wendy blinked awake. Dark and hard to make anything out.

She tried to move but fire burnt in her wrists.

She tried to move her feet. Same.

Tied up.

Someone had tied her up.

What the hell?

She kicked and thrashed and punched but she couldn't move.

Her breathing was fast and heavy. Coming through her nostrils. Something filled her mouth. A rag. It tasted all eggy. Dry. She couldn't open her lips. Couldn't even move them.

She was stuck here, wherever here was.

Who had her?

Why?

Why was she here?

Why had someone done this to her?

Everything hurt, like she'd been tenderised. Ready to be

cooked. Felt like her head was a marshmallow someone was toasting in a fire.

S'mores, right?

Thinking about something other than pain was good.

She tried to focus on what she could remember.

Nothing much. Sitting watching the telly on her own. She'd cooked a pasta bake, ate half. Took the bin out.

And that was it.

Someone attacked her.

She...

She could remember something. Two people. Hidden behind a wall of cheese inside her head.

Couldn't...

Did that happen? Were there two men? Or was it...?

Forget about that – she needed to figure out where the hell she was.

The heavy smell of oil.

Sounded like bullets hitting off a metal roof, but softened like it was far away. Raining.

A long swoosh. A car driving through the deep puddles.

Was she by a road?

If she could get free, she could get up and—

Someone muttered something under their breath.

She froze.

Someone was standing there. A man? Definitely. Light flashed and a phone did that camera shutter noise.

He spoke with a deep voice, even at a whisper. She couldn't make out the words. Wait, it sounded like stuff out of the Bible? What did they call it? Scripture? Was she in a church?

A light flicked on and burned her eyes. She had to blink a few times before she could keep them open. They stung like someone had poured chip vinegar into them.

He was looking down at her now. Short hair, thick beard.

Callum?

What the hell?

Was he here to save—

He grabbed her hair and lifted her head up, pain singeing her scalp, straining the back of her neck. He pressed something cold against her throat. Something sharp. A knife? 'Sorry, Wendy, but it's time.' His English accent used to sound soft and kind, but now it seemed harsh and cruel. 'I've got to do this, yeah?' He licked his lips and stared deep into her eyes. Those baby blue eyes, the ones she'd trusted, the ones she'd fallen in love with.

God.

She'd let Callum into her life and this was how he repaid her?

This was what he was doing all along? Kidnapping her just so he could kill her?

She'd been so fucking stupid.

He slammed her head back down with a crack.

She could see he was naked except for a butcher's apron, dark brown leather, covered in nicks and slices all the way up. He took out a knife sharpener and ran the blade against it, the sound like a shriek in her ears. 'Okay, so I'm going to—'

A loud trilling sound.

A mobile?

'Sorry, Wendy. I'll be right back.' He walked away.

He'd put the knife down, though. Near her hands. If she could grab it, she could angle the blade away from her and cut at her bonds.

Right?

She'd seen it in so many films.

That had to be real.

Didn't it?

She could see him, putting his phone to his ear like he was

talking to a mate. 'Hello, sir! Thank you for calling me back.' Far enough away that she could only hear his side of the conversation and only just. 'That's what I rang you about, yeah.'

She pushed her hands over and touched the tips of the fingers on her right hand against the cold steel.

Take it, cut her bonds, stab him, get out of there, get onto the road and escape.

She was struggling to reach it, though, her fingers just weren't long enough.

'Piss off. It's *always* been on your terms.' Pause. 'Because I need you to meet me on *my* terms for once. Not halfway. *My* terms. Okay?' Another pause. 'Don't make me beg. No. It's important. I need to talk to you.'

Forget stabbing him, she just needed to get out of here.

Get onto the road, flag down a car.

She heard another one passing. Must be a pretty busy street. She could maybe hide somewhere until another one came?

'We need to meet.' Pause. 'It's important. Okay, thanks. I appreciate it. Okay. Right. Yeah, I know the place. Twenty minutes. No? It's important I go back home first. It's on the way. So wait for me. Just... I'll be there.' Callum walked back over and snatched the knife from near her grasp. 'Sorry, Wendy, but I'm going to have to delay this, okay? I've got to go out. Won't be long.' His footsteps padded away.

She was back to being alone, lying on a table, squirming and desperate.

But she was still alive. She had that at least.

CHAPTER SIX

...

I stand in the rain, watching, waiting, listening to the hissing cars on the A68 just around the corner, speeding up away from the roundabout. Soaked through now because Derek's late. As ever.

The best things come to those who wait, don't they?

That's how the saying goes, right?

A deep rumble comes from the road, then a car swooshes onto the slip road, its headlights catching my own vehicle as it pulls to a halt in the old lay-by.

The engine rattles and dies, then Derek gets out into the rain, moaning about something under his breath. Typical. It's dark, but my eyes have adjusted and the full moon's visible through the thick rainclouds, so I can see him. He clearly can't see me from the wild way he's swinging his heavy-duty torch's beam around the place.

He catches me with it, but by the time the light swings back, I'm already walking away, feet splashing in the puddles. Some wooden benches wait at the bottom, carved to look like a train. The old bridge over the Tweed hangs under the modern road, but I walk away from them towards the viaduct.

I read about how the old bridge supposedly dates back to the Roman era, though it's surely been replaced in that time, at least once.

Some idiots thought Scotland hadn't been invaded by the Romans or that we'd heroically fought them off, but no – they came here, they saw us, they conquered. They just didn't fancy much north of the Forth. Down here, this would've been a glorious place to live back then, so long as you sided with them.

I'm going fast up the brae now, barely losing any breath.

I can hear Derek huffing and puffing behind me. 'Why are we meeting here?'

I don't reply, just keep on going up the hill, under the viaduct now, then I climb the steps up the steep bank onto the old railway line. A short clamber up to the mock Roman fort for children at the top, then a slower walk over to the old bridge.

Leaderfoot Viaduct, built by the Victorians to carry goods trains up to Edinburgh, full of Borders wool. Shut it after fifty years.

The big gate usually blocks it off, installed twenty years ago to prevent suicides, but tonight it's hanging open, the lock snapped with bolt cutters.

Who could've done that, eh?

I walk halfway across the bridge and wait for Derek to follow, leaning on the barrier at the side and staring down at the gurgling Tweed.

Derek stumbles towards me, panting like an overheated Labrador. 'Long way down, mate.' He doubles over, hands on his knees like a runner catching his breath. And Derek's no runner. 'Why are we meeting here?'

'This bridge is where the Tweed meets the Leader. The confluence. It's funny how one river gets to take the name, don't you think?' I point to the left. 'About seven miles that way, give or take, the Ettrick meets the Tweed between Galashiels and Selkirk. At that point, both rivers are about the same size and yet the Tweed carries the name until the North Sea, taking on the Leader here, then the Teviot, the Eden, the Whiteadder and others until the coast. A slight twist of fate and you'd be wearing your "ettrick" coat in Berwick-upon-Ettrick.'

Derek is upright now, but doesn't seem too interested. 'I don't follow.'

'Never mind.'

'Doesn't answer why we're meeting here?'

'Because there's nobody else around, Derek. It's a chance for us to speak without fear of being overheard.' I turn to face him, arms folded. 'And you called me first. What do you want to talk about?'

'I can't keep doing this.' Derek steps forward and I can see the bulge of a handgun in his thin jacket. 'The church in Melrose has been my saviour. I know I can't change what I've done, but I need to atone for my sins.'

And there it is.

Derek has finally cracked under the stress of living two distinct lives. The weight of all those secrets he's been keeping. All those lives ended and others ruined by his greed. Being on the run since that incident in London. Shooting a police officer like that. He didn't have to. He could've just fled, left them searching for him, letting the trail go cold.

But Derek Cameron is an impatient man. Incapable of restraint. Incapable of control, especially in the heat of the moment.

'You've been talking to the minister, haven't you?'

'I have been.' Derek beams at me. 'He's helped me see it all so clearly now.'

'How specific were you?'

'Oh, he's not got any grizzly details. I just talked about my guilt. My shame. About committing a crime. Several crimes. If I come clean to the police, then I'll achieve redemption.'

All I can do is laugh. 'That's the way it works with God, isn't it? You confess to all those murders and He lets you into the Kingdom of Heaven.'

Derek stares hard at me, those piercing blue eyes like signal fires in the dark night. 'Don't mock me.'

'I'm sorry. It's Saint Peter who lets you into Heaven, isn't it?'

Derek jabs a finger at me. 'I'm warning you.' The river splashes below us. 'Before I can move on, I need to get closure for my actions. All of them.'

'Derek, you've killed many women. You're a serial killer.'

'I... Yes. I am.' Derek runs a hand down his face. 'I need to save my soul for eternity.'

He really believes this.

The only solace Derek Cameron can take from his sordid life is the hope that Jesus Christ will forgive him his many, many trespasses.

'Derek, your soul's beyond tainted. If there's an afterlife, the place you're going to is very hot and lots of little red beings will poke you with red-hot sticks.'

Derek shakes his head. 'I knew you wouldn't understand or listen to what I had to say. I shouldn't have come here. This is a mistake.' He takes a deep breath, like he's thinking something through. 'I'm in constant pain.'

A metaphor, surely.

'Pain for what you did?'

'God no.' He reaches into his coat and aims his gun at me. 'You know too much.'

I just stand there, staring down the barrel of his gun. 'Is that the gun you shot that cop with?'

Derek looks at it, like it's the first time he's ever seen it. 'Guns are hard to come by.'

'Bullets a lot less so. You better have some in that thing.'

'Oh, I do. Believe me.'

'Derek, don't think shooting and killing me is going to help your situation any. You've abducted and murdered five women. That the police know about. You shot a serving cop and you've evaded justice for two years. I don't think there's an afterlife, but if there is – please don't kid yourself and think that you deserve to get to the good place.'

I turn and walk away from him, away from the car park. 'I'll see you around.'

'I'M POINTING A GUN AT YOU!'

I keep on walking. 'Shoot me, then.'

'Don't think you're safe at that distance.' He's walking towards me. 'You're a much faster runner than me, but nobody can outrun a bullet.'

I slow my pace until I can hear him behind me, still out of breath from the climb up here. I finally stop. 'Why are you doing this?'

'You know far too much. I need to stop you carrying on before I atone.'

'You said you're going to the police.' I turn back to face him. 'Why do you need to kill me first? Another death? Why?'

Derek frowns. He hasn't thought of that, has he? 'Right. That's... That's a good point.' He's staring at his feet, his gun arm hanging slack and aiming at the ground.

I reach into my pocket with my gloved hand and pull out my Taser.

He looks up, just in time to see it. 'What the—' He raises his gun, but I fire the Taser first.

One dart catches Derek in the top left of his chest, the other down by his right hip. He jerks, dropping the torch, dropping the gun, then he topples over to the side, landing on the guard rails. He swings around, his blue eyes full of relief that he isn't going down, at least. Still shaking.

I drop the Taser and unclip the darts from his flesh, then reach into his pocket for his phone, in a cheap Arsenal case. 'This'll help you pay for your sins, Derek.' I hoist him over the side of the bridge.

He can't even scream as he falls.

CHAPTER SEVEN

MARSHALL

Just after nine and the day was already heating up. Not quite 'cook an egg on the pavement' temperature, but it'd get there by early afternoon.

Marshall unbuttoned his suit jacket, then immediately regretted it. Sweat was pooling in his armpits.

Aye, he really needed to lose weight.

He sucked on the latte and felt his temperature rise a few degrees. That thing about drinking hot stuff when it was hot must be a myth – all it did was make you sweat.

When he'd first moved to London, you could see Wembley Stadium from street level around here. Now it was so built up you'd need to be on top of that crane to see the giant arch.

An ambulance pulled in at the side of the road and a paramedic hopped down. Green uniform, curly hair tightly wound into lines – cornrows, Marshall thought it was called – with his face dusted with stubble.

Marshall ambled over and took out his warrant card. 'DI Rob Marshall. Serious Collision Investigation Unit.'

'Troy Stockdale, paramedic.' He gave a high-pitched laugh. 'Can't be ages here, mate.'

'Just need you for ten minutes, then you can be back on your way.'

Troy nodded slowly. 'What you want to know?'

Marshall waved over at the crime scene guarded by two uniformed officers. A smashed-in Toyota Prius next to a Ford Sierra Cosworth resting on its roof, more rust than car at its age. Four detectives were doing their analysis.

Marshall looked back at Troy. 'You were the first on the scene, correct?'

'That's right.' Troy looked Marshall up and down. 'I know you from somewhere?'

Marshall winced. 'Just got one of those faces.'

'Not many Scots down here.'

'More than you think. Some of our lot can even pass for human beings.'

Troy arched his back and squealed with laughter. 'That's funny, man.'

'Listen, there's been a fatality, so please cut the—'

'He died?' Troy's eyes were wide. 'Seriously?'

'The Sierra driver. Half past four this morning.'

'Man, I took him to hospital.'

'I'm sorry.' Marshall wasn't sure what else he could say. 'Anyway, we got called out. My guys are doing our advanced forensics just now to see if there's any fault in the Prius driver. We just need a detailed statement from you.'

'The car was upside down when I got here. Had to wait for the fire—'

Marshall raised a hand. 'Sorry, it's not me who'll be taking your statement.'

'Oh.'

Marshall put his fingers in his mouth and did a football-manager whistle. All four of his team turned around. 'Mark, Dean, can you...?' He thumbed at Troy.

They walked over, brothers from another mother. Bean-poles with skinheads who thought this heat warranted a three-piece suit. 'Cheers, boss.' Mark tilted his head to the side, navigating Troy and his mate away.

Leaving Marshall on his own. With *those* thoughts and the rest of his coffee. In the heat.

How he'd ended up doing this, of all jobs. For his sins. For his many, many sins.

And this was his old patch. Even investigated a murder in those flats over the road, all curved and sleek. Must be people turn up here for the League 2 play-off final, pissed out of their skulls from drinking on the coach all the way from Lincoln or Bradford, and think those flats were the football stadium.

A Mondeo pulled in, bumping up onto the pavement. Del Amitri blasting out *Roll To Me*.

DCI Tina Rickards stepped out and stretched like a monkey in the zoo. 'Rob.' She shuffled over, smoothing down her hair. 'You look like someone's pissed in your coffee.'

'Tastes like it.' Marshall finished it and put the empty in through the pool car's window. He'd recycle it when he got a minute. No way would he let it become another part of the island of crap in the rear footwells. Nope. 'Just ruminating on this case before we move the cars back to our nick. Need to analyse them in situ, obviously.' He thumbed over to the crime scene. 'Take it you've caught this as a murder?'

'Why would you think that?'

'It's a death on your patch.'

'Nope. Not mine.'

'What, you don't still lead the Brent MIT?'

'Oh, I do, but this isn't about that.' She buttoned up her suit jacket. 'I would've waited for you to get back to your nick, but you're still as much of a workaholic as ever, so I've had to come find you.'

'If this is about why I'm leaving the Met...'

'No.' Rickards laughed. 'Even on the way out, you're still giving it your all. Most would be on the golf course.' She blew air up her face. 'Why are you leaving?'

Marshall could no longer deny it to himself. Didn't have a coffee cup to hide behind. Sod it, she deserved the truth after all that time working together, even with all the bad blood stuck to the hatchet lodged between his shoulder blades. 'Honestly?'

'I've always asked for brutal honesty from you, Rob.'

'Truth is, I feel wasted doing this.'

'Serious Collisions is an important role.'

'Aye, it's important work, sure, but it's not why I joined the police. I'm not making a real difference here. Any cop could do this.'

'Arrogant as ever.' Rickards giggled as she patted his arm. 'Just kidding. Going back to your old profession, though, you'll be just as frustrated as before.'

'True. Thinking I'll go and count penguins in Antarctica for a couple of years.'

'Are you serious?'

'I saw something on the internet about it. It's that or running a pub on Benbecula.'

'Before you take the long boat to the South Pole or the short one to one of the Hebrides, I need a little bit of your time.' She hit him with her laser vision. 'I've had to clear it with your current boss, Rob, but you're being seconded to an investigation.'

'Young didn't fight it, right?'

'Old Man knows when to fight. Trying to keep someone who's just quit isn't a hill anyone should die on.'

'So what is?'

'Derek Cameron's body's been found.'

Marshall felt a throbbing deep in his stomach. A queasiness. Made him sweat more. His head was a bell someone had struck with a hammer. Made him feel a bit dizzy. 'Where?'

'That's the weird part, Rob. He was found near your hometown. Melrose in the Scottish Borders.'

Felt like something was going to crawl up his gullet. He tried to swallow it down.

'We need you to help Police Scotland investigate the death of the man you hunted for over a year.' She rubbed his arm. 'You're someone who needs closure, Rob. Pack a case and get up the road. These smashed cars will still be here when you get back.'

CHAPTER EIGHT

Marshall pulled off the motorway and followed the back road from Carlisle into the deep unknown of the Cumbrian countryside.

Dog tired after six hours' solid driving.

Assuming dogs could even feel this knackered.

Should've taken a break around Birmingham. Definitely by Manchester. But no, he'd ploughed on, fuelled by increasingly warm tins of energy drink.

A curving carriageway, thick with trees on both sides. Stuck behind a lorry, a haulage firm based in Arbroath. Down here was a long way from home for them.

And where the bloody hell was the—

Ah. Houghton Hall. A hulking great glass garden centre, the evening light glinting off it. Looked like some corporate headquarters on the outskirts of Edinburgh or Newcastle.

He got into the right-turn lane, then slammed through ahead of a Volvo with flashing lights, his mind screaming FLOOR IT. Still in motorway driving mode. He needed to calm down.

The car park was half-empty, so he took it slowly as he rolled across the gravel.

Got a flash of lights from a silver Skoda, so he parked next to it. Ran a hand down his face but that didn't cut it, so he dug the heels of his hands into his eye sockets and that seemed to jolt some energy into his flagging body. He opened his door and got out at the same time as John Hulse.

Hulse didn't react to seeing his old boss for the first time in two years. He'd lost a lot of weight, so the scar running down the side of his face was even more prominent. Hair clipped even shorter and he was now clean shaven. Made him look like a hardened criminal rather than an ex-cop.

'Hi, John. Long time, no see.'

Hulse got in the passenger seat. He was carrying something, but Marshall couldn't see what.

Marshall stretched out until everything clicked. Wet, thin slashes of rain cut through him. Christ, it was freezing up here. Curiosity got the better of him, so he sat back in his seat. 'How you doing, John?'

Hulse passed him a coffee beaker. 'Here.'

'Thanks.'

'Owed you from the last time.' Hulse snorted. He took a sip of coffee through the lid.

'No greeting for your old mate?'

'Hi.'

A man of so many words...

'Thanks for this.' Marshall tore off his coffee's lid. 'I didn't know you'd moved from London.'

'Eighteen months now. Mum died. Got her old cottage.'

'In Carlisle?'

'Hexham.'

Marshall's geography of this area was spot on. He knew Newcastle like a second skin, only forty miles separated it from

Carlisle – when you looked at the map, you could see why Hadrian built his wall there, it was so narrow from coast to coast. Hexham was about a third of the way over. 'Sorry to hear that, John.'

'Are you? You didn't call.'

Marshall held the coffee cup in both hands, letting the heat sink into his palms. 'John, I've called you loads, but this morning was the first time you've answered.'

Another snort. His breathing had a harsh rasp.

'I get it, but it's...' Marshall took a sip of coffee. Sweet and caramel. 'We were partners, John. You wouldn't let me see you in hospital after the... after the incident. I came to your flat and you wouldn't answer the door. Kept calling and you wouldn't answer your phone. What was I to do?'

'Stop trying?'

'I can take a hint, John.' Marshall took another sip. He adjusted himself in the seat, trying to unkink everything. The last time he'd been in a car like this... 'Why did you answer now? After all this time?'

'Want a medal for saving my life?'

'Is that what you think? That I'm that shallow?'

Hulse shrugged.

'Come on. I chose to stay with you. I drove you to hospital.'

'We lost him.'

'But I didn't lose you, though.'

Hulse shut his eyes.

'You don't like talking about it, John, I get that. You don't like talking about many things. Worked well in suspect interviews. You ask a curt question, then you just sit there until the suspect answers. And they always answered. But it's okay to give voice to your feelings.'

'Almost lost a lung. Wish I had. What's left barely works.' Hulse was breathing hard now, the wheezy rattle of someone twice his age. 'You slipped back and saved your own life. I got shot again.'

'I'm so sorry, John.'

'Some days are hell. Can't get out of bed. Pensioned off. Medical settlement on top.' Hulse took another sip. 'Need very little, mind. Get bored, though. I'm working. Taxi driver for my uncle.'

Marshall craned his neck around and caught the Skoda. No signage, just a silver car.

Another sip through the lid. Hard to tell what was the rattle of the drink and what was the rattle of his damaged lung. 'Why we meeting?'

'Because Derek Cameron's dead.'

Hulse slumped back in his seat and let out the deepest groan. Seemed like two years of tension slid out of his body just like that. 'Sure?'

'I've not seen the body, but I have it on good auth—'

'What happened?'

'Late hours of Saturday night, they found a body. Wallet had some ID in the name of Callum Davidson. But they did a DNA trace yesterday and matched him to Derek Cameron, AKA Donald Calder, AKA David Crichton, AKA Douglas Cunningham.'

Hulse took a long gulp of coffee and rubbed at his chest. Right where he'd been shot by Cameron. The second bullet. 'Just like your profile.'

'All those women's lives ended. Him having a seemingly endless supply of made-up identities.'

'Murder or suicide?'

'That's the thing. Cameron took a header off a bridge. Whether he was helped, they don't know yet. But it was near my hometown.'

'Weird.'

'Tell me about it. If it's murder, I don't understand why someone would kill him now. Or who.'

'Me neither.'

'But I'll find out. They've seconded me to the investigation.'

'Happy?'

'Hardly. Back home in the arse end of nowhere. Great place for someone like Cameron to hide out, but not exactly... I've trained in finding serial offenders. There are barely offenders back home, let alone serial ones.'

'Or serious accidents.'

Marshall looked over, smiling, but Hulse wasn't looking at him. 'So you've been keeping tabs on me?'

'Rickards. Checked up on me. Know how she is.'

Oh aye, he did. Boy did he.

'John. There's no easy way to ask this, so I'm just going to come out with it. Have you been in contact with Derek Cameron?'

Hulse jolted into life, rocking forward in the seat. 'What? Of course not! You think I'd keep it to myself if I had? You think I'd meet up with the man who shot and wounded me? Fuck sake, I'd have taken him to the nearest nick myself. Who do you think I am?'

'I know you, John.' And Marshall could tell he was rattled by the way each sentence contained enough syllables to require at least a second hand to count them on. 'I worked with you for a few years.'

'And after all that, you honestly think I killed him?'

'Not saying that.'

'What *are* you saying?'

Marshall took a moment to think it all through. Every word had to be as careful as a step in a quiet house after everyone had gone to bed. 'John, I'm worried you tried to take him to the nearest nick, but he overpowered you and you accidentally killed him.'

Hulse shook his head, jaw clenched tight. 'Did *you* do it?'

'Do what?'

'Kill him.'

'What? Why would you think that?'

'You know the lay of the land up there. Your old stomping ground. Maybe you heard he was up there, decided on a bit of extralegal justice.'

Funny how Hulse became very eloquent when he got enraged.

'No, John. I didn't.'

'Sure about that? Because I might've been shot and pensioned off. Burst lung and damaged knee. But you, the great and mighty Rob Marshall, you were side-lined too.'

'Serious Collis—'

'—isn't Traffic. Yeah, I get it. But still, it's hard to take with your ego, eh?'

'My ego?'

Hulse finished his coffee and crumpled the cup. 'Forget it.'

'I'm serious. You think I'm egotistical?'

'I don't *think* it, Rob. I know it. We worked together for years. You are egotistical. You're this great profiler who had to become a cop because we fuck everything up. Your standards are higher than ours. It's... It's what makes you a good cop, man.'

'That's lovely of you to say, John.'

'I'm serious. You were running a serial killer investigation and now you're checking out damaged cars.'

Marshall hated to hear the truth. Especially as it tallied with his own thoughts. But it tied up with this inertia, at not being able to break free from the Met.

'And look where your ego got me, Rob. I was happy. Had a

job I loved. Now I'm driving bell ends to airports and old ladies to supermarkets. I wake up in the night and I *can't breathe*, man. Some days, Rob, I wish you'd just let me die.' Hulse opened the door and put his foot down on the gravel.

Marshall grabbed his sleeve. 'You don't mean—'

'Get off us!' Hulse tugged himself free. 'I do, man. I fucking do.' He stood up and limped off. 'Wish I was dead.'

Seconds later, his car was whirring back and he shot off through the car park in a fug of diesel fumes.

That hadn't gone as badly as Marshall feared.

CHAPTER NINE

Marshall knew every inch of every mile of the A68. Based on some old Roman road, winding from County Durham up to Edinburgh, slicing a wedge through his home county. The Scottish Borders.

Back then, his mum drove them around, Marshall in the back alongside Jen until he was promoted to the front passenger. Then she moaned about it and she got there.

After he passed his test, he drove around with a car full of idiots.

Then on the rare occasions he'd come back from Durham as a student. And afterwards.

And this was the first time in a few years he'd been within even a hundred miles of the place. Not that it'd changed much.

This stretch was lush with ancient trees, that empty decadence he grew up with. Made a great change from the brutal landscape of the A7 between Carlisle and Hawick, which made him feel like he was driving on Mars.

Two cars idled at the roundabout, waiting to turn left

towards Melrose, his hometown. Instead, he cut into the right lane and swept on towards Edinburgh.

Trying not to think about it. About anything. He'd even taken the slow route over the hills between Hawick and Jedburgh to avoid coming close to the town. And now he was past the Eildons, the three-headed hydra of a hill, and he just...

He tried to focus on John Hulse wanting to be dead.

Marshall could understand that thinking. The complex surgery he'd undergone to save his life had taken a toll on him. And of course he blamed Marshall for it.

Could just as easily have been Marshall who'd been shot.

Could just as easily have been both of them left to bleed out and die.

Just lucky that Derek Cameron had run out of bullets.

But accusing Marshall of killing him...

Aye, Marshall deserved that.

He'd been the one going in there with accusations.

Marshall slowed for the slip road, then eased in. At some point, this was a back road along the Tweed towards Newstead and Melrose, but now the council had closed it to cars, leaving it for cyclists, horses and dog walkers.

None of them at this end today, though, just columns of police cars like a Roman legion.

Marshall pulled in behind the last car and got out into the quiet evening. Absolutely perishing here, especially this close to the river, sucking in what little heat the air held. At least it wasn't raining. Yet.

The last time he'd been here, with his sister and his niece, the place had been a family picnic destination. Thea had played on the train, then on the fort up at the top of the viaduct. They'd walked to Melrose and had ice cream, Marshall glad to see the back of it and not feeling any better.

Now it was a crime scene. Police tape flapped in the breeze, a giant bear of a uniform guarding entry. Even bigger than Marshall himself, and the first flushes of cauliflower ear gave him away as a rugby player.

Marshall handed over his Met warrant card and let him inspect it, then took the clipboard and signed in. 'Looking for a DI Elliot.'

He got a grunt. 'Over there.' He pointed over to the train benches.

'Thanks.' Marshall gave him the clipboard back and wandered down.

DI Andrea Elliot was sitting on the engine, talking on the phone. Short hair, parted with a long fringe over to one side, exposing only one ear which was occupied with her mobile. She looked around at him, her eyes like green marbles dropped in the mud and left to set, forming dark, heavy bags. She looked absolutely exhausted. More or less exactly how Marshall felt. She held up a finger. 'Aye, Jim, think that's him now. I'll call you later.' She stabbed a finger off the screen. Then again. And again. 'Bastard thing.' Muttered, but loud enough for Marshall to hear. She put her mobile away and held out a hand. 'Andrea Elliot.'

He shook it. 'Rob Marshall.'

'We've been expecting you, but you're early.'

'Didn't take a break until Carlisle.'

'You must have some bladder.'

'They call me the camel.'

She laughed, then tucked her fringe behind her ear. 'Okay, so let's get you up to speed, shall we?' She gestured at the rear carriage of the children's train. 'Please, have a seat.'

'I've been sitting for eight hours, so I prefer to stand if it's all the same.'

'Suit yourself.' She leaned forward, rubbing her hands together. Made her look like some giant attacking the train.

'Okay, the bad news is you've been seconded to our ragtag team of misfits and miscreants. We're not that bad. Seven of us work for an outreach of the Edinburgh Major Investigation Team, covering serious crimes down here in the Scottish Borders. If you're into that kind of thing, it's Division J of Police Scotland South's Lothians and Scottish Borders region. Not to be confused with Lothian and Borders, which doesn't exist anymore.'

'I've kept up with all that, aye. We've got a similar structure in the Met.'

'Bully for you. We were set up following a recent screw-up in a case.' She sucked at her teeth. 'Local lot messed up a murder. Lost most of the evidence and lost a bloody suspect.' She sighed. 'Anyhoo. Think of us as another MIT but, let's be honest, we don't get a lot of murders down here.' She leaned forward and spoke in a quiet tone: 'My boss spends most of his time on the golf course.' She sat back, a wicked look on her face. 'But we've got more than a few cases on just now, so my boss's handicap is slipping, hence him putting me under ridiculous amounts of pressure to solve this.' She shrugged. 'Which I can handle. Been doing this twenty years now. Glasgow, Edinburgh and now here.'

'That's some—'

Her phone trilled out, a soft chorus of birds. She got it out of her jacket and checked the screen. 'Ah, scrotal sack. Better take this.' She answered it and turned away. 'Kirsten, you better have answers for me.'

Leaving Marshall on his own.

He had a good read on her already – Elliot was a female cop who'd worked her way up the greasy pole and wanted everyone to know it.

In other words, the complete opposite of Marshall.

He couldn't bring himself to look up at the bridge. Couldn't even think about it. About what happened there. That sick feeling he'd had back at Wembley had returned with all its mates and family members.

'Sorry, yet another call.' Elliot was back. 'You okay? Seen a ghost or something?'

'I'm fine.' Marshall gave her a smile, but it felt fake even to him. 'Just taking in the site.'

'You know this place?'

'Years ago. Before I moved away.'

'Right. Notorious suicide spot until they put a gate up there. Kind of a glamorous place to go, guaranteed to pop your clogs.'

Marshall swallowed hard and managed to look at the viaduct spanning the Tweed. Arches of vaulted blocks, the rest brick. Tall legs like giant stone flamingos. So many of them, hard to count and be sure you'd got the right number.

'Okay, well.' Elliot stuffed her hands into her pockets. 'I don't want you to feel like you've been forced on me.'

'But we both know I have.'

'Oh, come on, that's—' Her phone went again. 'Sorry.' She put it to her ear, not facing away this time. 'Shunty, can't you do it yourself? Okay, well ask Dr Owusu to speed it up. Personal favour to me. Thank you.' She ended the call with a roll of her eyes then put the phone away. 'Okay, so where was I?'

Marshall grinned at her. 'Making me feel completely unwelcome.'

Elliot laughed. 'I'll show you his car.' She powered back up the hill towards the car park.

The big uniform was messing about on his mobile. Daft sod hadn't muted it so it was all bleeps and bloops.

Elliot charged past him. 'Not on my time, Constable. Put it away.'

A gaggle of CSIs were processing a souped-up old Peugeot, a tiny town car modded into a monster of the roads. A few figures worked away inside it like they were doing one of those challenges to fit as many people as possible into it.

'Evening.' A CSI stepped out and tugged her goggles free. Bright green eyes that caught the light. She was tiny, about a foot shorter than Marshall, and waved a gloved hand towards him. 'Kirsten Weir. I'm the lead forensics officer for this case.'

'Rob Marshall.' He waved at the vehicle. 'That's definitely his car?'

Kirsten nodded. 'Registered to a Callum Davidson.'

Marshall snorted. 'That'll be another alias.'

'Right.' Kirsten pursed her lips. 'It matches the name in his wallet. We've run the registration details. Bought it three months ago from someone in Walkerburn. Still, it's registered to Callum Davidson. Looks like he's done extensive work to the car since.'

Elliot was staring at Marshall. 'Well?'

'Well what?'

'That the kind of car he drove?'

Marshall nodded at both women. 'That's the kind of car *Derek Cameron* drove.' He walked around the vehicle, noting the Transformers Autobot sign where the Peugeot badge should be. 'After each kill, he kept changing his identity and leaving his rented accommodation. When he... eh, eventually evaded capture, we dug deep into his life. Every alias always had a souped-up car of some description. Registered to them. Part of the identity process, we think. This is just the latest incarnation. But he also had a van, we think. Never recovered it but witness statements say it was an old white van with no signage.'

'All that in your profile?'

'You haven't read it?'

'Took a while for me to even get access to it, and I'm kind of busy here.' Elliot tucked her hair behind her ear again. 'But I'll read it, don't you worry. Chapter and verse.'

'I'll look forward to all the questions.'

Elliot patted Kirsten's arm. 'I'll let you get on. Mind and get that report into my inbox by sleepy-by time.'

'Sure thing.' Kirsten put her mask and gloves into the discard pile. 'I'll go and see what's what.'

'Good girl.' Elliot marched off back down the hill. 'Better bring you up to speed, aye?'

Being away from home for so long, Marshall had forgotten how they even spoke around here. 'Aye' was like a three syllable word, rising from aw to oo to aye in a smooth motion. Got even worse down in Hawick, which sounded like Hoik. Elliot's accent was more Galashiels or Selkirk, so understandable by most human beings.

He smiled at her as he got out his notebook. 'Sure. If you had an ID, how did you connect it to my case?'

'Therein lies the rub.' She powered on at close to a jogging pace away from the train benches to the steep climb towards the viaduct. 'Case like this, we treat it as murder, so we got pathology and forensics to fast-track his DNA. And, as you can imagine, we got a lot of hits and a lot of different names. None of which were in his wallet.'

Marshall was avoiding looking anywhere but at his notebook or his feet.

'All relating to your case in London. Derek Cameron. Five minutes after I look up his record, I get a call from DCI Rickards in the Met.'

'My old boss.'

'Seems charming.' Elliot rolled her eyes. 'A flagged case, eh? Had a look through HOLMES. You're not the named contact anymore. Why's that?'

Marshall followed her up the narrow steps carved into the bank. 'Long story.'

'We've got time.'

Marshall tried to disarm her with his smile. 'Would rather help you than go over outdated Met office gossip.'

Elliot focused on him for a few seconds, then set off again. 'Don't worry, I'll get it out of you. Or I'll find some other sod down there to dish.' She led past the child's fort at the top, bereft of kids pretending to be Romans.

Last time Marshall had been here, a massive gate blocked access to the viaduct. Now it was hanging open and Elliot strode on through. 'The padlock on the gate was cut off, but there's no sign of the bolt cutters. Probably at the bottom of the river, dragged halfway to bloody Berwick.' She stomped over the viaduct's trackbed, wide enough for only one train line, but long since removed. Three long rows of security bars ran along either side, but it hadn't stopped Derek Cameron going over.

Marshall followed her across the gravel path, acid bubbling in his gut, lights flashing in his vision.

Keep it together, you idiot.

Elliot stopped and peered down at the river.

Marshall joined her, but had to hold onto the railings. Below was the Tweed. A white tent glowed in the late evening sun, catching the last rays down there in the valley.

'Kirsten's CSIs are working away over there.' Elliot pointed at it. 'That shower are looking for evidence, but not finding much.'

'That shower?'

Elliot's lips twitched, then she leaned in. 'Between you and me, she's not exactly the best. Young, inexperienced and over-promoted. You know how it is.'

He did, but he also knew how it was with older and experienced officers who badmouthed everyone to strangers. 'That's the back road towards Gattonside, aye?'

'Aye.'

'And that's where the body was?'

'Aye.'

Down below, two CSIs emerged from the tent.

'He landed on the road?'

'Lucky he didn't hit a car on the way down.'

Marshall peered at the barrier and saw some scuff marks in the ancient grime. 'So, either he snapped off the bolts and walked along this end to jump off, or someone else did it and chucked him over the side.'

'That's your reading of it?'

Marshall felt a flush of heat up his neck. What was she keeping from him? And why was she testing him?

The gate at the far end of the viaduct was still intact.

'Okay, so you've ruled out suicide?'

'Never rule it out completely, but I think it's unlikely. Takes a lot of effort to snap bolts just to top yourself. Also, hitting the water from this height is like hitting the road.'

Marshall's mouth was dry. He looked away from the river, back along the viaduct. His eyes were stinging and not from hay fever. 'So you think he would've killed himself by jumping from the middle?'

'Right. Or over that side. Coming all this way, just to land on the road? Bit weird.'

'Who found him?'

'Guess.'

Marshall laughed. 'It's usually a dog walker, but they'd be on the old road on the other bank. I'd guess a car saw him.'

'Good guess.'

'So, what was it?'

'We got an anonymous tip-off just after midnight on Sunday night.'

'So, a car?'

'Nope. It was from a phone we found near his body, smashed to shite, wiped clean of prints and DNA. Had an Arsenal case on it.'

'That certainly makes it not seem like murder.'

'Quite.' Elliot looked around at him with those beady eyes. 'You know him best – could he have killed himself?'

Marshall winced. 'Truth is, I did a profile on him and led the investigation into his crimes, but I never spoke to him. Well, once, but...'

'But he was on your radar?'

'Right. Just came up as an associate of the first victim. Two DCs interviewed him. Just a statement about a schoolfriend. Never got him into an interview room.'

She grimaced, like she was confirming that his presence here was a complete waste of time. Or it was oversold.

Hard to disagree with that.

'Can I see the body?'

'You want to make sure it's actually him?'

'Want to drive a stake through his heart, fill his mouth with garlic and chop his head off.'

Joking aside, it was gnawing at him.

Derek Cameron had shot and injured his partner.

He'd abducted, raped and murdered five women.

They'd done the DNA, sure, but Marshall *had* to know it was him.

Had to.

She laughed. 'His body's at the Borders General.'

CHAPTER TEN

Elliot's shoes squeaked as she walked along the dim corridor, which stank of harsh chemicals, softened by a strawberry aroma. Whoever had cleaned hadn't done a great job of diluting the stuff – Marshall's eyes were stinging. Upstairs, the hospital had colour-coded directions to departments, but down here in the basement was just a black line leading to Pathology.

Elliot stepped into the office and crept over to the hatch at reception like someone was going to spot her and run off. 'Hello?'

Marshall joined her. Nobody here, just a few half-empty buckets of supermarket biscuits and cakes on the desk where a receptionist should be.

Elliot got out her mobile and checked the screen. 'You born here?'

'How do you know I'm from around here?'

'It's on your record.'

'This place opened just before our time.'

‘Ours?’

The more he widened the smile, the less honest it felt. ‘Mine. Born at the old Peel hospital by Caddonfoot. You?’

She nodded. ‘Peel.’

‘That’s something we’ve got in common, at least.’

She didn’t seem to notice him saying anything. ‘Come on.’ She opened the door and charged off along yet another corridor, both shoes squeaking. ‘You never met Derek Cameron, then?’

‘No, I did, just not in an interview room. Met him when he shot my partner in the chest and leg.’

‘Right, right.’ Elliot rapped on a door. ‘Didn’t go after him?’

‘John would’ve died if I hadn’t stayed with him.’

‘Sure about that?’

‘Sure.’

‘Bugger this.’ Elliot opened the door and stepped into the pathology lab.

The room was ice cold. Marshall felt the chill deep in his bones. Bliss. And then the sweat on his shirt was chilling too.

Elliot walked through the space, white surfaces all scuffed and faded. ‘Belu? You here?’

A black woman rose up from behind a desk, frowning. Hair clipped even shorter than Marshall’s own, but she didn’t have to contend with his premature greying; her stubble was a lush black. She folded her arms over her scrubs. ‘You brought him here, eh?’ South African accent, but it could almost be Zimbabwean. ‘I thought you wouldn’t bother until the morning.’

Elliot gave a curt smile. ‘Dr Belu Owusu, DS Rob Marshall.’

‘It’s DI.’

Elliot scowled at him. ‘Is it?’

‘Last I checked.’ Marshall got out his warrant card and held it out to her. ‘Thought you’d read my record. See?’

That seemed to piss her right off.

Owusu threw her head back and roared with laughter. 'You thought he was here to work for you, eh, but now you know he's here to take your job!'

Marshall raised his hands, as much for Elliot's benefit as anything else. 'I'm not here to take anything from anyone. Just seconded to the investigation for as long as I'm needed. If that's tonight, then cool, I'll be back on the road tomorrow morning.'

Owusu was still smiling. 'I'll be doing his post-mortem tomorrow, but I've had a decent-enough look at him beforehand. What do you want to know, big guy?'

Despite the temperature, Marshall was blushing. 'I just want to know if it's him.'

'Come on, then.' Owusu swayed across the room towards a set of mortuary fridges, her fluid grace like she was a plant underwater. She tore one open and it rolled out with a rumble. 'Here you go.'

Marshall stared down at the body on the slab, feeling the ice coming off in waves.

It wasn't Cameron.

He let his breath go. 'That's not him.'

'Eh?' Owusu stared into the drawer. 'Ah, shit.' She slid it shut and hauled open the top one. 'Wrong guy, eh?'

A crumpled body lay on the slab. Posthumous bruising and cuts all over his face. His neck was at completely the wrong angle.

Marshall crouched to inspect him.

All he could see was those bright blue eyes, those hands aiming the gun at his head, taunting him and Hulse.

Those same eyes stared through him.

A wave of tension eased from his shoulders.

He stood up again. 'Now that one is Derek Cameron.'

Elliot clapped his arm. 'Fantastic. You can get home now.'

'Hey, not so fast.' Owusu folded her arms. 'This guy here isn't a formal identification.'

'You've not got his dental records?'

'I've asked, but you know the state of dentists just now. Absolute chaos, eh?'

'He's got a birthmark.' Marshall pointed at the body. 'On his left hip, shaped like a long teardrop.'

'How do you know that?' Elliot's gaze swept across the body like a security guard outside a concert. 'I thought you didn't have a surviving victim?'

'I wish they'd all survived, believe me.' And he wished he'd gone after Cameron. 'After he shot my partner, I spent a lot of time unpicking the life and times of Derek Cameron. Interviewing anyone who'd crossed his path. And I mean *any*one. That detail came from a girlfriend at high school. He took things a bit too far in bed, if you know what I mean.'

Elliot nodded, shaking her fringe free to flop down again. 'I know precisely what you mean. Escalation path to rape, which leads to murder.'

'Can lead to it, yes. Some just stop at sexual crimes, which is bad enough.'

'Let's see.' Owusu pulled back the sheet covering Cameron. His tiny penis was shrivelled up and looked like a foam mushroom sweet. A painful-looking rash covered his left hip. 'Okay, so I thought that was some kind of sexual kink but I'd say these marks are consistent with him trying to scratch off the birthmark. Some abrasive material, like steel wool. Have to say...' She shook her head, eyes wide. 'That's going to *hurt*.'

Marshall inspected the area and saw the faint outline of the teardrop. 'It's growing back, right?'

'Going to keep doing that, eh? Impossible to get rid of a birthmark without laser surgery.'

'And that's expensive?'

'Can be, why?'

'From what we've learnt, Derek Cameron was living the kind of life Jack Reacher, the Littlest Hobo or the Incredible Hulk would. Just upping and leaving whenever things got bad. London's so densely populated that moving ten streets away's like moving across the whole of Scotland. Easy to disappear from people's lives.'

'And you think he couldn't afford it?'

'Right. The guy worked as a mechanic. Didn't own a garage. Parents both died without leaving anything behind. That kind of peripatetic existence, you don't build up savings or own property. All of his money was spent on maintaining his lifestyle and having other identities to fall back on.'

Elliot got out her phone and started tapping at the screen.

'What are you doing?'

She looked up at Marshall. 'Just making sure we get hold of Callum Davidson's bank records.'

'Trying to prove me wrong?'

'No, I've just got a shite team who keep forgetting things.'

Marshall stared at the body now. At his face. Hard to think of him as being the man who'd caused so much damage, so much pain. He had very short hair, not shaved on top, but trimmed. Made it easy to add a wig so he could change his appearance. Those plain features too... He was like the starting point for an identikit, to be adjusted and moulded into any other face. Thirty-two, but he could pass for fifteen years in either direction. Derek Cameron was still a chameleon.

Save for those piercing blue eyes.

But they could be covered with non-prescription contact lenses.

Elliot pocketed her phone again. 'Who's helping him?'

'A good question.' Marshall let out a halting breath that caught in the air. 'His profile is that of a loner. He was identifying targets from the night bus he—'

'I know all of that, aye. But to change identity like he has, he'd need help.'

'Like a passport forger?'

'That kind of thing, aye.'

'Those guys are ten a penny in certain parts of London. Good enough to get anyone on a flight would be expensive, but the cheaper ones are still good enough to get a bank account and a credit card.'

Owusu yawned into her fist. 'Sorry.'

Elliot chuckled. 'We keeping you up, Belu?'

'No, no. It's just late. And I've got to get home, so if you're done here, then—'

'When did he die?'

Owusu pursed her lips. 'Usually the first question your lot asks me, so bonus points for delaying it.' A slow breath hissed out of her nostrils. 'Sunday night, around midnight. Died on impact from the fall. Broken neck.' She dipped her head towards Elliot. 'Andrea says there was a mysterious phone call around that time, so I'd say that matches up with what I'm seeing here.'

'All those injuries were from the fall?'

'No. Some have been there a bit longer than Sunday night. His left cheek has some ecchymosis that's yellowed and a laceration that's scabbed over.'

'Bruises and cuts, please...' Elliot was fiddling with her mobile. 'Think he's been in a fight.'

Marshall waited for her to look up. She didn't. 'You got any reports of—?'

'Team are on it.' She put the mobile away and hissed out a

sigh. 'I obviously don't know how to run a murder investigation, so thanks for your advice.'

Marshall raised his hands. 'Just trying to get as much data as we need, that's all. Have you done the blood toxicology?'

'It isn't complete due to our colleagues in Edinburgh being total dickheads, but I found traces of a white substance in his nostrils. Just finished the tests on it and my suspicions were correct – cocaine. We don't know how much he'd been taking. Stuff's so cheap just now. And he smells strongly of alcohol, so there's going to be a fairly colourful blood tox report on this guy.'

'And that's—' Elliot's mobile rang again. 'Sorry.' She stomped off. Didn't care who knew how pissed off she was.

Owusu chuckled. 'Girl's always on a call, eh?'

'Comes with the job.' Marshall wondered what the hell meant she was on so many phone calls. 'Bosses always want chapter and verse on a case.'

'Tell me about it. Sometimes we can only give them a vague outline.'

Marshall focused on Owusu. 'Have you ruled out suicide?'

'Not easily.'

'But you have?'

'Why are you asking?'

'Elliot seems to think it's not likely to be.' Marshall walked away from the corpse. 'You know alcohol and drugs increase suicide risk by a factor of like sixteen or something?'

'I do, but I wouldn't hope that your serial killer suddenly developed a conscience over his actions and decided to kill himself.' Owusu prodded the dead flesh with a finger. 'Your guy has two marks on him, neck and his other hip, which are consistent with a Taser hit.'

Marshall sighed, looked at the door. 'So he was attacked?'

'Correct.' She leaned in close. 'See the scarring here?'

'Doesn't look like a good, clean hit to me.'

'Oh, it's as good as you'd get from fifty thousand volts slamming right into him. Two puncture marks with slight burn from the arcing electricity. He would've been stiff as a board. Easy to push over the side.'

'Any clues as to who attacked him?'

'Not from that. But with a Taser like this, you have one foot of spread for every seven of distance to the target... So with that spread his assailant would have to be ten to fourteen feet away.'

A distant attack from behind pointed to a surprise. 'Have you found the electrodes or the darts?'

'Not to my knowledge. You'd need to ask Andrea.'

First name terms. Interesting.

Elliot came back, mobile in her hand. 'I'll not put this away in case Shunty phones again. I swear some people just aren't up to being police officers.' She shifted her gaze between them. 'What's up?'

'DI Marshall was wondering if you'd recovered any of the Taser?'

Elliot was still looking at her mobile. 'No joy on that score. Scoured the road and the banks.' She looked up. 'Why?'

Marshall gave her as smug a grin as she'd given him. 'Not sure how many firearms cases you lot deal with up here, but I suspect most will be drunk farmers firing shotguns at trespassers. With Tasers, the manufacturer packs AFID tags into each cartridge, so—'

'Aphids?' Elliot was scowling. 'Like greenfly?'

'Anti-Felon ID tags. Tiny dots of paper with the cartridge number on them in very fine print. You can't clean them all up and they're left behind to ID the cartridge they came from, which may lead to the purchaser.'

Elliot was back to hammering both thumbs off her mobile

screen. 'I'll get Kirsten to double down on that, then.' She looked at Owusu. 'Anything else?'

'Nothing.' Owusu raised her eyebrows. 'We done here?'

Marshall nodded slowly. 'Not sure, but you can go.'

'Thank you.' Owusu walked over to an office desk in the corner and grabbed a bag. 'You guys lock him away, eh?'

'Sure thing.' Marshall stared at the body one last time.

All that pain and suffering... He couldn't do it anymore. Nobody else was going to die because of Derek Cameron.

'Listen, I forgot something.' Owusu was clutching a bag and a long coat. 'I think Cameron had sex the day he died.'

Marshall shut his eyes. Felt like his heart skipped a bit. 'Shit.'

'We had traces of vaginal secretions on what measured out to be a well-below-average-sized penis, showing the sex was with someone else.'

Marshall's throat had clenched, so tight it felt like he'd not be able to eat or drink again for hours.

Elliot frowned at him. 'You okay?'

'I'm...' Marshall swallowed down his revulsion. 'I'm concerned he's still doing it.'

Elliot's frown deepened. 'Didn't your boss brief you?'

'She told me he was dead. What am I missing?'

Elliot pinched her nose. 'Wendy Malcolm. Seventeen. Reported missing on Sunday. We think Cameron took her on Saturday night.'

Felt like someone punched Marshall in the stomach. He couldn't breathe. Sweating, even in this ice-cold room. Stars dotted his vision.

'Why?'

Elliot held up a finger. 'She'd been seeing a Callum Davidson.'

Marshall clutched onto the words like a drowning man at reeds by the side of the river.

Elliot's face twisted into a glower. 'My problem, and why I've got so many phone calls, is that the only person knows where she is...' She gestured towards the fridge. 'Is lying there, dead. We've got to find Wendy, and soon.'

Assuming she was still alive.

CHAPTER ELEVEN

...

I've got to kill Wendy.

I hate knowing their names, makes it so much harder to do it.

But I've got to. She can't talk to the police. They can't find her. Not alive, anyway.

I open the door and step inside. Even in the height of summer, it's cold in here. The thick walls prevent the heat getting in.

My footsteps echo as I walk up to the back.

The table's empty.

Shit.

She was here.

I can see her in my mind's eye, lying on that table. Tied up, drugged. Not resisting.

The part we both enjoyed.

Stupid prick.

Just had to kill Cameron, didn't I?

She was right here. Cameron took her here, like we discussed.

Now I don't know where the hell she could be.

CHAPTER TWELVE
WENDY

Wendy rocked forward. Awake. Alive. Just.

Everything was a blur.

The light was too bright. Everything glowing and smudged.

Still tied down.

Still couldn't move.

That rag filled her mouth. Still tasted eggy, but it was stuck to the roof of her mouth. Dry now.

How long could people survive without water?

Three days?

She'd been... What, a week? That couldn't be right.

She'd no idea how long she'd been here. Or how long since Callum left.

The only moisture on her body was the tears she cried when she thought of him. How she'd let him into her life.

How he'd...

How he'd done this to her.

Focus on now. Focus on getting out of here.

Silent outside, so it had to be a different day. No sounds of puddles or rain, so it was dry outside now.

Nobody was going to find her.

She was going to die of thirst, wasn't she?

No.

She couldn't think like that.

She just couldn't.

A harsh rattle, like jailer's keys.

What was that?

Again. Someone was rattling a door. Or a chain anyway.

Quite far away, but that's what it was.

Was someone here?

Was it Callum?

Had he come back?

She tried calling out, but it was just a dulled 'Mmmf.'

Another rattle. 'Dirty bastard! Get out here, you paedo prick!'

Sounded like a kid.

'Mmmf!'

Rattle.

'Mmmf! Mmmf! Mmmmmf!'

Nothing.

'Mmmmmmmf!'

Wendy listened hard, but all she heard was several footsteps running away.

CHAPTER THIRTEEN
MARSHALL

Marshall stepped out into the evening. Darker than it should be at this time of year, this far north and at this elevation. Eerily still, though.

Yarrowford nestled between severe hills, a sprawling hamlet a few miles west of Selkirk. Anywhere this side of Galashiels was going to be like that – the Southern Upland Way ran a couple of miles north, all the way from Stranraer to Dunbar. Something like that. No wonder there was a border here; no army could easily get over that.

Marshall yawned. He needed his bed. Or whatever hotel they'd checked him into. Assuming they had. Maybe they expected him to stay with his mother or his sister, but he hadn't spoken to either of them in... well, two years.

Elliot was still in her car, a rusty pink Golf, talking on the phone yet again. In years to come, when everyone had chips in their heads to do all that phone stuff, at least she'd save on wrist strain and having something pressed to her right ear ninety percent of the day.

The realisation of what the call was about jerked him out of his fatigue. A missing woman. Seventeen, the lower end of Derek Cameron's target age.

Jesus Christ – this was on Marshall.

He'd let Cameron escape. Two years later, he could do this to Wendy Malcolm.

Everything in him clenched, hoping this wasn't Cameron's doing, that she'd just absconded somewhere.

Elliot got out of her car. 'Come on.' She yawned her way up the path and hammered on the door like a drunken ex-wife. 'That's Wendy's car, still here.' She pointed at a lime green Fiat 500, a tiny wee thing cowering next to a 4x4 Volvo. 'Dad reported her missing on Sunday morning. We're combing her house right now, speaking to her pals, you name it, but we've got nothing.'

'Was she taken outside or elsewhere?'

'Why?'

'We think Cameron took his victims outside.'

'That would be a theory to test, wouldn't it?'

'And are you?'

'Am I what?'

'Testing it?'

'We are.'

'Okay. Good.' Marshall inspected the house. An old farm cottage, standing alone in dishevelled grounds. Lights blazing away inside, the barbecue smell of kerosene as the boiler kicked in and plumed out smoke.

The door opened and a big lump in a suit frowned out. Brown skinned with an immaculately trimmed beard. Mid-twenties, if a day. 'Ma'am, you need to look at this.' He passed Elliot an iPad.

'Thank you, Shunty.' She held it out for Marshall to see.

CCTV footage, timestamped Saturday night. 19.14. Taken from across the road.

A souped-up Peugeot pulled up outside. The one registered to Callum Davidson. A man got out and hoiked up his jeans. Baseball cap with a dark ponytail poking out the back. Denim jacket with Metallica and Iron Maiden patches. He looked around and the camera caught those eyes again. Even in black and white, they glowed.

Derek Cameron.

He hurried up the drive, much like Marshall and Elliot had just done, then thumped on the door. Seconds later it opened and a woman stepped out, then kissed him. He led her down towards his car and it drove off.

Marshall sucked in a deep breath. 'That's not proof he took her.'

'No, but it's a bloody good clue.' Elliot handed the iPad back. 'A serial killer was last seen with the deceased? Come on. You do agree it's him, right?'

'Aye, it's him. Stupid hat and a ponytail. We wondered if he wore a wig to disguise himself, but this proves it.' Marshall looked around, expecting an introduction, but whoever Shunty was had disappeared. He looked back towards their cars, where he imagined the video had been captured from. No sign of any recording equipment, though, just some trees and a low fence. 'Who took this?'

'The farmer is their landlord. Doesn't trust any of his tenants, so he's installed a sneaky camera in the woods there. Denied it existed, but we managed to persuade him to share it. My DS has four other sightings of that car in this area over the last week, so we think Cameron was visiting Wendy regularly.'

'You run the plates yet?'

'Aye, but no joy. Unlike in Edinburgh or Glasgow, the Automatic Number Plate Recognition system is sparser than the hairs on a baby's arse. Bottom line, no cameras in the immediate area. No information on his movements.'

'What about where there are cameras?'

'No hits. One on the A7 leaving Gala, one by the petrol station at the far end of Selkirk.'

Marshall knew this area, though. There were a hundred different back roads he could've taken. Slower even than the A7, but if you were an expert at evading detection? Aye, you'd choose that way.

'Only question in my mind is where he's taken her.' Marshall pointed down the valley. 'Ton of old shepherd huts that way. Winding roads up into the hills that nobody ever goes down.'

'We're asking around, don't you worry.' Elliot smoothed her hair over her forehead. 'Forgot to say. Kirsten called me on the way here. Forensics have finished going through Cameron's car. The passenger seat has traces of hair matching the colour of Wendy's.'

Unlike the others, she hadn't been knocked out and chucked into the back of his van.

Maybe she hadn't been taken somewhere, raped, then killed.

'Need you to take it easy in here, okay?' Elliot led him inside.

Whatever they were paying in rent, none of it was going on the upkeep of the place. The decor was old-fashioned and sparse. Heavy old furniture that had seen better centuries. Cracks lined the walls.

A man perched on the sofa, head in his hands. Big Santa Claus beard, but ginger rather than white. Lumberjack shirt and three-quarter-length shorts. Lemon-yellow flip-flops. He looked up at them. 'Any news?'

'Nothing yet.' Elliot sat next to him. 'Aidan, this is DI Marshall. He led the case into your daughter's abductor down in London.'

Aidan Malcolm glowered at him. 'Heard you let him go.'

'It's a decision I've played over several times since, sir. Chase after an armed man or save my partner's life.'

'Guessing you chose the coward's way out.' Aidan snorted hatred through his nose. 'If you hadn't chosen that way, my girl would still be here.'

Language was sometimes critically important in cases like this – if he jumped from 'missing' to 'dead' this quickly, that would move him over to the suspect column.

'I've thought those thoughts myself.' Marshall perched on an armchair opposite Aidan. The stuffing puffed out of a burst seam on the left side. 'But we don't know that Wendy's dead.'

'You don't know she's alive, either.'

'I gather your daughter works in Selkirk?'

Aidan shook his head. 'No, Gala. She left school at sixteen. Last summer. Told her not to, but she wouldn't listen, would she? Got a job washing hair. Not even cutting it. At the college, sure, but she's not earning much. Didn't stop her buying herself a bloody car!'

So she drove to work rather than... Who was Marshall kidding? No buses around here. She'd have to get to Selkirk first.

And no night buses meant a different way of targeting his victims.

'Were you here on Saturday night?'

'Away with the boys down to Leeds. Rugby club annual thing. League country down there, really, but it was a good time. Watched a match, played a couple, had some beer and a curry. Didn't hear from Wendy on Saturday night, wasn't picking up. Got back Sunday afternoon and she wasn't here. Fine, I thought maybe she was with that boy she's been seeing.'

'You get a name from her?'

'Callum. Don't know his surname.'

'How long's she been seeing him?'

'A couple of weeks? He's picked her up a few times.'

'Have you got any other family?'

Aidan squeezed at his nose, like he was staunching the tears. 'Her mother died ten years ago. Car crash on the A72, overtaking a bus just past Walkerburn. Hit a motorbike, swerved and ended up in the Tweed. Dead on impact. Lost our baby too.'

'I'm sorry to hear that, Mr Malcolm.'

'Sure you are.'

'What about friends?'

'Not that I know of. Why are you asking? You should be out finding her!'

'To stand the best chance of doing that, we need to build up a picture of her life. And we need to find any alternative explanations to her disappearance. Such as deciding to run away to Ireland or France. London, even.'

'Right, well.' Aidan looked away. 'She's... She's Wendy, that's for sure.'

'Is your daughter impulsive?' Keep in present tense, stoke those flames of hope.

'Not always, but... Aye, she could be.' Aidan ran a hand through his hair. 'My lassie has issues trusting anyone. Never saw any laddies in school. Or lassies. I'm as liberal as they come. Don't care, just so long as she's happy. But somehow that laddie broke down her defences.'

'You know how they met?'

'Sorry. Think it was online. Sits in her room a lot, on her phone and that.'

'You know why she doesn't trust anyone?'

'Hardly. Never speaks to her dad, does she? But... The boys

at school were cruel. Spoke to the headmaster about it, but what could he do? The girls weren't much better.'

'This is Galashiels Academy, right?'

'Right.'

'I know it well.' Marshall gave a polite smile. 'Does she have any female friends?'

'Hmmm.' Aidan leaned back and his T-shirt rolled up to show off his paunch, bald like it'd been shaved. 'None that I know of.'

'She give any idea where she was going on Saturday?'

'Very cagey about it, to be honest. Respect my kid's privacy, but... I... Christ, I wish I'd paid more attention. Wished I'd forced her to tell me. You know?'

'I can imagine.'

'Aidan, you can't beat yourself up, okay?' Elliot clamped his thigh and gave it a squeeze. 'We're doing everything we can. Okay?'

'Okay.'

The floorboards in the hall creaked. A woman peered in. Marshall would've thought she was Aidan's missing daughter – the same natural blonde hair and girlish face – but her grey trouser suit and pink blouse were tell-tale signs of a DC. 'Mr Malcolm, wondering if you'd be able to look through some names for me?'

He stared at Marshall. 'You got enough out of me, son?'

Marshall was about the same age as him, but he didn't correct him. 'I think that's enough to be getting on with for now, aye.' He got to his feet and followed Elliot over to the door, then stopped and looked at Aidan Malcolm. 'Please focus on the fact we haven't found your daughter. We can't give you any promises about her condition, obviously, but we won't rest until we find her. We will do everything we can. Okay?'

'That supposed to reassure me?'

Marshall deserved that. It sounded insincere and clichéd. 'What might help more is the knowledge that when Derek Cameron abducted his victims, he killed and dumped them nearby. People found those bodies. But he had them for up to a week each time. If he took Wendy, it was Saturday night. He was dead himself just a day later. So I think there's a very strong possibility your daughter's still alive. In my opinion, we're not looking for a dead body, Mr Malcolm, we're looking for your daughter, still alive.'

Aidan stared at him, frowning, then looked over at Elliot's DC with newfound vigour. 'Let's see that list, hen.'

Marshall took one last look at him, then followed Elliot back into the hall, then outside into the cool air.

Elliot had her mobile out again. 'You get anything out of that?'

'I don't think he knows where she is or what happened to her. He's just a dad, stressed out his kid's missing. Feeling guilty for not asking more of her. But he's not involved in what's happened.'

'Agreed.' Elliot put her phone away. 'As far as I can tell, Aidan's completely in the dark.'

'You know him?'

'Know most people around here, aye. Aidan's my mum's neighbour's cousin's son.' Said with no note of confusion. 'Used to play with him when we were wee.' She looked away, swallowing. 'I was based in Edinburgh when Sharon died. Absolute tragedy. Helped him come to terms with it and they let me work the case to make sure.'

'Foul play?'

'No, but I wanted to know if it was her fault or someone else's. Sad fact is, it was all hers.'

'Poor guy.'

'Aye, he's okay.' She coughed. 'Anyway. I've got Jolene in there going through Wendy's socials.'

'Another of your team you haven't introduced me to.'

'Do I need to if you're going back to London in the morning?' She let it hang in the air. 'From what Jo's found, Wendy had an active online life.'

'He said she had trust issues?'

'Right. Not many real-life friends, but a lot of interactions on the socials.' Elliot opened her car door, but didn't get in. 'My guess is the lonely are ideal for people like Derek Cameron to prey on.'

'Sounds like you've done your reading.'

'All in your case file, Marshall. Got the subtitles for the hard of understanding from Jolene. Socially isolated women who were night owls, who worked late shifts. So your night bus theory fits *your* cases down there, but up here, there's no such thing.'

'The internet's a pretty big bus.' Marshall grinned at her. But it soon faded. 'So you don't know how he met her?'

'That's right.'

'What about Wendy?'

'Member of sixteen groups online, active in five. Trying to track down people who'll go on the record is tough.'

'If she has a tendency to go deep in friendships online, we might find someone she confided in.'

Elliot gave a flash of her eyebrows. 'We?'

'Okay, you.'

'Fine, but how's that going to help?'

'We might find something.'

'I can't allocate staff based on a "might" and a "something".'

'Callum's her knight in shining armour. Could be the place

he's taken her was somewhere she'd been to. And she might've mentioned it to someone.'

'Fine.'

Another phone call blasted out. Elliot stared at her phone like she was going to throw it against the wall. 'Better take this. Let's go back to the station.'

'Hawick?'

'God, no. Melrose.'

And Marshall had that tightness in his gut again.

CHAPTER FOURTEEN

The long row of old houses was a grand way to lead into any town, but in Melrose it seemed that bit grander. Hardly any had been subdivided into flats, by the looks of it. Even if Marshall sold his London flat, he doubted he could afford one. Still, he could probably buy half of Galashiels, just a few miles down the road.

At the bend, the old church he used to attend was coddled in sheets and scaffolding. The roof tiles were off too. Looked like a big property development going on, the giant hoarding flogging executive apartments. The price was eye-watering – who was buying them here? Still, it looked like the build had stalled, with no signs of any active equipment, just a security light on inside.

He passed the rugby stadium, a small grandstand surrounded by playing fields. The narrowest turnstiles in the world – surely no rugby player could fit through. In April, the place would be filled with temporary stands for the Melrose Sevens. A few days of bacchanalian excess masquerading as a rugby tournament. Long time since Marshall had played there.

The police station was a tiny box, incongruous with the town's Victorian opulence, but the Sixties brutalism blended well with the surrounding policeman's cottages, probably now sold off to private owners.

Two floors, each pretty small. Hardly the ideal place to base a large investigation.

A stream of traffic blocked the entrance. A traffic jam at this time of night. Unusual.

No sign of Elliot in either of the car park's spaces.

Sod it, he drove on around the one-way system.

The first change — the old post office was now a fancy gift shop. Seemed to offer craft classes as well.

At the corner, the abbey was lit up, showing the building's broken grandeur. As much a casualty of the brutal wars with the English as the people.

The car park had just two cars next to each other, lights off, windows down, music pumping. Facing opposite ways so the drivers could sit and chat.

Marshall took the bend and trundled towards the market square, stopping behind a silver Seat. On the corner, a woman chatted with her friend, hands windmilling in the air.

His mother.

A horn blasted behind him.

He should get out and speak to her.

Another honk.

He looked behind him and it was Elliot, motioning for him to go.

Bloody hell.

He put the car in gear and eased through the tiny roundabout, then right through the square with its solicitors' offices and hotel bars, then back on towards the turning and the police station, now on his left and mercifully clear of traffic.

Marshall pulled into the lane running past the station and bumped up onto the pavement. Nobody would need to get past at this time, surely? If they did they could squeeze a bus through.

Elliot had the same idea, parking right behind him.

Marshall let out the yawn he'd been stifling. Boy did he need his bed. He'd have to settle for someone else's, hoping his sleep mask and ear plugs helped him. He got out into the cool air.

Elliot was already out, phone in hand but not talking into it or checking the screen for once. 'What happened back there?'

'Where?'

'Outside the hairdresser.'

'Thought I saw someone I know.'

'And?'

'And you honked your horn and acted like I'd just cut you up at a roundabout.'

'Was it them?'

'Don't know, I drove on.' Marshall thumbed back the way. 'There's a Co-op now where the furniture shop used to be.'

She set off towards the station, checking her phone as she walked. 'Christ, how long have you been away?'

'Long enough.'

Her tutting got worse the closer they got and the more she scrolled with her thumb. 'Bloody hell.'

'Everything okay?'

She put the mobile away. 'It's all fine. All hunky dory.'

Marshall dashed forward to open the door for her.

'Very chivalrous.' Elliot slipped inside and walked past the empty reception desk to swipe through the door, holding it open for him. 'After you.'

Marshall did as he was told, but once he'd stepped

through, he had to wait. Three corridors branched off. 'Which way?'

Elliot took straight ahead. 'What's it like being back?'

'It's not London, is it?'

'Well, no.'

'You know what I mean. It's very quiet here. Even with that traffic jam back there.' Marshall shrugged. 'Would've thought you'd be all down in Hawick where CID used to be.'

'Only the boss is down there. Choice of three decent golf courses, and another half an hour away from the brass up in Edinburgh. The actual work gets done here and Gala.' She stopped outside a door. Someone had stuck a Post-It note to it, marked with 'WATCH YOUR BALLS'. She smirked as she tore it down, then entered her office.

Marshall followed but didn't know where to stand or sit. It smelled of ripe Stilton cheese and floor polish. The two chairs in front of the desk were piled up with box files. He shifted one lot onto the edge of her desk.

Elliot hung her coat on the rack and sat behind a computer. She switched on a big TV hanging off the wall, tuned to Sky News. One tut at the political clusterfuck in Westminster, then she was logging in to her computer and ignoring him. She was just as bad with that as with her phone.

Marshall grabbed the scrunched-up note from the desk. 'What does this mean?'

'Lads in the station call me the Ballbuster.' Elliot smirked, her eyes flicking up and down her screen. 'I arrested someone in Glasgow five years ago. Things got out of hand and, well. You can imagine the rest.'

'You punched him in the balls?'

She laughed. 'Did worse than that.' She leaned back and folded her arms. 'Twat had a knife. He stood over me, ready to slit my throat. I hit him with my keys. So hard I punctured a testicle.'

'Jesus Christ.'

'So watch yourself.' She turned to jab a finger at him, though he couldn't tell if the threat was a joke or not. 'I skimmed your profile earlier.' She tapped the screen. 'Seems pretty thorough for someone investigating serious collisions.'

'I was a criminal profiler before I joined the police. Based at the University of Durham. Worked a few cases in the north-east, then a couple down in London for the Met. Then I joined the police.'

She scowled at him. 'You're a direct entry?'

'As a DI.'

Elliot shook her head, seeming bemused by it. 'So why are you now investigating serious collisions?'

'Long story.'

'Got all night.'

'Oh, this needs a few days.' He looked away from her. Needed to trust her a lot more before he shared that detail with her.

She snorted, staring at her computer screen. 'So, Derek Cameron hasn't been seen nor heard of in two years. Why's he here? Why now?'

'I wish I knew.' Marshall finally settled down opposite, but the chair had a wonky leg. So bad he felt he was going to topple right over. 'I don't get why he's been hiding out in the Borders of all places.'

'You don't think he was passing through?'

'Not if he's taken someone, no. His MO is all about monitoring victims over a long period of time, making sure he knows everything about their lives. It minimises the opportunity for someone to spot him abducting his victim.'

'So you think he was just meeting someone up on the viaduct?'

Marshall raised a shoulder. 'See your point, but you used the J-word.'

'J-word?'

'Just. Anytime someone uses it, expect a bloody nightmare.' Marshall leaned forward, which seemed to balance the chair a bit better. 'Of all the rural places in the British Isles he could've hidden out – Cornwall, the Highlands, Wales, even Ireland – it's a huge coincidence that you found him here of all places, isn't it? Two miles from where I grew up.'

'Putting yourself front and centre, eh?'

'Hardly. I was Deputy SIO on a five-victim serial killer case. Fair enough if he was found in Wembley or Brent. But as far as I know, I'm the only Met officer from the Scottish Borders. This is where I was born and raised, not like Hawick or Kelso. That bridge...'

'Sometimes coincidences happen, Marshall.'

He wasn't getting much out of her.

She reached into her drawer and pulled out a box of protein bars. 'You want one?'

'I'm fine.'

'No, you're not. You drove here from London pretty much without stopping, then you've been at a crime scene, a pathology lab and a victim's house. You haven't mentioned eating. Now, you could be a superhero, but I think even you need food.'

'Fine, thank you.'

She tossed him a peanut and raspberry bar.

Not his favourite, but he devoured it in two bites.

She took a dainty nibble of hers. 'You know Derek Cameron best. How do we find Wendy?'

Now he'd eaten, Marshall realised he was starving. His

stomach was an empty void, numb to hunger. He could destroy the rest of the box, then raid the vending machine and it still wouldn't come close to satisfying him. 'In London, Cameron took his victims someplace secret. A week later, they were dumped and the bodies found. Up here, well. I just don't know.'

'He had some kind of secret underground lair?'

'In London, he had a lock-up in Surbiton. Wasn't underground or much of a lair.'

'But we're looking for a lock-up or abandoned building somewhere, right?'

'Probably, aye. Thing with serial abductors is it's all about control. Controlling their victims. Controlling their environment. They take someone and basically own their very existence for as long as they want. Having that power over another human being can be the thrill. Now, if Cameron wasn't completely in control of the location, someone could come in and interrupt.'

'Like Wendy's father, say?'

'No. God no. I mean a random member of the public or maybe a family member. Or a friend. Wherever he's taken her, it's got to be somewhere only he has access to.'

'Like what?'

'We know Cameron doesn't have any living family, so he could be staying with a friend. Could even be that he's hiding in plain sight, acting like a normal human being. Living in a flat, with neighbours. He can't afford a sprawling country pile. But I'd be looking at garages or derelict buildings.'

'Plenty of them around here. Old mills along the Tweed.'

'That kind of thing. The garage in Surbiton was rented in his own name, would you believe? As far as we can tell from the forensics, he held his victim there for a week, raping her until he'd had enough, then strangled her.'

'I'm going to have another one.' Elliot tore into the box and tossed a bar towards Marshall. Coconut and blueberry. Hearing the graphic details of a serial killer's MO didn't seem to faze her. 'They were all strangled?'

'Pretty much. Figured that he did it as a sex act. The first tentative victim, he—'

'The girlfriend at school?'

'Right. He tried choking her. She liked it. He loved it. Then he tied her up and it freaked her out.'

'Okay, so he strangles these women to death as part of one last sex act?'

'That's what I think, yes.' Marshall got up and walked around the room. Both whiteboards were filled with statistics. Nothing clean that he could write on. And he needed to write when he was thinking. Otherwise, the sheer number of thoughts clouded his brain. Getting it down onto the page or the board meant the thoughts were dealt with. Managed. Then he could connect them and divine noise from the chaos.

'You okay there, Marshall?'

He grabbed his protein bar and opened the wrapper. 'We need to dig into the life of Callum Davidson. Find that special place for him with personal significance.'

'Any ideas?'

'It's a lot of work. We need to find where he worked. Who he spoke to. Interview them in the hope that he's dropped clues or mentioned something.'

Elliot grinned. 'We?'

'The collective we. You. Your team.' Marshall bit into the bar. 'And we don't have long to unpick his life. Wendy's been missing for over three days now. He's been dead most of that time. She's dying. Or dead.'

'Marshall, I've got a ton of resource scouring the area. Half of the Edinburgh team, as well as the local lot who know the lay of the land. We're doing everything we can.'

'Is it enough?'

'I've got to hope so.' She finished her bar, narrowing her eyes as she chewed. 'What I would love to know was what the hell Cameron was doing up on the viaduct at midnight, high as a kite. That might lead to who would kill him. And maybe we can find Wendy that way.'

'That doesn't seem like something you need me for.'

'How are you proposing to help, then?'

'I could go back to London tomorrow.' Marshall felt a tickling in his nostrils like he might cry at any point. He waved a hand at her computer. 'But I could update my profile.'

'What with?'

'Wendy Malcolm is an extra data point. We might be able to connect her with the others two years ago. There are differences, sure, but some of that is because rural Scotland and urban London are chalk and cheese. But there might be similarities. Something that could narrow things down. The best way I can help you, Andrea, is to dust off the old profile.'

She seemed to bristle at the use of her forename. 'You don't think it's a waste of time?'

'No, I think it could be. But it could be important.' He smiled at her. 'Have you got me somewhere to stay?'

'We haven't, no.'

Marshall clenched his fists, curled his toes. 'But I've drive—'

She burst out laughing. 'Of course we do. Presidential suite at Taylor's Hotel.'

'Take it you mean the cheapest single bed there?'

'Their finest wanking chariot is all yours.'

Marshall got up and stretched out. 'Where can I get a strong coffee at this time?'

'In Melrose? No idea. Hotel's probably shut the kitchen. There's a McDonald's the other side of Gala. Their coffee's okay. You planning on doing an all-nighter?'

'I need to, don't I?'

'See, I had you pegged as a martyr and now you've just confirmed it.'

CHAPTER FIFTEEN

There was one place in Melrose where Marshall could definitely get a strong coffee at any hour.

He took a deep breath and held it in his lungs.

Should he do this? Could he?

Stop being a coward.

He let his breath go and knocked on the door.

Almost dark now, just the last few rays of light making it over the hills to the west. Cold, with the whisper of rain on the breeze. The fast road was propped up over the town, an ambulance screaming over with flashing blue lights, heading back to the hospital.

Where Derek Cameron was resting.

Hard to believe he was actually dead.

Hard to believe Marshall's quest was finally over.

Almost.

They still had to find Wendy Malcolm.

Hopefully still alive.

He peered in through the kitchen window.

A teenage girl was doing the dishes, earbuds sticking out, bopping to some music as she rinsed a plate free of suds.

Christ. He had the wrong house.

And his mother had moved and hadn't told him.

That was on him. Took two to tango, but he was the one who had shut down, who hadn't even spoken to her in years.

Sod Elliot, he should've got out of the car and spoken to her when he saw her in the town square. Apologise for his part in the frostiness.

If he was being honest, that was about ninety percent of it.

He stepped away, taking one last look inside.

And saw her.

His mother.

Janice Simpson.

Her blonde hair was now mostly silver. Still had her figure, despite constantly moaning about how her kids had ruined it. The kind of joke said with a smile, but which stuck with both of them.

Wait, so the girl washing the dishes...

Shit, it was Thea. Marshall's niece. She'd grown about a foot in the two years since he'd last seen her. He hadn't seen much of her in her life. Not recently, anyway.

Marshall rapped on the door again.

Mum opened it. 'Robert?' She looked him up and down. 'Is that you, Robert?'

'No, Mum, it's an evil me from a parallel universe.'

'Robert, what are you doing here?'

'Nice to see you too.' Marshall reached over and gave her a big hug. She smelled the same but felt smaller and frailer. 'How are you doing?'

'I'm well. Just a bit surprised to see you, that's all. Sorry. I... It's been a long time.' She laughed. 'Come in, come in.' She led him back inside.

He walked in and got that blast of his childhood. The smell of her cooking, tinged with that vinegar. Maybe it was how she cleaned the surfaces.

No sign of Thea now.

'Place has hardly changed.'

'Is that a criticism?'

'No, it's nice being home.'

'I haven't seen you in over a year.'

'It's three years. My cousin's wedding.'

'Right, yes. And you only stayed the one night, didn't you? In that hotel. Not here.'

'You know how it is, Mum. You had a full house. And I'm a busy man.'

She tightened her lips and narrowed her eyes. 'Too busy for your family.'

'No, I still text my sister.'

'Texting isn't seeing people, Robert.' She shut her eyes. 'Sorry, I'm being a cow. It's just...'

'I get it, Mum. Sorry, I should've called you first.'

'I... I've changed my number.'

Jesus, that stung his heart. That she hadn't told him. 'I should've called Jen and asked for it when you hadn't replied for the twentieth time. I just took a telling.'

Not the only time in his life he'd had that...

'Cup of tea?'

'That'd be lovely, thanks.'

'Tea's just brewing.' Mum walked over and poured from the same old green pot into the matching mugs. One had added a chip to the crack. 'What brings you home?'

He slid a hand down his face. 'I'm back here for a case. Just thought I'd say hi.' He waved at her. 'Hi.'

'Come on, Robert. You're staying here.'

'They've got me a hotel.'

'Cancel it. Please!'

Marshall stared hard at her. Almost exactly like looking at his sister. Nothing like looking in the mirror. And she was upset. Shocked, but also torn. 'I've got a ton of work to do. It's complex, but there's stuff I need to do. Sorry.'

'Okay. I see.'

'Going out, Gran.' A blur of blonde hair and gangly limbs stormed out the front door, slamming it behind her.

'Thea!' Mum raced over to the window and chapped on it. 'That girl will be the death of me.'

'How is she?'

'She's good. Doing well at the school. You missed her birthday.'

Marshall rasped a hand over the stubble. 'I'm sorry.'

'It's not me you should be apologising to.'

'I've messaged Jen, but haven't heard from her in a while either.'

'Robert, your own niece is sixteen and you forgot her birthday.' She shook her head as she tipped in milk. 'That's confusing for her.'

'I get it. Why's she here, though?'

'Well, your sister and Thea are staying with us.' Mum rested a cup on the table in front of him. 'Sit.'

He did, cradling the hot cup. 'Wait, what happened to Paul?'

'Long story. It's been a nightmare ordeal for her. For them both, really. After what Jen went through with your father...'

'We both went through it.'

'Well, you did, that's true, but she took it much harder.'

And Jen's twin brother hadn't been there for her, had he?

'She's bought a place in Clovenfords. Be out of here in a couple of months.' Mum tilted her head back up the hill. 'Stay the night and speak to them, Robert. Please.'

He should. At least to see Thea.

But...

'No, Mum. I've really got to get on, but I'll stay for a bit, okay? Maybe see you tomorrow night?'

Arms folded tight across her chest, scowling at her son. 'Well, how are you doing? Any females on the scene?'

Females... Great...

CHAPTER SIXTEEN

Taylor's Hotel was a hulking great building on the high street, resting between two competing butchers, with a hipster coffee shop taking up half the ground floor. Three stories, making it one of the tallest buildings in Melrose, save for the abbey's remnants and the many churches.

Marshall was still fizzing with energy when he pulled into the car park at the back. He grabbed his luggage from the boot. A slight mark on the suitcase, but it looked presentable. He unclipped it, then wheeled it over to the hotel's rear entrance.

The interior was all heavy furniture, dark mahogany and green carpet. A grandfather clocked ticked away beside the hotel reception, even heavier wood surrounding a wee hatch.

Marshall dinged the bell and waited.

No sign of anyone.

And he finally noticed the typed sign:

AKS IN BAR

Marshall didn't know whether 'Aks' was a typo, someone's name, someone's nickname or a bit of slang. He wandered through to the bar and found someone. People. A lot of people.

The giant screen was showing a tennis match, the sound almost deafening. Under the roof, probably. His flat wasn't a million miles from Wimbledon, but he'd never made it to a match.

Marshall looked at the crowd watching the tennis. Mostly men in their forties and fifties, clutching pints. He scanned each face. Nobody he recognised – wait, the guy in the lime polo shirt. He was in his year at school, wasn't he? Then he heard him speak with a London accent. Nope. Mistaken identity.

Pool balls clacked, but Marshall couldn't see a table anywhere.

The barman was cleaning a glass, the TV reflected in his thick glasses. Hard to tell if his mutton chop sideburns ran into the porn-star moustache or if there was a gap between them. Maybe the hair was just thin there. 'Help you, son?'

'Got a reservation. Rob Marshall.'

Still didn't look away from the tennis. 'The cop?'

'So much for discretion.'

'Hey, you need discretion, you – go on, my son! – should stay elsewhere.'

'Didn't book it.'

'Right. Sure.' He threw his head back with a groan. 'Bastard.'

'Can I check in, then?'

'Oh. Aye.' For all that work, he hadn't seemed to have made much headway in drying the glass. 'Chantelle usually does the reception but her dog had a hysterectomy today, so...'

'That's a thing?'

'Seems like it.' The barman tossed a key on the bartop and a clipboard. 'Breakfast is seven till nine. Need a wake-up call?'

Marshall signed his name. Felt like half of his life was spent filling out forms. 'I'll be out of here before six, I should think.'

'Sure. Christ, man, I've got a tenner on this.' Seemed like the last money the guy had in the world by the way he was taking a straight-sets defeat. 'Can I get you a drink while you wait?'

'Wait for what?'

The barman looked at him like he'd grown a third head. 'The tennis to finish?'

'Not really into tennis. Can I get a coffee to take up to my room, then?'

'Filter do you?'

'Depends when it was made.'

'Half seven.'

'Morning or evening?'

'Evening, you cheeky bugger.'

Two hours stewing. Sod it, bound to be nuclear strength and enough to get him through the night.

'Sure, I'll have it. Black, please.'

'Fantastic.' The barman stepped over to a filter machine, focusing on the tennis, and got out a Styrofoam cup – surely they'd been banned in the Nineties? He poured, but tipped the jug onto his foot. 'Ah, for fu—' He kicked his shoe off. 'Sorry, sir, that's the last of it.'

'Can you put on another pot?'

A distracted sigh. 'Suppose I could, aye. In fact, I'll join you.' He set about emptying the machine and tipping the grounds into the bin.

Marshall looked around the room again. Christ, it had changed a lot. He'd been in here a lot as a kid. A dive bar that took a laissez-faire attitude to checking the ages of its patrons.

Had his first pint in here, the lemonade barely softening the harsh lager. Had to help Jen out after they'd tanned a half-bottle of vodka before coming in, going to see someone DJing at the club in Gala. Only thing she saw that night was in the inside of the toilet bowl.

A woman was frowning at him. Shoulder-length green hair, shaved at the left side and swept right over to the other. Sitting on her own at a laptop. Piercing green eyes. She stood and walked over, the frown deepening. 'Oh my. You're staying here too?'

Marshall leaned back against the bar and smiled. 'Sorry, I don't think we've met?'

'We have.'

He had to rack his brains for where he knew her from. Her accent was local, probably Gala. 'Were we at school together?'

'Don't be daft. I'm about ten years younger than you.' She held out a hand. 'I'll introduce myself again, so this time it might stick. I'm Kirsten Weir.'

That clicked it all into place. 'Crime scene investigator, right?'

'Now you've got it. I suppose you'd have recognised my hair if you'd seen it.'

'It is quite a statement. And sorry for not recognising you. Been a hell of a day.'

She reached over for her glass of rosé wine. 'You want a seat?'

Marshall checked on the barman's progress. Unlike the barman himself, who was watching the tennis. At least he'd put the machine on, but it was only just now getting up to heat and hadn't spat any hot water through the coffee grounds. 'Aye, sure.' He wheeled his case over and sat opposite her. 'Might not be much company. I've got a lot of work to do and I'm shattered.'

'Heard you're this shit-hot hotshot criminal profiler.'

'Whoever said that must've been drunk.'

'Why?'

'I was a criminal profiler, but I was neither shit hot nor a hotshot. I just... Wrote documents and interviewed people.'

'Hopefully not that way around.'

'What?'

'Surely you'd interview them before you wrote the documents?'

'No, I did it in that order. Read up on the suspects first to get the gen on them, then interview them to test my hypothesis, then refine it.'

'Sounds interesting.'

'Partly. Trouble is, you have to catch the bastards first for it to be a useful process.'

She stared hard at him with her green eyes. Matched her hair perfectly. 'And it's the ones you haven't caught that you want to focus on?'

'Exactly that.' Marshall sat back. Felt sweltering in here. Didn't want to give too much away with all these prying ears. 'You in to watch the tennis?'

She shook her head. 'Hate sport.'

'So why are you staying here?'

'What do you mean?'

'You've got a local accent.'

'So do you and you're staying here.'

'Touché. You don't live in London, though, do you?'

'Edinburgh.'

'Which is commutable.'

'Not in January when I started down here. Road kept getting closed. Managed to get them to put me up in here. Meant I could cancel my room in a shared flat in Gorgie and stay here rent-free.'

'Wise.'

'Don't tell anyone.' She tapped her nose. 'Back on secondment here to help with this outreach initiative. Absolute joke. Political bullshit.'

'Tell me about it...'

She sank some of her wine, the ice cubes clinking. Classy. 'But you're originally from the Borders, London boy?'

'Right. Grew up in Melrose as much as I did grow up. You?'

'Gala. Langlee.'

'Wow.'

'Come on, it's not that bad.'

Marshall laughed. 'People around here talk about the place like it's a circle of hell. Try going to London.'

'Or Edinburgh.'

'Exactly. It's actually not that bad.'

'Here you are, pal.' The barman put the Styrofoam cup in front of Marshall along with his room key. 'Forgot that, didn't you?'

'Sorry.' Marshall was blushing. 'How much am I due you for the coffee?'

'It's on the tab, pal.'

'Get you anything, Kirsten?'

'I'm good, Carlos. Cheers.'

And he was walking off, watching the tennis.

'Carlos?'

'Name's Carl, but everyone calls him Carlos.' She shrugged. 'Nicknames, eh?'

Marshall pulled the lid off and took a sip. Absolutely vile. Thin and yet somehow tasting stewed despite only just being brewed. He put the lid back on. 'I'd love to have a drink with you, but I've got to get on with my profile.'

'Never stops, eh?'

'Nope. Never does. Until we die. Maybe then we'll get some peace.'

She smiled. 'I'm actually working here if you want to join me?'

'Thanks, but I need absolute concentration.'

'Sure.' She seemed disappointed. Or he'd somehow misread the situation. Not the first time.

'Maybe see you at breakfast?'

'Oh, I don't eat until lunchtime. Intermittent fasting.'

He frowned at her glass. 'Doesn't wine count?'

'It's not wine. It's sugar-free squash.' She waved him away. 'Go on, get on with your profile.'

CHAPTER SEVENTEEN

Marshall eased off his noise-cancelling headphones and let the world back in. He was stripped down to his pants, but the room was baking. The room's heating seemed to only have one setting: BURNING HOT.

He reached over to open the window wider. Seconds later, a fug of cigarette smoke and drunken giggling came in.

On a Tuesday night.

Sounded like the match was in the fifth set by the rapturous cheers coming up from the bar.

The empty coffee beaker was still on the desk, so he dumped it in the bin, then went back to his profile, headphones back on.

He could barely focus on it. The words swam around the page. He managed to read a whole paragraph, but hadn't taken anything in. Might as well have been about MPs' expenses or the tennis match. Not even Sony's finest technology could help.

So much for pulling an all-nighter. Marshall needed his

bed. Assuming he could sleep in this heat. Maybe a cold shower would sort him out? Or a cold bath?

His phone was flashing on the desk.

Rickards calling...

He wanted to ignore it, but he knew that'd only make things worse. He answered the call through his headphones. 'Hey, boss.' Opening his mouth pulled out a yawn.

'You okay there, Rob?' She sounded like she was in the station's car park. Her voice was a glorious 3D sound that seemed to swallow him up.

'Sorry. I'm just tired.'

She clicked her tongue. 'Thought you'd be in your bed, but I just wanted to see how you were doing.'

'Reworking my profile on the Chameleon, AKA Derek Cameron.'

'Oh. Wow. Already? You getting anything out of it?'

'Nothing new so far.'

'Oh. Sorry to hear that. Not surprised you're too tired to focus on it, though. Only you would think about driving from London to Scotland, then try to pull an all-nighter to rework a three-year-old profile without having much additional data.'

He let the yawn go. 'Seemed like a good idea at the time.'

More clicking. And when she clicked, she lied. 'Keep at it. It might be what they need. Let's pick up in the morning, but get some sleep. Okay?'

'Okay. Will try. Catch you later.'

'Cheers, Rob.' And she was gone.

Marshall put the phone down and immediately it buzzed. Like working in a call centre.

Jen calling...

Only a matter of time...

He could visualise the string of text messages between his mother and sister, discussing him and his surprise presence.

Or they just discussed it when Jen got in from work.

He answered the call. 'Hey, trouble.'

'Not in the mood, dickhead. Mum said you were here?'

'Straight to the chase there. No build up, no exposition, no ramping up of tens—'

'*Rob*.'

'Aye, I was there.' Christ, he could hear the climbing 'aye' sound creeping back into his accent after only a couple of hours back.

'Didn't think to let me know, did you?'

'It's work. It's... Sorry. It's a long story.'

'You always say that. Just give me edited highlights.'

'Someone died. Someone I've been searching for.' He paused long enough for her to get half a sigh out. 'I hear that you're staying with her?'

'Waiting for my divorce to come through. Paul's buying me out of the house. Just about scraped enough to buy a place in Cloven.'

'Sorry to hear that.'

'It's nice!'

'I'm joking. I know it is. Maybe we should catch up for a coffee?'

'I'm kind of busy just now.'

'No time to see your twin brother, eh?'

'Shut up, dickhead.'

'I'd love to see Thea again.'

'Sure you would. Because someone who's keen to see his niece makes sure he doesn't go two years without seeing her. Then misses her birthday.'

'Come on, that's... It's totally fair. I deserve that. I've been a stranger and I'm sorry. I got lost in the job. The pandemic was tough on me and—'

'It was tough on everyone. But it wasn't a constant lockdown. You could've come up after they eased the restrictions.'

'That's true. I should've talked to you about it.' He paused to let her fill the gap, but she wasn't. She was just as stubborn as him. 'Jen, I want to make up for it.'

'Let me think about it.' She sucked a deep breath. 'This case you're here for. Is it the guy at the viaduct?'

'Can't really say.'

'Christ, Rob. I'm your sister. I won't tell a soul.'

'Okay, so what if it is?'

'Jesus, that must be tough.'

He swallowed a lump in his throat. 'It is what it is.'

'Rob, I know you. You'll be beating yourself up over everything. What happened up there wasn't your fault.'

He shut his eyes and felt the tears sting his cheeks. 'I know.'

'Seriously, Rob, it wasn't.'

'I know. I've been trying to come to terms with what happened since I was seventeen.'

'Are you any closer?'

'Jen. I need to get to bed. Can we rake these hot coals over coffee?'

'Okay. I'll check my diary. Sleep tight, dickhead.' And she was gone.

Marshall was buzzing again, that fluttering in his stomach and his chest. Like there were snakes down there. Or worms. Felt hard to keep anything down.

He stuck on some late Radiohead and went back to his profile, trying to piece it all together, trying to spot what he was missing. All those words he'd written three years ago after three victims. All the changes he'd made tonight, underlined in red. He'd been staring hard at the trees, but hadn't seen the wood.

Made him wonder.

Can't see the wood for the trees.

Was that wood as in forest or as in what people made stuff out of? Was it about missing the big picture or the small detail?

It hit him.

What he was missing was why anyone would kill Derek Cameron.

So many suspects, but who's the likely one? A father, a brother, a husband, a friend of a victim. A mother, a sister, a friend.

No husbands, but it still left a lot of people, someone who just had to track Cameron down and enact revenge.

Was that the motive? Revenge?

He couldn't see anything else.

Maybe it was someone who'd reported suspicions to the police which had fallen on deaf ears. Something to follow up on – trace through all the call records on HOLMES, anyone who'd reported a suspect.

But finding the murderer of a serial killer – if he'd even been murdered – wasn't the A-game here.

Wendy Malcolm could die.

And he was sitting in a hotel, wearing just his pants and expensive headphones. Absolutely melting and working at a laptop. Picking away at an old profile.

Was he looking at a forest or some timber?

And something dug into the back of his brain, like a deer tick snapping on. It wasn't just the dead women – and the potentially still alive one – who were victims of Cameron.

And look where your ego got me, Rob.

Some days, I wish you'd just let me die.

Those words had stung him. John Hulse had said them and

he'd been right – this was an ego thing for Marshall. He knew that, but he hoped it drove him to do good. To stop people like Derek Cameron.

But what if it betrayed something?

What if Hulse had got a lead on him and decided to go rogue?

Besides, Marshall didn't want to leave it like that, so he picked up his phone and tapped out a text to Hulse:

Sorry for earlier. I was too forceful.

His phone buzzed almost immediately:

You're a wanker. Been to hell and back over this. But I love you, man. Sorry for overreacting.

No need to apologise.

Marshall was just being polite. Hulse had been an arsehole. Both had and both needed to apologise.

His phone vibrated in his hand.

DS Hulse calling...

Christ, Marshall hadn't updated the contact entry since Hulse joined his team years ago. He answered it. 'John.'

'Mate. You really think I could kill someone?'

'I don't know, John. I don't think so, but I don't know you anymore. Not like we used to.'

Hulse grunted.

'The truth is, like you said, I was the one who let Cameron go. I chose to stay with you. And we didn't catch him. He's free —' Careful! 'He was free to do it again. And now he's dead without any answers. And... And I can't see why he'd be in this area.' He looked out of the window at the rolling hills on the other side of the Tweed, a spectral blue glow behind them. Wouldn't get truly dark. 'He's found where I'm from. Feels personal.'

'Like I said. Your ego.'

'No, John. Where he was found has personal significance for me.'

'What?'

Marshall couldn't speak. He grabbed the bottle of water off the table and took a long drink. Didn't cool him down any.

'You're freaked out, Rob.'

'Damn right. And more than a little bit.'

'Why are you up in Scotland?'

Fishing. Worrying Marshall was on to him. Try and focus him. 'There's another woman missing, John. It's definitely Cameron.'

'But he's dead?'

'That's what's so hard about it. We know Cameron took her, but we don't know where to. So she could be trapped and dying now.'

'Probably dead.'

'Probably. But I've got to try to find her. She's maybe got a day. Maybe.'

'Think this is personal, don't you?'

'John, ever since... it happened. Two years pretty much to the day. I've played over and over what happened. When Cameron shot you, he came up to the car first. He knew our names, John.'

'You think he'd been following us?'

'I do. Or maybe he'd been waiting to get on the bus and saw a car sitting there. Two idiots watching out for him and he decided to strike. Still, he knew us.'

'Know what's coming next.'

'What?'

'Him being here, abducting a woman. If you'd stopped him, she'd be okay.'

God, he'd missed Hulse's blunt honesty.

'You can blame yourself for what happened, Rob. My therapist said that's counterproductive, though.'

'I bet she gets a lot out of you.'

'Mate, it's a man and I'm really open with him.'

'Pleased to hear it.'

'My advice, Rob? Focus on what you can do now. How to save that woman. Ignore the noise. It distracts you. Do that profile. It might unearth the truth. You got this, man.'

'Thank you.' But Hulse had already hung up.

Marshall didn't know what to make of it. But to be effective, he needed to sleep.

CHAPTER EIGHTEEN

...

I put the phone away and stand in the square, Taser in my pocket, pretending to inspect the properties for sale in the window. Might be entering a recession, but you wouldn't think it here. Prices to make your eyes water.

A dog's sniffing at the bin, but its owner's glued to her phone, which lights up her face. Bless the beast, she couldn't pass an object without seeing who's been there before, could she? 'Come on, you.' The owner tugs at the lead, but she's still locked to her phone.

Gives me another chance to look over at the hotel.

He's still up in his room. Detective Inspector Robert Marshall. Head lowered as he works on a laptop, headphones on.

He had to come here, didn't he?

Maybe I acted too rashly in killing Derek Cameron, but I had no choice.

Could've predicted they'd send Marshall.

Not even Marshall will find me, though.

But if he finds Wendy first, then...

Shit.

The skin on my arms pricks up.

It's good to be back in the game like this. Makes me feel alive.

A van pulls up and the lad jumps out, dumping the newspapers outside the shop. It's gone before I notice, heading for the shop in Tweedbank, probably. I wander over and check out the front page of the *Edinburgh Argus*.

They're leading with the disappearance of Wendy Malcolm. Borders lassie, seventeen, taken on Saturday.

Right age, right profile.

Derek Cameron's doing.

I can't clear it up.

Shite.

I made a mistake there.

Wait.

She needs to be found.

Whoever does will be seen as a hero.

It can't be me.

I can't ingratiate myself – it'll draw suspicion. It has to be anonymous or someone else's doing.

That's got to be the plan.

If Marshall finds her alive, I'm in the shit. But if she's dead when he does, she can't talk.

I look up at the room again. Marshall is looking right at me.

His gaze darts around the square, then he draws the curtains.

If he saw me, it's game over.

I scurry off back the way I came. Can't do this again. It's way too risky.

CHAPTER NINETEEN

MARSHALL

So much for being out of the hotel before six.

Quarter to seven and Marshall was still rubbing the sleep out of his eyes. His cooked breakfast was staring back at him. A full Scottish he was struggling to get through.

'There you are.'

Marshall looked up to a flash of green sitting opposite.

Kirsten Weir, placing two coffee cups on the table. Smiling at him. 'Beaten by your breakfast, eh?'

'Can't eat any more.' Marshall pushed his massive breakfast plate away. 'When I get a fry-up, I expect the baked beans to be in a ramekin so they don't get everywhere.'

She scowled at him like he'd just insulted every single ancestor by name. 'You *what*?'

'Seriously. Nobody wants soggy, tomato-y bread or eggs, do they?'

'You use a sausage to stop the spread. Or...' She leaned across the table. 'Pro tip. When you're cooking beans, squirt in some brown sauce and overcook the beans until they congeal. Beautiful.'

Marshall narrowed his eyes at her. 'I'll try that next time.'

'Do it.' Kirsten slid one of the coffee cups over the table. 'Here.'

'For me?'

'Right. The stuff in the station is rank. Saw you turning your nose up at Carlos the Barman's lame attempts at coffee making.' She put a hand around her mouth and whispered, 'He uses instant.'

'Seriously?'

'He's like that advert when we were kids. Doing all the puff puff noises, pretending he's got a filter machine going. There are drums of stuff from that cheap shop by the station in Gala.'

'Might have to charge him with fraud… or administering a noxious substance.'

She laughed. 'Anyway, there's a good place next door.'

'Thank you. I'll get you one tomorrow. Assuming I'm still needed.' Marshall grabbed his coffee and stood up. 'You going in now?'

'Sure thing.'

'Want company?'

'It's not exactly a long walk to the station.'

'Still, it's Melrose. Anything could happen on the way. Drug gangs, packs of wild dogs, sentient killer robots from the future.'

She laughed again. 'Sure.' She strode out of the restaurant at a rapid clip. 'It's robots from a parallel universe *I'm* worried about.'

Marshall picked up his leather messenger bag and coffee, then followed her out.

Christ, she was fast.

Kirsten was waiting outside for him. 'You get anywhere with that profile of yours?'

'Need more data, really.'

'Six cases isn't enough?'

'It'd be plenty in normal circumstances. And sometimes it's not about the number of cases so much as the information we've gathered on them. Problem is, the sixth victim is very different to the first five. His MO and location have changed. Used to act in complete secrecy. Now he's been seeing her in public.'

'Getting braver?'

'Maybe. Could be he's entirely innocent. Could be anything. I need more data.'

'So another day shadowing Ballbuster Elliot?'

'We'll see.' As they walked, Marshall looked into Gibson Park, a place he'd played touch rugby as a kid, where he'd got drunk as a teenager, where...

He wiped away a tear from his eye before it fully formed.

She was frowning at him. 'You okay there?'

'It's windy. Must be grit.' He sipped coffee through the lid. Tasted lovely, nothing like the crud in the hotel. 'I'm just here to consult. It's Elliot's case.'

'I'll warn you now. She's a total arsehole.'

Marshall smiled at her. 'Pissed you off, has she?'

'Pissed everyone off. On a daily basis. Believe me, you cops can be total dicks at the best of times, but she takes it to the next level.' She entered the lane leading to the station, shaking her head. 'She's perfected being a total wanker.'

A car squealed, then bumped the kerb just inches away from Marshall's toes.

He jerked back, spilling his coffee over his shoes. 'Hey!'

The driver seemed to take no notice. A big lump got out, strapping on a backpack, big enough to make him look like a snail carrying his home. He plipped the locks and marched off towards the station.

Marshall recognised him – the cop at Wendy Malcolm's

home the previous night, the one who gave Elliot the CCTV on the iPad, who disappeared in a puff of smoke. She had a nickname for him that seemed to be apt.

He charged after him. 'Here, you almost ran me over there.'

Got a withering look back. 'Sorry, mate, no idea what you're talking about.'

Marshall grabbed his shoulder as he tried to enter the station. 'I'm talking to you, *mate*. You made me spill my coffee! What's your name? Shifty? Shonky?'

'It's DS Rakesh Siyal.' He stood up even taller, like his rank would protect him. 'Who are you?'

'DI Rob Marshall. I don't want to make a big thing of this, but you need to drive a lot more carefully. This whole town's a twenty limit and this is a *car park*.'

'Right.'

'You can apologise now, Sergeant.'

'Aye, and you can let me go and do my job.'

Kirsten got between them, blocking Marshall. 'Shunty, on you go.'

'Cheers, Weirdo.' Shunty slouched off inside.

Marshall was seething now. Heart pumping, fists clenched. 'You shouldn't let him—'

'No.' Kirsten gripped his arm. 'You don't get it. If he's not in five minutes before the briefing, Elliot will toast his nuts.'

'I don't care! He almost ran me over!'

'Shunty's one of the good guys, Rob. Trust me on that.'

Trust her? He barely even knew her. 'Fine, I'll let it go for now.'

Kirsten gave Marshall her coffee. 'There, all better. See?' She patted his arm, smiling. 'Come on, we shouldn't be late for the briefing either.' She strode inside.

Marshall stopped to get his pass out of his jacket pocket. Wasn't there. He searched both trouser pockets – no joy – then found it in the pouch on his messenger bag. Why on earth he'd put it in there...

He went inside and swiped his card against the reader.

Red light.

Bloody thing still didn't work.

The door clicked shut, with Kirsten on the other side.

At least there was someone on the desk today.

Marshall walked over and showed his warrant card. 'I'm here to consult on—'

'Mate, can you give me a minute?'

'Excuse me?'

'Have to add you to the system, Mr Marshall.'

'It's Detective Inspector Marshall.'

'Very pleased for you, sir, but your rank doesn't speed anything up.'

'So your chief constable wouldn't get through?'

'She'd be fine as her pass is a Police Scotland one, not a Metropolitan Police one. Now, just give me a minute. Aye?'

The outside door opened and Elliot barged in, lugging a giant cake box. 'Morning, David.' She stopped to get her card out, blew her hair away from her eyes, then pressed it against the reader. Green light.

Marshall walked over, smiling. 'Andrea, can you let me through?'

She looked Marshall up and down. 'Against protocol, I'm afraid. David's in charge of security here, not me. Got me into trouble for letting you in last night.' She bumped the door with her hip and slipped through. 'Don't be late!'

'Great.' Marshall rested his coffee on the counter. 'How long's this going to take?'

'Piece of string, mate. I'm at the mercies of our IT infrastructure and it's slower than my youngest getting out of bed on the weekend.'

Marshall adjusted his strap so it wasn't digging into his shoulder quite so badly. 'Come on, I'm a DI coming into your station. Please, just issue me with a temporary pass.'

'I'm updating your Met one now. Two ticks.'

Forget about ticks, this was going to take longer than the next bong of Big Ben.

Marshall tilted his head at the closed door. 'You know her?'

'My wife.'

Marshall widened his eyes. 'You're kidding me?'

'Nope. Andi's my childhood sweetheart. Married twenty years. She's the career-driven one. I do this fifteen hours a week. Rest of the time, I'm a househusband. Two teenaged girls and a nine-year-old laddie takes a lot of laundry.'

Maybe Marshall had been too harsh judging Elliot, which was a lot less harshly than Kirsten.

Two teenaged girls who could easily fall prey to the likes of Derek Cameron...

This case was personal to her in a totally different way to him.

'Have to do this through the back, chief.' Without even checking it was okay, David-the-receptionist-who-might-have-the-surname-Elliot slipped through the door.

Leaving Marshall on his own in reception. He got out his phone and sifted through the barrage of messages he seemed to have got over the short walk in, sipping his coffee as he marked them read.

Nothing to action, at least.

But Rickards had sent him a lovely photo of Zlatan, his cat, stretching out in the morning sun. Another reason to wrap this all up and get home.

Aye, London was home now.

Not this place, this godforsaken nowhere land between England and Scotland.

Who was he kidding? It was beautiful. Hills, lochs, fields, plenty of towns and villages, cafés and old pubs. Like Club Tropicana, all it was missing was the sea, an hour away in any direction, but unlike it, you had to pay for every drink.

God, that coffee was good.

The door tinkled.

Marshall didn't look over, just read a text from Hulse:

> Let me know if you want to meet up over the next few days. Busy. But doable.

He started thumbing out a reply.

'I thought I'd find you here, Robert.'

That voice.

He swung around.

Graham Thorburn stood in the doorway, hands in the pockets of his blood-red cords. Green tweed jacket. Salmon shirt. Still had dark hair, despite being early sixties and his skin a tan-bed brown. 'Have you got a minute, Robert?'

No sign of David with his pass.

'Due in a briefing any minute, but I'm yours until then.' Marshall paced over and gave him a hug. 'It's been a while, Graham.'

Thorburn nodded as he was let go. 'Hasn't it just?'

Up close, Marshall could see his blemishes. The patch he'd missed when shaving. The gap in his teeth. The splodge of porridge on his shirt. The open fly. Yeah, Graham Thorburn was getting on.

'Your mother didn't sleep at all last night, Robert. She's obsessed with you being home, but not staying with us.'

'Us?' Marshall took a drink of coffee.

'I... We...' Thorburn looked away. 'It's been a couple of years since I last saw you. Same with your mother. A lot's happened in that time. We've been back together pretty much all that time.'

'I'm pleased for you, Graham. Just... Don't leave her again. Jen had to pick up the pieces last time.'

'I'm trying not to.' Thorburn stuffed his hands back in his pockets. 'Son, Janice wants to spend time with you. Go and stay the night there.'

'I'm not here on holiday. I told her that. It's... This case...'

'You need a hand?'

'No, I'm the hand. But thanks for the offer.'

Thorburn raised his hands, his palms the only bit of him that wasn't tanned. 'You miss her. She misses you.'

'I know. I was there last night. I said I'd go round again. I will.'

'Robert, please—'

'I don't have time to do this right now, Graham, but dinner tonight will be great.'

David came back through and handed Marshall his card. 'Should work now, mate. Keep it in a different pocket from your mobile, alright?'

'Sure thing.' Marshall smiled at him, then at Thorburn. 'See you tonight.'

'Promise me we'll get time to speak, Robert. Promise me.'

Aye, they weren't getting any younger. He should spend time with them.

'I promise.' Marshall gave him another big hug. 'I swear.' He let go, swiped his card and walked through into the station.

CHAPTER TWENTY

No incident room here. Not even a meeting room. Just twenty-odd cops stuffed into the corner of an open-plan office area. Barely enough desks for half of them. Maybe the rest were based in Galashiels or Newtown St Boswells.

Elliot stood at the front, clutching that cake box. 'Happy birthday, Ms Weir.'

Kirsten was smiling, but her face was bright red. 'Usually I have to bring the cakes in on my birthday.'

Elliot laughed. 'That's not how I roll.' She pushed the box towards her. 'Go on, take it.'

Kirsten opened the box. 'Wow, this is amazing.'

Elliot was beaming. 'David baked it yesterday. I was up past midnight decorating it for you.'

Marshall got a good view of it as Kirsten showed it off. Chocolate frosting, covered in half-broken bits of Maltesers and stars. Marshall's breakfast was already repeating on him, so he doubted he'd have a slice, but it looked... astonishing.

'I'll have to thank him, then.' Kirsten took the knife from Elliot, but didn't cut the cake. 'How did you know?'

'It's on your record, daftie. I make sure everyone gets a nice birthday. *Everyone*.' She looked across the room. 'Ah, DI Marshall, nice of you to join us.'

'Sorry, the card reader wasn't accepting my Met pass.'

'Come over here. Don't be shy.' Elliot beckoned him into her corner like she was hauling something by a rope. 'Do I call you DI or Doctor?'

Marshall joined her, hiding behind his coffee. 'Prefer DI.'

Elliot clapped his arm and looked around the room. 'This lovely laddie might solve this case for us. His skills are hopefully worth the three quid Kirsten just spent on his coffee.'

Aye.

There was a darkness to her humour. An unkindness.

Giving Kirsten the cake bought her brownie points to spend on belittling him in front of the team. A team that had only room for one DI.

'I'm two pound fifty's worth at best.' Marshall raised his eyebrows. 'And I'm just here to consult on the case. That's all.'

Elliot smiled. 'How about you give us your profile of Derek Cameron?'

'I've done some work on it, but it needs a lot more data to be useful to man or beast.'

Elliot waved a hand around the room – Christ, it was like being in the front row of a stand-up comedy gig. 'Most of us worked our way up through the ranks or at least spent a good few years on the street, but DI Marshall here is a brain box. Used to be a criminal profiler, isn't that right?'

Marshall gave her a nod while he sipped coffee.

'When do you think you'll finish the work, then?'

Marshall's neck was hot like sunburn. 'To be honest with you, the important thing is finding Wendy Malcolm. Alive. We know who did it, but her abductor's dead. Finding her is your priority.'

A scowl flashed across her face, then Elliot grinned at him. 'Let's catch up after this, okay?' She shifted her gaze around the room. 'I asked for you to investigate the loved ones of victims. Jolene's team are still compiling a cross-reference, but we'll get there.' She stabbed a pen off a notebook. 'Kirsten, before you cut into that cake like it's a lover's heart, how about giving us your team's update?'

Kirsten rested the knife down. 'We've finished scouring the area near the bridge for forensics and, like I warned you, we've found nothing. Pair of bolt cutters cut the lock, as suspected. No trace of them, so it's likely our killer took them away with them. Or it was unrelated. That said, we did find traces of her hair in the car.'

Marshall frowned at her. 'Is it possible Wendy's in the river?'

Elliot shook her head. 'Had divers down that whole stretch to Dryburgh, then boats all the way to Kelso. No sign of her. No sign of anybody.'

'Okay. Just wondered.'

'No such thing as a daft question.' Didn't seem like it from her glazed eyes. 'Oh.' She reached over to a desk and produced an evidence bag, then tossed it towards him.

Marshall caught it. Heavy. Cold.

A gun.

Shit.

The gun Cameron used to shoot at him and John Hulse.

His mouth was dry. 'Where did you find this?'

'Up on the bridge. Why? You recognise it?'

'It's Cameron's. Or the same model at least.'

'Cool beans.' Elliot shifted her focus to Kirsten. 'How about at Wendy's home?'

'Nothing much there, either. DNA traces from Wendy, her father and an unidentified female.'

'Is Aidan not playing ball?'

'Not for me to say. Shu— DS Siyal was leading on that.'

Shunty was staring at the floor. 'Asked him about it, ma'am, but he refused to say. I think he's got a new lover.'

'Typical.' Elliot charged over to the board. 'I'll have a wee word with him. He probably thinks he's protecting his late wife's memory or something. No shame in moving on, is there?' She scribbled something illegible, then swung around to Kirsten. 'That you?'

'For now.' Kirsten checked the fancy smartwatch on her wrist. 'Listen, I'm waiting on some DNA results, so can I dash off?'

'Cool beans.' Elliot waved her off. 'We'll save your cake for your return.' She watched Kirsten leave the room. 'Shunty, you're up next.'

Siyal still had his backpack on. Maybe he was part snail after all. 'The main progress has been made at the crime scene, vis a vis securing eyewitness testimony.'

Elliot rested a fist on her hip. 'In words of one syllable or less, please?'

'Fewer.'

Elliot glowered at him. 'What?'

'You use fewer when you're taking about quantities. It's like you wouldn't say "how much days left".'

'Ladies and gentleman, this is what a direct-entry sergeant looks like... You get edumacation but not results. And now today's grammar lesson is over, how about you give us your update, vis a vis get on with it?'

'Sure.' Shunty took off his backpack and rested it on an office chair. 'We received a phone call from a lorry driver who'd been transporting cattle from near Hexham to Pathhead, a few miles north of here. Said there was a car at the car park around the time of the murder.'

'He was shifting cows at midnight?'

'He'd got lost, ma'am. He pulled in to check where he was going on his phone.'

'He's sure about this?'

'Call record shows it. Matched it to his phone's GPS and the cell sites back it up.' Shunty flicked through a pink and green notebook. 'He distinctly remembers Cameron's Peugeot. Guy's into car pimping, so he took a wee look at it.'

'If you could get a tower dump vis a vis confirming connections to the same cell tower that Cameron's phone made the 999 call to. Not to mention a call dump of all of his calls. And check out this guy, vis a vis him not being our killer.'

Shunty nodded, but he wasn't making eye contact with her.

'Cool beans.' Elliot clapped her hands together. 'Okay, I doubt we'll get anything out of it, but I'm a persistent woman. I expect you to be the same, Sergeant.' She held up a finger. 'A persistent man, not a woman.' She giggled. 'Though what you get up to on a Saturday night's entirely up to you.'

Shunty stared at her, locking his gaze with hers. 'That's transphobic.'

Elliot scowled back. 'What?'

'Alleging that I have some kind of kink for wearing clothes from the opposite gender, or that there's anything wrong with that if I did.'

'Guess who's had his wokey-bix this morning!'

Shunty stood his ground. 'I'm serious.'

'And I was making a joke to lighten the mood, sergeant.'

'Imagine if—'

'Which I shouldn't have done.' She held up a finger. 'I'm booked on a course next week, so if anyone wishes to discuss this matter further with me after this, then please do. My door's always open. And I'm sorry if I've upset anyone. It's a force of habit, from being in rooms like this as a young cop, when they were staffed by dinosaurs, long since retired. For the record, my middle child's currently identifying as non-binary, so I know it's not a joking matter.'

That seemed to pacify Shunty, who was nodding along with it.

'Now, I do expect persistence from you all.' Elliot cast her gaze around the room. 'Despite Derek Cameron being suspected of serial murder, we still need to do our best to catch his killer. Cameron abducted his victims, raped them, killed them and dumped them. People found those bodies. But he had them for up to a week each time. If he took Wendy, it was on Saturday night. He was dead hours later. So, there's a very strong possibility she's still alive. We aren't looking for a dead body, but we're looking for Aidan Malcolm's daughter, still alive.'

Pretty much word for word for the speech Marshall had given to her father the previous night.

Impressive memory, but she had no shame.

Elliot pointed at Marshall. 'And the headshrinker here's right. We need to find Wendy as a priority. Maybe both tasks are the same, so can you please outline your profile so we're all on the same page?'

'Now?'

'Yes, Inspector, now.'

'Okay.' Marshall reached into his leather messenger bag for his laptop. Not that he needed it – he could recite the text in his sleep. And had spent a good chunk of last night doing just that, drifting in and out as the faces of his victims passed through his mind. 'Okay, so I want you to think about the common or garden killer we deal with. A perpetrator with one identity, one name, one car, one job. After enough time and evidence, we can just go and arrest him.' He paused, for effect rather than to think. 'Now, who the press down south dubbed "the Chameleon" wasn't like that. When you throw in multiple names, places, vehicles, occupations and homes, we in law enforcement have huge problems. No leads, but a shared MO across multiple years and, sure, we had DNA from each attack, but there was no sample on record to match it to. Not even a hit from those commercial genealogy databases, so we didn't even get a relative on file.'

Shunty was writing furiously in his notebook. Marshall hoped it was about this case and not trying to solve today's Wordle.

Marshall rested back against the table the laser printer squatted on. 'Derek Cameron was a chameleon. During the day, he worked different jobs. Car mechanic, electrician, plumber, cleaner, painter, joiner, handyman, kitchen busboy... Gig jobs, which let him work to suit his addiction. Derek Cameron abducted, raped and killed five women. He spotted them on the night bus north from Hammersmith, then he stalked them over weeks, building up the patterns of their days, until he knew when he could strike.' He thumped the printer.

Shunty jumped. Made him look up from his notebook.

'He held his victims in a location for up to a week. Not less than five days. He raped them repeatedly. Then he killed them.' Another punch. 'He dumped them in waste ground in the middle of the night. He was never spotted, either abducting them or dumping them. Once he'd finished with them, he'd disappear. The garage, the builders, the office, the restaurant, whoever it was he was working for, they'd never hear from him again. He was an everyman and a no-man.'

Shunty looked up from his notebook. 'Why did he do it?'

'Why does anyone? Power, domination, control. Plus, based on the pathologist's assessment of his anatomy, compensating for a very small penis. He would "inflict" himself on his victims to show what his equipment was capable of, but not giving them a choice to decline or laugh at it. He's either a sadist or anger-retaliation rapist. I'd need to know more about his behaviour during the assaults or what tips him off on victim selection. Does he just pick weak ones to hurt them? If so, he's a sadist. If he's perceived some wrong against him, it'd be anger retaliation. Hard to say without a series of psychological interviews with him and his victims. I only spoke to him once for a matter of seconds before he shot my partner right in front of me.' Marshall rubbed at his right ear. 'My hearing's a bit damaged on that side, so please talk to me on the other one.'

Nobody laughed. They just seemed a bit shocked.

'I did a geographic profile, which revealed how he targeted the victims. Like I said, on the night bus. We were staking it out and that's when he saw us. But we knew him. Derek Cameron had been interviewed as part of the case. He was a friend of victim one, Erin Geraldine Nash. He'd put us off on a wild tangent, costing us weeks of work. All the while, he'd been working on victim two, Deanna Casey.'

The room was deadly silent. Not even Shunty scratching notes.

'To answer your question, DS Siyal, I think Cameron was looking for resolution to some childhood trauma. I believed he was someone who lost his parents young, or who suffered an abusive childhood, potentially at the hands of his mother. And this was him re-enacting that trauma, attempting to cure himself of it, if you will. He could cast off an identity like a snake does skin. Using aliases like he did potentially showed he was from a care background.' Marshall raised a finger. 'And he was. Derek Clive Cameron. Born in Croydon, South London. Aged two, his mother left his abusive father and moved to Harlesden, West London. My old patch. Probably means nothing to you lot, but it's not a great place. Pity the people who have to live there. It's not their fault, society inflicted it on them, but you wouldn't wish it on your worst enemy. Derek Cameron had a difficult childhood, there's no doubt about it. The social workers couldn't get near him. Series of uncles, possibly at least one abusing him. Then his mother died when he was just six years old. They couldn't find his father or any other family. That was when he was put into care.' He left another pause. 'But he'd already started harming animals by then. So he showed all the signs of being a sexual sadist.'

Elliot was shaking her head. 'Sounds like a nasty piece of work.'

'That's one way of looking at it.' Marshall stuffed his hands in his pockets. 'I don't believe people are born evil, but Derek Cameron had all the help he needed to *become* evil. After he was fostered, he just never stopped. He escalated to raising fires, but was never charged with anything. Then he was quiet for a bit, had a good foster mother. Stabilised him, let him be normal. Until a girlfriend at school suffered a choking incident. And then over the next five years, from aged sixteen to twenty-one, we have a number of casual hook-ups he'd taken things a bit far with. Then several sexual assaults where the culprit matches his description.' He looked up at the ceiling tiles, more water stain than pristine pattern. 'Since shooting my partner, we've been searching for him for two years, but it's easier to gather evidence retrospectively when you know who did it than in a linear fashion when you've no idea. And we obviously didn't find him. You did. I wish he was alive, so he could pay the price for—'

'Thank you.' Elliot stood up, arms folded. 'These rapes you mentioned. Do you think they are his?'

'We think so. We investigated Cameron retrospectively to rule him out or in as a suspect, but found nothing conclusive and nothing that could help locate him. But those rapes... The first three we know about were a year apart each, but then he raped another four with a four-month gap, so his lust was getting stronger. Or it could be people didn't report earlier ones. Not everyone does; there's a stigma. He may also have utilised the services of prostitutes who are less inclined to cooperate with police, or travelled to other jurisdictions, wilfully or as a matter of circumstances. And that's just what we have on record – it could be there was no gap, and we just don't know about the victims.' Marshall swallowed down the last of his cold coffee but it didn't touch the sour taste in his mouth. 'The first murder victim, Erin Nash, was known to him. He used his birth name with her as they went to school together in Harlesden before he was expelled. He was taking a big risk with her. Maybe there's a clue to his motivations in that risk. A connection to his history, his upbringing. Maybe he was getting closure on some perceived slight from her, which is back to anger reassurance, but he didn't stop with her. He'd got a bloodlust.'

The room hummed like a broken fridge.

Elliot walked over to the cake and plunged the knife deep into the chocolate. She didn't make another cut, just left it sticking out, and turned around. 'So, our priority here is to find Wendy Malcolm. We're combing the area, looking for clues. DI Marshall is here to help us find her using what he knows of the inside of Derek Cameron's bonce.'

Shunty raised his hand again. 'Ma'am, to move a live body or dump a dead one, you really need a van... and with him being in the trades it would probably be a work van, something that blended in, so nondescript or minimally liveried. And if there aren't any suspicious ones out in the open, then we need to look at garages and barns where one could be parked inside.'

'That's very impressive stuff, Shunty.'

'Like DI Marshall says, Cameron is a chameleon, so a generic vehicle would help him blend in.' Shunty was looking at his notebook. 'But he's also a car guy so he may have customised it.'

Elliot smirked. 'A sleeper car...'

'A what?'

'Looks like a dog, but runs like a deer.'

'Well, yeah. You can modify it so the engine is a lot faster than it appears. Also, get a control box to switch the turbo charge on or off. And since DI Marshall's team never found one through all his identities, he may still have the same one. A PNC check under his aliases may reveal a make and model.'

Basic stuff and Marshall was glad someone was saying it, especially if Elliot didn't.

'Add that to your list, Shunty. Now, I can't help but wonder if Cameron stopped after that night two years ago until now, or if he kept it up.' Elliot stared at Marshall. 'How do we find Wendy Malcolm?'

Marshall felt insects crawling all over his skin, down his throat. He played it through, but he just didn't have enough data to make a decision. Not that a room full of sweaty cops cared about his data. They just wanted a direction to march in. 'The honest answer is I don't know yet. And we're probably looking for Wendy's body.'

'Thank you.' Elliot walked over to him and patted him on the arm. 'Now, I suggest you all read Dr Marshall's report and see what *you* think. There might be something in there that, when paired up with your local knowledge, gives us something that can help us find Wendy Malcolm. Because that's what I want to do. Let's find her today. Alive. Okay?' She clapped her hands together. 'I've got the post-mortem this afternoon, but I need you all to work your arses off. Let's find her, people.'

The room exploded into chatter.

Marshall stopped Elliot getting past. 'I told you I'd rather not be called doctor.'

'Why, you earned your doctorate, didn't you?'

'Still.'

'Finish the profile.' She walked off towards her office.

Marshall felt spent. Like he was a sponge someone had squeezed out.

Kirsten stood over him, clutching a sheaf of papers. 'You okay?'

'It's hard reliving it all, you know?' Marshall held up his empty cup. 'Nice coffee, by the way.'

'My cousin owns the place. Dean Taylor.'

Marshall frowned. 'I think I went to school with him.'

'He's an old bugger too, so it's possible.' Kirsten brushed his arm. 'Listen, I need to see you and Elliot.'

'What's up?'

But she was walking away. In the direction of Elliot's office.

CHAPTER TWENTY-ONE

Marshall took the seat opposite Elliot.

Kirsten sat next to him. 'One thing you've stressed to us, Andrea, is what'll help this case is for us to distance ourselves from any emotion.' She looked between them. 'These were women's lives, whose last few days were horrific, to be ended in the most brutal way. But if we treat them as data points, being distant might help to see new patterns.'

Elliot drummed her fingers off the wood. 'What have you got?'

'The reason anyone got close to Cameron two years ago is because DI Marshall did geographical profiling on the five victims he knew about. London's a city with the population of a country, so it's easier to profile and see the pattern – the victims took the same bus every night. So they had an opportunity to identify him. After shooting John Hulse, it's possible Derek Cameron stopped and Wendy Malcolm's abduction was him starting up again – two years of being in the clear, so he felt safe to do it again now. Maybe he stopped, but maybe not.'

Elliot sipped from a Gregg's coffee cup. 'I don't follow.'

'Didn't think you would.' Kirsten passed the papers across the desk to Elliot. 'These are all from ViCLAS. That's Violent Crime Linkage Analysis System.'

Elliot was drumming her fingers on the table. 'I know what it is.'

'The NCA have run the analysis for me. Based on DI Marshall's profile, I've found three murders in the last two years who all match Derek Cameron's MO.'

Marshall could only sit there, pulse racing, mouth tasting like an ashtray.

Elliot rocked back in her chair with an almighty crunch. 'You didn't think to share these with DI Marshall last night before he reworked his profile?'

'It's not just him who does all-nighters, Andrea.'

'Take us through it, then.'

Marshall leaned forward, resting his elbows on his knees.

Kirsten held up the first page. 'Okay, eight months after Rob's incident in Hammersmith, there was a murder in Northwich near Manchester. Same MO, same victimology.'

Elliot looked at Marshall. 'I think Dr Marshall here should be the judge of that.'

'Of course.' Kirsten held her gaze. 'I'm just raising these to help, seeing as how you asked me because the NCA have stopped answering the phone to you or Jolene.'

Elliot cleared her throat. 'That's enough of that.'

Kirsten turned to another page. 'Then four months later in Kirkby Lonsdale in Lancashire. Another four-month gap and we've got one in Carlisle.'

Elliot took the pages and sifted through them. 'But we don't know they were him, do we?'

'Correct. Like I say, they all match on MO and victimology,

but the forensics were... There are gaps in their work, let's put it that way.'

'So we can't match them to him?'

'That's by the by.' Kirsten narrowed her eyes. 'Like you said, we need to find Wendy Malcolm before she's a corpse.'

Elliot sat back and folded her arms, gaze drilling into Marshall. 'Like Kate Pierce.'

She knew...

Of course she knew...

Kirsten frowned at Elliot. 'Who's she?'

Elliot snorted. 'Why don't you tell us, Dr Marshall?'

He folded his arms across his chest. 'Why don't you?' His throat was dry. The words were a croak.

'After the incident where Dr Marshall's partner was shot, Derek Cameron panicked and fled. Dr Marshall here was hunting across London for him. He identified a missing woman, taken the day before he saw Cameron. A victim who matched all of Cameron's hallmarks. But it took a week to unpick his life and find her in a lock-up garage in Surbiton, rented by one Donald Collins. But it was too late. Kate Pierce was dead.'

Marshall's head hung low. It felt like it was happening all over again.

Storming across the car park between the garages.

Snapping the lock himself.

Getting in there first to find a corpse tied to a workbench.

He sat back, eyes closed.

'You okay?'

Marshall opened his eyes again. 'Wendy Malcolm is like Kate Pierce, but this time I can save her.' He stabbed a finger on the page. 'There's a pattern here. Assuming it's him, he's travelled up the west side of England, then due north towards Edinburgh, stopping at Selkirk. But there are two eight-month windows between Kate and the first victim, then from the Carlisle one until Wendy Malcolm.'

'Agreed.' Kirsten had another sheet of paper. 'The NCA are checking partial matches for some unreported victims. Again, when the press gets ahold of this and we announce that the Chameleon is dead, more people may come forward with abductions and rapes.'

Elliot was on her feet, staring at the whiteboard. 'You think getting found in London may have cooled him off?'

'Right. Maybe he re-evaluated his strategy and became more forensically aware. One step back, two steps forward as he rethinks his MO. Could be something in Northwich awakened a beast in him. But that's a big gap, so maybe there are unknown victims in Northampton or the Cotswolds or Birmingham.'

Elliot wiped a chunk from her board. 'And he's getting further and further north, further away from London. He's leaving his trauma behind him. Assuming these are all him.'

Kirsten nodded. 'I'm pretty sure.'

Elliot uncapped a pen. 'Okay, so we've got three distinct phases to his MO over time. First, there were tentative date rapes. Then he escalated to kidnapping, raping and murdering in London. And there's now, going up the country.'

Kirsten nodded again. 'He's cleaned up his act, become a lot more forensic. The threat of the police catching him in London made him change to protect himself, maybe. It's possible he was now using contraception and became even more obsessed with a forensically inert scene. Like him cleaning that car.'

'Or it's someone else. This was all in the public domain two years ago.' Elliot paused, drumming her fingers on the board. 'Marshall, I need you to investigate these victims.'

'I want—'

'—to help us find Wendy Malcolm. Aye, I get it. But I've got twenty cops for that. Basic officers. You're the only one who can do this profiling magic. I need you to speak to the other three victims today, get your extra data points.'

'That's not how it works. Way before I'd speak to the victims and make them relive their traumas, I'd pore over the files then confirm with the detectives.'

'Sweet. I'll call the lead cops today, get appointments for you, but you're getting on the road. Hope you don't get car sick, 'cos you're going to do a lot of reading.'

'It's going to take the whole day, though. Maybe two. Assuming the lead cops are on shift or still around, assuming the friends and family want to even speak to me. Whether they know anything.' Marshall felt that tightening in his throat. 'And I'm not sure it'll save Wendy Malcolm.'

'Please try.'

Marshall sat back. Hulse was right. His ego got in the way. He wanted to be the one bursting in to save Wendy Malcolm, carrying her out in his arms, driving her to hospital. Saving her life. Talk about a hero complex. 'Okay. I'm willing to do whatever it takes.'

'Thank you.' Elliot smiled. 'Get your arse down to Carlisle.'

CHAPTER TWENTY-TWO

Seemed to be more cops in the station's tiny smoking shelter than there was space for. Two were smoking, at least four vaping. All of them checking their phones. Might as well have gone for a walk rather than standing around ignoring each other.

Not that Marshall was much better, loitering with his phone to his ear.

Down the line, Rickards was clicking her tongue. 'I hear you, Rob.'

'But?'

'I'm thinking.'

'Listen, I'm not here to mess about.' Marshall walked back down to the main street through the town, but didn't want to get too far from the station. Otherwise, before he knew it, he'd have walked to Edinburgh. 'I feel like I should stay and find Wendy Malcolm.'

'Rob, I don't want to patronise you, but what you do best isn't basic policing. From what I gather, DI Elliot has more than enough basic cops to go around. That right?'

'Those are her words, aye.' Hard to escape the feeling he was being ganged up on. 'But I—'

'But you bring something special to the table, Rob. You're pretty unique, especially on a weird case like this. If you focus on the profile, it might accelerate the search. Okay, so you might not get your superhero moment, but it might help DI Elliot and team find Wendy.'

She was right.

But it still felt like passivity in the face of another Kate Pierce. Somewhere around here, a woman was dying.

Or dead.

'What makes you special, Rob, is your ability to spot patterns. We need to find Derek Cameron's killer, which is a secondary concern, but we also need to understand what he's been doing between then and now. If his death is anything to do with these murders or it's something else entirely.' More clicking. 'And we need to know if he has killed these other women. If he has, then there are grieving families out there. People who lost a sister, a daughter, a girlfriend, a wife. It's important for them to know who did it.'

Marshall stopped, feet balancing on the edge of the kerb opposite the rugby ground, the trees swaying in the breeze. Couldn't say anything.

'I know you want to find Wendy, Rob. Nobody else can blend policing and profiling. Focus on what you're great at. Or what you used to be before you asked to get moved sideways.'

All he had for that was a sigh. Anger coursed through him, fizzing in his stomach like gunpowder ready to ignite.

'Remember. Your skills almost caught Cameron.'

'That's bollocks. We just lucked out. Sitting there while he—'

'Shush.'

Marshall gritted his teeth. 'I'm a cop. I want to help.'

'Focus on that word. Help. You were sent there to *help* them, not to scratch an itch or overcome a tragic history. Play along with Elliot. Do what you're good at. This isn't your case, Rob, it's theirs. And you can help.'

'Fine. I'll let you know how it goes.' Marshall ended the call and felt the rage flood his veins. Then it fizzled out, leaving behind calmness. Serenity.

She was right.

Not to get too big-headed about it, but he was there to *help* find Wendy Malcolm. It wasn't his case. If he could find who killed Derek Cameron, all the better. Maybe it would help, like she said. And maybe all he could do was help grieving family members begin to get closure on the senseless deaths of their loved ones.

Marshall reached into his pocket and found the car key. He pressed the remote locking button and scanned the car park for his pool car.

Only the left indicator on a purple Audi winked in response. 08 plates, so over fifteen years old, but looking even older than he felt.

And he was supposed to get to Manchester and back in it?

He peered in and, sure enough, whoever had last been in it had spent a lot of time at McDonald's and Dominos. Smelled like something had crawled in and died, rotting under the bags and bags of cardboard burger containers. Enough pizza boxes to...

He didn't have the words.

Jesus wept.

'Hey.' Kirsten was hovering around, scratching at her hair. 'You okay?'

'This car's...' Marshall sniffed. 'How can I get to Manchester in that? I doubt I'll even get to Gala. Hell, Tweedbank's going to be a struggle.'

'I meant about...' She walked over, smiling. 'Listen. I'm sorry to hear about what happened to you in Surbiton.'

'Turns out Elliot's been chatting to my old boss about it.'

'And he's okay talking about what you went through?'

'She. And seemingly.'

'That why you ended up working in Traffic?'

Marshall tossed the key in the air and caught it. 'I couldn't do it anymore.' His mouth was dry. A parched riverbed and no amount of saliva could lubricate it. 'There are so many deaths down to me. The five... They were statistics to some. Data to add to my profile. But they were also women whose lives had been cut short. I spoke to their friends and families, all traumatised by their loss. *All* of them. Death is death, never easy, but at the hands of someone like Derek Cameron – and in that way – it's incredibly difficult to come to terms with. He ruined the lives of the living.'

'And you blame yourself for Kate Pierce, right?'

He could tell her to piss off, to swallow down his self-disgust, but... 'People always say not to blame yourself. To keep your own sanity, you need to compartmentalise it. But how can I not blame myself? I was Deputy SIO on the case, leading the investigation. As soon as we got word of a possible abduction, that was it. I didn't sleep until we found her.' He swallowed, tasting blood in his throat. 'And it was too late.'

'Had she been dead all that time?'

'She died five days before we found her.'

'How long had you known about her?'

'Three.'

She gave a kind smile and stroked his arm. 'Rob, you couldn't have done anything about her.'

'Didn't feel like that at the time.'

'I can tell you're beating yourself up about Wendy Malcolm. From what I gather, Kate Pierce isn't in your profile?'

Marshall caught her perfume – a sweet scent he recognised from his childhood. He tried to ignore it, focus on the here and now. Or a different there and then. 'No. Kate was discovered afterwards, so I never got around to adding her.'

'Well, then. Maybe those two extra data points can help? And those extra victims I found...'

Marshall couldn't look at her. 'Maybe you're right.'

'I am. I'm here for you, okay? If you need anyone to talk to, well, we're staying in the same hotel. If you need anyone to run anything past, I'm here. Okay?'

'Thank you.'

They stood in silence for a few seconds, the summer wind kicking around more grit, a lot of it landing in Marshall eyes.

A hell of a lot.

Sure, that's what it was.

Grit in his eyes.

Sure.

'Key.' Shunty stepped between Marshall and the car, holding out his hand, both straps around his shoulders. 'Key.' Face was tripping him, as his mum would say.

'Sorry, Sergeant, I've booked this car.'

Shunty unslung his rucksack from one shoulder. 'Aye, but the boss ordered me to escort you down to Carlisle.'

CHAPTER TWENTY-THREE

Marshall looked up from his laptop at the street rumbling around them, his computer bouncing and knocking his knees. He knew Carlisle well enough to know Shunty had taken a wrong turning. They were trundling up a long single-track road up the back of some shops, heading to – aye – a dead end. On the left was a goods yard for the big Tesco on the main road. The street entrance at the end was blocked off. Looked like it had been that way for a few years.

'Great.' Shunty stuck it in reverse and swung back around into the Tesco's entrance. He put it in gear, but didn't drive off. 'You knew, didn't you?'

'Knew what?'

'That this was a dead end.'

'I was working on my laptop when you took the turning, so no.'

'Probably think I'm a total fanny.' Shunty drummed his thumbs on the dashboard. 'Wasn't blocked off when I was here last year. Must've done it recently.'

'It's okay, Sergeant. I don't think you're a *total* fanny.'

Shunty looked like he was going to cry.

Jesus, this guy wasn't cut out to be a cop.

Marshall tapped the desk-mounted screen, pointing a few streets away. 'Satnav said it was the other way. I'd never try to out-think one of them.'

'Map hasn't been updated in ten years, at least. Thing threw a wobbler last time I drove over the new Forth Crossing.' Shunty grunted and set off back the way they'd come. 'You managed to get anything from your profile there?'

Marshall sighed. 'I've just sat here, looking at maps and case files, trying to get something more than my initial reaction.'

'You think Cameron was working his way north?'

'Seems like it. No idea where his eventual goal was or if he even had one. It's less than two hours from here to Melrose, unless it's you behind the wheel.'

'You got a problem with my driving?'

'No, but you're slow for a cop. Did you do advanced driver training?'

'Booked on it in October.'

'Right. Okay. My point is there's not much between here and Melrose. It's possible Cameron lingered around Carlisle a while after he killed the victim. Or he drove straight to Melrose, then didn't kill anyone in the gap. I just don't know.'

But he did know the later three and Wendy Malcolm had less in common with Kate Pierce and the first five. Subtle differences, but so many of them it built up into a massive gulf. Or so he thought.

Aye, he needed to speak to someone. Interview them.

Shunty pulled right at the end, barrelling the wrong way up a one-way street. 'Isn't knowing about this sicko what you're here for?'

Marshall was gripping the oh-shit handle above the door so tight that half of it snapped off. 'You know this is a one-way—'

'Ah, here it is.' Shunty pulled into a space long enough to do it front-ways. The only car pointing this way. He reached over Marshall's knees and opened the glovebox.

A load of sweetie wrappers fell out onto his lap. Sticky, horrible mess.

Shunty got out a parking disc and slammed the glove box shut, then set the time on it and stuffed it into the window.

Marshall stared at him. 'You mind clearing that up?'

'Not my mess.' Shunty got out into the street.

What a guy.

Marshall had sympathy for him. Scotland liked to portray itself as a forward-leaning nation, but it still wasn't great on race. An Asian police officer was going to get a lot of abuse, especially one with a Glasgow accent.

He stuffed his laptop into his messenger bag and got out. Much warmer than when he'd met Hulse the previous day, about five miles east, but still nothing like London. Close to ten now and it'd be a decent day down there. Here, there was more cloud than blue and it was cold in the shade.

Shunty was walking towards someone, head bowed.

A bald-headed man, leaning back against a Volvo and tapping his watch. Dark suit, black tie, like he was on his way to a funeral. He stood up tall and squared up to Shunty.

Aye, he was dressed for Shunty's funeral.

Marshall hurried over, getting close enough to hear them.

'You were supposed to be here an hour ago!'

Shunty folded his arms. 'Not breaking the speed limit for anyone.'

'The speed limit? You must've done forty all the way here!'

'There were tractors and...' Shunty noticed Marshall and shut up, deciding to look in the bookshop's window instead.

Marshall smiled at the guy, holding out his hand. 'Foxton, right?'

'DI Shaun Foxton at your service.' He grabbed his hand. 'You must be Marshall?' He didn't wait for an answer and charged off down the street, hands in pockets.

Marshall followed, but didn't get a chance to speak to Shunty. Didn't look like he wanted to be spoken to.

Foxton opened a door and went inside.

Marshall let Shunty go first but he didn't want to, so instead he led into the stairwell and started climbing.

Foxton's heavy footsteps were like two bowling balls falling upstairs.

Foxton knocked on a door and waited, arms crossed over his chest, pulling his suit jacket tight across his meaty shoulders. 'This is my case, so I'm leading here, alright?'

'Alright.' Marshall joined him by the door. 'But I wanted to have a word with you beforehand.'

'Tough.'

Right. One of those cops who controlled their territory like a master with a pack of dogs. 'You know Andrea Elliot, aye?'

'Good friends, aye. Don't get too many cross-border crimes and most are with Dumfries and Galloway, as was. But we get enough of them to let us get to know each other. Usually it's missing kids from Hawick or Galashiels running here rather than Edinburgh or Newcastle.' He paused to laugh. 'Poor sods.' He thumped the door again. 'Audrey? It's Shaun. Open up, would you?'

The door became a thin slit. A bloodshot eye poked out, focusing on Marshall, Foxton and Shunty in order. It shut with a slam. Then opened fully.

A gaunt woman stood there, bright flowery top with green

leather trousers. Early twenties. Eyes that searched everywhere except their faces. Bare feet padded away across floorboards into the flat, hair stretching down to her backside.

Foxton let them go first, so Marshall took charge.

The kind of flat you saw anywhere. Roomy hallway with cream walls and tranquil pictures on the walls.

Audrey Ewing – he presumed – was sitting on an armchair in the living room, knees curled up to her chest.

Foxton stopped Shunty, speaking in a low tone, 'Go make us some tea, kid.'

Shunty sighed, then scuttled off into the small kitchen stuffed between a bathroom and the living room.

Marshall followed Foxton in. Ice cold inside, window wide open. Marshall made to shut it.

'Don't. Don't touch that.'

Marshall looked over at Audrey, who was glaring at him. 'Okay, I won't.'

Good view of the bookshop opposite, which seemed to extend into several adjacent units. Despite the window being open, the room they were in smelled of incense, but he couldn't see any sticks burning. Thrashy music played on a very low volume, a blast of angry punky noise at odds with the vibe of the place.

Foxton sat on the sofa, casual like he was waiting for a haircut. 'Why are the windows open, Audrey?'

She nibbled at her thumbnail. All of her nails were chewed. Twitchy and edgy, like the music she listened to. 'Getting rid of the evil spirits.'

Foxton frowned. 'I thought you got rid of them last month?'

'I did.'

'But?'

'Someone came here.' She shifted her sharp focus between

them. 'Pretended to be a friend of my sister's, but he was asking too many questions. He was a journalist.' She leaned forward, resting her elbows on her knees. 'Stupid to trust people.'

'You're not stupid, Audrey. Not by a long shot.' Foxton was shaking his head along with that. 'Listen, we need to ask you about David Carruthers.'

'No.'

'No?'

'*No.*'

'My friend here.' Foxton waved at Marshall. 'Rob. He's a specialist in this kind of crime. He investigated this exact case in London. We believe he's searching for the same guy who took your sister.'

Audrey's nostrils were out of control, like she was going to hyperventilate. 'David Carruthers has done this to other people?'

Foxton nodded. 'I know this is difficult to think about, but we want to give you closure.'

Audrey kicked her legs down and stood up. Buzzing with energy. Clapping her hands independently, fingers against palms. 'Karla reported a leak in the shower. A plumber came around to check it. It turned out to be grout needing replacing, but he'd made a mess investigating it. Huge hole in the wall. The plumber couldn't fix it. Wouldn't. But he had a friend who could do it. David Carruthers. A handyman. From London. Karla agreed to let him do it.' She was nodding, way too fast.

'Audrey, it's okay.' Foxton was on his feet now, hands out to placate her. 'We need to—'

'Karla got him to fix a few loose floorboards and build a chicken run in the yard out the back. I went away on a retreat. That night, Karla was taken from here in the middle of the night. A week later, she was dumped on the lane two streets away. Dead.'

The lane Shunty had driven up. Probably as good a place as any in central Carlisle.

That need to return them to near where he'd taken them was textbook Derek Cameron. No matter how dangerous it was, he had to do it. As dangerous as the abductions themselves.

Marshall waited for her to make eye contact, but she walked over to the stereo and changed track. 'Audrey, to understand things a bit more, I need to ask you some different questions about—'

Shunty clattered into the room, carrying a tray laden with a teapot and some mugs. 'Sorry, she's only got green in.'

'Don't drink black tea.' Audrey was shaking her head. 'It's carcinogenic.'

Foxton took over, pouring one for her, then for himself. He handed her a cup with a floral pattern and settled back against the window with his own, a black mug with FUCK YOU written in angry orange letters. 'Audrey.' He left the space for her. 'David Carruthers is dead. His body was found near Melrose.'

Her eyes danced around the room. Despite what Foxton had hoped, the news didn't seem to give her any closure. Quite the opposite, in fact – she was shaking.

'Audrey, we think David Carruthers has taken someone else. We think she's still alive. We need to find her.'

Marshall swallowed down some scolding tea. 'When you spoke to him, did he ever—'

'I *told* the police everything!'

'Audrey, it's okay.' Marshall rested his cup down on the table. Foxton was shooting him a warning look, which he ignored. His mouth was on fire. 'I hear you. Everything you're saying. It's difficult repeatedly going through all of the trauma you've experienced over the loss of your sister. I'm so sorry it happened. But, like DI Foxton said, there's another woman missing. Now, you've been amazing, Audrey, you've told us all about what happened to her. But I need to ask you some questions about him. About David Carruthers.'

She was looking at him. Right through him, in fact. A stare like a power drill.

'Audrey, David Carruthers was a fiction he created. His real name is Derek Cameron. Like DI Foxton told you, we found his body up near Melrose. He abducted a woman called Wendy Malcolm on Saturday night, before he died. We think she could be still alive, so we want to—'

'Anything.'

'Okay.' Marshall tried a smile, but that intense look was... He shook it off. 'When he was here, fixing your walls and your shower, did you speak to him?'

'He spoke to me.'

Marshall smiled at her. 'I'm guessing it was more *at* you, right?'

She giggled. 'Right.'

Even amongst the trauma of her sister's death, she was still there.

'What did he talk about?'

'The weather. He was always talking about the weather. Moaning about it.'

'Always?'

'He was here for four days. One day to do the wall. Another to do the bathroom. Then two for the chicken coop. We never got around to getting hens.'

Marshall left her a brief gap. 'Did he mention any hobbies?'

'Football. He had the radio on. TalkSport. The constant drone of it. Talking about Arsenal a lot.'

'Was he an Arsenal fan?'

'I think so.'

'Did he mention going to any matches?'

'He said he was a season ticket holder but it lapsed. He went to some away games with his brother.'

'His brother?'

'That's what he said.'

'He give his name?'

She shook her head. 'Went to see them at Manchester United. And at Burnley. Lost them both, he said he was cursed. Talked to me about how bad they played in both games. The referee was biased against them.'

Both clubs were in the target area for his victims. Marshall would have to look into those fixtures and see if it tallied with his time there.

'I like football.' Audrey was smiling. 'The noise of the crowd is soothing.'

'Not when you're at a match.'

'No. I went once and had to leave. But I like it on TV.'

'What about anything else?'

She frowned.

'Audrey, did he speak more to you or your sister?'

'Equally.'

'Okay, so he talked to you about football. Did he know you were into it?'

'I was watching *Match of the Day* when he came around first.'

So he was targeting his story, tailoring it to her.

She took a sip of tea. 'He talked to Karla about his van.'

'His van?'

'Said he'd had it ten years. Kept updating it himself. Was replacing the engine.'

Here we go.

'Did he say anything else about it?'

'Not to me. And she didn't say anything.'

'Was Karla into cars?'

Audrey nodded. 'Formula One.'

Right. Another targeted story.

'Did he talk about any hobbies or any other events he might be attending?'

She shook her head.

Marshall had a couple of tiny nuggets to ponder over in relation to the profile, but the fact he was still exhibiting social chameleon tendencies, fitting his stories to the listener, was only part of it.

What he shared of it might be key.

Fixing up your own van, modifying it, that meant he had a local workshop.

Probably where he'd taken Karla.

Could be Wendy was down here.

Marshall got to his feet. 'Listen, if there's anything you can—'

'Please. Leave. Mum will be here soon.'

Marshall looked at Foxton and got a tight nod from him. 'Okay, Audrey. I'm sorry for what's happened to your sister. For the trauma it's taken out on you. We'll leave you be now. Okay?'

She nodded.

Marshall led them out.

Foxton pointed at Shunty and hissed out an instruction, 'Can you clear up the tea?'

'Haven't finished mine.'

Foxton plonked his mug on the tray. 'Tidy ours while you do it.'

CHAPTER TWENTY-FOUR

Marshall followed Foxton outside into a brief flurry of thin rain, already smelling of toasted ozone. 'Thanks for arranging the meeting.'

'Polite to a fault.' Foxton was striding across the street. 'Sorry you didn't get anything out of that.'

'It's not as fruitless as you might think.'

'Oh?'

'The questions you were asking, I could've got from the report. In fact, I did – as we drove down here. The other stuff was useful, how he targets the information to the listener. I can check those football matches, see if they match the timelines of the other victims further south. An Arsenal away loss to Man United isn't that unusual these days, but a Burnley one is. And the stuff about his van? That's golden. It's filling in detail for his MO.'

'I'm excited for you, pal. Really, I am.'

'One thing, though: it doesn't say if she was taken from inside the flat.'

Foxton seemed more interested in checking out the display in the window of the bookshop. 'We believe so.'

'The report said you didn't get any DNA?'

Foxton turned around. 'Audrey's a freaky cleaner. Obsessive. Should employ her as a crime-scene cleaner. I got involved in this after her sister had been missing for four days. The windows had been open all that time and the flat cleaned *twenty* times. A day.'

Marshall grimaced. 'Bad luck.'

'Nothing on the body when we found her, either.'

A dead end to Foxton but this was triggering synapses in Marshall's brain, sparking connections. 'She's autistic, right?'

'Audrey? I mean, can't you see?'

'No, I saw. But I was wondering about Karla?'

'She had what used to be called Asperger's and is now part of just autism spectrum disorder. Least, I think that's how it works. Hard to keep up with it these days, to be honest.'

'You seem to know a lot about it.'

'My youngest is autistic.' Foxton leaned close to the glass, like he'd spotted a book he wanted to buy for his kid. 'A teacher spotted it at an early age. It's not about her being a problem, just stopping the world being a problem for her. She's just different, that's all. She'll never be normal, but what's normal? Who wants to be normal? She's normal for her. We have to adapt.' He looked around at him, fixed him with a hard stare. 'Bottom line, though, is Karla had relatively unimpaired language skills and intelligence. Autism's a spectrum and, as you can see, Audrey's on the border between functioning and non-functioning. The death of her sister's hit her hard. Set her back a lot in her coping with the world. They lived together because their mother struggled with them. She didn't want them in the house. Soon as Karla left school, they got that flat.'

'They're twins?'

'Year apart. Audrey's younger.'

'Did she work?'

'Karla did. From home. Telesales stuff. Got through hundreds of calls a week, much higher success rate than anyone else. Earned enough to pay for both of them, pretty much. Mother helps out, but...'

Foxton seemed like a man beaten by his life and Marshall knew why. Having an autistic kid was one of the biggest strains anyone could have. Designing a life that prevented even the mildest diversion from their routine, that blocked any surprise. Aye, it was a lot to take on, a lot to maintain. He'd seen it work well for the kids, but it took a toll on the parents. Still, every parent wanted what was best for their children.

Scratch that – he'd seen those that didn't care about them.

But he had to cling to the knowledge that most did.

He joined Foxton looking at the bookshop display. A lot of names he didn't recognise. 'I know it doesn't feel like a lot, but it's good for me to be here to build up the picture of the life of a victim. Thanks for arranging that. I know it's hard for Audrey, but hopefully it'll help her get some closure on her sister's death. Same for their mother.'

'In time, maybe. Listen, I usually want to be repaid by you catching the bastard, but if he's dead? If he's really dead?' Foxton swallowed hard. 'Is it definitely him?'

'Definitely. Is it worth me speaking to the mother?'

'Nope.' Foxton puffed up his cheeks then blew the air out. 'Mother's a difficult woman, not got the patience her late husband had. But she's stepped up since Karla... went. She's been looking after Audrey. Poor thing wants to stay in that flat, but she'll struggle to pay the rent.' He whispered, 'What a world.' He looked over at Marshall. 'Were the other victims autistic?'

'Not to my knowledge. Maybe some were undiagnosed, but if I had to hazard a guess, I'd say they weren't.'

'Interesting.'

'In what way?'

Foxton shoved his hands deep in his pockets. Seemed to be about to say something, but he folded his arms instead. Then he opened his mouth to speak, but rubbed his chin with his right hand. He sighed. 'Andrea... DI Elliot said you've got five victims in London?'

Marshall felt that cold slap on his cheek. 'Six.'

'And she said another two cases in Kirkby Lonsdale and Northwich?'

'That's right. So including Karla, that's nine cases where he's abducted and killed. Wendy Malcolm, our missing woman, is number ten.' Marshall held Foxton's gaze for a few seconds. 'I don't want this to sound callous, but I'm building a profile of Derek Cameron. The more we understand about him, the better chance we've got of finding Wendy.'

'So he kidnapped her and died?'

'More like he was murdered.'

'Rather you than me, mate.' Foxton's eyes were like dinner plates. He laughed, cold and hollow. 'The lasses in Kirkby Lonsdale and Northwich, what happened to them?'

'We haven't visited them yet. Why?'

Foxton was back looking in the shop window, stroking his chin.

'Why do you ask, Shaun?'

Foxton dipped his head. 'I might have another data point for you.'

'Go on?'

'The flag on the system from those bonny lads and lasses in the NCA alerted me to this case being connected to your others. There might be another.' Foxton swallowed hard. 'A woman was abducted from Longtown few months ago. Found in the lane at the back of the vets a week later.'

Marshall knew the town, one of the small settlements between Hawick and Carlisle, on the English side of the border.

Geographically, it was between Carlisle and Melrose, so it matched the direction of travel.

Timewise? Slap bang in the middle of the eight months since Karla Ewing's murder. Meaning there was no cooldown – Derek Cameron could've just kept on killing.

Marshall felt a shiver on his arms. 'You worked that case?'

Foxton grimaced. 'Found her on St Patrick's Day. Town has a whole celebration that night. Don't know why, it's not particularly Irish, but we shut it all down while our missing person's case spread all over the news.' He pinched his nose. 'We thought it was a date rape, you know? Had this local idiot in for it. Guy called Norman Norman. Joke's always on him in that town. Didn't even have a middle name he could use.'

And Marshall was beginning to get that feeling that Norman Norman was a patsy. An easy conviction. The local weirdo was always the target of people's prejudices. Guy was probably much more interested in IT architecture, train timetables or building dry-stone dykes by hand than in raping and killing.

'She have any workmen in?'

'That's what's got me thinking.' Foxton snorted. 'Roofers replaced all of the tiles on her roof three weeks previously.'

And roofers weren't really a specialised trade. Sure, you needed to know what you were doing, needed training, but the most important skill in the job was having no fear of heights and being prepared to be up there in all weathers. Well, most of them.

But it was the perfect job for Derek Cameron. Somewhere

he could fall into a gang, keeping up the earthy banter to help him fit in, but all the while he was searching for more victims.

Sounded like he'd found one.

Marshall looked around at Foxton. 'Okay, well it kind of fits the profile.'

'Kind of?'

'I mean, I need to see. Can you send the case file to DI Elliot? And get me a payroll from the roofers?'

'Sure thing.' Foxton flipped out a notebook and jotted something down.

Shunty trudged out of the flat door, head low, hands in pockets, then walked over to the pool car.

Foxton walked over. 'She okay?'

Shunty was nodding without looking at him. 'As okay as she can be. Had to put her crockery back exactly as she wanted it.'

'She say anything else?'

'She didn't seem to acknowledge what'd happened to her sister.'

Foxton winced. 'That's Audrey.'

The biggest change in her life had happened.

Her sister was gone, leaving a huge gap.

Something she just couldn't face.

Marshall focused back on Foxton. 'This victim. Any family I could speak to?'

Foxton frowned. 'You don't want to speak to her?'

Some ray of light warmed up Marshall's ice-cold stomach. 'She's not dead?'

'That's why it wasn't flagged.'

CHAPTER TWENTY-FIVE

Marshall sat in the passenger seat, hunched forward over the laptop, though his seatbelt kept tugging him back. He had to look up as they took a bend, though Shunty drove so slowly it didn't give him that plunging feeling in his gut he usually got.

His diagram filled the screen, the six London data points laid out in chronological order, with Wendy Malcolm over on the far right.

Hopefully the last data point, but there was always the possibility of another Wendy Malcolm they didn't know about. Extremely unlikely but still not impossible.

In the middle, Karla Ewing was a new point in the same colour as the potential victims in Northwich and Kirkby Lonsdale.

He'd added Caroline Reynolds between Karla and Wendy.

A giant question mark surrounded those cases, but it was a pattern both in the way Derek Cameron's geographical path weaved out from London to Manchester then to the Scottish Borders. But also in time – whatever made Derek Cameron commit those crimes, he was doing them every four months on average. Some a week early, others a fortnight late, but most a day or two either side. Like the phases of the moon were driving him.

The gap from Kate Pierce in Surbiton to the Northwich case was a yawning chasm, just like there'd been between Karla and Wendy. If there was one consolation to all this work, it wasn't identifying additional data points, but additional victims. Giving their friends and family a fighting chance of grieving, rather than living in the unknown.

Seeing it all laid out like that, though...

It was sickening how Cameron had kept up that bloodlust, especially knowing the police were hunting for him. Something brazen and arrogant about it; he knew he was one of the most wanted men in Britain but kept on doing it. Kept listening to the compulsion, kept feeding it.

And nobody had connected these particular dots on ViCLAS until Kirsten.

Marshall was kicking himself – despite being sidelined, he should've checked it. That DI whose daughter went missing, he'd done the same for ten years. Marshall should've checked for unreported victims at least weekly.

Now Cameron was dead, more people might come forward with rapes and attempted assaults. More data points. But that wasn't going to be quick enough for Wendy.

Marshall could've stopped those additional victims if he'd chosen to go after Cameron instead of saving Hulse...

That was something he was trying to swallow down.

Something he kept having to swallow down.

He looked up again. They were going through a short stretch of lush woodland on both sides of the road. You'd think you were in Middle England, with its flatness, not merely a few miles away from some of the most brutal hills in Britain.

He stared at the diagram again, trying to conjure pattern from all the noise.

Marshall's profile was panning out, at least when it came to victimology – Cameron targeting vulnerable women, preying upon their social isolation, increasing the chances he'd get away with it.

Which he had done until someone had caught up with him.

While Marshall was still nowhere near identifying Cameron's killer, at least he had a thread to tug on.

One thing he was actually good at was tugging at threads until he could identify if it was golden or if he'd pulled apart the whole jumper.

The car jerked to a stop. Made Marshall rock forward in his seat and the belt bite into his shoulder. He looked up from his laptop.

They were stopped on an American-style main street rather than a curving high street or market square. Longtown – sometimes an English place name was as literal as anything in German.

A road worker switched off the traffic signals and hauled the device into his van's trailer.

Shunty sat there, the engine rumbling.

'Why aren't you going?'

Shunty looked over at Marshall. 'Who has right of way?'

'You! Both of you!'

Now, a car was closing in on them and, of course, Shunty pulled out into traffic and got a blast of horn. He darted in and shot on through the town, ten over the limit.

'It's a thirty.'

Shunty looked around at him. Blinked hard a few times, then looked back at the road. 'Okay.' He slowed down.

'Did I annoy you there or something?'

Shunty focused on the road as they weaved over the bridge leading out of the town, back towards Scotland.

'Slow down.'

'I'm doing thirty!'

'No.' Marshall pointed to the right. 'That's the vet where Caroline Reynolds was found. Where she worked.'

'With you now.' Shunty pulled in to the side of the road.

Marshall stuffed his laptop into the door pocket, stuffing down a thick wedge of empty biltong wrappers like a hen lying on eggs. He got out into the stiff wind and buttoned up his jacket.

They were on the outer limits of the small town. A sprawling country garage on this side, the site filled with cars that looked like they'd been there for years, made it seem more like a scrapyard. Opposite, the vet surgery was in a small square with some shops. A builder's merchant, a bike shop.

The lane where she was found seemed to be a pipe manufacturer. At least, that's what Marshall took it to be. A rough track led into a yard, surrounded by trees and at least two mobile phone masts. Single-storey brick office at the front. A man in a high-vis jacket sat on the kerb outside, munching his way through a stack of sandwiches wrapped in tinfoil.

Shunty joined him on that side of the car, hands in pockets. 'Seen enough?'

Cheeky sod. Marshall folded his arms. 'What do you think?'

'Me?'

'Aye, you.'

'Why are you asking me?'

'Because you're a DS. Surely you've got some insight into this?'

Shunty shrugged.

'That's it? You've got nothing?'

Shunty shrugged again.

'Are you—' Marshall stopped himself. 'Are you okay?'

'Why wouldn't I be?'

'You don't seem to be on your A-game.' Marshall left him a gap, but he didn't fill it. The wind blew between them. 'Unless this is your A-game?'

Shunty turned around and stared deep into his eyes. 'I'm wondering why you aren't focusing on the fact someone survived their ordeal.'

Woah, more than two syllables in that sentence. 'Go on?'

'You've got six victims in London. Wendy's disappeared, presumably still alive but we've got a race against time. Karla Ewing is a suspected seventh murder, that you know about, that you can confirm.' He waved his hands back towards the town. 'Caroline Reynolds is someone who fits the pattern exactly. Isolated. Lives in a rural town. Abducted a week before she was dumped. But Cameron didn't kill her. Why?'

Sometimes people who didn't speak were empty vessels who didn't have anything to say. But sometimes they were just sitting there, observing, soaking everything up. And sometimes they'd been cowed into silence by bullies.

Marshall nodded along with it. 'What does that make you think?'

'Could be he was careless. He thought he'd killed her but he hadn't. Or it could be he was regretting part of his actions. The part of what he didn't like about his *hobby* was killing them. Abducting and raping, sure, he was fine with that. But actually murdering someone? He'd regretted doing it.'

Maybe Shunty wasn't an empty vessel, after all.

'That's a pretty interesting—'

Marshall's phone rang:

DI Elliot calling...

'Better take this.' He put it to his ear, blood thudding in his ears. 'Andrea, what's up?'

'I got your text. Shaun Foxton actually found it in his heart to call me, though. Get your arses back up to Melrose, Marshall. I've arranged a video call with that lassie.'

CHAPTER TWENTY-SIX

Elliot's office window was open a crack, filling the place with the harsh smell of smoke mixed with her perfume, so strong that Marshall could almost taste it. Roses.

Marshall couldn't figure out if the smell was coming in from outside or if Elliot'd sneaked a crafty cigarette while she waited for them to drive up, too lazy to go out into the summer rain with all the smokers out there.

The TV hanging from the wall was on, showing an empty interview room in a police station. A light flickered in the background. The date and time was printed at the top right, below a corporate logo, showing it was a live feed.

Elliot sauntered in, clutching a lighter and a white box that read SMOKING KILLS in giant black letters. 'There you are.' So she'd been outside, then.

'Here I am.' Marshall sat in the chair to the right of the TV. 'Have I missed it?'

'No, no. Just fetching her.' Elliot stuffed her cigarettes in her handbag and took the seat next to him. Absolutely reeking of perfume. 'Where's the clown?'

'The clown?'

'Shunty?'

'DS Siyal shuffled off somewhere.'

She shook her head, sighing.

'You're pretty down on him.'

'Kid's a clown.'

'No, I get that's what you think, but what's he done to earn the name Shunty? Why does he have a nickname?'

'First day, he shunted a pool car against a bridge. Wrote it off. Smashed his head against the steering wheel. Blood everywhere. The suspect he was transporting got away. A murderer. Hence the name Shunty. Hence him *needing* a nickname.'

'Clearly not lost his touch.'

'What's he done?'

'Oh, nothing really.'

He'd driven like an idiot, been caught out, then paid the price with a name and lots of bullying. Most people could put up with a bit of it, but cops could be *brutal*, taking it way past the joke. A gang, all intent on belittling the new sergeant.

But Marshall had seen a side of Shunty that Elliot clearly hadn't. He was thoughtful, cerebral, insightful. Marshall's type of cop.

A wee barrel of a man sloped onto the screen. Barely five foot tall and as much around his waist. He perched on the seat. 'Inspector, are you ready up there?' Thick Cornish accent that made him sound like a Hollywood pirate.

'We are.' Elliot sat back, hand over the microphone. 'That's DI Marcus Trescothick of Devon and Cornwall Police. Don't get how Scotland is all one force, but those clowns down there still get to have their own fiefdoms.'

Clowns.

She loved that word. Ineptitude was something she perceived in everyone. No doubt Marshall was 'that profiling clown from the Met'. She probably felt like sending him down to the English north-west was getting him out of her hair. He'd show her.

Elliot lifted her hand off the mic. 'I've got a meeting with DCI Pringle down in Hawick, so we need to hurry this along, if that's okay?'

Marshall frowned at her, then cupped the mic with his hand, but Trescothick had disappeared. 'This is going to take as long as it takes.'

'Not for me it's not.'

'What's the meeting?'

'The boss is trying to get the TV news clowns playing ball. You'd think a live abduction would get them all juiced up, but no. All that shite down in Westminster is *still* dominating.'

'How about you go to your meeting when you need to. I'll stay and interview her for as long as I need.'

Elliot nibbled at her top lip. 'Fine, but please—' She held out a hand. '—make sure she's not too stressed, okay?'

'Of course. Is there any chance we could visit Mr Norman in prison?'

'Norman Norman.' Elliot was cackling like a drunk schoolgirl. 'Poor guy.'

'Can we?'

'I put in a request. He's refused all contact since his arrest, so I wouldn't hold out much hope.'

'He's on remand, right?'

'Awaiting sentencing.'

'He entered a guilty plea?'

'Offered a deal. He took it.'

'But he didn't attack her?'

Elliot shrugged.

Anyone can convict the guilty, but start convicting the innocent and they promote you…

Onscreen, a woman joined Trescothick, perching on the chair next to him. It didn't move, like she wasn't there. She was young, maybe eighteen, and looked like a ghost. Silver hair, dyed presumably, severe makeup stretching her eyes out so she looked like a cat. Her feral gaze shot around the place, not settling on anywhere in particular, but specifically avoiding the camera. Thick scarf around her neck, despite it being the best part of thirty degrees down there in Helston.

Caroline Reynolds.

The survivor.

Shit. That scarf, it was covering over the strangulation marks. How Cameron had tried to end her life. How he must've thought he'd done.

Marshall leaned forward, clasping his hands together, not smiling – especially not after her ordeal – but trying to keep his face friendly enough. 'Caroline, my name's Rob Marshall. I'm a police officer in the Met, specialising in serial crimes. I've been seconded to this case up here, but we believe—'

'Aye, aye.' Caroline stared at the camera with a fierce intensity. 'They've told me about you.' Her accent was supercharged Scottish, all lilting and rolling, the kind you only really got in border towns, where the national identities seemed to push the accents to harsh extremes. 'Heard about how you didn't catch him.'

Marshall could deny it, could fight it, but nope. He was owning this now. All of it. So he nodded. 'That's right. We didn't.'

Those feline eyes narrowed. 'So why the hell should I help you?'

'Did they tell you there's another abductee?'

She shut her eyes. 'No, they didn't.'

'We're racing against time to find her, Caroline. I hope—'

'How can I help? He took me and...' She broke off, rubbing at her scarf.

'Caroline, I gather you moved away?'

'Right. I couldn't live there, not after... I... I moved to Cornwall to live with my brother after... After what happened.'

'Are you from Longtown?'

She shook her head. 'Eyemouth.'

On the other coast, an active fishing town, one of those ones that didn't quite like incomers. A good two hours away from Longtown. A bloody awful one given the roads around here.

'I moved to Longtown last year. Six months ago... Because of my work. At the vets. I was a nurse there. Just opened a new branch, asked me to help set it up.'

She was away from home, a drive away from friends and family. Aye, that isolation was strong in her.

'Caroline, I've spoken to the investigating officer and—'

'Shaun.' She was smiling.

'Right. DI Foxton said they'd arrested a man called Norman Norman.' Saying it out loud seemed preposterous. Marshall didn't know how the poor sod must've felt growing up with that. Or how Caroline must feel hearing something so daft next to something so serious. 'Is that true?'

'Norm's a friend. At least, I thought he was. Still can't believe he'd do that to me.'

'Caroline, it's possible he didn't.'

'But... He abducted me.' She thumped the table, which seemed to wake up Trescothick. 'Held me, raped me. Dumped me a week later, outside my bloody work. Thinking I was dead.'

'Are you sure it was Mr Norman?'

'I...' Her fists were clenched, but resting on the table. 'I didn't see his face. He was careful like that. Always wore a mask when he... When he...'

'Caroline, this is important. Are you saying you don't *know* it was Mr Norman who attacked you?'

'No.'

'I know this is painful, Caroline, and I know a lot of police officers have asked this, but can you take me through what happened the night you were taken?'

She sat back, arms across her chest, her eyes thin slits. 'Norm was a customer at the vets. Had two wee cats, Pumpkin and Pickle. We got chatting once when it was just me in there. He asked me to go out for a drink. I went. It was fun. But I left with a peck on the cheek. Then walking home, I thought someone was following me, but I couldn't see him... Then I did and he's running at me. I told Shaun that I didn't get a good look at him. It was dark and I tried to run, tried to escape, but he... He caught me. He... I... He caught me.'

Marshall held her gaze for a few seconds until she looked away. He gave her a few more seconds to recover from that attack of honesty. From reliving the trauma. 'Caroline, where did you stay in Longtown?'

'It's... It was a room in a house on Lover's Lane.' She pounded the desk with both fists.

'What kind of house was it?'

'Brick. Post-war. Old couple lived there. Jean and Mike. Needed a bit of money, so I rented it off them. Could walk to work. There was a massive field across the road I could walk their dog in.'

'This might sound daft, but I gather they'd had the roof redone?'

'The roof?' She threw her hands up in the air. 'What the fuck? The *roof*?'

'Caroline. Please. It's important.'

'Right. Mike arranged it, aye. The tiles were off for a week.'

'Did you speak to any of the roofers?'

'What are you talking about?'

'Caroline, did you speak to any of the men working on the roof.'

'They were there before I went to work, couple were there after I got back.'

'Shaun said you spoke to—'

'One of the lads was very chatty.'

'What was his name?'

'Callum Davidson.'

Marshall felt a pit open up in the middle of his chest.

Cameron.

But...

He'd reused a name. That was new.

Could it be because Caroline had survived he couldn't bring himself to change his identity?

Could it be he'd just run out of them?

Or could it be he was getting lazy?

Marshall grabbed his laptop and hefted it up to show the screen at the camera. 'Caroline, is this him?'

A tight nod. 'That's him.' No hesitation, no delay. 'That's Callum. You think... You think *he* attacked me? It wasn't Norm?'

'Caroline, this man's name is Derek Cameron. Callum Davidson is an alias he's used. He's... He's done this multiple times, to multiple women. There's an urgency to this. A woman called Wendy Malcolm was taken from near Selkirk at the weekend. We're trying to find her before it's too late.'

'Why do you think I can help? Why don't you just find him?'

'Because Callum's dead.'

She ran a hand down her face. Her shoulders sagged. It

looked like she was going to slide off the chair onto the floor. 'Oh my god.'

'Caroline, we need to find Wendy. And soon. Any information he passed on to you is going to help us.'

'Like what?'

'An address. Something he might've slipped in about where he—'

'He said he lived in Galashiels.'

Marshall sat back in his chair. That was interesting – just under an hour's drive away. 'You're sure about that?'

'Said they didn't like Cockney wankers like him there. Mentioned a place called Langlee.'

Everyone in the Borders knew of Langlee.

Notorious, but nothing like as bad as you'd get up in the Central Belt or any of the English cities. Nothing like the places he'd seen in London. But it still had its moments and the locals were there for life. Some wouldn't take too kindly to an English guy living there.

'Did you see a car? Maybe a work van?'

'A van, definitely. White, but... I don't think there was any signage on the side.'

'What did he talk to you about?'

'Football. Drinking with his pals. His kids.'

'His kids?'

'Two boys. Keith and Edward. I think. Separated from the mother. She lived in Sunderland. He...'

'Sunderland, definitely?'

'Could be.'

'Could be or it is?'

'I don't know.'

'Caroline, it's important you—'

'I don't remember much else. Sorry.' Caroline got up and shot off out of the screen.

Marshall stared at Trescothick, clearly stunned by it. 'Look after her. Okay?' He hit the end call button, then sat back and looked over at Elliot.

She was standing up, fiddling with her phone. 'So, Callum Davidson. Same name as with Wendy. You any idea what that could mean?'

Trouble was, Marshall had way too many ideas. He crunched back in the chair. 'The only time Cameron's been careless before was with his first victim. Erin Nash. He targeted a school friend. Serial offenders tend to get more careful as they go, not less. Usually they're caught because of something they've overlooked, a pattern we can see but they can't. Not like this. This feels... odd.'

'Could be he's out of fake IDs. Needs a lot of work to get all that background and keep it plausible.'

Marshall thought about it, but a man who abducted and murdered women every four months wasn't playing by normal rules.

'Let's hope this is the fuck-up we need.' Elliot put her phone to her ear. 'Shunty, it's me.' She rolled her eyes. 'DI Elliot. Your boss. Put your lunch down and listen! You know how you've been searching for Callum Davidson's address? Get any hits in Langlee?' Another roll of the eyes. 'I told you to stop eating.' She sighed. 'Okay. Have a look.' She stabbed her phone with her left thumb then put it away. 'Asked Shunty to look for him yesterday, before you pitched up, but the useless clown takes twice as long as anyone else. Swear he couldn't find his arse in his pants with two hands and a torch.'

Marshall didn't play the game. Just kept it straight. 'No luck so far?'

'No, but knowing Cameron's been living in Langlee is a good thing. Not that Langlee is a good place at all.' She smirked. 'Ach, it's not too bad. Grew up there.'

'Has DS Siyal got any other leads on him?'

'DS Siyal? Oh, Shunty. Right. No. Nothing. But Cameron's obviously getting some help from someone shady as there's no paper trail on Callum Davidson.'

'Standard Cameron MO.'

'Need a favour.' Elliot clamped a hand on his shoulder, pinching the skin through the fabric of his fighting suit. 'You seem to have a soft spot for Shunty. Good thing, because Jim Pringle asked me to assign him to you for the duration.'

CHAPTER TWENTY-SEVEN

The sun was clouding over, leaving Galashiels in a dark grey. The train line ran on one side, hidden behind a tall fence, a giant brick retaining wall climbing up to stop the houses above sliding down here. The town centre was buried away in an elaborate one-way system. Marshall didn't want to see how badly decimated it was now. Last time had been brutal, the last two chain shops shuttered with no likely replacements.

Shunty pulled up at the roundabout, indicating right. He waited for the column of traffic to clear, then eased around it, feeding the wheel like a learner driver. 'Was our morning worth it?'

'What do you mean?'

'A lot of fuel and time gone. Did you get enough out of it?'

'Aye, I got something out of it. And if we hadn't gone there, we wouldn't have got this lead. That's good, right?'

Shunty didn't say anything, just drove on.

The new train station was on the left, an innovation since Marshall had lived there. Into Edinburgh in an hour. Felt like it should be a lot less time, but it was probably a good thing for house prices and business in the town. God knows it needed it.

The heating was on full blast despite it being July, that burning sensation hitting Marshall in the face and making him yawn. He reached over and turned it back down. 'Where did your nickname come from?'

Shunty pulled up at the pedestrian crossing to let a couple with a pram across. The light hit green but he waited for them to finish, then eased off again. 'Wrote off a car on my first day.'

'How?'

'Driving too fast.' That explained his driving now. Over-compensation. 'Slid on the ice, lost control. Smashed into a wall.'

'DI Elliot said it was a bridge.'

'The wall was on a bridge.'

'Was it your fault?'

'According to DI Elliot it's all my fault. I totalled the car.'

'But?'

'Bloody pool car had been driven into the ground, brakes were buggered and it was icy.'

'What was it?'

'Eh?'

'The car. What was it?'

'Oh. Right. Same as this. Green. Three letters lower on the plate.'

'Stood no chance, then.'

'Why? Do you think it's not my fault?'

'God no. You were just unlucky. Rule with police cars is you break 'em, you fix 'em. Can't fix 'em? Get a new one. Down in the Met, the boss's strategy to update the fleet was to give the shittiest car to the fastest driver and hope something jumped out in front like a big black dog, which would run away. Many a bad police car has fallen fate to that dog and, as far as we know, it's still out there.'

Shunty was rubbing at his forehead. There was a patch of lighter skin, presumably where he'd been cut.

'You don't like the nickname, do you?'

'Shunty?' He took the left up the brae, away from the centre and out towards Melrose. The much quicker way, but that bridge was being repaired yet again. 'I *hate* it.' He shrugged. 'I suck it up, though. Don't want to seem difficult.'

'Elliot gave you it, right?'

'Right.'

'You know it's workplace bullying, right?'

'Don't have to tell me twice. It's not like a micro-aggression, it's more a macro-aggression. But I'm a police officer. I'll get a lot worse from the public because of the colour of my skin.'

Marshall clocked him for more of what he was. Not just an officer from an ethnic background, but a Gen Z kid. A Zoomer or whatever the latest thing was. Care about the environment and their personal pronouns. Very sensitive too.

Marshall didn't doubt why he was struggling to make it as a cop.

Still, he'd risen to DS and that didn't stack up.

Marshall folded his arms as they passed the old school, now yet another development site. One thing Gala had going for it was a lot of old buildings ripe for turning into flats. 'You said that happened on your first day?'

'Right.'

'A PC was driving a pool car?'

'No.'

'You were a DC?'

'No. DS.'

'Wait, you're a direct entry?'

'Never hear the end of it. Supposed to be her number two, but she sidelined me straight away. I've only got a team of two and they're both the ones she doesn't want. Like she's daring any of us to quit the force. Meanwhile, Jolene is an Acting DS, managing the rest of them. It's not fair.'

'It's tough, isn't it?'

Siyal looked over at Marshall. 'Eh?'

'I'm a direct entry as a DI.'

'Huh.' Despite the whole town being a twenty, Siyal was speeding up past thirty. 'They don't think we're good cops just because we didn't walk the beat. Not sure how chasing some idiot across a train line or down a back street makes you a good detective.'

'What did you do before, Rakesh?'

He looked around at Marshall. His grimace was maybe because Marshall had used his name instead of a nickname. 'I was a lawyer. Human rights firm in Edinburgh. All the team joke about how I was just filling in forms to get Polish lap dancers their residency post-Brexit. They've no idea. I was born here but Scotland can feel like a foreign country at times. Not easy for a brown guy like me.'

'I wish they had one percent of your braveness.'

Siyal looked away. 'Hardly.'

'Direct entry hires like us are under a microscope. In the Met, there's the temptation to treat what happened with me as another reason not to continue with direct entry.'

'What happened?'

'I was sidelined on my own case.' Marshall shut his eyes and felt the rumble of the car through his whole body. 'In light of my partner's shooting and my failure to find Kate Pierce in time, I... I couldn't handle the stress. Or at least, that's how they saw it. I hadn't been toughened up enough, so the decision was made that I needed to be off that case... But I'm not going to sit there as an admin officer, messing about with spreadsheets. I'd joined the Met to solve murders. Serial murders. It's what I'm good at. It's what I'm trained for. But if they didn't want to use me, then sod them... I took an opening in Serious Collisions. Not exactly my wheelhouse, as they say, but it'd give me a chance to get some distance between what happened. Maybe show them some convictions. Unearth some murders.'

'But?'

'You know how the Met is. Or maybe you don't. Everything is politics.'

'Welcome to Police Scotland, my friend. It's just the same.' Siyal took a left turning up towards a Spar, a Chinese takeaway and the Woodcutter pub, a grotty little box with four mobility scooters parked outside. A modern church sat behind them, but it looked sad and neglected.

Siyal took the turning before it, heading for a clump of Sixties tower blocks. White-harled, four-storey things. Looked recently renovated, freshened up with paint jobs and carpentry. In Edinburgh or London they'd be surrounded by concrete playparks ruled by street gangs, but here a council worker whizzed around on a ride-on mower, scooting around a mature apple tree.

Siyal pulled into a space, perfectly distanced from the two shining cars either side. 'I appreciate your honesty, sir.'

'Please. Call me Rob.'

'Sure about that?'

'Sure. I'm not a knight of the realm. And I'm on your side.'

Siyal laughed. 'Nice to have a DI on my side.'

Marshall opened his door but didn't step out. 'Look. Just because Elliot doesn't rate you, that doesn't mean you're a bad cop. Or you haven't got the potential to become a great one. Elliot's old school, just play her game and earn her trust.'

'Easier said than done.' Siyal sighed. 'I'm trying, but she's tough.'

'Aye, and rough as arseholes.' Marshall smiled at the guy, even got one back. Aye, this was part of the job he enjoyed, getting through to someone. Battering down their defences. Then helping them. 'Anyway, are you sure Cameron lives here?'

'Lived.' Siyal got out his phone, a giant Samsung beast that was more tablet than phone. He played a video, CCTV of the car park. Derek Cameron's Peugeot was parked right in their exact spot. 'Not had time to scan it for signs of Cameron taking a woman inside, but—'

'This is good work.'

'Thanks, sir. *Rob*.' Siyal sniffed. 'While we were in Carlisle, my team were doing a search on the potential addresses for Callum Davidson, including going door-to-door. Found it on the council tax system.'

'See, that's the sort of shoe leather stuff you missed by being direct entry.'

'Exactly. Trouble is, there's nothing on the rental agreement for Callum Davidson. That flat's registered to a Jean Paton. A lady in her seventies, but the neighbours insist it has a young man inside. Called around earlier and we couldn't get in. Nobody there. Asking for a warrant, but it's going to take time.'

'Can't anyone in the council help with that?'

'Just in time.' Siyal pointed at a van with Borders Council markings on the side, wedging itself diagonally across two spaces. 'Here we go.' He got out into the rain. 'Pegsy?'

Marshall followed him over.

'Morning, Rakesh.' Pegsy looked like he'd been stretched out on a rack to seven foot tall. Like a lamp post, with dull eyes. No idea how he'd even fit in that van. Knees must be up at his chin. Still, his curly hair would be a good-enough handle for anyone trying to fight him. 'How you doing, man?'

They did a weird handshake, an elaborate system of slaps and grips and bumps that ended with them slapping each other on the back.

'Gina at the office said you need access to the flat of one Callum Davidson?'

'That's right.' Siyal pointed to the block on the left. 'Top floor here.'

'Thing is, I checked the system and there's no Callum Davidson living there.'

'I know. That flat's registered to a Jean Paton, but we think she's in a home down in Jedburgh.'

'Right. There's only one way to find out who lives there.' Pegsy set off over the path towards the entrance.

Siyal jogged to catch up with him.

Marshall took it slowly, giving Siyal space to fight his mate and win.

'You've got the key, right?'

'Right. I'm just not sure I can go into some old dear's flat without a serious—'

'Mate.' Siyal was holding the door open. 'You owe me for the last time. That wee scumbag staying in his grandad's flat?'

'Aye, aye. Come on, then.' Pegsy charged up the stairs, three at a time, pulling out a giant ring of keys as he ran.

Siyal was keeping up with him, but Marshall had to follow at a much slower pace. He was out of breath by the top floor, but at least Pegsy had knocked on the door. 'Mrs Paton? It's Gregor from the council.'

Siyal was leaning against the doorjamb, sucking deep breaths.

'Mrs Paton? We're coming in. Okay?' Pegsy opened the

door and crouched down. He showed Siyal a wad of envelopes, then started going through them. 'Paton, Paton, Paton. See?'

Siyal grabbed them off him and flicked through much faster, scowling until he got halfway down. 'Davidson, Davidson, Davidson.'

'Shite and beans.' Pegsy got out his phone and started thumbing through it. 'Need to call my boss.'

Siyal glowered at him. 'You're saying we should get a warrant?'

'No, but I don't want whatever you pair dig up here to be on my head.' Pegsy showed them inside the flat. 'Sod it. Fill your boots, lads.'

Marshall went first, snapping on blue nitrile gloves as he entered. Heart thumping now and not just from the climb.

The fear that maybe they'd find Wendy Malcolm or her body.

The fear that they wouldn't find anything.

Or worse, the hope they would.

The flat was an absolute pigsty. The furniture looked like it belonged to Jean Paton. Floral three-piece suite, nicotine-yellow melamine table by the window, dreary landscapes on the walls. The full bong, crushed cans of Stella Artois and residue of a line of white powder on the coffee table were all Derek Cameron's, though.

Aye, that matched Owusu's initial assessment.

Cameron was a cocaine user.

A PlayStation 5 and Xbox Series X rested on the floor in front of the massive LG telly. Giant floor-standing speakers hooked up to a tiny wee stereo.

Siyal was crouched in front of the consoles, nodding slowly. 'Hard to get hold of one of these bad boys, let alone both.' He winched himself back up. Looked like he was going to totter over again. 'There's the drugs, but not really a sign of Cameron being a dealer.'

Marshall scowled at him. 'What are you talking about?'

'Elliot's theory is this is a drug deal gone wrong.'

'That's bullshit. Cameron's not into drugs in that way. Just recreational use.'

'Leave you to fight that battle.' Siyal opened a cupboard door and whistled through his teeth.

Marshall walked over and inspected his discovery. Various brand names. Blister packs, not prescriptions. Oxycodone by any other name is just as addictive.

Ah shite, maybe drug dealing did have something to it.

'We need to accelerate the blood toxicology.'

'On it.' Siyal got out his phone and put it to his ear. 'Dr Owusu, please. I can wait. Tell her it's Rakesh.'

Marshall walked around the room, scanning everything. The surfaces, the doors, the cupboards, the telly.

There we go.

Behind the TV was a tiny door, barely big enough to stick an iPad through. Maybe a wee elf lived in there or it was a portal to another dimension. But it was much more likely to be something sinister.

Marshall muscled in, wedging himself between the TV and the wall. Almost pushing the telly over, but he got enough of his arm in to open the door. Took a few goes, but eventually the catch gave and it popped open. Hard to see at this angle, so he picked up the telly and rested it on the floor between the games consoles, then went back to the panel.

Shite and beans, indeed.

Rolls of gaffer tape stacked up. Ziplock bags filled with cable ties. Two ball gags. Three hoods. A length of rope coiled up like a snake. Everything the pro-amateur rapist needed to abduct and attack his victims.

At the back was a little white tray stuffed full of pots, tins and clear bottles. Marshall inspected the labels – Christ, they were forensic crime scene cleaning materials. Dark Web jobs too, coming from America and Germany. The kind of stuff that would clean a location really quickly, but so bloody toxic you'd give yourself cancer if you weren't wearing hardcore PPE.

He needed to get Kirsten to bring her CSIs round here to dust the place.

One last look, though, with his phone's torch.

The light caught something tight at the back.

He took a photo and checked the display.

A pair of USB sticks were taped to the wall.

Marshall might've been a direct-entry arsehole, but he still knew when to leave well enough alone. Preserve it all until it could be catalogued. He looked over at Siyal, still on the phone. 'Where are the nearest IT forensics analysts? Edinburgh?'

'Seriously?'

'Seriously.'

'Mate, Kirsten Weir is a pro.'

CHAPTER TWENTY-EIGHT

Marshall waited in the hallway outside the flat. The door was open, but nobody was getting in there without his express approval. He could smell pungent deodorant creeping out from somewhere. His stomach rumbled, loud like it was someone else's. But he hadn't eaten since half-destroying that fry-up. Too many coffees meant he was bursting for a pee.

Made him dance from leg to leg. He could go in the flat, but he didn't want to destroy any forensic traces. Could be anything in that toilet. If Elliot was right, the pipes could be swimming with flushed substances.

A door at the end opened and a woman peered out. Long hair shrouding her face, like a folk singer transplanted in time from Sixties San Francisco to present-day Langlee. 'Can I help you, mate?'

'Police.' Marshall took out his warrant card and held it for her. 'Wondering if I could—'

The door slammed.

Great.

Back to the one-man jig.

The downstairs door shut and two pairs of footsteps climbed towards him.

'I mean, I just put up with it.' A female voice, local accent. 'Why can't you?'

'Sure, but you're you.' West coast accent. Must be Siyal. 'I hate "Shunty" but you don't mind people calling you "Weirdo".'

'Well, I am weird.' She laughed. Kirsten. Finally. 'Besides, your reaction to it just encourages them. Try and be zen about it. Then it'll pass.'

Siyal grunted.

Marshall didn't know what to do with himself. He wanted to spring into action, rush down there and get them to hurry up while he shot off in the pool car to Tesco or Ashworth's to use their toilet.

He couldn't leave the flat. And, as much as he was giving Siyal pep talks, he couldn't trust him yet. Couldn't trust any of them.

Kirsten's green hair finally appeared over the top of the banister, followed by the rest of her. She gave him a nod as she walked over, carrying a plastic bag. 'Hey there. Holding the fort like a brave little soldier, aren't you?'

Marshall laughed. 'Someone's got to.'

Siyal stepped up to join them. 'Uniform are coming now, sir, so you can be relieved soon.'

'It's me I need to relieve.' Marshall was having to take long strides to distract himself.

'Oh.'

'I can wait.' He couldn't, but he did need to put a brave face on things.

Kirsten hefted up a carrier bag. 'Got you something to eat.' She handed it over, then slinked inside the flat, snapping on her own gloves.

Another two sets of footsteps climbing up, much faster and not discussing their nicknames.

Siyal was lurking at the top of the stairs, trying to peer into Marshall's bag.

'Excuse me, Shunty.'

Siyal had to step aside to let them past. An odd couple, a tall woman and a tiny wee man, both dressed in matching crime scene investigator suits, lugging equipment.

Marshall showed them inside, then managed to check the contents of the bag. Two boxes of supermarket sushi, a bottle of Coke Zero and a bag of fizzy sweeties.

Absolutely spot on.

Siyal burped into his fist. 'Weirdo got you that.'

'It's perfect. How did she know what I'd like?'

'You're part of the metropolitan elite, aren't you? That's as exotic as you'd get in Gala, unless you count a Gregg's steak bake or a McSpicy as fancy food.'

Marshall got out the bag of fizzy Charlie the Seahorse sweets. 'These are hardly exotic.'

'It was that or a stick of rock.'

'I'll have to thank her.' Marshall put the sweets back and tore the lid off the first tub of sushi. He dashed soy sauce all over the salmon and avocado. Shoved one in his mouth and chewed. It wasn't too bad. Pretty good, actually. He realised how hungry he was.

Flashes came from inside the flat.

Marshall popped another long nigiri in his mouth and shifted around to watch the photography.

Kirsten's two were over by the telly, one photographing the rape cupboard, the other jotting it all down on a clipboard. The wee guy put it down and reached into the cupboard. He had to go right up to his armpit to reach the USB drives, which his pal captured with a bright flash, then he handed them over to Kirsten. Soon as she took them, he was jotting them down on his form. Lights flashed.

Kirsten came back outside and picked up her rucksack from the floor tiles.

Marshall hadn't even seen her drop it before she went in. 'Thanks for the sushi.'

She smiled at him. 'You strike me as the type. Ashworth's supermarket is as close to a proper sushi restaurant as you'll get down here. Couple of okay ones in Edinburgh, if that's your bag.'

'Been to a few excellent ones in London.'

'Get you.' She pulled out a rugged laptop from her bag and rested it on the banister. Didn't seem too worried about the prospect of it dropping, but the thing would probably survive re-entry from space let alone a wee drop down a stairwell. She slotted the USB stick into a device, then stabbed it into the side.

Marshall swallowed down an avocado roll. The wasabi he'd scraped on the top was burning his sinuses. 'What did you do there?'

Kirsten looked over at him. 'Using a USB condom.'

'A what?'

She tapped the stick. 'These things can have anything on them. Don't want it to take over my machine. The condom just lets me get at the contents, so I can clone it and upload the disk image to the cloud.' She leaned forward, clicking the pad a few times, swiping her fingers across the surface. A final click and she let out a sigh. 'Great. It's encrypted.'

'Dead end?'

'Unless you've got the encryption key it is, aye.'

Marshall had been here before on cases, before and after he'd joined the police. In America, they treated encryption as a munition on the grounds it allowed bad actors to do stuff in complete privacy and secrecy. Here it was as badly frowned upon, just not as heavily legislated against. He looked over at Siyal. 'Can you go through Cameron's stuff and look for anything like a password or a code?'

'You know that if he's gone to the trouble of locking the sticks away, he's not going to leave the password on a Post-It note.'

Marshall towered over him. 'A woman is going to die if we don't find her. If it's sitting around and—'

'Don't need to tell me twice.' Siyal darted back into the flat.

Kirsten swapped over to the second stick and slotted it in. Then grimaced. 'Same story with this one, sorry.'

Marshall couldn't understand what was on them. His secret identities? Wait, there was no sign of any documentation – passports, driver's licenses – so maybe he *was* on his last one. 'Why would he do that?'

'What, lock away two drives but leave them without the encryption key?' She smirked. 'Because he doesn't want you seeing what's on them, you daftie.'

'No, I get that. It's just... Is there any chance you could—'

'There's an Israeli firm who specialise in it, aye, but they cost a few million quid per drive and the success rate is less than twenty percent. Good luck getting approval for that. Besides...' Kirsten shrugged. 'Could just be his MP3 collection or football highlights of videos he's snatched from YouTube.'

'Or it could be something entirely critical to why the hell he'd been doing this. Or to why he's been killed.'

'Aye, but I can't see anyone stumping up that cash, not without some clue as to what's on it. Maybe if Derek Cameron had been involved in some terrorist activity. But his crimes – no matter how severe – won't warrant that kind of spend.'

Sweat slicked down Marshall's back.

Wendy Malcolm's life had a value placed on it.

'I'll take this back to the station and get a second opinion.' Kirsten snapped her laptop shut and popped the drives into an evidence bag. 'But you should watch what you're doing with Rakesh.'

'What I'm doing? I'm being friendly.'

'You call shouting at him to get him to search the flat friendly?'

'No, it's not, but...' Marshall ran his hand over his bristly scalp. 'I mean... Aye, I've been friendly to him. Asking him questions, even getting him to talk about the shite he puts up with from Elliot and company.'

'Good.' Kirsten put the laptop back in her bag. 'But you're clearly traumatised by not finding that woman back in London and it's not Rakesh's fault, so don't take it out on him. Okay?'

'I'm—' Trying to deny it. Marshall nodded at her. 'You're right. I'm sorry. I am probably triggered by this.'

'It's okay.' She patted him on the arm. 'I know you mean well, but there are enough egotistical wankers around here. We don't need another one.'

Siyal strode out of the flat again. 'Nothing looking like a code, sir. Sorry. But the guy's a hoarder. Place is stuffed full of shite. Going to take days to get through.'

'He's only been here a few months.'

'Right, aye.' Siyal looked back inside. 'It's probably the old lady's stuff. Looking through that for a code? Talk about needle in a haystack... I mean, if it's the name of his cat, then cool.'

'He's got a cat?'

'No, but like in those films where they're guessing someone's password based on all the stuff on a desk. Kid's names, birthdays. That kind of thing.'

'It's not likely, is it?' Marshall dropped his empty second

sushi box back into the bag. 'And if it's going to take days... We don't have that time. Wendy doesn't have it.'

Kirsten shook her head. 'Listen, it's not just the Israelis who've got advanced techniques. I'll clone both drives, then I can try to brute force them with all your Password123 nonsense without losing the originals. Maybe I can get in.'

'Okay, good idea.' Marshall looked at Siyal. 'Can you rustle up a few extra bodies and search this flat. Every room, once over. Anything that looks like a code. Don't take more than two hours; we're just looking for the obvious.'

'Rob.'

Kirsten winced at Marshall. 'Oh, forgot to say. Reason I was getting your lunch is Elliot told me to expense it. The cost is you attending the post-mortem for her.'

'Great.'

'She said you should take your laptop and update the profile while Dr Owusu does it. Maybe there's something in Cameron's death that gives a clue as to where Wendy is.'

'Big maybe.' Marshall focused on Siyal. 'Any chance you could take me to the hospital?'

'Don't suppose I've got a choice, do I?'

'No, and if we could stop on the way. Somewhere with a toilet?'

CHAPTER TWENTY-NINE

...

I park the van not far from the jetwash place, close enough for it to seem like I'm going to use it, but instead I wander off back towards the town. When you drive down here, you miss the beauty in the trees, each one with its own history. I keep looking back over my shoulder but there's nobody about, certainly nobody interested in me.

I close in on the garage, but it looks pretty knackered. Big old building, pretty much the first on the way into Galashiels, if you accepted the carwash was outside the town. Probably some kind of mill or service building for any of them.

Derek had talked about having a garage for his car. That stupid little piece of shit he'd shoved a turbo-charged engine into.

Aye. This certainly fit the bill.

Trouble is, how do I get inside?

The doors are locked. Windows boarded up. Auction sign up, but that's older than the pandemic. No idea if anyone bought it. Only one door big enough for a car and that's got more locks than the average prison.

'Can I help you?' Big fat bastard is walking his super-lean greyhound. Eyeing me up like it's me who's been shitting on his lawn instead of his dog.

'Giles Armstrong.' I barrel over there and hold out my hand. Sod doesn't shake it. 'I'm a property developer. Pass this building every day on my way to work.' I thumb up at the auction sign. 'Just wondering if anyone's bought it?'

'Way I hear it, a pair of brothers from Northern Ireland did.'

'You know them?'

'Nope.'

Why are you so fucking interested in me, then?

'No idea how I could get hold of them?'

'Land Registry would be my bet.' He leans in close. Massive big bastard, towering over me. 'Thing is, with a lassie missing, some creepy bastard hanging around a building like this is going to raise questions. You got any answers, pal?'

I give the boy a smile. 'Heard about that. Awful business. And you're right – I'll try and get in touch with the owners myself.' I set off back to the van.

'You do that.' He's watching me all the way back. 'CREEPY BASTARD!'

I can't come back here in a hurry, can I?

CHAPTER THIRTY
WENDY

Wendy opened her eyes. The lids were sticky and dry. She could barely move, couldn't even move her legs against the tape and the cable ties, let alone fight against them anymore.

The rope was a bit slacker around her throat, not that it gave her any extra room to shake free.

Everything hurt. Her skull felt like someone was chiselling away at it. Even her skin felt dry now.

Shafts of light cut through the smashed glass in the window, past the wooden boards. Meaning it was now day. When had that happened? She'd... She remembered it being night, but now...

Must've been here for days.

People outside. A dog barked. A man shouted, 'Aye, you run, you creepy bastard! Stay away from here!'

'Mmf.' She can't move. She tried, throwing everything into it, kicking, lashing. 'Mmmmmf!'

She needed to be saved.

But the only sounds were passing traffic.
She was on her own again.
And she felt so tired.

CHAPTER THIRTY-ONE
MARSHALL

The last time Marshall had been in here was to identify Derek Cameron's corpse. The room had been ice cold then but now, it was like dark midwinter, the deep chill that sucked the warmth from your bones. Felt like you'd never get warm again.

Dr Owusu was working away, slicing at Cameron's skin to get at another organ. She wasn't much of a talker, keeping her voice low as she spoke into her microphone.

Five hours he'd been in here, listening to her mutter. Hard to escape the feeling Elliot just wanted him out of the way at the same time as ticking off a task on her to-do list. She'd no doubt sell it later as him taking one for the team.

But those hard hours hadn't got him any further forward with the profile. The thin laptop weighed heavy on his lap.

Marshall focused on Cameron's face. In death, he still looked hardened. He'd caused so much misery during his life, but did he deserve to die like that? If anyone did, it was him. Probably deserved much worse for what he'd done.

The relatives of his victims deserved justice, closure, to

know he couldn't do it again. To see his head bow in court as the judge passed down a longer-than-expected sentence.

All they had was an investigating officer passing on information.

It'd take weeks, months or years to process fully. And longer to heal.

Still, Cameron wasn't going to kill anyone again.

Marshall's profile was stuffed full of eight definites, two possibles, a likely gap he needed to fill.

And Wendy Malcolm.

Scratch that thought – even in death, he was still killing.

He was stuck here, doing Elliot's job for her, while Wendy Malcolm was... what, dying? Already dead?

The room swayed around him. Neither Owusu nor her assistant seemed to notice.

Focus.

Get your head in the game.

Marshall was no closer to gleaning why Cameron had been killed. Most murders suffered from a paucity of plausible reasons, but with Cameron there were far too many people with a genuine motive for murdering him.

Christ, even Marshall would be a suspect if he didn't have the cast-iron alibi of being on shift at a fatal crash site at the time of Cameron's murder.

John Hulse was definitely one, but any relative or friend of any of the victims had to be on a list stretching into the hundreds now.

'Get your hands off each other!' Elliot waltzed into the room, smirking as she pointed at Marshall then at Owusu. 'Honestly, Belu, I can't trust you with anyone, can I?'

Owusu looked back down at the corpse. 'Thank you for finally showing up, Andrea.'

'Come on, that was funny.'

'Nope.'

'Of course it was.'

Owusu took a lump of butcher meat over to her scales, then muttered something into the recorder.

Elliot was glaring at Owusu, angry with her for not reacting to her terrible joke. She shifted her focus to Marshall. 'How's it going?'

'Getting nowhere, really.' Marshall slammed the laptop lid shut so he wouldn't be tormented by the screen. 'I've finished updating my profile, but it's not given anything new.'

'So your trip this morning was a waste of time?'

'Hardly. We found Cameron's address and we've been inside his flat. The gear he had stowed away was proof that he'd been abducting people, or at least interested in it. We know how he was able to render sites and victims forensically inert. And if Kirsten can crack those USB drives, we might be able to close the case.'

'Close the case, eh? You mean find Wendy Malcolm?'

Marshall swallowed it down. 'That, aye.'

'But that's not going to be any time soon, is it? We haven't found her yet and it's getting to the point when we probably won't, at least not alive. The good lady doctor here's going to have another corpse on her slab.'

Dr Owusu didn't look up from stitching Cameron's chest back up.

Marshall stared at Elliot. 'How's DS Siyal getting on finding the encryption key?'

Elliot put her fists on her hips. 'I'm not exactly rolling in the aisles about you requisitioning several of my officers to join his merry gang without my say-so.'

'You're serious?'

She stepped forward, close enough to smell stale cigarette smoke and the mint she was using to cover it over. 'This is *my* case, Marshall. You want cops, you need to go through me. Okay?'

'Tell me you've not—'

'God no, I'm not that petty. I'm just warning you that if you push me, I will be.' Elliot sighed. 'Shunty's got a team of numpties going through that flat. It's going to take them an age of man to finish going through all her junk. And I doubt they'll find anything.'

'You've been there?'

'Aye, I paid a visit after my little ding-dong with Mr Little Ding-Dong down in Hawick.'

Owusu looked up, her eyebrows arched, then went back to it with a quiet mutter.

Marshall stood up and felt a throbbing in the base of his spine. Aye, he needed to do some stretches. 'I presume that's your boss you're talking about?'

Elliot laughed. 'Aye, though I've got him to send me another ten skulls to help with this fool's errand.' Another sigh. 'Cameron's only been living there for a maximum of eight months.'

'What makes you think that?'

'That's when the dear old Mrs Paton was turfed into Broadfoot nursing home in Jedburgh.'

'Have you—'

'Spoke to her myself. Nice wee place between Hawick and Jedburgh.'

'Get anything out of her?'

'Oh absolutely tons, but unless hearing the story about her seeing the Beatles in Edinburgh in 1964 three times is going to find Wendy Malcolm, I'd say it was a bit of a waste of time.'

'Dementia?'

'Sadly. And I had a wee shufti at the flat. Definitely looks like it's all an old lady's stuff, so are you sure Shunty's going to find what you're looking for?'

Marshall had already been through that in his head. 'There's two possibilities, right? First, aye. It's all her junk and Shunty's shufti is—'

Elliot roared with laughter, like it was the funniest thing she'd ever heard.

'That DS Siyal's hunt is indeed a waste of time. That they find nothing of note in there. But what also makes sense to me is keeping all of her stuff gives him a great opportunity to hide what we're looking for more easily.'

'But why? Why hide it at all? And what is he hiding?'

'I don't have answers for you, Andrea. But I still think we need to keep looking for that code.'

Elliot scowled. 'We'd be better using the resource to search online.'

Marshall couldn't see any logic in it. 'Was he very online?'

Elliot shrugged. 'We don't think so.'

'So why look there?'

'He might've been using certain forums or what have you. Those crime scene cleaners came from the dark web, right?'

'Correct. But we don't know if he got them from there or from someone who had. Besides, we don't have a computer there. We've got two USB sticks, but nothing to put anything on them. Or to search "certain forums" with.' Marshall held her gaze. 'It's not where we should be devoting resources, Andrea.'

She laughed. 'Remember that you're consulting on *my* case, okay? I'll allocate the resources where I like.'

'This isn't a dictatorship. If you waste time or make too many bad calls, I'll speak to your superior officer about it.'

'Ooh, get you and your threats.'

Marshall stared her out. Being seconded to a case where

the SIO was absent and the deputy was a maniac. Aye, this was so much fun.

'Okay, if you've finished your lover's tiff?' Owusu was raising her eyebrows. 'I've got my initial findings for you.'

Marshall picked up his laptop and followed Elliot over to the slab.

Cameron lay there, eyes open looking up at the ceiling.

'Cause of death is as per my original findings.' Owusu made two fingers look like legs. Held them up in the air, then dropped down towards the floor. 'The fall from that height was enough to kill. And I'd suggest the scarring from a likely Taser needle indicates murder.'

Elliot made a winding motion. 'Can you get to the good bit?'

'Andrea, I'm...' Owusu huffed out a sigh, but she was smiling at least. 'The full blood toxicology confirms our suspicion of cocaine use, backed up by a severely damaged septum. His blood alcohol level was three times the drink-driving limit.' She shifted her gaze between them. 'And there are traces of opioids. Strong traces. Strong opioids.'

'Getting high off his own supply.' Elliot flashed her eyebrows. 'Our overriding theory is this was a drugs thing. He was yet another Gala dealer who took on too much. Bad guys caught up with him.' She smacked her hands together. 'Splat. End of story.'

Owusu was frowning. 'You're serious?'

Elliot nodded. 'Makes perfect sense to me. Sure, he might've been a filthy wee murdering rapist, but he was clearly a coke fiend. And finding smack in his system... Clincher.'

Marshall stared at the body, scanning his wrists for track marks, his biceps for bruising. Nothing. Whatever he was taking, it wasn't injecting heroin.

He didn't want to jump in – this was Elliot's case, Elliot's fuck up.

Elliot was looking up and down the body. 'We found packets of Oxycodone in his flat. On brand and off.'

Owusu ran a hand across her mouth. 'That tallies with what I'm seeing here.'

'Recreational?' Elliot laughed. 'Of course it was. I mean… Obviously. He's taking these pills to get off his bonce, right?'

Owusu fixed her with a harsh glare. 'Andrea, you don't take these to get out of your box. You take them to self-medicate. The X-ray reveals that he had bone cancer.'

Elliot bowed her head. 'Shite.'

'It's pretty advanced. Late Stage III, I'd say. And it looks like it's spread to his lymph nodes. I'm not an oncologist – I only get to see them once they've popped their clogs, eh?'

Marshall winced. He hated to think it was a suicide. That he'd been so sadistic to let Wendy Malcolm die like that.

No, the Taser marks. You don't kill yourself by shooting yourself with a Taser.

Owusu raised a finger. 'Listen, I've got an appointment booked with the senior consultant to go over the results with me, but that's tomorrow.' She walked over to the computer. 'In the meantime, I can't find a diagnosis on the system. Not for any of the names you've given me.'

Marshall waited until she looked his way. 'So you think he didn't know he was dying?'

'Right. That kind of cancer is very, very painful. Not that you have any that aren't. But it begins with a dull ache and gets progressively worse until it's all he can feel.'

Elliot stood up tall again. 'So he's been numbing the pain using illegal oxy?'

'My supposition would be along those lines, yes.' Owusu shifted her gaze between them. 'Bottom line, guys, is he was dying.'

CHAPTER THIRTY-TWO

Marshall sat in the passenger seat of Elliot's car, his knees pressing hard against the dashboard. He would move the seat back but the rear footwell was stuffed full of shite. Boxes of paperwork and empty tubs of supermarket brownies. He hugged his laptop bag and tried to avoid being thrown around by her crazy driving as she weaved in and out of traffic on the way back to Melrose.

'What's your take, Rob?' His old boss's voice boomed out of the speakers. Rickards sounded like she was out walking somewhere.

Marshall had done nothing but play it through since they'd left Owusu's lab. 'I think this changes things a bit.'

Elliot was glaring at him. 'Go on?'

'Despite the lack of a formal diagnosis, Cameron's clearly been in severe pain, given the self-medication. Maybe he knew he was dying or suspected it heavily. He'd be in constant agony, feeling like his bones were aching all day.'

Rickards clicked her tongue. 'Can you diagnose bone cancer without a series of invasive tests?'

'Exactly.'

'Eh?'

'After a blood test, you'd need a biopsy of the affected area of bone. Then an X-ray or an MRI scan. If it was the case, our question would be where, when, who. Which hospital, which consultant. All of that. Which identity he used. It might be he didn't have any left.'

'Right.' Elliot pulled up at the lights. 'Tina, Owusu's been looking into it for us and she's got nowhere. He wasn't seen at Borders General or either hospital in Edinburgh.'

Marshall tried to squeeze his bag back down to his feet, but it wasn't happening. 'It's possible he could've had it years ago, maybe even been treated for it and was in remission. But he can't get treatment for it now, for fear of being found. Hence him self-medicating.'

Rickards paused. Sounded like a bus pulled in next to her. He could picture the exact stop, right opposite their old nick, next to the café they'd decamp to when the shit hit the fan. 'That sounds a bit smart for him.'

'Hardly.' Marshall reached for the handle above the door as Elliot scooted off through, taking the long way to Melrose. 'He was fastidious with crime scenes.'

They passed the grand old train station, a few miles away from any live service and now an Italian restaurant with a day care at the back.

'Well.' Rickards clicked her tongue a few times. 'I don't know where your supposition leaves us.'

Marshall had an idea pop into his mind fully formed. 'Maybe it is a form of suicide.'

Elliot pulled out to overtake a coach, but her car wasn't up to it, so she slipped back in. 'What are you talking about? He was hit by a bloody Taser! In the back!'

'Exactly. I'm thinking he's too narcissistic to commit suicide – serial rapists and killers are psychopaths, so self-preservation is paramount. I'm wondering if Cameron could've paid someone to kill him.'

Elliot was silent, hugging the rear of the coach waiting until she was able to blast out.

Rickards was clicking her tongue.

'This is a man who used to be incredibly capable.' Marshall hugged his bag. 'He's worked in a lot of physical jobs that require a high degree of fitness. But he's now in crippling pain all the time. He's taking ridiculously strong drugs just to function. And the drugs are making him careless. Maybe explains why he recycled his ID. Not that he couldn't get a new one, just that he forgot.' He was drumming his feet, warming to the theme. 'And it could explain why Caroline Reynolds wasn't killed. Why he left her alive. It mirrors the escape he had as a child from his own ordeal when he was fostered. Maybe it's him proving to the world or just to himself that it wasn't a random event.'

Elliot took the exit for Melrose. 'Sounds like psychobabble to me.'

'That's how the theory goes, but one has to stack up against reality.' Marshall held his feet in place. 'Problem is, no matter how much pain he was in, Derek Cameron was still more than capable of overpowering Wendy Malcolm.'

'Okay, so you guys still have no leads on Wendy's whereabouts.' Rickards clicked her tongue yet again. A clear sign she was getting more stressed. A lot more. 'Okay, Rob, you need to find where she is.'

'Like we're not trying...'

'Yeah, I know, but seriously. We're all counting on you.'

'Will do. Bye.'

Elliot reached over and ended the call. 'What a charming woman.'

'Tell me about it.' Marshall sat there, staring into empty space, feeling like he was wearing a backpack like Siyal's, but it was filled with giant rocks, weighing him down and he couldn't shrug either shoulder off, couldn't shake the weight.

Elliot slowed as she entered the town centre, but had to stop at the narrow gap between two pubs, letting the oncoming traffic pass through. 'I empathise with your plight. DCIs, eh? Got to love them. At least yours *does* something other than golf.'

'Aye, she gets on my case and stays there. And she's not even my line manager anymore.'

'No, but you're both assigned to this case.' Elliot tightened her lips. 'I'd give anything to be shot of my clown.'

'Where is he? That's like a day I've been here and he's not introduced himself.'

'Relax, it'll happen.'

'Is your boss actually on the golf course?'

'Nope. DCI Pringle's up in Edinburgh, managing the media fallout from the case. Kind of like a nuclear bomb going off up there. I'll brief him afterwards, but I bet he's got himself a tee time at Muirfield.' She laughed at her own joke, easing through the gap towards the station.

Marshall looked over at her. 'You got any plans for this evening?'

'First, I'm going to check up on my team, then I'll head out to Cameron's flat and give Shunty a hoof up the arse. Then I'll make my way home. Back in at six tomorrow to do this all over again. Lather, rinse, repeat.' She pulled up outside the station. 'What about you?'

'Can I walk you through my profile?'

'Sounds riveting. I'll print it off in case I can't sleep tonight.'

'It's important work.'

'Sure, but have we found Wendy Malcolm?'

Marshall was used to this kind of truculence, both before and after he joined the police. Senior officers brought in a profiler to cover their arses with the media and rivals at their level. Cops like Elliot were landed with him and hated being told what to do, even if it caught a killer. 'What's the point in me being here if you're not going to listen to me?'

'Look. Neither of us has eaten. Let's talk over some food. My treat. Might unearth something, but it'll help us both think more clearly.'

Marshall realised how hungry he was. Couldn't remember the last time he'd eaten. The sushi at the flat? 'Okay.'

'Excellent. Let's dump our stuff, then go to Burt's.' She got out of the car and slammed the door.

Marshall watched her enter the station, thumbing her phone's screen. He got out into a spit of rain and crossed the car park. By the time he got to the front door, it was absolutely tipping down. He entered the station and the place was roasting, like being inside a bread oven.

'Robert!' A voice came from the public waiting area to the side. His mother climbed to her feet and tottered over to him on heels way too high. She leaned in to kiss his cheeks, giving him a blast of her sweet perfume and her sweet wine breath. 'I keep expecting you to call again, but you're not going to, are you, and Graham said you were here, so. Here I am. Your tea's in the oven and—'

'Mum, I'll need a rain check on that.'

Elliot was over by the security door. 'I'll see you inside, Rob.'

Mum was frowning at the closing door. 'Is that your boss?'

'Long story, Mum.'

'Is she or isn't she?'

Aye, everything was black or white with her.

'No, but she's running the investigation I'm seconded to.' Marshall dumped his bag at his feet, a barrier between them. 'Sorry, I'm a bit busy just now. What's up?'

'Dinner. Now.'

'Mum, I've got to—'

'No, you're not getting out of this.'

'Seriously, I've got to work. There's a—'

She pinched his cheek like he was a daft wee laddie. 'That's no way to talk to your mummy, Robert.'

A laugh came from the door. 'It's okay, Rob.' Elliot was still there, hands on hips. 'You've worked hard today, you deserve a rest. Some time with your family.'

Marshall shot her daggers, but they all just bounced off, so he focused on his mother. 'Let me get up to speed, then I'll come over. Ten minutes.'

'Good.' Mum kissed his cheek and tottered out of the station.

Marshall took his time grabbing his bag. 'She doesn't take no for an answer.'

'I can see the family resemblance.'

'Are you sure you don't need me?'

'Positive. I might be a prickly bitch at times, but you've done this case a power of good today. We still haven't found Wendy Malcolm but we've got a fighting chance now because of you.' Elliot smiled at him. 'You've done your part. We just need to do the donkey work to back that up. Okay?'

Marshall stood there, thinking of a hundred things he could get on with. Maybe that was the problem – too many possibilities.

Elliot tapped her card on the reader. 'Rob, we all need to put a little petrol back in our tanks. Take two hours and be with your family. I'm doing the same – Lord knows why David stays with me. We'll meet back here then and I'll update you if anything happens in the meantime. Deal?'

CHAPTER THIRTY-THREE

'I made your favourite, Robert.' Mum poured some more red wine into his glass. He still hadn't drunk any of it. 'Made it specially for you. The best lamb from the butcher's. Got her to give me the best cut.'

'Thanks.' Marshall stared down at his plate. Roast lamb, roast spuds, all the veg. Half of the greengrocers was on his plate, while Mum just had a few carrot batons on hers. A world away from his lunch of supermarket sushi, but much closer to his heavy breakfast. 'It's lovely, thanks.'

She pushed over a gravy boat filled with mint sauce that smelled like toothpaste. 'You not hungry?'

'I'm... I've had a hell of a day, that's all.' Marshall didn't take any, but sliced into the tender lamb and put some in his mouth. Whatever disagreements he'd had with his mother, she was still a great cook. 'This is brilliant. Thank you.'

'Door's always open for you, Robert. You know that.'

The front door rattled open and a grumpy teenager tumbled in, her coat's hood wrapped around her face just like Marshall's snorkel parka when he was a kid. She opened it and her hair tumbled out, then she tore off her coat and dumped it on the back of a chair. 'Absolutely *soaked*.'

'Summer rain.' Mum was on her feet, grabbing the coat and sticking it on the coat rack and handing Thea a towel that Marshall hadn't even seen, then pecking her on the cheek. 'Christ, lassie, you're freezing.'

'Only started when I was halfway up the hill, Gran.'

'Doesn't take that long to get here.'

'Not *that* hill, the other one.' Like that narrowed it down any. If there was one thing the Borders had in abundance, it was hills.

'Go and say hello to your uncle.'

Thea seemed unsure what to do or say. She wore a smiley-face Nirvana T-shirt – Kurt Cobain was only a vague early memory in Marshall's life, let alone in his niece's. 'Hey you. Long time, no see.'

'Hey. Yeah. Sorry about that.' Marshall couldn't maintain eye contact. 'Fan of Nirvana?'

'They're the *best*.'

'I was more a Strokes guy.'

'A *what* guy?'

'Nevermind.' Marshall held up his hands. 'That's unintentional.'

Thea was frowning. 'What was?'

'I said "Nevermind". That was their album. Right?'

'Was it?'

How could she be a fan of the band and not know their biggest album? Then again, kids these days all streamed music on Spotify and were all about certain songs. Just like his mother with her singles – Clash, Pistols, Siousxie, Jam, Altered Images, Cure. Maybe Thea's kids' generation would never get albums. Then again, Marshall still had a drawer full of mixtapes he'd lovingly made...

'Where have you been?' Marshall took another bite of lamb.

Thea sat at the head of the table, opposite end from her uncle. 'Seeing some pals in Peebles. Got the bus back on my own.' She dipped her head. 'Mum's *such* a dick.'

'Thea!' Marshall's mum was putting the kettle on. 'What do you mean by that?'

'Supposed to pick me up, right? But she got held up at work.'

'These things happen, my girl. Have you eaten?'

'Aye.' But Thea was looking super stressed. Fidgeting with her hairband. Fingers dancing across the table.

'You haven't, have you?'

'Had a banana.'

'That's not enough. Growing girl like you. I'll get you some.' Mum reached into the cupboard for a plate, humming along to *Love Will Tear Us Apart* on the radio.

Marshall finished chewing and leaned in towards Thea. 'You okay?'

'Why wouldn't I be?'

'You just seem ill at ease.'

'I'm fine.'

'What's up?' Marshall held her gaze finally. 'Is it me? I know I've not been the world's best uncle, but—'

'No, of course it's not you.' Thea snorted. 'Just... you know. School shit.'

'School is shit, you're right.'

'Also. Supposed to be meeting my friend, Alex, to go to the cinema. They lost their school essay. English. It's like *way* late, but they got dispensation to deliver it late. So they're restarting it.'

'Lost how?'

'Laptop swallowed it. They can't find the file *anywhere*.'

Marshall smiled at her. 'Aye, that happened loads of times to me over the years. I'm bloody useless with computers. Lost my PhD thesis.'

Her mouth hung open. 'Tell me you got it back!'

'Nope. Had to rewrite it from scratch. It wasn't as slow as I expected. But I've lost so much work stuff over the years that I might have an idea. I had to undelete stuff once. Usually it goes into your trash but sometimes it just deletes the file without a trace.'

'So you could get it back?'

'Right. One could. It's... The way it was explained to me was, it's something like the file's still there on the disk, but what's been deleted is... Think of it like an index card in the library. As long as something else hasn't overwritten the book, then you'll be fine and you can get your file back.'

'Overwritten? You mean if someone's taken the book out again?'

Marshall felt like he was being tripped up by an analogy he barely understood himself. 'No, I think I mean someone's put another book in its place. Or a bit of it.'

'Right. Kind of with you now.'

'I'll get some recommendations for apps that might help your pal.'

'It's a Dell.'

'On it.' Marshall scribbled it down on a piece of paper, then smiled at her. 'Listen, I wondered if you wanted to get some food sometime? Or just catch up?'

'Sure. I'm off cycling with my friends tomorrow. Day after?'

'Cool. As long as I'm still here. But if I'm not, I'll come and see you before I go.'

'Sounds good.' Thea sat back as Mum put a plate in front of her. Like with him and Jen as kids, she was trying to 'feed the girl up'. 'Gran, I'm vegan?'

'Oh, well, I won't tell if you won't.'

Thea rolled her eyes. 'That's not how it works.'

The door clattered open and another damp figure stormed inside. 'In the name of the wee man, it's feral out there.' Graham Thorburn slid off his coat and tossed it onto the rack, water spraying all over the wall. Thea's was next to it, dripping onto the tiled floor. 'Good evening, Robert. Nice to see you here.' He kissed Mum on the cheek, his hand on her hip. 'And you too, my darling.' He put a bag in front of Thea. 'Picked this up for you in town.'

She opened the bag and her eyes bulged. 'Wow!' She got up and hugged him. 'Thank you!'

Marshall tried to see who the author was but it was already back in the bag. He got up and walked over to Thorburn, wrapping him in a big hug. 'Been a while.'

Thorburn broke off first. 'I saw you this morning?'

'I know that. I just... It's been ages since I've seen you properly. That's all.'

'Hasn't it just.' Thorburn looked up at Marshall, his eyes sparkling. 'I'll just go and get changed out of this.' He sloped off out of the room.

Marshall took his seat again. 'When did you and him get back together?'

'A year ago, but you'd know that if you'd been in contact with your darling mother.' Another wag of the fish slice. 'Living in London was getting him down, too stressful. He got a job in Edinburgh and he was down here one day for a meeting and—'

'—I bumped into your mother in a café.' Thorburn was back in the room, already changed into khaki trousers and an 'Old Guys Rule' T-shirt. 'And we met up again for a walk. Then dinner. One thing led to another, and you know how it is.' Thorburn took the seat between Marshall and the door. 'It has been a while, Robert.' He smiled at Mum. 'Robert and me used to see each other in London.' He frowned at Marshall. 'But we lost touch.'

Mum was scowling at them both. 'You pair were meeting up in London?'

Marshall slumped back down into his chair. 'Mum, you'd know that if you'd been in contact with your darling son.'

'Ha bloody ha.' She aimed the fish slice at him. 'It's not funny, Robert.'

'Oh, Janice.' Thorburn poured himself a glass of wine. 'We'd meet up every now and then. Robert's just like a son to me.'

Marshall shrugged, reduced to acting like a teenager. His brain knew why he was feeling these dark emotions.

Childhood abandonment.

Teenage trauma.

Daddy issues.

But he couldn't stop feeling them. The burning hole in the pit of his stomach that Thorburn had filled over the years, stoked by his repeated withdrawal.

'I didn't know you were back in her life, Graham.'

'I'm back. And we're in love.'

Marshall felt a spear in his heart. Thorburn had been an on and off presence in her life for years. And Marshall knew more than most how difficult his mother could be. But she was at her most stable when Thorburn was around. 'I'm pleased for you both.'

'I'm sorry we lost touch, Robert. That's on me.'

'It's more my fault than yours.'

Thorburn picked up his wine glass and took a sip. 'Oh?'

'Just... You know what happened.'

Thorburn was smiling at his quasi-stepson. 'Dr Marshall here was on track to be the pre-eminent criminal profiler of his generation. He was certainly working with the best. Jacob Goldberg at Durham.' He reached over and grabbed a potato off Mum's plate. 'Robert and Jacob were some team.'

Thea was shifting her attention between them, like she was watching a tennis match.

'But a case broke Jacob, didn't it?'

Marshall stared deep into his wine glass. The heavy scent was all he could focus on.

'Same time as Robert became a police officer in London. I worked with him on some cases. As senior lecturer in criminology at Imperial College, I was often asked to consult. The last case I helped Robert on... We came up with the idea for a geographical profile. He almost caught a serial killer off the back of it. Derek Cameron.'

'You helped me with the early profiling work, but...' Marshall scraped his chair back. 'We didn't catch Cameron. We spooked him and he fled. He got away. And...'

'You can't blame yourself for what happened, Robert.'

'No? A woman died because of me, Graham. It's my fault.'

'I hold myself responsible too.'

'Me and only me.' Marshall stared into his plate. Congealed fat sat where the meat had been. He was burning up inside. 'I'm thinking of leaving the police. Maybe returning to academia.'

Thorburn winced. 'You're still young, Robert. You can still make great changes in the direction of your life. I'm back up here. Head of Department in Criminology at Edinburgh. I could put in a word for you?'

Marshall looked him in the eye. 'That would...' He looked away. 'Maybe. I don't know. It's nepotism. Listen, I carried the can for what happened. Took a sideways move.' He laughed. It was the only way he could get it out. The pain, the disappointment, the regret.

'One thing I'd say to you, Robert, is you might miss the involvement in cases.'

'I thought that's what I wanted, but you know that saying? One victim is a tragedy, but a thousand is a statistic? It'd be nice to be able to get that distance from the brutal truth of what I deal with every day.'

'I've got to hand it to you, Robert, you identified a hole in the system. Where you could be special and unique. Jacob thought you threw it all away when you became a cop, but you wanted to help directly. There are thousands of cops out there, Robert, but none had your experience as a criminal profiler.'

'But I'm useless in both fields.' Marshall got up. 'Mum, I was going to wash up for you as a thank you, but I need to walk and clear my head.'

'Robert, I'm sorry.' Thorburn stood up, slowly, and put a hand to his back. 'I can be crass at times. Please don't go on my account.'

'It's not about you...' Marshall made for the door and grabbed his coat off the rack. He needed to say more, so he turned back. But the words wouldn't come out.

Thorburn sat there, chewing another purloined potato. 'You shouldn't blame yourself for what happened with Kate Pierce.'

'That decision to not go after Derek Cameron cost her life.'

'But it saved...' Thorburn's lips twitched. 'What's his name?'

'John. John Hulse. I met him yesterday and... He's in a bad way. All because of me.'

'You saved his life, Robert. He's breathing because of you.' Thorburn reached across the table to take Mum's hand. 'I've learned a lot of hard lessons in this game. You need to learn to forgive yourself for what happened, Robert. It wasn't your fault.'

No. It was yet another stone weighing Marshall down.

He gripped the door handle. 'Bye, Mum. Thea – I'll get that app recommendation for you.' He opened the door and stepped out into the howling gale. 'And thank you, Graham. I appreciate you trying to talk me around, but I know what I did. Whose fault all of this is.' He shut the door and powered down the hill towards the hotel, letting the cold air bite at his face.

CHAPTER THIRTY-FOUR

Marshall knew he should just get inside the hotel and go up to his room. Not that he'd be able to sleep, but he could channel the fizzing energy into his work, read the profile again. Spot the glaring errors and maybe unearth a new path through it. Maybe it would congeal into something he could action, some insight into why Derek Cameron had done this. Why he'd been killed. Where Wendy Malcolm was.

But he was too keyed up to focus. That tingle of panic sat at the top of his stomach, above the fatty dinner he'd managed half of.

He walked right past the hotel.

Rain thudded down on him. Soaked already, but sod it, he needed to get all this shite out of his skull. He sloshed past the butcher's where his mum had bought that lamb. Half the town seemed to be butcher's shops. The place hadn't changed that much since he'd lived here, and certainly hadn't been ravaged by the pandemic, but there were differences, mostly in the shops. A new café where an interiors shop had been. A new interiors shop where a café had been. A new bookshop wedged between two units he thought had changed too, but he wasn't sure. The old bookshop was now a gift shop.

The police station was up ahead.

Go inside, see what Elliot had to say, if she'd eaten, see if there was an update. Or just get on with the profile. Taking time out for a family meal was a luxury, and he couldn't afford luxuries.

No. If there was an update, Elliot would've phoned. Or Siyal.

Marshall checked his mobile and he just had six emails from Amazon and a spam text.

Unwanted by anyone.

Stop feeling so sorry for yourself, dickhead.

He wiped the raindrops off the screen and pocketed his phone.

Besides, Elliot would no doubt ask how his family dinner had gone and he just didn't want her to know anything more about his family life on top of the slight details she had. Elliot seemed the sort to—

Paranoid, much?

Instead, Marshall took the right turn and walked around the one-way system, passing another old pub they used to drink in underage, which was now a Greek restaurant.

The rain was getting heavier and he was a stupid twat for doing this. His jacket was soaked through and would unlikely be dry by the morning. He hurried on, desperate to get back and into the shower, cutting up past the ice cream shop, still open at this late hour even though the bored teenager behind the counter didn't have any customers. Marshall hurried up to the square. The wine shop was still there on the corner.

Open.

Warm.

Tempting.

Bugger it. A glass of red in his room to stop him obsessing about the case. Or to help him.

Aye.

He pushed in and got a *meep-maw* from the buzzer.

No other customers, but the big shop was crammed with posh booze. Some displays mounted on old whisky barrels. Two bulging racks of red, two of white, one for summer rosé, then a spirits selection where gin and single malt whisky battled it out for supremacy. A final rack of beer cans, all with high-concept designs and daft names. Lilt, Overlapping Centre Halves, Old School IPA.

Just one guy working. Big lad with a rugby player's frame, his lumberjack shirt tucked into belted jeans short enough to show his cyan Chelsea boots. Bushy beard tapering to a suede-head. And he was staring at Marshall. 'Rob?'

Took Marshall a few seconds to place him. 'Dean? Dean Taylor?'

'Robert bloody Marshall!' He stormed across the shop floor and wrapped Marshall in a bear hug, then broke off and looked him up and down. 'How you doing, man?'

Marshall stepped back from him. 'Had better.'

'Never change, Rob. Never change.' Dean chuckled. 'Haven't seen you in yonks, mate. Not since Anna's funeral.'

Marshall looked away, acting like he was checking out the display of Dunpender single malts. Definitely not crying. 'You know me. Like to keep myself to myself.'

'No. That's not you at all.' Dean was smiling but his eyes were narrowed. 'Life and soul of the party.'

'People change a lot in twenty years.'

'Guess they do.' Dean grinned. 'What brings you back?'

'I'm a cop now.'

'Wow. Oh. That case up on the viaduct?'

Marshall looked away again. 'Can't talk about it.'

'Bet it is, though. When did you become a cop?'

'Ten years ago.'

'Thought you were some psychologist or something?'

'I was.' Sometimes being vague was preferable to giving the whole truth. Lying by omission rather than commission. 'How long have you been working here, Dean?'

'Working here?' Dean laughed. 'I own it, man.' He winced. 'Dad and his brother technically still do, but they can't be arsed running it, so I've a third share in the whole business and I've got—' He scratched at his beard. '—all these grey hairs to show for the stress of it all.'

Marshall couldn't see a single one. Then again, it was bright in there. 'What whole business is that?'

'This place and, obviously, Taylor's hotel.'

'I'm staying there.'

'Shit, really? Should get the charge cancelled for you.'

'God no. Appreciate the offer, mate, but Police Scotland are picking up that tab and it's good to support local businesses, right?'

Dean bellowed with laughter. 'Here.' He grabbed an expensive bottle of red. 'Take this. It's on the house.'

'Thank you.'

'Call it a late birthday present.' Dean wrapped it in red tissue paper and popped it in a hessian Tweeddale Wines bag. 'I'm sure cops are allowed to have birthdays, right?'

Shite!

It was Kirsten's birthday. He should get her something, especially after she helped him out earlier.

'Can you give me two bottles and I'll pay for one?'

'Compromise. I like it!' Dean repeated the wrapping with a second bottle. 'Though if you're going to just tan both bottles in your room, I've got some white spirit under the counter here?'

'Very good.' Marshall handed over a tenner. 'That enough?'

'Just about, aye.' Dean clicked his fingers and did pistols with his fingers, both trained somewhere near Marshall. 'I own Dean's Beans too.'

'Below the hotel?'

'Right. Come in for a coffee tomorrow morning.' Dean scratched his thick beard. 'It's the one business I actually own outright.'

Marshall smiled at his old friend and held up the bag. 'Will do.' He left the shop with another sad *meep-maw* then bundled through the pissing rain across the square to the hotel, carrying his bag with two bottles.

He went inside and it sounded like half the town was in the bar, so he wandered through.

No sign of Kirsten in there, though most of the tables were filled with an equal number of men and women playing cards. Bridge, by the looks of it.

Marshall smiled at the barman and walked back through to the reception. He still had his key in his pocket, must've travelled down to Carlisle and back, so he walked up the stairs.

'Rob Marshall?'

He stopped and turned back around.

A skeletal woman stood in the doorway to the bar, arms folded. Hair dyed too dark for her age. Smooth skin where laughter lines should be. 'Thought it was you. Can't believe you'd have the gall to come back here.' She refolded her arms. 'Then again, I actually can.'

Anna's mother.

The last person Marshall wanted to see.

He fixed her with a hard stare. 'Mrs Kelso, I'm so sorry for what happened to—'

'Sorry?' She stormed across the tiles then hit him. Again and again. '*Sorry?*' Again and again and again.

Marshall blocked her blows with his arms.

She was fast, too fast for him. 'Sorry doesn't cut it!'

He could only parry her and hoped she'd tire.

She stopped. 'How can you say you're sorry?'

'Because I am. I'm sorry for what happened to your daughter. To Anna.'

'But not for what you said?'

He still held his arms up, waiting for the next blows. 'No, I'm not.'

'Jesus Christ!' Another blow, but this time Marshall caught her wrist. She slapped him with the other hand, a sharp sting to his cheek, but he caught her wrist on the rebound. 'My husband died because of you! It wasn't his fault! The stress of what you did killed him!'

Marshall held her wrists tight, no matter how hard she was struggling, he wasn't going to let her go. His cheek was stinging from the slap, like she'd pressed an iron to his skin. 'That's not how—'

She stared at him, fury burning in her eyes, then she wilted and all the rage disappeared. She seemed to crumble.

'Mrs Kelso, I'm sorry for what happened to Anna.'

'Don't call me that. You're not a laddie anymore.'

'I truly am sorry. Nobody's more upset by what happened than me.'

'How can you *say* that?'

'Because it's the truth.'

She shook her head. 'I heard someone else died up there.'

'On Sunday night.' Marshall kept his distance from her. 'I'm a cop now, Cathy. I'm working the case.'

'You arsehole.' A rasping slap bit into his left cheek this

time. She walked off, leaving him with a face on fire, both cheeks burning.

Still, he couldn't blame her. Poor woman had been through so much. Lost so much. Not that he was much different.

'You okay?' Kirsten was standing by the front door, frowning. Tugging off her raincoat and letting the water spray out.

Marshall brushed his cheeks. 'I'm fine.'

'Rob, did she hit you?'

'Seriously. It's okay.'

'What was that about?'

'Long story.'

'Okay, I get that, but I want to listen.'

'She's just… someone I used to know. It's nothing, really.' Marshall eased a bottle out of the bag then held it out to her. 'Here, happy birthday.'

Now she was looking like she was the one who'd been slapped. Bright red cheeks, pursed lips. 'Wow.' She laughed. 'Seriously?'

'What?'

'That's a forty quid bottle.'

Now he was blushing. Bloody hell, Dean…

'Take it as a thank you for helping at Cameron's flat.'

'But that's my job?'

'Still, you could've got someone else to do it. Someone who didn't have your skills.' Not that it had got them anywhere. Aye, this was looking daft. 'But it is your birthday, so take it as a gift.'

'Aye, not that I've got anything in my life…' She tilted her head to the side. 'At least share it with me?'

'Just a glass. I'm not worth any more than that.'

She winced. 'Come on, that's not true. Listen, there's a residents' lounge upstairs with some glasses.' Before he could argue, she was charging up the stairs.

He followed her up, wrapping his soaking bag around his shoulder, carrying his very expensive freebie from Dean. 'You must know about file recovery, right?'

She glanced back down. 'I wrote the book.'

'Cool, maybe you can help.'

'I mean it, I wrote a book about it.' She led him into a large lounge area, stuffed with fussy old sofas and low tables. Big lights on an atmospheric setting. Comfortable.

Marshall dumped his stuff and waited for her to sit first. 'My room's up another flight in a much more functional area of the hotel.'

'I was in there. Then I had a word with the receptionist and got her to move me to here.' She picked up two wine glasses and a corkscrew from a table, then perched on the sofa and yanked the foil off the top of the bottle. She dug the corkscrew in and twisted until she got the faint pop. 'You're making the place looking untidy.' She patted the sofa next to her. 'Sit.'

Marshall eased off his soaking coat then did as he was told.

She poured out a healthy measure of wine into a glass. 'What kind of machine?'

'Machine?'

'That you need to recover data on...'

'Right. Eh, a Dell.'

She poured out another glass and passed one to him. 'Windows or Linux?'

'Eh, I don't know.'

'What do you mean, you don't know? You lost the file, didn't you?'

'My niece's friend did.'

'Oh, right. Let's assume it's a Windows machine. A Linux user would be in there undeleting the files themselves. What kind of file was it?'

'Word document. It's... their essay.'

'Right, well, that'll be easy enough. Small file. It's either there or it's not. I can recommend an app to undelete stuff from the laptop's hard drive. Also, I can give you all the stupid file locations Word can store stuff.'

'That'd be magic, thanks.'

'Don't mention it.'

'I'm mentioning it.' He took a sniff of the wine. Didn't smell like forty quid's worth, but he was much more of an Aldi man where good wine was cheap.

'Okay, I'll text you the instructions, you can send it to your niece.'

'Thank you.'

'If that doesn't work, I could have a look at it.'

'You don't have to.'

'No, I like helping.' She raised her glass and chinked it against his. 'Here's to my sodding birthday.'

CHAPTER THIRTY-FIVE

It might've been early, but it was already bright. Last night's rain had cleared off, leaving a morning that was too bright for Marshall. The dark clouds hovering over the hills on the horizon gave that little bit of threat, or a promise that the day wouldn't be so bloody bright.

Still early and he was so tired.

Not that he'd had too much to drink, but anything after about seven broke his sleep patterns.

Not that he'd managed much.

Marshall entered Dean's Beans and got a *weep-waw* for his trouble, a sadder version of the same sound in the wine shop.

Spartan furniture in there, all mismatched tables and chairs like some Hackney after-hours burger joint but without the tins of Red Stripe under the counter.

Self-roasted here in Melrose

Smelled dark and smoky too.

Marshall checked the board above the counter and hadn't

seen such a range of coffees in years. Peak hipster – a few coffee names even a Shoreditch barista wouldn't know. And in Melrose of all places.

No staff to order from and no customers to follow the lead of. Marshall leaned against the counter and shouted, 'Shop!'

Dean Taylor marched through and stopped. 'There you are.' He stuffed a few boxes of chicken and avocado salad into the fridge at the front. 'What can I get you, man?'

'An Americano.'

Dean clicked both fingers in time with the Simply Red track playing on the stereo. 'You ever try a long black?'

'Never even heard of it.'

'Coming right up, then.'

Marshall winced. He'd made that mistake before. 'Will I like it?'

'Relax, it's just an Americano made the other way round.'

'What does that even mean?'

'An Americano is an espresso topped up with hot water. A long black is an espresso tipped into hot water.'

'That's a thing?'

'Big difference. Less bitter and creamier. Think of it as an Australiano.' Dean battered the tamper on the counter then filled it with coffee and pressed it against the machine. 'Takeaway?'

'Aye. Listen, about that wine last night?'

Dean turned around and grinned. 'Good, right?'

'It wasn't a ten quid bottle, was it?'

'Well, no. But it was the least I could do, man.' Dean flipped a tap and steam hissed out of the espresso machine. He filled the cardboard cup, then looked past Marshall. 'Morning, you.'

'Morning, *you*.' Kirsten was yawning into her fist. 'Hey, Rob. You're here.'

'I think I am, yeah.' Marshall smiled at her. 'Can I get you a coffee?'

'After you got me that wine? No way. This is my shout.' She barged past him to the counter. 'Long black, please.'

'Making two already.' Dean gently poured an espresso into Marshall's cup then attached the lid. 'Enjoy it. Swear, it's that bit nicer than an Americano.'

'It really is.' Kirsten swept her green hair back, watching Dean disappear through the back again. Chapping her card on the counter didn't seem to hasten him back. She looked around at Marshall. 'How's your niece getting on with the laptop?'

'Texted my sister your instructions, but she hasn't got back to me.'

'Like I said – I can take a look at the laptop. Least I can do after that wine. Still got half a bottle left if you want to do it later?'

'You sure?'

'Aye, of course I am.'

'It's a huge help.'

'So you didn't actually read the instructions, did you?' She smiled. 'All I'd do is download an undelete app. Any one. It's pretty basic stuff. Then run it and cross your fingers the file's still there.'

'Cool.' Marshall got out his phone, but sure enough – Jen hadn't replied. Nobody had. To anything.

Dean slid her coffee over the counter and held out the card reader. 'Get a room, you two.'

Marshall was blushing.

Kirsten's mouth hung open. 'Eh?'

'Oh, come on. It's written all over your faces!'

'You're talking shite.' Kirsten tapped the card off the reader. Her phone blasted out. She checked the display. 'Christ. Right, Rob, I'll see you inside the station.'

Marshall let her go, then arched his eyebrow at Dean. 'Mate, what are you playing at?'

'Come on, man, I can see she's into you.'

Marshall's skin was like sunburn now. 'That's not on the cards.'

Dean winked at him. 'Having a romantic drink with her in the hotel, though.'

'How the—'

'Rob, Rob, Rob.' Dean tapped his nose. 'I own the hotel you're staying in, remember?'

Marshall took great care removing the lid of his coffee. No milk in it, so he grabbed the jug of semi-skimmed and tipped a load in. Just about enough.

Dean looked like Marshall was putting graffiti all over the Mona Lisa. 'You're butchering my coffee!'

'It's mine now so I can do what I want to it.'

Dean laughed. 'Let's have dinner tonight and catch up.'

'Fine. Seven?'

'Half past. Got a new starter in the wine shop I need to supervise. That okay?'

'Cool, see you then.' Marshall stepped out into the bright morning.

'Still here.' Kirsten was leaning against the butcher's window, staring into her phone. 'Dean does well, doesn't he?'

'In what sense?'

'Well, you wouldn't think a small town would take too kindly to someone of that persuasion.'

'What persuasion?'

'Eh... He's gay?'

Marshall raised his eyebrows. 'I didn't know, but good on him.'

'Relax, you're not his type.' She charged off along the street towards the station. 'He's into otters and twinks.'

'Whats and whats?'

'A criminal psychologist like you isn't up on gay slang?'

'I've forgotten more than you could ever know, young padawan.' Marshall smiled at her. 'Never had a gay serial killer case.'

'Always women?'

'Not always, but mostly.' Marshall clenched his teeth as they walked. 'The worst I had was—'

'Oh, jings, crivens, help ma boab.' Kirsten stopped outside the station.

Elliot was standing in the shelter, checking her mobile, exhaling cigarette smoke then sipping on a Gregg's coffee. Despite the crowd out yesterday morning, it was just her today. Funny that.

Kirsten slipped inside the station before Elliot could spot her.

Marshall was too late.

Elliot blew smoke out the side of her mouth. 'Rob Marshall. How goes it?'

Marshall couldn't just walk away, so he sidled up to her. 'Take it you haven't found her?'

'Would've called if we had.'

Marshall felt a throbbing behind his eyes, like someone had stuck an ice-pick there.

'How was your dinner with your mum?'

'Oh, family get togethers are the *best*.'

Elliot looked at him like she knew he was talking shite and trying to laugh off his trauma. 'Your mum seems forceful. Like you.'

'What's that supposed to mean?'

'The way you've managed to go from being an advisor to a central member of the team. That's forceful.'

'Have I? All I've done is what you've asked me.'

'Until you found Cameron's address in Langlee. Then you're grabbing Kirsten and giving Shunty half of my team.'

Marshall was in no mood to play office politics. He'd had more than enough of that in the Met. Seemed like half the job was arguing with idiots about stupid stuff. 'I'm sorry if I've overstepped any boundaries. It's... personal.'

She raised an eyebrow. 'Not a long story?'

'Right. No.'

'You want to talk about it?'

'Thanks for the kind offer, but I'm good.'

'Don't want you distracted by "personal".'

'It won't impact my ability to do my job.'

She exhaled smoke out of the side of her mouth again. 'Aidan Malcolm isn't going to appreciate the lead detective on his daughter's case being *distracted*.'

'What? I'm not the lead detective.'

Elliot shrugged. 'Still, for all the work you've done on your profile, it won't be useful in time, will it? And we're clearly getting nowhere in finding her.'

Aye. Something was going on here. Marshall waited for her to blow out another puff of smoke. 'What's up?'

'Nothing.'

'Sure about that?'

'Sure.' But she was looking away. However good she thought she was, Elliot was no poker player. 'Why do you think something's going on?'

'Andrea, we're both DIs, you can talk to me, whatever it is.'

'So you can do all that psychologist mumbo jumbo on me? Piss off.'

'No. I mean it. Whatever's going on, I'm here for you.'

'Barely know you. Why should I talk to you?'

'Might be good for you. I won't judge you. I'll just listen. I might even be able to help.'

She side-eyed him, then took another drag of her pungent cigarette. 'Pringle's threatened *me* with being sidelined.'

'Seriously? Why?'

'It's something to do with a missing woman being dead or dying...' Despite all the hardness, he glimpsed a gentle side to her. She blinked away some tears and smiled at him. 'I'm okay.'

'I understand what you're going through.'

'Go on?'

'Long story.'

'You know you keep saying that?'

'Probably. Nothing in my life is straightforward, Andrea. I wish it was. I've lived through my own version of your nightmare. I didn't rescue Kate Pierce... My soul's been riven with guilt ever since. If I didn't let Cameron go in the first place, I could've saved her. Could've saved all of these other victims.'

'Yup. Got the set.'

His head dipped.

'What's the plan today, Marshall?'

'I was thinking of taking a drive down to Kirkby Lonsdale and Northwich. Dig into those other victims. I mean, I could do it over the phone, but sometimes you just want to press the flesh.'

'Boss!' Siyal was running down the road, his lopsided gait looking like he was going to trip up at any moment. 'Guys...' He doubled over, sucking in breath.

Elliot grabbed his arm and leaned over. 'Shunty, what's up? Are you okay?'

'Got something.' Siyal stood up, grimacing. Breathing hard. 'All of the shite in Cameron's flat... We haven't found an encryption key, but I've got this.' He passed Elliot an evidence bag containing a payslip. 'Looks like Callum Davidson's been working as a mechanic.'

CHAPTER THIRTY-SIX

Sometimes business names matched their roles.

Dean's Beans was definitely one of them, but Max Power was certainly another. A tiny wee garage up a back street near Aldi at the far end of Galashiels, huddling under the trees on the hill, wedged between a 4x4 specialist and the bus depot. A long single-storey building in black and neon yellow. Three wide doors, all raised up and showing mechanics working away to the din of chart radio.

Marshall gestured into the building. 'Your lead, Sergeant.'

Siyal frowned briefly, then walked up to the reception door.

Marshall followed him into a tiny space even smaller than Elliot's office back at the station. Wood panelling and a fancy desk that wouldn't look out of place in a high-end dentist. Still, it was covered with five open ring binders. Three chairs for waiting customers, two of them occupied by women in their fifties, despite the fact the business seemed to specialise in pimping pocket rockets.

Who was Marshall to judge – maybe they liked whizzing

around the backroads on the Tweed's south bank in a Mitsubishi strapped onto a nuclear rocket.

He swallowed hard, though – Wendy Malcolm might've sat in one of those chairs. Probably had done.

He joined Siyal by the desk.

A skinny wee rake of a guy was hammering the keyboard of a beige computer that sat side on to the desk, muttering under his breath. He turned to face them, groaned, then took another bite of the triple-link sausage butty he was tucking into. In case that wasn't enough, a second one sat next to it, grease oozing out onto paper. He was only interested in his breakfast and whatever he was up to on that computer.

Siyal leaned forward. 'Excuse me, sir.'

Nothing.

'Mate. Excuse me.'

Still nothing.

The side door opened with the din of clanking machinery and Korean pop music. A tall guy with a tidy beard and smooth hair stepped in, rubbing his hands on a rag. He took one look at Siyal then Marshall, then tapped his skinny colleague on the shoulder. 'Max. Customer.'

'Can't get the bloody thing to connect to Citroën.' Max sat back with a sigh, then wheeled around to look at Siyal. 'Can I help you, pal?' Local accent, but deep and bassy. He had a dollop of brown sauce on his chin. Didn't seem to notice.

Siyal smiled at him. 'Need to speak to the owner.'

'That's me.' His Ss were whistles. He finished chewing, then hoisted himself up to standing. 'What's up, sir?'

'You the owner?'

'Max Power, aye.'

'That's your name?'

'Aye. What of it?'

'DS Rakesh Siyal.' He flipped out his warrant card. 'This is DI Rob Marshall.'

Max seemed to recoil, the chair trundling backwards. 'Listen, pal, can this wait? Got two guys off and a ton of MOTs to run today, with nowhere near enough time.' He was speaking low so his customers wouldn't hear. But the room was far too small for that.

Siyal nodded. 'Would one of the absentees be Callum Davidson?'

Max laughed. 'Depends what he's done.'

'Have you heard from him?'

'Not since Saturday.' Max exhaled slowly. 'What's there to say, eh? Lads here called him Cockney Wanker, like the character in the Viz. I mean, I think he was a Cockney. From London anyway. Good lad, mind.'

'Good lad how?'

'Pal, I've no idea what you're looking for.'

Marshall joined Siyal leaning against the desk. 'Did he talk about his time in London?'

'A fair amount. Big Arsenal fan, eh? Season ticket holder at the Emirates, or so he says. And that was about it.'

'Any friends you know of from that time?'

'Not really. Never talked to us about mates, like. Just vague shite, you know?'

'Oh, I know.' Siyal grinned like he was one of the lads. 'What about friends locally?'

'Just drinkers. Liked his lager. Usually went to one of the three or four boozers in town that hadn't barred him yet.'

'What do you mean by that?'

Max winced. 'Sorry, just a joke. Not aware of him being barred.'

'Mention any girlfriends?'

Max scratched at the splodge of brown sauce on his chin, then licked his finger clean. 'Was seeing a lassie, like.'

This was new.

In all of Marshall's previous interviews with employers or friends, there hadn't been a single mention of Cameron claiming to be involved with someone.

Usually his relationship with the victim was private. That final hurdle, where he unearthed some deeper intimate details of their lives to plan out their abduction. Always secret to prevent any suspicion falling on him.

The only thing they'd ever found was a Facebook post about Erin Nash being involved with someone.

Still, this girlfriend could be just chat.

Didn't have to mean Wendy Malcolm.

Siyal had his notebook out. 'You get a name out of him?'

'Mate, what's this about?'

'We found his body. Monday morning, just after midnight.'

'Ah, blimey Charlie.' Max slumped back into his chair. It wheeled backwards until it hit the wall and juddered to a halt back where he'd started. He looked at his mate then up at Siyal. 'Sure it's him?'

A nod. 'We believe he was murdered.'

'What? In *Gala*?'

Like Galashiels didn't have the occasional murder...

'Aye, sir. Well, over past Melrose.'

Max looked at his mate again, then back to Siyal. 'That boy at the Leaderfoot Viaduct?' His eyes were bulging. 'That's *Cal*?'

'I'm afraid so, sir. Now, we'd like to find his killer, so any information you could give us on him would be appreciated. We just need to find out who could've murdered him.'

'I don't think it would've been that lassie he was seeing.'

'Why not?'

'Stands to reason.' Max laughed. 'Read about it in the paper this morning. No lassie's going to be able to do that to a boy.'

Sexist prick.

Siyal leaned closer and whispered, 'Did you know about the murdering or just the raping?'

'The what?'

'Mr Davidson, as you know him, was a serial murderer. He abducted a series of women and murdered them after a prolonged sexual assault.'

Max slumped back into his chair, then sighed like a clapped-out car's exhaust. 'This serious?'

'I'm afraid so.'

'I don't know anything about that, okay? What happened when he was off the clock, I've no idea. We bantered about any old shite, but that was it for us. Banter. Right, Shug?'

His mate was staring at his phone, though, scratching his thick beard. 'Sure thing.'

'Any of the other lads know him?' Siyal was looking at Shug. 'Like him?'

Shug put his phone away. 'What's up?'

'Cops, man.' That seemed to spook him. 'Asking about Cal.'

'Cockney Wanker? What about him?'

'Did he ever mention his bird to you?'

'Nah. Kid was a bit of a loner. Mentioned her once like, how he was taking her out for dinner, but that was it. Not sure she exists. Like at school, when some wee virgin would swear he had a girlfriend but you wouldn't know her because she went to a different school.' Shug didn't seem to care that he was talking to the cops. 'Why you asking?'

Marshall shifted his gaze between them, watching the minute shifts in body language at the mention of a missing woman's name that had been all over the TV and papers. The *front* pages, which probably didn't help when it came to guys like them. 'Did he ever mention an Aidan Malcolm?'

Max frowned. 'Hang on a wee minute. Boy who lives out Yarrowford way?'

Marshall nodded. 'Was he a customer?'

'Aye, always asks for his car to be collected and dropped off. Pays for the privilege, like, but it's a bit of a ball ache having two of my lads out for that time. One to take the car, the other to get them back. Why, what's happened?'

'His daughter's gone missing.'

Max's mouth hung open. 'You think he... He... What?'

'We believe Mr Davidson is involved in her abduction.' Again, Marshall shifted his focus between the two men. Eyes wide, mouths hanging open. And it looked genuine too, that they didn't know what their colleague did. 'Callum Davidson's real name is Derek Cameron.'

Max scowled. 'You what?'

'He used a series of aliases. We believe he took Wendy Malcolm, just like six women in London and another four in the north-west of England.'

'Shite, shite, triple shite.' Max was sitting there, head in hands. 'I had no idea.'

'I get that.' Marshall left him a gap. 'Trouble is, Derek Cameron's dead, and we believe he's the only person who knows what's happened to Wendy.'

Max shifted his gaze between them. 'I want to help.'

Shug joined in, nodding in almost the exact same timing.

'Let me check.' Max reached for one of his many ledgers and flipped through it. 'Aye, here we go. Malcolm. Fiat 500. 19 plates too. Eighteenth June. Oil change, new battery.' He looked at Shug. 'Says here you did it?'

'Aye... Me and Cal drove out to collect that boy's kid's car a few weeks back.' Shug held up his hands. 'I was too busy with that footballer's car, mind? Cal took it back himself. Said he'd do it himself. Think he got her to drop him off in Gala.'

Max tutted. 'Shite, aye.' He swallowed something down. 'That's around the time he mentioned seeing a lassie.'

Marshall looked around the office, then back at Shug. 'Here?'

'Nah, in the pub.'

'Thought you didn't go drinking with him?'

'I went a couple of times.'

'Just a couple, eh.'

Shug shrugged. 'Cal's a bit of a pisshead. I mean, I like a drink, don't get me wrong, but he used to tan the lagers like tomorrow wasn't a work day. Never seemed to faze him, mind. Think he liked a wee toot, you know?' He tapped his nose.

'Any idea where he got the drugs?'

'Hardly.'

Siyal slapped the desk. 'You do know where he got the drugs from, don't you?'

'Woah, woah, woah.' Shug stood up tall, jaw tight, fists clenched. 'Listen very carefully, son. I lost my brother to heroin. I don't touch anything stronger than lager. You hear me?'

'I hear you.' Siyal held his gaze. 'We found traces of cocaine and Oxycodone in his bloodstream.'

'Shite.' Shug ran his oily hands through his greasy hair. 'What's Oxycodone when it's at home?'

'Big pharma heroin pills. Can get them on prescription. We think he was dying of cancer.'

'Cancer? Shite.'

Max was shaking his head too. 'News to me, man. I mean... Nope. Seemed to have a bit of pain in his back, but... Said it was a sprain.'

That all tallied with everything Marshall knew about

Cameron's last few months. Dying of cancer, whether he knew it or not, meant he was self-medicating with drugs. Obviously was with booze too. 'He say what the pain was from?'

Max grimaced. 'Joked that it was from too much fighting.'

'Fighting?'

'Reason I stopped going to the boozer with him...' Shug leaned in closer. 'He'd get lippy. Get himself into trouble, you know? I mean, I'm from Gala and these people are my mates, you know? Boy from England goes in and acts like that?'

'Anyone who took a particular dislike to him?'

Shug raised a hand. 'Nothing much in it, like, least not the ones I saw. Just a bit of smacking and slapping and that. Then buying each other pints afterwards and bonding over a game of pool. Know how some lads are.'

'Any of these fights ever go further?'

'Not to my knowledge. Most were just banter, you know?' Shug laughed but nobody joined in. He looked around like someone was listening in, despite the juddering and thudding coming from the garage making it hard to pick out half of the words he said. 'Thing is, Cal had a right shiner for the last week, still hadn't faded on Saturday.'

'You any idea where he could've got that shiner from?'

CHAPTER THIRTY-SEVEN

A nightclub and an Italian restaurant sat opposite a grifty boozer stuck next to the back entrances to some shops.

Marshall couldn't remember the name of the back lane they were in, running between the two main streets in Galashiels. Bank Street with its funky cafés, bakeries and a park that was a miniature Princes Street gardens in Edinburgh. Channel Street, the busier shopping precinct, that rumour said was now mostly empty or given over to charity, but Marshall was surprised at how many new places were opening up. Of all the towns to have two boardgame shops within spitting distance of each other...

Still. Five to eight and GG's Sports Bar was already open and serving.

Siyal held the door for Marshall.

The place reeked of bacon, spilled lager and burnt toast. A stage ran across the back of the room, presumably set up for local bands, but now just had a giant projection screen showing Sky Sports News. The twenty or so punters dotted around tables looked like hardened workers, but they must all be hard of hearing given the ear-splitting volume.

Siyal sidled up to the bar and flipped out his warrant card. 'Police.'

The barman was pouring out the second of three pints of golden lager. He kept on pouring as he shifted his gaze between them. 'What's this about, boys?' Trying to act all calm, but there was something going on here. Boyband skin, death metal tattoos.

Siyal gripped the edge of the bar then recoiled, deciding against it. 'You the manager?'

'Owner.' He stopped pouring and got the third glass. 'Greg Gallagher.' He thrust out a hairy hand. 'The GG behind the name. Used to get called "Horsey" at school. Pleased to meet you.'

'And you.' Siyal shook it. 'Need to ask you about a Callum Davidson.'

Greg thought it through then, forehead creased. 'Sorry, mate. No idea who you're talking about.'

'Heard he got into a fight a week ago.'

'Not in here. And not anyone called Callum.'

'He might've had a London accent.'

'Oh. Aye, but he wasn't a Callum.' Greg's lips twisted together, his forehead creasing. 'Declan, I think.'

'Declan?'

'Aye. London lad. Arsenal fan. Had to have a word with him shouting some abuse at the screen on the final day of the season. Veered on the antisemitic.' Greg pointed at a stool. 'He used to sit there, talking shite to anyone who'd listen. Said his old man came from Cork, I think.'

Siyal held out a photo of Derek Cameron. 'This him?'

Greg scratched at his chin. 'Aye, that's him.'

Marshall couldn't process it. Cameron had used another

name, one that hadn't shown up in any of the previous cases. So why had he recycled Callum Davidson?

Greg's nervous gaze shot between them. 'What's he done?'

Siyal rested his hands on the bar top and leaned across to whisper shout, 'He's a serial murderer. Good news is he's dead. Bad is he's abducted another woman and we don't know where he has her.'

'Ah, Jesus Christ.' Greg hauled the beer tap and poured the third pint. 'Jesus Christ.'

'We gather he got into a fight here.'

'I was in the kitchen when it started. Came out, smacked their skulls together. Declan got a bit lippy once I'd got them outside. Threatening me, then tried to stick the nut on me. I gave him the right hook. Down like a sack of spuds. Pure instinct, you know? Used to be an amateur boxer, know how to handle myself.' Didn't seem to have any of the injuries a boxer might have, but there was a decent gym in an old church in Gala.

Siyal tilted his head to the side. 'Did you go back for round two and kill him?'

Greg switched off the beer tap, cool as you like. 'Nope.' Like someone had just asked him for tomato ketchup.

Marshall looked at Siyal. 'What do you think?'

'I don't know what I think.'

The daft sod wasn't playing along. Some bad cop Siyal was making... Marshall sucked breath over his teeth. 'I think we've got a suspect here. Someone to take in and interview.'

Greg was shaking his head. 'No way, man. Nothing to do with me!'

'You took him out, right?' Siyal shrugged. 'Maybe you finished the job later. Could be some other reason. Either way, we're doing this down the station.'

'Mate, I did nothing.' Greg gave a deep sigh. 'That night,

Declan was in here, talking shite, hammered, out of his skull. If I was a betting man, I'd say coke and lots of it. He didn't get it in here, okay?' He pointed a finger at both of them. 'Stumbling around, shouting the odds at people, offering them to fight. But I took him outside. Dragged him over the road. And left him. Didn't give him the shiner.'

'You know who did, right?'

He stared down at the floor. 'My mate booted the shite out of him.'

'Your mate?'

'Keith lives next door. Found out Declan had been at it with his wife while he was working the rigs.'

CHAPTER THIRTY-EIGHT

Marshall trudged up the last few steps and had to wince. Whatever was going on inside Cameron's flat, they were making a hell of a lot of noise about it. Crashing and thumping, shouting and the sort of swearing police officers were best advised to keep under their breath. He waved a hand at the door, which didn't have a name tag on it, just a number. 'So that's how your lot catalogue items, is it?'

Siyal shut his eyes. 'Please don't tell *her* about this.'

Marshall smiled at him, trying to encourage and reassure, but it was hard when he had his eyes closed. 'Listen, if Elliot gives you a bollocking, you need to make sure she's being fair.'

'What do you mean by that?'

'I mean, I've been here two days and I can see you're the subject of workplace bullying from her.'

'That's not true.'

Marshall stepped close to him, keeping his voice low. 'Is it a race thing?'

A slight shake of the head. 'She's incredibly careful for it not to be. Most of the time.'

'The stuff I've seen isn't cool. I worked in the Met, as I've no doubt bored you witless about already. There's guys from a number of different ethnicities there, butting up against each other and it all sort of works out. Here, though, it's locals. And you.'

'If I looked like you, I'd still get it. She just doesn't like anyone who calls out her bullshit.'

'Might be wiser to have those chats in private?'

'Believe me, I've tried.' Siyal rubbed at his eyes. 'Let's see if they've got anything.' He walked over to the door, but stopped. 'Shite.'

'There you are.' A female officer was standing in the middle of the room, fists resting on her hips. Marshall recognised her from Wendy Malcolm's home and the briefing he'd attended, but he couldn't name her. Blonde hair, fierce eyes despite her young looks. Jolene, maybe? She stormed over to them. 'You've just let them work away here without any supervision, you clown.'

Elliot's favourite word. The apple hadn't fallen far from the tree.

Siyal was just standing there. Shoulders bowed. Defeated. What the poor guy seemed to endure daily would break the strongest. And he clearly had been broken by it.

Sod this.

Marshall blocked Siyal off and got in her face. 'Jolene, isn't it?'

She was looking up at him with a sneer. 'Who are you?'

'DI Rob Marshall. Your boss might've mentioned me at yesterday's briefing.'

She brushed her hair back and plastered on a smile like cheap makeup. 'Yes, sir. Sorry, I didn't recognise you there.'

'It's a pleasure to meet you, Jolene. Heard a lot about you.' Marshall held out a hand for her to shake. Her grip was weak and she wouldn't look him in the eyes. 'I'm working with DS Siyal here. He's supervising the team cataloguing the victim's possessions. As you're aware, the victim's a serial murderer.' He whispered now: 'This is his operation, not yours. Please, let the team do their job. They're adults, after all.'

'I don't report to you.'

'I know you don't.' Fight fire with fire. 'But you're a DC, I'm a DI and if you don't want me to report your behaviour to DCI Pringle then...'

Despite the fact Marshall hadn't even met him yet, Pringle's name was enough for her. 'Sir.' Jolene scuttled off out of the flat, getting her phone out of her pocket.

No prizes for guessing which clown she was going to call.

Marshall turned his focus to Siyal. 'You're the one who bollocks DCs, not the other way around.'

'No sweat.'

'What's that supposed to mean?'

'It means, I can handle her.'

'It didn't look like that to me.'

But Siyal wasn't listening or didn't seem to want to discuss it any further. Maybe he was playing a long game with her, but it didn't seem like it. He picked up a tablet, chunky and old enough to run off steam, and tapped in a code. 'They haven't found anything resembling ID for a Declan.' He handed the tablet over to Marshall. 'Maybe he was winging it?'

Made sense to Marshall – nobody in a bar had to know your real name, or what you were pretending was your real name. Pay cash or tap a card on a reader and they wouldn't have to read your name. So maybe he was winging it there.

Marshall finished scanning through the catalogue, even though his mind was a million miles away. Or just next door. The neighbour who thought Declan was sleeping with his wife.

Siyal's team had found a lot of stuff, but it amounted to a whole heap of sod all. He put the computer back down. 'Shall we check this neighbour, then?'

'Right-o.' Siyal left the flat, taking it slowly like he was scared Jolene was still around. Instead of following her down the stairs, he walked over to a nook in the corner. Two doors sat opposite each other, locked in a staring competition.

Siyal knocked on one with a door plate reading:

Phoebe 🩶 Keith

It hadn't been there the day before when Marshall had asked about using the toilet.

Siyal tilted his head towards the door. 'One of the Edinburgh cops hasn't been able to get an answer from here.'

Marshall scowled. 'A woman answered yesterday but shut the door in my face.'

Siyal put his ear against the door now. 'I can hear loud voices in there. Do I have—'

'Out of the way.' Marshall nudged him and listened.

Early Wu-Tang Clan blasted out, the guttural roar of ODB rapping some hideous filth over a lazy beat.

'I didn't!'

'Jesus fucking Christ! You did! I caught you!'

'I swear! I didn't do anything!'

'Fuck it.'

A sound like meat slapping off a chopping board.

Marshall thumped the door with his fist. 'Police!'

A scream.

He kicked the wood. 'Police! Open up!'

Nothing.

Marshall pointed at the door. 'Open it.'

Siyal looked at him like he'd gone mad. 'What?'

'He's trying to kill her! We need to get in there!'

Siyal looked at the door again, frowning, then shoved his shoulder into it.

All he achieved was a pathetic squeak.

Marshall pointed back at Cameron's flat. 'Get them!'

Siyal staggered over to the door, rubbing at his shoulder.

Marshall stepped back two steps, like a rugby kicker. Deep breath. Then he shot forward, knee up, foot high and kicked it just below the handle. His momentum took him through. The door smacked back against the wall, the handle wedged into the plasterboard.

The sign was split in half at his feet, right down the love heart.

'What in the name of fuck is going on?' A wee guy wearing a navy tracksuit and acid-yellow trainers stood over a woman, his fists clenched, his face a snarl. Hair shaved to the bone at the sides, clipped short on top.

The woman – Phoebe, presumably – cowered behind her hands. Her folk-singer hair was tied back in a ponytail, fronds hanging free. Blood trickled down what little of her face Marshall could see. Seemed like a cut above her left eye.

While Marshall hadn't risen up from uniform, he'd seen his share of domestic violence. The psychology was all over the place, hard to predict which way things would go. Instinct kicked in – control the situation, get a read on the psychologies, then act.

'Police.' Marshall flipped open his warrant card. His other hand was gripping his baton, tucked away behind him. 'Need you to come with me, sir.'

'Think you can come in my fucking house, eh?'

'I do if you're acting like you're going to murder someone, aye.' Marshall stepped forward. The room was thick with cigarette smoke and hip-hop. He probably weighed double

Keith's weight, but he'd never bet against the smaller guy if they had anger on their side. 'You know someone called Declan?'

The name seemed to throw Keith. 'What?'

'Heard how you kicked the shit out of someone called Declan.'

Keith stood there, nostrils twitching. Didn't say anything.

Marshall stepped forward, angling himself between Keith and Phoebe. 'Is Declan your neighbour?'

'Fuck you, shithead.'

Siyal barged into the room, holding his arm, accompanied by two big lumps in fighting suits.

Marshall waved at Keith. 'Get him out of here, please.'

The big bear men grabbed hold of Keith, but he was determined to shake them off.

Marshall found the stereo and killed the violent music. He crouched down and offered her a hand. 'It's Phoebe, right?'

She looked up at him, tears streaming down her face, mixing with the blood from her temple. A wound like that didn't come from a slap. Or just one punch. Unless the punch was reopening an old wound.

'My name's Rob. I'm a police officer. We are going to arrest him. Is his name Keith?'

She watched Siyal's two lumps drag him out of the flat, then her shoulders deflated. 'Keith.'

'Okay, Phoebe, can you tell me what happened here?'

She just shook her head, eyes shut.

'Was this about Declan?'

'Keith thought I'd been seeing him behind his back.'

'Declan lives next door, right?'

'Right. Since his auntie Jean died, aye.' She dabbed at her forehead and stared at the blood on her fingertips like it was normal. Like it was okay.

'Fucking prick!'

A shout erupted behind Marshall. Footsteps thundered towards him.

Phoebe screamed.

Marshall barely had time to turn around before Keith knocked him over, cracking his skull off the wall.

Keith spat on him, then raised his boot.

Siyal nailed Keith with his forearm, wrapping it around his throat, then hauling him down to the floor. He yanked Keith's arm up his back and the wife-beating shite squealed.

Marshall eased up to standing, wiping the spit off his cheek. Stupid mistake, turning his back like that. Siyal's two pals were on their knees out in the corridor. Christ, Keith had taken them both out.

He was snarling like a feral dog that had been abused since birth, turned into a fighting machine.

But Siyal had him on a lead, muzzled. 'Keith, stop.'

Keith tried to speak, tried to lash out, but Siyal had him right where he wanted him. 'Been away on the rigs and that slut's been shagging that Cockney prick behind my back.'

'Declan?'

'Aye, Declan the fucking English cunt.'

Phoebe was up on her knees, like she was praying. 'It wasn't like that.'

'I fucking know it was, you bitch!'

Marshall needed to separate them. Getting her out of the flat was preferable to him. 'Come on, Phoebe.' He held out a hand. 'Let's get you out of here, okay?'

She took it and he helped her out into the stairwell.

The two big lumps went back inside.

Thumping and crashing came from the flat.

Siyal yanked Keith up to standing. 'You're going to be away from home for a different reason, son.' Weird how he could be like that with members of the public, but wilted under the glare of colleagues. He passed him to the two massive uniforms who led Keith down the stairs.

Phoebe was staring at Marshall. 'What's Keith done?'

Marshall met her gaze and held it until she looked away. 'Phoebe, Declan is dead.'

She swallowed, making eye contact again. 'You think Keith killed him?'

'That's what I want to find out.' It wouldn't locate Wendy, but if Keith had killed Derek Cameron, it'd answer one big question. 'How did you know Declan?'

'Neighbour.'

'Okay, but you got on well, right?'

'Right. Keith's been away a lot. Like, a *lot*. Offshore for the last month. Doing electrical work on the rigs up off Aberdeen. Double time all week. Hard to say no to that, right? Earning well for the first time in his life. But I'm lonely when he's not here. And Dec... He came around one day, asking for sugar. You know how it is.'

Marshall knew about twenty different ways it was. Some of them would fuel her husband's fears. Some would dampen them down. Others might even allay them. He left her the space to come out with the truth.

'Dec and me... We used to chat. The best chats, you know? We'd put the world to rights. He was a good friend, you know? A great listener.'

'Keith seems to think—'

'I *never* had sex with him. Never even kissed. He was just a good friend. That's all it was. I'm married and I thought I loved my husband.'

Marshall could see that Phoebe was matching Derek Cameron's MO. He was grooming her like all the others, but he hadn't got to the point where he abducted her, raped her and killed her. Maybe the fact she was so close to home saved her, or maybe he was saving her for a rainy day, when the bloodlust returned. 'Okay, this is going to be hard, alright? Declan's real name is—'

'Callum, I know. He told me.'

'What?'

'He's an undercover cop.'

Jesus, this was new.

An elaborate fantasy life created just for her.

Judging by her eyes, Phoebe believed it too. 'He's living here to entrap a drug dealer.'

'Did he ever talk to you about his investigation?'

'Said it was confidential. I'd be in trouble if I heard anything.' Phoebe nibbled at her thumb nail. 'But I saw Dec speaking to someone.'

'Who?'

'A man.'

'Once? Twice?'

'Quite a few times, actually. He came to the flat. Heard them talking. No idea what it was about. Seen him in the staircase a couple of times on his own.'

'You ever ask Declan about him?'

'Nope.'

Derek Cameron was a loner, someone who hunted and abused solo. This would make a big difference to the case, to his profile.

Might even explain who killed him.

And maybe Elliot was right and there was a simple explanation to his death.

'Was this guy a drug dealer?'

'What? No. Dec didn't touch anything stronger than beer.'

'We found cocaine in his system. And Oxycodone.'

'Shite.' Phoebe was staring into space. 'Shite.'

'Phoebe, he wasn't a police officer. And he was neither Callum nor Declan. His real name is Derek Cameron. We've been investigating him for the abduction, sexual abuse and murder of several women in London and in the north-west of England.'

Phoebe slumped back against the wall and screamed. 'No!'

Marshall gave her a few seconds to react, but the poor woman was broken by it. Living with Keith, the vile wife-beater and now hoodwinked by a serial killer?

'You're talking shite. Dec's the nicest guy in the world. You've got the wrong man.' She folded her arms across her chest. In her mind, she was right and he was wrong. The co-operation had dried up.

'Phoebe, it's the truth.' Marshall was trying to make eye contact with her, but she was avoiding it at all costs. 'This has eaten up my life. Six women in London. Others between Manchester and here. I've spoken to the families of the victims. Their loved ones aren't coming back. I can't give them justice now, because he's dead.'

She looked at him now.

'But there's a woman missing, Phoebe. We need to find her. Help me. Tell me all you know about Declan.'

'I have.' She leaned back against the wall and huffed out a sigh. 'This that woman in the papers?'

'Her name's Wendy Malcolm. She's seventeen.'

'Jesus Christ.'

'We need to find this man he was talking to, Phoebe.'

'Saturday.'

'What about it?'

'There was this van outside. Sitting there all night. Until Sunday. Drove off after Dec.'

Shit, this had to be something.

'Do you remember anything about the van?'

‘It was a car, actually.’

‘You said a van.’

‘I know. It was a car. Think it was white or grey.’

‘What make?’

‘A Ford.’

‘That’s good.’

‘Or a Saab or a Volvo or a Vauxhall.’

Three-quarters of the cars on the road.

Magic.’

‘The plate began NB.’

‘Okay, that’s good.’ Marshall focused on Siyal. ‘Sergeant, can you...?’

He nodded at Marshall. ‘On it.’

Phoebe shut her eyes. ‘He’s definitely not a cop?’

‘Absolutely. Any undercover cops keep that fact secret. Same with secret agents. He was trying to be alluring. Mysterious.’

‘Shit. Well. He told me he was targeting who he was getting his gear from him. Was going to arrest him for drugs.’

‘Who?’

‘Neil.’ She looked up at him. ‘His hairdresser.’

CHAPTER THIRTY-NINE

Scott Street in Galashiels. Anywhere else, it'd be a back street, some residential housing and local shops. Here, it was one of the two main routes through the town. Or the one you took if you were coming from the west and wanted to avoid the snarl up in the centre's one-way system.

A curving row of flats that rolled with the hills they were built upon. In the sunshine, the stone would be golden, but it was thundering down. Columns of rain bouncing off the pavement. Cars slushing through the stream filling the road. Even so, there was a shaft of sunlight in the direction of Peebles. The flood wouldn't be biblical, just seemed like it.

Siyal pulled in, but neither of them were in a hurry to open their door. 'You want me to take a lead in here?'

Hairdressers filled the ground floors of the three-storey terrace. Curl Up and Dye was wedged between Utopia Hair Design and Bev's Barbers, both geographically and market-wise. Wooden interior, with a cream sofa and coffee table. Two women worked away at elderly customers while a man sucked from a coffee mug, listening to the phone. He scribbled something onto a ledger, then put the phone down and drank more coffee.

Marshall could see it play out. Two customers in for an hour each, but how many would be going through the books? 'Any of these known as money laundering businesses?'

Siyal looked around at him. 'That's where your brain goes?'

'No, mine goes to much darker places than that. But it's an obvious supposition. Cash businesses, low levels of policing. Especially if Neil Inglis really is a hairdresser who deals drugs. What did your guy say?'

'Hardly my guy…'

'Okay, but the guy in the Edinburgh drugs squad you spoke to?'

'It's on their radar.' Siyal reached over and turned up the heating. 'Word is, you pop in, get a bit of a trim from him, but drop a wee codeword. "My uncle Charlie's coming to stay." "Oh aye, how long?" "Two weeks." Then a colleague drops two grams of coke into the sweetie tray by the till. My auntie Mary, my auntie Molly and my friend who's just been in Hong Kong.' He looked over at Marshall. 'China White, get it?'

'Aye, I get it. But it's hardly subtle.'

'They don't need to be subtle. A hairdresser's is busy and noisy. Dryers and music on. So much noise.'

'True enough.'

Siyal scratched at his chin. 'This guy Phoebe swears she saw. None of my team have found anything on him.'

'We know it's not Neil. She knows him. Meaning she's probably had her uncle Charlie or auntie Mary visiting.'

'So, if he's not his drug dealer, who is it?'

Marshall didn't have an answer for that, so he gave Siyal the benefit of a shrug.

'Somebody was getting Cameron all those painkillers we found. Is it someone working for Neil?'

'Good point.'

'Were they even his? Was he dealing them?'

'Oh, Cameron was on them.'

'What?' Siyal scowled at him now. 'I haven't heard anything back from Doctor Owusu regarding the blood toxicology.'

Marshall twisted around to look at him. 'We've got them back.'

'No, we haven't.'

'I was at the post-mortem.'

'Were you?' Siyal punched the wheel. 'It'd be helpful if Elliot actually talked to me or, like, we had a briefing.'

'Following leads is better than attending briefings, Sergeant, so count your lucky stars. Get on top of that car, okay?' Marshall got out his phone and called Elliot.

'Well, if it isn't the Lone Ranger. How's Tonto?' She laughed. 'Actually, don't answer that. What's up, Marshall? You're seeking approval to speak to Neil Inglis?'

Marshall left a pause. He could hear the anger in her voice. 'That's it, aye.'

'No.'

'No? Why—'

'Because after Shunty spoke to someone about Mr Inglis, my phone's ringing. Edinburgh's drugs squad are conducting an investigation into that business, especially him. I want to keep us out of it.'

So, Siyal's guy hadn't been too pleased about it. And territorial pissings were the bane of Marshall's life. 'Andrea, you yourself put this murder down to being a potential drug hit.'

'That's right. Which is why I've been speaking to the Drugs DI in Edinburgh about doing this in a strategic way.'

'That's great, but we've found a report of someone visiting his flat a few times.'

'Oh aye?'

'We've got a suspect in his murder. Could be entirely innocent but, in my opinion, we've got to progress this. This seems like the sort of racket I've seen in London a few times. Cash businesses to support drug gangs laundering money.'

'We get them up here too, sunshine. The last thing I need right now, when I'm trying to recover Wendy Malcolm, is noise from upstairs about you scuppering a long-term drug investigation.'

Marshall scanned the street. Chances were, one of those cars was surveilling the shop right now. 'This might help us find Wendy.'

'What? How?'

'We know he took her. We don't know who killed him. If it was a drug thing, maybe they're close. Cameron might've told this guy something that—'

'But you probably won't get the square root of hee haw.'

'I'm fed up with probabilities. We need to be doing everything we can to recover her.'

'Saying I'm not?'

'No, but this is something we can do. Right here, right now. Let me "play the daft laddie" and see what I can shake loose. Please. I just need a word. Or two. Okay?'

A sharp intake of breath. 'Fine. But don't mess this up, okay? There's a lot of drug money in this town.'

'Lot in every town, especially London boroughs. I know what I'm doing.' Marshall ended the call and let out a sigh. 'So, I'm going in here to see what I can find. Trouble is, I'm no use at that kind of work.'

'You were bluffing?'

Marshall shrugged. 'How hard can it be?'

'I can go in, sir.'

'Have you got experience of it?'

'No, but I can do it.'

Marshall patted him on the arm. 'Thanks for the kind offer, but you stay here. Chase up your team for anything on this Declan character.'

'Right.' Siyal folded his arms over his chest. 'Great.'

'Thanks for understanding.' Marshall didn't have time to massage Siyal's fragile ego right now. He got out into the downpour and sprinted across the road. Headlights on at this hour. Unreal. He slipped in through the front door, dripping water onto the floor and smiled at the man behind the counter. 'Sorry about this, but is there any chance I could get a haircut right now?'

'Give me a second, sir.' He checked the book. He was wearing a Paul Weller *Stanley Road* T-shirt, though it had seen better days. His own hair was cut in that mod style, wonky high fringe, back-combed on top and sort of hanging everywhere else, especially over his ears.

Marshall got a stab of regret.

John Hulse used to call the men who wore that cut 'Wellends'. And every time he'd point out how it was a portmanteau of 'Weller' and 'bell end'. Every time. Pretty much the only thing that made him laugh. Now, Marshall doubted even that would.

He pursed his lips. 'Sorry, sir, we're a bit busy just now.'

Marshall looked around. 'You don't seem it.'

He raised his eyebrows. 'Excuse me?'

Marshall glanced at the appointment book. It looked full, despite them sitting outside for ten minutes and not a single customer entering or leaving.

Money laundering? Oh aye.

He leaned on the counter and spoke in the quiet tone he'd reserve for complaining in a hotel. 'Listen, it's Neil, isn't it?'

'Right, aye. Why?'

'Today's my twin sister's wedding day and my hairdresser's cancelled. Some shite about a flooding from the flat above. Don't know whether to believe him or not, but he recommended you. And Jen *will* kill me if I go there looking like this.' Marshall ran a hand through the stubble that really should've been clipped a week ago.

Neil examined his hair like a butcher examining a carcass. 'I suppose I could fit you in.' He led over to a spare chair and tucked Marshall in. 'Number one or two?'

'Two, thanks.'

Neil clicked a guard into place on the clippers and started buzzing away at Marshall's hair. 'Don't worry, I'm not going to ask you about your holidays.'

Marshall smiled at the reflection in the mirror. Tried to avoid looking at himself – he looked exhausted and his skull was the shape of a wonky potato. 'Tell you, I'd kill to go on a holiday.'

Neil arched his eyebrow. 'Oh?'

'In a lot of pain. Lower back feels like someone's driven a car through it. Bloody doctor won't prescribe anything.'

'Sounds brutal.' Neil sliced another strip of hair off the top. 'How long's your sister been engaged?'

'Four years. Supposed to get married in March 2020.'

'Oh, don't. Got so many friends doing that.'

'Aye. Worst part is I'll have to sit for *hours* at Jen's wedding today with this throbbing back. I'll be a complete mess by the end.'

'Try necking as much prosecco as you can get, maybe?' Neil grabbed Marshall's shoulders and shifted him to the side. 'You tried the hospital?'

'Two trips to A&E in the last six months.'

'That's rough, man. What does the doc think it is?'

'Hard to say. It comes and goes. Right now, it's come.' The

top of his head was almost finished now. He locked eyes with Neil in the mirror. 'Mate of mine, Declan, he had the exact same thing, but he got these pills for it.'

'Declan?'

Marshall nodded. 'Lives in Langlee. Londoner.'

Neil slotted in a different guard and ran up the back of Marshall's hair. He needed to be careful not to spook him before he finished, otherwise he'd be walking around with a stupid half-haircut all day. 'Think I know him. Used to come in for a cut every fortnight.' He stood back, hands resting on his hips. 'Weirdest thing. I swear I met him under a different name last year.'

'That's really weird, aye.'

'Mate of mine got us invited to a party down in Kirby Lonsdale. Lovely wee town, sort of in the middle of nowhere. Not really near the Lake District, but not far off. I swear his name was David something, then.'

That name wasn't on Marshall's radar at all. Then again, he hadn't dived into the two cases in that neck of the woods.

'That's really weird. Which one is the real name?'

'Impossible to know, isn't it?' Neil switched to the little white trimmer and set about lining around the top of his ears. 'See a lot of guys like that, though. Often in the closet, so they use an alias so their wife doesn't find out.' He shifted to the other ear. 'You're his mate, though. What's your take on it?'

'Wouldn't say we're mates, exactly. Work together.'

Neil frowned. 'You work at the garage?'

'Scrub up well, don't I?'

Neil laughed. 'Aye, maybe.'

'Anyway, you were saying about that party?'

'It just seems weird. Why use a different name?' Neil stepped back and held up a mirror for Marshall to inspect his neck and then the sides. 'Sorry that was so quick. How is it?'

'It's good, actually.' Marshall shook his arm free from the gown and ran a hand through his firm stubble. 'Listen, my uncle Charlie's needing a cut too. Can I send him in?'

Neil smiled. 'Sure. What kind of cut does he get?'

'Same as mine, actually. Number three, though.'

'Doesn't take it as short as you?'

'Says you can see his head's shaped like a potato. Mine is and I don't really care.'

Neil hauled the gown off in a spray of discarded hairs. 'That's fifteen quid for the haircut.'

'Pay at the desk?'

'Aye, come on over.' Neil walked to the till and waited there.

Marshall followed him, smoothing down his stubble. Sure enough – a little ball of white powder was sitting in the sweetie bowl. He leaned forward. 'How much am I due you?'

Neil kept his voice level. 'Call it an even hundred.'

Three grams of coke and a functional haircut. Bargain.

The door honked behind Marshall. He caught sight of Siyal entering the salon, hands in pockets, smiling at Neil but keeping a distance.

What the hell was he doing here?

Marshall reached into his pocket for his wallet. He always carried at least a hundred quid. Never knew when you'd need it in London. He handed it over, but Neil wasn't looking at him.

Over by Neil's chair, Siyal opened a cabinet and pulled out a huge bag of weed. Pill blister packs fell onto the floor. He looked over to Marshall and held it up. 'Smelled it, didn't I?'

Marshall stared at Neil. 'I'm arresting you for—'

Neil bolted for the door.

Marshall blocked him off, gripping his skinny arms and pushing him back into the salon.

Both other hairdressers were looking over, mouths hanging open.

Neil reached for a pair of scissors, pink disinfectant spraying through the air, and wielded them like a knife, ready to stab.

Something landed in Marshall's eyes. Stung like lemon juice. He shut them instinctively, trying to claw out the stinging liquid.

Something pressed against his chest and he stumbled backwards, landing on a chair. It wheeled backwards across the floor.

He managed to open his eyes just in time to see Neil darting through the entrance.

Siyal crashed his forearm into Neil's throat. The hairdresser hit the deck and Siyal leaned on his chest, saying something Marshall couldn't hear.

Marshall got up and blinked his way out into the downpour. 'Well done for getting him.'

Siyal snapped out a pair of handcuffs and slid them onto Neil's wrists. 'Sussed out where he was going and went there first.'

CHAPTER FORTY

The rain hammering off the station's car park made Marshall feel that Galashiels was in the early hours of an Atlantean submergence.

He'd forgotten how the weather in the Borders ran in vertical strips, south to north. But here it was in action.

Elliot was out there, huddled under the tiny section of roof in the smoking shelter.

Marshall was buggered if he was going to cross over to speak to her. He tried waving but she wasn't looking at him. He texted instead:

Lawyer's here. See you inside.

He swiped his card and walked back into the station. Must've been built around the same time as the Melrose station, though it was much bigger – it needed to be. Was actually staffed, too, with pairs of uniforms roaming the corridor, instead of braving the downpour.

Marshall opened the interview room door.

Neil Inglis sat there, stock still. Back straight, facing forwards. Barely blinking. Like he was on a meditation retreat somewhere in the remote Himalayan foothills, rather than inside a police station. 'Is he here yet?' Didn't shift his gaze.

'My colleague's just gone to get him.' Marshall sat back and folded his arms. 'Do you want any time alone with him?'

'Nope. I've not done anything, so why should I?' Sure, all those bags and blister packs of drugs weren't his. 'I'm just going to give you the truth and be judged by it.'

The door opened and Siyal stepped inside. 'Here we are, sir.'

A creepy wee gargoyle followed him in. Mark Davidson. Neil's lawyer. His thick glasses didn't hide his beady eyes shooting around all over the room, latching onto every surface and cataloguing. His beige suit was topped off with a green shirt and a red cravat. Like he'd been dressed in the dark by someone who absolutely hated him. He sat next to his client, his big gut straining at the buttons of his suit jacket. 'Let's get on with this, shall we?'

Marshall motioned for Siyal to commence recording.

'Interview commenced at ten thirty a.m. On—'

Marshall's phone blasted out.

Unknown caller...

The mobile number below wasn't something he recognised off the top of his head, either. He switched the ringer off and pocketed it, letting it ring away in silence.

The room was hot, as though the rain outside had passed on an instruction to the boiler to make it overheat.

Davidson was focusing on him. 'Sorry, are we boring you?'

Marshall gave a warm smile like he wasn't seething. 'No, I

just wanted to make sure your client wasn't interrupted by my phone.'

'That's very noble of you.'

'All part of the service, sir.'

'Mm.' Davidson smiled at Siyal. 'Let's get this underway, then.'

Siyal returned Davidson's smile. 'You don't recognise me, do you?'

Davidson narrowed his eyes at him. 'Can't say I do, no.'

'Okay, well that's interesting.' Siyal opened his notebook and ran his finger down the page. 'Rightio. Just...' He sighed, then looked up. 'You're an Edinburgh lawyer, aren't you?'

Davidson nodded. 'My firm is one of the most prestigious in Auld Reekie.' Did that really annoying thing where he put on a very Scottish accent for those two words, in contrast to the neutrality of the rest of it. 'Why?'

'Just wondering how a Galashiels hairdresser can afford an Edinburgh lawyer with your reputation.'

'I beg your pardon? My reputation is unimpeachable!'

Neil reached over to whisper into his lawyer's ear.

Davidson snarled at Siyal. 'We would formally request a brief moment to discuss some pressing matters.'

'Very well.' Marshall stood up and sloped out into the corridor. 'Knock when you're done.'

Siyal shut the door and leaned back against it. 'Something doesn't add up.'

'No.' Marshall glowered at him but he wasn't looking. 'You goading him didn't help.'

'I know him from before I joined the cops.'

'Oh? Anything I should worry about?'

'No. Just don't trust him.'

'He's a criminal defence lawyer, Rakesh. Never trust them.' Marshall yawned into his fist. 'Time for another coffee.' He set off along the corridor in the direction of the smell of rancid instant. 'A small-town hairdresser gets a big-time, big-city lawyer for one reason and one reason only. Drugs.' Another yawn caught hold of him. 'Though Christ knows what this means for Wendy Malcolm's case.'

'You okay there?'

Marshall stifled the yawn before it formed. 'I'm fine, why?'

'You're limping a bit.'

Marshall reached down to rub his aching calf. 'I'm bloody sore. Built for comfort, not for speed. I know this DCI in East London who's always in scrapes like that, chasing down the streets.'

'A DCI?'

'Aye, exactly. Should leave it to one of his team, but hey ho. You can hear his knee cracking from the other end of Scotland Yard.' Marshall entered the station's tiny wee kitchen.

'There you are...' Elliot was in there, clutching a cardboard tray with four Gregg's coffee cups. 'Thought you'd appreciate a little pick-me-up.' She handed Marshall one with an M scribbled on the side. 'Could slip a gram of coke in it, if you want.'

'Rather just stick with the caffeine, thanks.' Marshall took a cup and opened the lid. The liquid was black as night, steaming out. He took a sip. 'Thank you, Andrea.'

'Come on, boys.' Elliot led them down the corridor, handing another one to Siyal like she wanted him to drop it and spill boiling coffee all over himself. 'This better be worth it.'

'Got one for me, Andi?' A tall man in a sharp suit was waiting outside the interview room, grinning. Perfectly sculpted quiff held in place with hair gel. Rower's physique, his wide shoulders contrasting with his slim waist. He pulled his hand out of his pocket and thrust it towards Marshall. 'DCI Jim Pringle. Finally we meet.'

Marshall shook it. 'Finally.'

Pringle sucked air over his teeth. 'I can only apologise for my tardiness. Bit of a manic time down here just now. Hoover, that's no excuse.' He was grinning.

Did he really say 'hoover' rather than however? The way he was smiling, he clearly thought it was a joke everyone would find funny.

Marshall gave the most polite smile he could muster, then hid it behind a sip of burning coffee, which didn't make it past his lips. 'You don't have to tell me what it's like being busy, sir.'

Pringle took the last remaining cup from Elliot's tray. 'I'm sure we'll see the benefarts from your presence soon.'

Benefarts?

Jesus wept.

Marshall struggled to hide the grimace. Elliot had warned him that Pringle was a lazy sod. She didn't warn him about his eccentric sense of humour. 'Well, sir, I'm as frustrated as anyone else that we don't have Wendy Malcolm in a safe place.'

'I know it's not through want of—' Pringle whistled like a bird. 'Anyhoo, just been stuck on a conference call with the big brainboxes up in Edinburgh. We've got a smattering of intel schmintel on that shop, but unfortunately not on Mr Neil Inglis himself.'

Marshall bit his cheek. This guy... No wonder he was stuck down here. 'That doesn't stack up for me, sir. We found enough drugs in Derek Cameron's flat to supply the Borders for a few months.'

'So I gather, but wee willy winky won't be able to connect that with anything relating to him popping his clogs.'

Marshall focused on Elliot, glad she could at least speak like an adult. 'So you now don't think his death is a drug motive?'

'No, I'm not saying that.' She hid behind drinking from her coffee cup and grimaced at the taste. 'Just that we've got no intel on Cameron dealing to anyone. One Declan Connolly has come up as *buying* a lot of product from there, sure, but none of the usual informants – and I mean users – are naming him. So I'd say it's just for personal use.'

'Could be Neil's in with the in-crowd, or just dealing to a very selective one.' Pringle was scowling at Siyal. 'Not impressed with you, sunshine. You were given explicit approval for intel gathering, not an arrest. Jumped the gun, didn't you, laddie?'

Marshall knew he could land Siyal in it here. Curry favour with Pringle and Elliot. But he'd been the one to make the choice, not them. And one thing he'd learned was to have the courage of his convictions. 'Sir, it was my decision to arrest. Sorry if I overstepped the mark, but we had enough material there to take him down.'

Pringle swivelled around to inspect Marshall, stroking the stubble on his chin. 'It's not him we want to—' More whistling. 'He's a cog in a machine. Actually, he's a leaf on a branch. We want the whole tree.'

'I do know how drugs investigations work, sir.'

Pringle didn't say anything, but his glare was a hundred percent aimed at Marshall.

'And I know I'm merely on secondment to this case, but I'm thinking Wendy Malcolm's life trumps a drug dealing operation?'

'Nice try, Sonny Jim.' Pringle smirked. 'But I'll give you both a free pass if you find her.' He sauntered off, sipping his coffee. 'I'll be watching you. Every step you take.'

Marshall watched him walk off, whistling in tune now.

Elliot leaned in close. 'For God's sake, make sure you lead, okay?' She tilted her chin at Siyal. 'Don't let that clown make an arse of it.' She said it loud enough for someone in London to hear, let alone Siyal.

Marshall watched her charge off towards the observation suite, then looked around at Siyal. 'You know to ignore them, right?'

'I do, but all that rage has to go somewhere.' He knocked on the door. 'Thank you, sir.'

Marshall looked over at Siyal. 'What for?'

'You could've buried me there, but you took responsibility for it.' Siyal sighed. 'Pringle is... He... Doesn't *care* about this job.' He looked over at Marshall. 'I heard he's reluctant to have you on the case.'

'What, why?'

'He wants to get the glory for himself, but the powers-that-be insisted on bringing in you and your boss to help out.' Siyal tapped his nose. 'Never trust him...'

Loud footsteps pounded back towards them. Elliot, clutching her coffee like a grenade. 'On second thoughts, Jim and I have decided that I'm sitting in on this interview. Shunty, can you go back to supervising the search of Cameron's flat?'

Siyal gave a flash of his eyebrows, then swanned off down the corridor. 'Thanks for the coffee, ma'am.'

'Hope you enjoy it. *Clown*.' She left the coffee area. 'Come on, Marshall. Let's do this.'

CHAPTER FORTY-ONE

Elliot thumped on the door. 'We're coming in.' She opened it and stormed inside. 'Morning, lads.' She took the seat Marshall was in and leaned over to restart the recorder. 'DS Siyal has left the room, replaced by DI Andrea Elliot.' She sat back and cracked her knuckles. 'Where had you got to?'

Marshall sat next to her and took a drink of coffee. 'Mr Inglis was just about to confess to the possession of illegal drugs and the murder of Derek Cameron.'

'No, I'm not!'

'Oh come on. There's a ton of charges hanging over you. That huge bag of cannabis we found, plus several bags of pills and powders. They're all being analysed just now. I'd guess it's cocaine, ecstasy, heroin and a lot of prescription drugs provided without possession of a pharmacy license.' Marshall smiled. 'That's a long time at Her Majesty's Pleasure.'

Davidson rested on his elbows. 'Andrea, nice to see you again, but I think you need to be aware that you've got severe issues regarding possession of your evidence.'

'That right?'

'The drugs weren't found on my client. I gather they were in an unlocked cabinet where others could have had access.'

'You think I'm some wet-behind-the-ears rookie, don't you? If he had access, was standing that close that anyone could smell the marijuana and people would have to walk past him into his work area to get it, then that's the definition of constructive possession. Knowledge, control, consent, ipso facto he's nicked.' Elliot leaned forward, cracking her elbows off the table. 'Besides, there were two customers present during our discovery of your client's illegal stash. Both are now in another room backing it all up. My officers will be typing up their statements and getting them signed off.' She focused on Neil. 'Mr Inglis, there's just no way you're getting out of this, even with a fancy lawyer.'

Neil pursed his lips then turned to face his lawyer. Neither said anything, but a trove of information passed from eye to eye.

'Now I think about it, there is one way out of this.' Elliot finished her coffee and set the empty aside. 'I can think of two ways, but I doubt you'll grass on your supplier, will you?'

Neil shut his eyes, teeth gritted together.

Elliot splayed her hands on the table. 'Which leaves you talking to us about Declan Connolly.'

'What about him?'

She tossed the cup into the bin. 'Let's start with you selling him the drugs.'

'Not going to talk about that.'

'You did do it, right?'

'Said I'm not going to talk.'

'Okay, then let's move on to you murdering him.'

'No comment.'

Marshall smiled at him. 'You're not surprised that he's dead, though, are you?'

Neil seemed a bit rattled by the questioning. Selling drugs was one thing, but killing someone? That was clearly too much for him. His steely resolve was melting. Fingers trembling.

Marshall leaned forward, head in his hands like he was bored and chatting to a mate about football. 'Where were you on Sunday night, Neil?'

'I was gaming.'

'Xbox or PlayStation?'

'PC. Got a gaming PC.'

'What game were you playing?'

Neil seemed to relax a touch. 'It was this online thing. *Indignity*. I did a raid with some mates. A bank job where we... robbed a bank. Got in and out without killing anyone, which was the challenge.'

Marshall nodded. 'I know the game. Bit of controversy around it a couple of years ago, wasn't there?'

'No idea. Just play it. Can show you the logs.'

'Cool.' Marshall looked away like that was it. Then shot his gaze back to bore into him. 'Doesn't prove it was you playing it, though.'

'Eh?'

'It shows someone used your machine to play it. You could've paid someone to take your place while you murdered Cameron over a drug deal.'

Neil shook his head. 'Not who I am.'

'Sure about that?'

'I cut hair. I play videogames. That's it. That's me. That's Neil Inglis.'

'Okay. You did a good job of the haircut.' Marshall ran a hand over the stubble. 'But when you say it's not who you are, that makes me think of Declan Connolly. You said his name was David when you met him last year. That what you're doing? Giving yourself another name to compartmentalise your actions?'

He sighed like he was bored. 'I am only Neil Inglis.'

'Thing is, Neil, you were wrong on both counts. Declan, David, whatever. His name is actually Derek Cameron. And he's a serial murderer.'

Neil shrugged like he'd been told his milkman's brother's cousin had just lost his job in America. 'Had no idea. I just cut his hair and talk about games with the lad.'

'You didn't sell him drugs?'

'I don't sell anyone drugs.'

'And yet we found a ton of them in your place of work.' Elliot sat back, shaking her head. 'Thing is, Mr Inglis, Derek Cameron abducted a woman on Saturday night. He died on Sunday. She's still missing. Now he's dead, there's a race on to find her. If we don't, she'll die. Probably is, but we've got to keep trying.'

Davidson whispered into Neil's ear. Neither said anything else.

Elliot narrowed her eyes at them. 'I hope she's still alive. Of course, whoever helped us find her would be a hero. If they'd, say, been dealing drugs, it would be taken into account in their prosecution.'

Davidson leaned over and whisper-shouted, 'You should talk.'

Neil took a deep breath, shifted his gaze between Marshall and Elliot, then ran a hand down his face. And held it there. 'Okay, so I provided Declan with the prescription meds. I've no idea what for. He wouldn't say.' He looked at Marshall. 'You were good, though. When you came in for your haircut. I believed you when you asked me about that. Thought you were actually a friend of his. But it was coke you were after, wasn't it?'

'And you gave me it. Three grams of the stuff.'

'Can't prove it.'

'Oh, we can.' Marshall was smiling. 'Did you ever visit his home?'

'No. Never. Only interacted in the hairdressers. Only there. Always. I actually did cut his hair, you know.' Neil's hand was shaking. 'Did he really kill someone?'

'Six definites. At least another four probables. And Wendy Malcolm is still missing.'

Neil shut his eyes and the weight of him seemed to slide out of his feet. 'Sorry. I'm scratching my brain here.'

'We have a witness statement placing Mr Cameron with someone outside his flat several times. Was that you?'

'Told you, no.'

'What about your people? Did they ever visit?'

'No. I don't have any people.' Neil swallowed something down. 'Except for Ashley in the salon.'

'Is she the one who puts the drugs in the sweetie bowl for you?'

'No comment.'

Marshall sat back and apprised him. His breathing. The way his gaze locked onto the tabletop. No matter which way he cut it, it just didn't seem like Neil was involved. He stood up and gave a cut-throat gesture to Elliot.

She leaned over to the microphone.

'Listen.' Neil was frowning. 'There might be something else.'

Elliot sat back, the machine still running.

Marshall stayed on his feet. 'Go on?'

'A couple of times, instead of a cash transaction, I gave him... a haircut in exchange for services rendered.'

'Sexual?'

'Fuck off.' Neil sat back arms folded. 'Just because I'm a hairdresser doesn't mean I'll fuck anyone for money.'

'Didn't say that. Just wondered if that's what you meant by services rendered.'

'My car, you homophobic prick.'

'I'm sorry.' Marshall jerked forward, hands raised. 'I don't mean to cause any offence by it. I'm not a homophobe, okay?'

'I'm not even gay. Jesus Christ.' Neil winced. 'Whatever. I've got an old BMW. It was my dad's. G-reg Alpina 3 series. Beautiful car. Declan, or whatever he's really called, serviced it for me.'

'Did you take it to the garage he worked in?'

'Nope. Declan did it himself.'

'Where?'

'Don't know. Told us he had a workshop in Gala. Used it for his own car and some homers.'

This was it.

A secret hiding place for Derek Cameron to stow away his victims.

And Elliot knew it too. She was on her feet, getting her phone out of her pocket. 'Do you know where it is?'

'Nope. Just something he did for me, in exchange for a haircut or two. Picked it up from the salon, then he dropped it off, good as new.'

'You've no idea where?'

Neil pinched his forehead. 'Said he's working on restoring an old motor there. Think it was an old Corsa or something. Plan was to turn it into something that could go so fast it could travel back in time.'

Marshall wondered if that wasn't a joke but Cameron's actual motivation, that all the pharmaceuticals and narcotics made Cameron blur reality until *Back to the Future* seemed less a film and more a how-to guide. 'Thank you for your honesty. I hope this helps us. We'll be back in a minute.' He followed Elliot out into the corridor.

Pringle was already there. 'That's a mighty fine breakthrough there, boys and girls.'

Marshall couldn't help but nod. 'A garage is the sort of place that matches my profile. Where he'd take a victim and hide her. Where he'd kill her.'

'I think you're right.' Elliot was nodding, hands on hips. 'But does laughing boy in there actually know?'

Marshall shook his head. 'If he knew, he would've told us. He might be a drug dealer but he genuinely wants to help us find Wendy. And I don't think he killed Cameron.' He shifted his gaze between them, making sure they listened. 'But I'd suggest getting your best two cops to sit with him and document everything – and I mean *everything* – he knows about Cameron. Maybe something will slip out. Something he doesn't know. Or maybe I'm wrong and he does.'

Pringle was stroking his chin, giving a harsh rasping sound. 'You don't think he knows—' Whistle. 'Do you?'

'Nope. Theirs was a purely business relationship. Looks like it went both ways, sure, but they probably had good reasons to keep a distance from each other.'

Inspiration hit him like a lightning bolt. 'But I know someone who might have an idea.'

CHAPTER FORTY-TWO

Marshall was first out of the car. While Elliot parked up properly, he stomped across the soaking pavement towards the garage, splashing pavement water up the back of his trouser leg. He had to step aside to let an old lady race off in her Subaru, turning to get a look at the spoiler and the chunky exhaust pipe.

He turned back.

Max Power was vaping in his office. Didn't look up at Marshall as he entered. 'Sorry, sir, I'll just be a minute.'

'Mr Power, it's the police.'

Max looked up now and huffed out a blast of thick vapour. 'I've got six MOTs piling up and now a third lad's gone home with suspected bloody covid!'

'I'll be quick then.' Marshall kept his distance – he didn't want to catch it again. First time had been brutal. Second wasn't a picnic but at least he'd had his booster and omicron wasn't anything compared to the original flavour. 'Did you know Callum was doing homers for people?'

'Was he? Sneaky wee shite. In here?'

'No. We think he had a garage elsewhere for his own car. We believe he fixed up a car for a pal.'

'It's muggins here who locks up every night and I make sure this place is *tight*. When you said that, I was worried the wee sod had broken in and using my tools!'

'So, do you—'

Max cupped his hands around his mouth. 'Earth to Shug!'

In the garage, Shug slid out from under a Honda SUV, then sat up like he was crunching in the gym. T'Pau played on the radio. 'What's up?'

Max was charging towards him and crouched next to the car. 'You hear about a motor Cal was doing up for a mate?'

'Sorry, Maxine, but don't have any idea.' Shug clocked Marshall. 'Like I said earlier, he just talked about drinking and football. Never about the work.'

Marshall joined them, but he couldn't even consider squatting like Max. 'It's possible the woman he kidnapped is being held there.'

'Sorry, pal.' Shug looked like the apology was genuine sorrow. 'No idea about that.'

And just like that, the hope that Max or Shug had known about it was dragged from Marshall's fingers. He let a sigh go. 'Okay, lads, well. If you think about anything...'

'Actually.' Max was scanning through his phone screen, vape stick between his lips. 'A mate of mine was in a few months back. Said he was looking for a short-term tenant. Tam's a right chancer, so he'd speak to anyone. And now you mention it, I think Cal did his car.'

Marshall knew it was an outside bet, but it might just pay off.

CHAPTER FORTY-THREE

WENDY

Wendy couldn't even open her eyes. The gummy thickness had dried to a crust. Her head was like someone had struck it with a sledgehammer. Over and over and over again. She felt so heavy. No idea what time it was.

Voices.

'I'd need to think about it.'

Muffled, coming through the door.

'You do that, pal. You do that.' Scottish, local. Deep and reassuring.

Was that Callum?

Was he back?

She tried to scream but her mouth was a husk. The rag was still in there. She couldn't move her feet or arms. No strength now.

Nothing.

'It's nice and about the right size, but I need to think it all through. You know how it is.'

'Aye, I do.' English, high-pitched. Rasping. 'Sure you don't want to have a look through in the workshop?'

'Isn't your tenant here?'

'Haven't heard from him in a while.'

They were coming in here.

They had to!

She needed them!

She put everything into lifting her head up. Pressing her chin into her chest, bone against bone.

'He won't be in. It'll be cool.'

The wiring on her bra was exposed. Shit. She could maybe do this.

'Aye, just not sure. Feels a bit weird. How would you like it if someone came into your garage?'

She leaned forward, catching the end of the rag on the exposed wire and it snagged.

It had bloody caught it!

She let her head fall back and the rag rasped out of her mouth, just half of it stuck to her tongue. She had just enough saliva to get her tongue separated. Two heaves from her aching throat and she managed to get the rest out.

'Help.'

Her voice was a whisper. Shrill, harsh. She could barely hear it. How could they?

She lay there, waiting. Breathing hard. It was all she could do.

'If you clear it with the boy, or clear his stuff out of there, then sure. But I'm not happy with this. Makes me think you'd do it to my stuff.'

'Course I wouldn't.'

'Help!' At least she could hear that, but her throat was exposed wire.

'You hear that?'

'Oh, aye. Get a lot of wild birds in here. Nesting little shits.'

'And you want me to rent the place off you?'

'It's not a problem anymore, but one of them might've returned to the scene of the crime. I'll get my boy in later. Come on, then. If you don't want to have a look, let's go and talk over some food.'

The door clattered shut.

Keys jangled, dulled.

Then the clunk of a lock.

'Help!' That was loud. Loud enough for them to hear.

If they were still here.

Wendy lay there, head splitting. Throat raw.

She tried shouting again, but nothing came out.

All she could do was close her eyes.

She didn't have long left.

CHAPTER FORTY-FOUR

MARSHALL

The old mill building wasn't so much in a bad state of disrepair as fed up with nobody demolishing it, so had decided to start on the process itself. The roof was in three triangular sections, sharp angles slicing the air, and all were bowed down in the middle and missing a lot of their tiles.

Two hulking meat wagons blocked the A7 in both directions, their drivers out with their caps on, directing traffic back through the town or north to the road to Clovenfords.

Now the day had shifted from pissing rain to baking sunshine, Marshall suspected heavy snow in the middle of July was possible. The weather here was always strange, but living away for so long made him appreciate just how weird it was.

Elliot was on the phone to someone. Always. She jogged over to the roadblock and waved at a Mitsubishi truck. One of those heavy things with an open back. Never saw them in London, but Marshall had seen a hundred of them back here.

He followed her over. 'That your guy?'

Elliot glanced back at him. 'Indeed it is.'

A hulking brute got out and marched towards them. Lumberjack shirt and hiking trousers tucked into desert boots. 'Andi. Swear you get more beautiful every time I see you.' He had the voice of a nine-year-old boy. One who lived in the Cotswolds, not the Scottish Borders.

'Always the charmer, Tam.' Elliot stood there, letting him come to her. 'We need inside.'

'Not even going to buy me dinner?' Tam grinned at Marshall. 'Tam MacDougall. Pleasure to meet you.'

'Rob Marshall.' He smiled, but every piece of him wanted to open that door.

Right now, Wendy Malcolm was Schrodinger's abductee, both dead and alive at the same time. Like the quantum physics thought experiment, he'd only know which she was when he opened that door.

'Can we get inside?'

'Told you when you rudely interrupted my lunch, you're wasting your time.' Tam brushed a hand through his thick hair, resetting the centre parting. 'I was just in there with a potential client about actually getting work started here.' He laughed. 'There are no abducted women inside.'

Marshall snorted, struggling to hide his impatience. 'But you did rent it to Callum Davidson, right?'

'It wasn't so much *rent*, as in a formal agreement, so much as him paying me cash in hand to let him work there until I got the—'

'Sounds a lot like rent.'

'It's not. I mean, I don't technically own the building.'

'You don't seem to technically do anything.' Marshall stepped closer to him. 'We need access to the building. Now.'

'I don't think I—'

'Max Power mentioned your name.'

'No idea who that is.'

'He owns the garage where you met Callum Davidson. Who you rented the building to.'

'I'm just renting it out until the owners knock it down to turn it into a hotel.'

'You're building a hotel here?'

'Airbnb apartments. Work's been scheduled to start by the end of the year, but it's on pause because of everything hitting the fan politically at the one time, so I'm trying to put a transitional rental agreement in place. Never a quiet moment these days, eh? Remember the Nineties? Swear all that happened in 1994 was a World Cup and that Nirvana guy shooting himself, but now? Christ, centuries happen every week.'

Marshall was trying to be patient with him, but this twat could talk and every second counted. 'Come on. Let us in.'

'It's just a car workshop in there. Have you got a warrant?'

'Okay.' Marshall squared up to him. He was about the same height and size as him. He wasn't going to batter him, but persuade him to do the right thing. 'Let me tell you about Callum Davidson. He's a serial killer. Six in London and a few others we haven't confirmed but are very, very likely. There's possibly a woman in there, right now. You could help save her. She might be here, might not. But I will do anything I can to find her. So please. Open the door.'

Tam was frowning. 'Callum's the one who abducted that woman?'

Marshall nodded. 'Her name's Wendy Malcolm.'

Tam scowled, but didn't say anything.

'What are you hiding here?'

'Nothing.'

'Are you in league with him? Were you—'

'No! Okay, fine, whatever. Let's get you in there.' Tam stormed over to the door, unfurling his giant ring of keys as he walked. 'Think it's this one.'

Marshall stood next to him, fists clenched.

All he could think of was the same exercise in Surbiton, waiting outside the garage Derek Cameron had trapped Kate Pierce inside, the squad of uniforms waiting behind him as one of them used a pair of bolt cutters to open the chain.

Elliot had a squad of uniforms behind her just like he'd had, all ready to tear the place apart and find her.

Back then he'd had hope of finding her. Now, he expected to find a corpse.

Tam opened the door and stepped aside.

Marshall was first in.

The place was dark, shafts of light criss-crossing the space from holes in the walls. It stank of damp and mushrooms. His eyes were slow in adjusting to the gloom. Three walls were stacked with shelves, each one filled with big boxes. A giant door filled the fourth wall, on the right. A smaller one led to the left.

Cops swarmed the stairs at the back like ants up a tree.

Elliot was pointing at things and shouting.

Marshall set off towards the big door. He gripped the handle and hauled it. Bastard thing was wedged shut. He looked around. 'Andrea, we need another way into this room.'

'On it.' She stormed back outside.

Marshall gave the door one last tug and something cracked. It slipped off the rollers and fell towards him.

He jumped back away from it.

The door tumbled over, landing centimetres from his toes.

Through the gap, he could make out the shape of a car under a tarp. Tools dotted around it, stacked up and tidied away.

He stepped into the workshop, which stank of motor oil and rust.

Something thumped against the door. Elliot's lumps with the Big Key battering ram. They hadn't got the message.

Behind a tall metal unit, a table was pressed against the far wall.

A figure lay on it.

Bonds around their ankles and wrists.

Marshall shot over.

Wendy Malcolm wasn't moving. She looked dead.

He was too late.

Way too late.

Fuck.

Fucking hell.

Again.

It had happened again.

He reached over and pressed his finger against her artery.

The faintest pulse throbbed against his skin.

She opened her eyes to narrow slits. 'Help.'

CHAPTER FORTY-FIVE

Marshall clutched the ambulance door with his left hand. The hot metal burnt his skin so he pulled it away. Cold sweat soaked his shirt, chilling him when the sun went behind a cloud.

He was breathing more easily.

For the first time in years.

Wendy Malcolm lay on a bed in the back of the ambulance, a drip wired into her wrist. Her skin there was cut and bruised, same as the other side and both ankles. She must've been struggling against her bonds for days.

As much as he hated the cliché, she was a fighter.

'Come on, pal.' The bulky paramedic hopped down from the ambulance, leaving his skinnier colleague in there. 'Need to get her to BGH.'

'Sure.' Marshall stepped away from the vehicle. 'Will she survive?'

'I'm not a doctor, but my assessment, for what it's worth, is she's at death's door.'

It slugged Marshall in the gut. The cruellest blow would be to save her, only for her to die.

'Almost dehydrated to death. Delirious, when she's conscious. Another couple of hours, maybe, and that would've been it for her.' He turned to give a smile. 'But you saved her.'

'Thank you.' Marshall caught one last look at Wendy. She was away with the fairies. Hopefully she wouldn't be away with the angels for a long time. The faint pulse he'd felt was now a stronger breath, so he had hope.

He had to hope. And keep hoping.

The paramedic slammed the door and darted around the side. Seconds later, the engine growled and it shot off, running blues and twos towards Gala, following a squad Volvo doing the same. They rounded the corner and the siren started up, the noise fading into the distance.

Tam McDougall was stuck between a pair of detectives, arms folded, truculently refusing to comply with their instructions. 'I didn't know anything about it! Until you confirm that I'll have a lawyer present, then—'

'Of course you'll get a lawyer.' Jolene grabbed his arm and got him to shift. 'In my experience, the truly innocent people can't stop explaining how they didn't do something, but if you think you need a lawyer, maybe you *are* guilty of something.'

Marshall sat down on the edge of the pavement, feet planted on the ground, head in his hands.

It was over.

Wendy Malcolm was safe, her life in the hands of medical professionals rather than fate.

The reason he'd been brought up here...

Who fucking cared who killed Derek Cameron?

That piece of shit was dead and he wouldn't be buried. Nobody would mourn him, but a trail of families and friends now had justice and the knowledge their loved one's killer wasn't going to do it again.

If Wendy didn't pull through, she'd be the last victim.

He had to hope she'd be the second survivor. That the doctors would prevent a homicide that had already started to happen.

And he'd been the one to find her. His work had pieced it all together, joined the dots until he could repeat enough of Cameron's steps to rescue her.

This time he'd found the victim alive.

He was used to complex stuff, building psychological profiles of victims and killers, knitting everything together, but this had been shoe leather work. Police work. The stuff he'd missed out on by taking direct entry into the service.

He let his breath out in one long, slow exhalation.

'Hero of the hour.' Kirsten was standing over him, her green hair catching the sunlight. 'You okay down there?'

He sighed. 'I'm exhausted.'

She dumped a bag on the ground and sat down next to him. 'We weren't up *that* late, were we?'

'No.' Marshall couldn't even smile. 'I mean, the constant stress of this case. It's been two years since I found Kate Pierce in that lock-up. I've barely slept in all that time. And now...'

'Now you've saved Wendy, Rob.' Kirsten was smiling at him, like she was trying to encourage him. 'If she survives, it's because of you.'

'Feels like a big if just now.'

She play-punched his arm. 'Try and look on the bright side, Rob. We've found her. You saved her. Her dad's got her back from the dead. Take the win.'

She was right.

He looked over at her and chanced a smile. 'I'm so used to battering myself over the skull with blame.'

'I get that. But you've done your job.' She hefted herself up to standing again. 'Now, I've got to brave Shunty and get my guys inside that building so we can scour it forensically to find out who was here.'

'It was Cameron.'

'Sure, I know. But you guys are still trying to catch Cameron's killer. I'll confirm Cameron was here, sure, but you need as many clues as to who his killer was, right?'

'At some point, the brass will tell Elliot to ease off. It'll be pretty soon, I suspect.'

'I'm determined to help out while we still can.'

'Thank you.' Marshall looked up at her. 'I know I'm a grumpy sod at times, but I appreciate you trying to perk me up here.' He rasped his hand over his stubble. 'It's been brutal, Kirsten. Finding someone like that. After Surbiton... This... This is different. This time, I have a kernel of hope she'll pull through.'

'Hope is important, Rob.' Kirsten picked up her bag. 'And if you ever need a chat, you know where I am. Still got half a bottle of that very nice wine to drink. Shame to do it all alone.'

Marshall mustered a smile. 'Could do with some right now.'

She brushed his arm and walked over to the garage.

If that's what it was. An old mill building, the last one in Gala, though the town was spreading west with a new housing development climbing the hill opposite a jet wash place.

Good place for Cameron to do what he wanted to Wendy.

A horrific place to die.

'Come here often?' Pringle took Kirsten's place on the kerb. 'Well done, Inspector. Finding the damsel in distress. Full marks, son.'

'Sir, there's... At least wait until we know she's going to be okay?'

'Indeed.' Pringle sat there, lips twitching. He looked like he was going to say something, but shut his mouth. Did it again. Then he pulled himself up to standing. Again, like he was going to say something. He frowned. Stuffed his hands in his pockets. Then cleared his throat. 'Thank you for your efforts, Inspector. You've made an excrement contribution to this. Now my team's solved this case, you can make your way back to your own patch. We can manage the rest from here without you.'

That's how he was going to play it?

Fine.

Marshall stood up too and dusted off his hands. 'You're happy with someone getting away with murder on your patch?'

'I didn't say that.'

'You did, though. Or your actions did. Derek Cameron was killed. Someone met him. Either here or elsewhere. Used a Taser on him. Pushed him off the side of the bridge. There's so much we don't know about this case. And it's blind luck that we managed to find Wendy Malcolm.'

'It's not luck, it's hard work.' Pringle smiled. 'Believe me, sunshine, I know it's all your work. Alright?'

'No. It's not alright. There are other victims. Not just the gap between London and Northwich, but afterwards. Phoebe Thomson, his neighbour, follows the pattern. Cameron seems to be escalating in frequency as his cancer worsens. What if there's another Wendy Malcolm?'

'And what if the moon crash lands into St Boswells this afternoon?' Pringle stared up into the sky at the thin crescent floating in the mid blue, like there was a possibility it could happen. 'It's all over, not least from that perspective. You saved the girl and the guy's dead, that's got to be a win.'

'Cameron was going to kill Wendy Malcolm.'

'Probably, but Wendy is on her way to BGH. She will

survive, I hope, but she'll be deeply traumatised. But she will still be alive. Well done, Inspector, you won.' His grin widened. 'Thank you for your help. You've been a total rock star.' He thumbed behind him. 'Now, one of my lads will drop you off at your hotel.'

CHAPTER FORTY-SIX

If Marshall had a tail, it'd be stuck between his legs right now.

Siyal pulled up outside the hotel and turned off the engine. 'It's been good working with you.'

Marshall opened his door but not far. 'Has it?'

'It has. You're the first cop who's bothered to treat me with respect.'

Marshall laughed. 'If you want my advice, I think you should respect yourself more. Trust your instincts. I see a lot of promise in you. Make sure Elliot and Pringle see that too.'

'Will do.' Siyal was looking into his wing mirror.

'See you around, Rakesh. And don't let them call you Shunty unless you want them to.' Marshall got out, wondering if Siyal would pay heed or if it'd already fallen on deaf ears. He walked over to the hotel in the baking heat.

Eight hours in the car, if he was lucky. Down the M6, praying he could get around Manchester and through Birmingham without hitting either rush hour. The A1 might be better, but he'd hit Newcastle at the worst time.

Either way, he was feeling wiped out.

Scrubbed clean.

Wrung out.

Knackered.

Starving.

Sod it.

He went inside Dean's Beans and was disappointed to see Dean Taylor wasn't serving.

The hipster behind the counter looked around from the espresso machine. Hair tied up in a manbun. Rings studded his eye sockets. 'Can I help you, mate?'

'Can I get a table for lunch?'

'There's one in the window.' He smiled. 'What can I get you?'

'A long black coffee and—' He scanned the board's food selection. Typically tiny, just six items, all fancy versions of comfort food. '—a cheese and onion chutney sourdough. Wholemeal.'

'Coming right up.'

Marshall walked over to the window seat and collapsed into the chair. Left his phone in his pocket and watched Melrose bustle through the window.

Two couples in their sixties outside the newsagent, laughing about something.

A mum pushing a pram waving at someone in the butcher's next door.

One of those towns where people still went to the butcher for high-quality meat rather than settling for whatever was in the supermarket.

A little old lady lugged a shopping trolley behind her, scowling at Marshall through the window. For once, her ire was directed at the world instead of just at him.

He got out his phone and dropped it on the table. A couple

of missed calls from Rickards. Aye, he wasn't going to return them in a hurry.

Still early enough to get home before it was dark. Back to see if Rickards had been feeding Zlatan. No, he knew he'd been fed from the security cameras. The big fat sod would eat any food given, that was his problem.

Same as Marshall's.

That saying his mum used all the time...

You get like those you bide wi'.

Aye. Poor Zlatan was both biding with him and eating like him.

'Here you go, amigo.' Dean Taylor slid a plate in front of Marshall, orange cheese oozing from the sourdough onto the red serviette. And now Marshall noticed the sign above the till saying the sandwiches were toasted. 'Didn't you have a breakfast this morning?'

'Skipped it. Got a long drive ahead of me.'

Dean frowned. 'You're leaving?'

Marshall leaned in close. 'We found her.'

'Congratulations, man.' Dean clapped him on the back. 'That must be a good feeling.'

'Only if she pulls through.'

Dean scratched at his neck. 'I was wondering if you fancied a pint later. But if you're heading...?'

'Can't drink beer. Wheat allergy.'

'You just ordered a sandwich on bread?'

'Sourdough, mate. Doesn't count.'

'Right.' Dean winced.

Marshall sighed. 'It is sourdough, right? Proper sourdough?'

'Baked by my own fair hand.' Dean grinned. 'No, I was just thinking we should have a glass of very nice red wine to celebrate your success. But if you're going...'

Maybe Marshall should hang around.

Even if he didn't do anything directly involved with the case, he could try to mend fences with his mother.

He reached into his wallet but it was empty. Shite, that hundred quid was in the salon's till. 'Do you take cards?'

'Where do you think you are? Of course we take cards!' Dean laughed. 'So, tonight? Drink?'

Marshall smiled. 'Sure.'

'Half seven in the hotel bar. See you there.' Dean waltzed off. 'I'll fetch your coffee. See you must've liked your long black.'

Marshall slumped back and took a bite of his sandwich. Sour and tangy. And that was just the bread.

That hadn't taken a lot of persuading.

Maybe it'd be good to reconnect with the town. See a few old faces. Exorcise some ghosts.

Tackle the long drive tomorrow. A good night's sleep, then on the road at four.

Or the day after...

He bit into the sandwich again, actually savouring the mix of tangy cheese and sour relish. For once, food was a source of joy rather than fuel or a consolation of loss.

'You okay?' Elliot was standing outside the toilet, eyebrow arched.

Marshall put his sandwich down and finished chewing. 'Surprised to see you here. Thought you were at the hospital.'

'Got called on my way there. Wendy needs a bit longer until I can speak to her.' She stepped forward, beaming at him. 'You saved her, Marshall. That was great work.'

'Thank you.' He couldn't look at her. That smile... 'Pringle's told me to leave.'

'Seriously?'

'Also heard he doesn't want me around.'

'Nobody wants you around, you clown.' She held up a hand, grinning at him. 'I'm joking. You've been great to work with. Easy.' She gestured at the chair opposite. 'Mind if I...?'

'Sure.'

She grabbed her bag, coffee and panini off another table, then sat. 'I warned you about Jim Pringle. Behind all that bene-farts and whistling nonsense, there's a tiger. Don't trust him.' She grabbed his hand. 'Never trust him.'

'I won't.' Marshall pulled his hand away. 'And I don't have to anymore.'

'You're driving home?'

'Think I'll stick around until tomorrow. See a friend, speak to my mum. My sister. My niece.'

'Oh. Okay. Cool.' Her lips were twisted up. She dropped her panini back onto the plate. 'What's your take on Pringle?'

Marshall didn't want to get dragged into a turf war. Office politics was his least favourite part of the job, not least because he was so crap at it, but also because it was so pointless – it was nothing to do with solving crimes or making people feel safe, it was just about ego. Pure and simple.

Playground bullshit.

Still, maybe Pringle was that living example of the Peter Principle, promoted to the point of incompetence. He seemed to want to close this case off, take the victory and ignore the fact he had the unsolved murder of a serial killer on his patch.

'I don't really have a take, I'm afraid. Just pleased that his ego hasn't got in the way of us pursuing justice here.'

'Right. That sounds a lot like a take. I've worked with him, on and off, for five years. He's a lazy sod. He's taking finding Wendy as a win.'

'I can see that side of things. Budgets are tight, blah blah blah.'

'Problem I've got is Pringle asked if we should be considering the killer to be a woman as it would explain the Taser. I pressed him on why. He said a man could've just chucked him over the side so perhaps a woman or a young girl, maybe a former victim. I mean...' She picked up the sandwich and bit into it with a loud crunch.

Marshall sat back. 'I can sort of follow the logic, to a certain extent, but I'd make sure I put heavy caveats around saying it out loud. After all, men and women are both a spectrum of sizes and strengths. You could probably deadlift more than Pringle, for instance. Besides, nobody uses a Taser because they're weak. You use one to incapacitate your target for a few seconds.'

She nodded when she seemed to realise Marshall was saying the same thing as her. 'It's sexist bullshit is what it is.'

'Hard to disagree with that assessment.'

'See what I'm dealing with here?'

'I do.' Marshall blew on his coffee. 'Still, I'd certainly flag it up as a possibility and attach a probability score to it. Make sure it was actively being investigated. After all, we still don't know who killed Cameron, do we?'

'Nope.' She thumped the rest of her sandwich back on the plate and chewed angrily, mouth open. 'I knew they wouldn't care about that. Focus on saving the girl. That's the headline. Let it take centre stage. And finding who killed a serial killer? Nobody seems to care about that.'

'I do.'

She took another bite of her panini and eyed him. 'Do you?'

'Pringle might want to brush it under the carpet, but I *hate* loose ends. And that's kind of tearing the fabric apart for me.'

'I hate it too.'

Marshall finished the first half of his sandwich in silence. 'But it's not my case anymore.'

'Still, you're the guy who profiled Derek Cameron, who

chased him for so long. What do you think happened? Who do you think killed him?'

'I just don't know.' Marshall took a drink of coffee. Much harsher than this morning. 'I found Wendy, so I'm trying to take that as a win.' He swallowed a bite of sandwich down. But he could feel himself dragged back into the case.

Trying to stop it all flowing and connecting together, but his mind was already going through all of the options.

Jesus Christ, his brain was fizzing.

'Wonder if you wanted to speak to Wendy Malcolm?'

'Been told not to.'

'I'm offering you the chance to close it all off. To hear her ordeal, see how it matched up with your profile. To see if she can help us catch whoever killed Derek Cameron.' She dabbed at her lips with her serviette. 'After all, someone who's killed once and got away with it could do it again. Even if Pringle doesn't want to, I need to know who killed Cameron.'

Marshall picked up the last lump of sandwich, now cold and gloopy.

He couldn't say no.

CHAPTER FORTY-SEVEN

...

Come on, come on, come on.

Across the street, I can see Marshall, sitting in the window of Dean's Beans, talking to a woman. Think she's the cop he's been working with. Guy's too damaged to be after her, for there to be romance on the cards.

I take another sip of tea and the cup's cold, so I top it up from the pot.

Marshall hasn't found the girl, that I know.

Derek's last victim.

Our last victim.

She can't have much time left, if she's still alive.

I look back up. Bugger, they've disappeared.

Shite. Marshall's staying in that hotel. Have they gone for a shag?

Not his style.

I get up, grab my coat and drop a tenner on the table. Too much for the pot of tea, but time is marching.

Out on the busy street, there's no sign of them.

Going into the hotel car park's going to be too obvious.

Crap.

I'll inspect the butcher's window. Pretend I'm after some sausages or pork chops.

And bugger me, a car pulls out of the hotel.

Marshall's in the passenger seat. She's driving.

I need to follow him, see if he's leading to Wendy.

My phone rings and I check the screen.

Thea calling...

I have to take this.

'Hello?'

'I know.'

'What do you know?'

'Everything. Where's Wendy?'

'I'll take you to her.'

CHAPTER FORTY-EIGHT
MARSHALL

Marshall charged after Elliot along the hospital corridor, close enough to the windows looking into the middle, where the garden caught the sun, but it didn't light up the rest of the place.

'She's up here rather than down in Pathology thanks to us.'

She was right.

Marshall followed her around the corner and stopped dead.

Elliot was flagging down a nurse in navy scrubs. Senior charge nurse.

Big arms wrapped around Marshall, almost knocking him over. 'Thank you, thank you, thank you.'

He had to prise himself away so he could get a good look at his assailant.

Aidan Malcolm, eyes glowing, grinning ear-to-ear. 'Thank you for saving my baby girl.' He shoved a bag into Marshall's hands. 'Here. Take this.'

The bag contained the same expensive bottle of red wine

Marshall had been gifted by Dean Taylor and a special edition Dunpender whisky.

'Sir, I can't take this.'

'Nonsense.' Aidan clapped him on the back. 'You deserve it.'

'Sir, I don't drink.'

'Oh, well. I'm sorry. I misread you.' Aidan snatched the bag back and shook his hand. 'Thank you for saving her life.' He clapped his arm, then hurried off down the hallway, clinking like a Scottish fishing trip.

Leaving Marshall on his own.

Elliot was over with the nurse.

The way she was shaking her head... She didn't have time for her. 'Nope. Nope. Nope. It's out of the question.' She tried to barge past.

Elliot blocked her. 'Seriously?'

'Seriously.' She looked around at Marshall, frowning. 'Rob?' Like she'd been jolted by an electric wire.

Marshall smiled at her. 'Hi, Jen.'

Elliot tilted her head to the side. 'You guys know each other?'

Jen thumped him on the arm. Hard. 'Robert here is my twin brother.'

'Oh shit.' Elliot barked out a laugh. 'You're serious?'

Jen rolled her eyes. 'Can't you see the similarity?'

'Like, no.' Elliot was scowling. 'Male and female twins? How does that work?'

'We're fraternal twins. Non-identical. It's... Think of us as brother and sister but born at the same time.'

Elliot was shaking her head now. 'He must've taken up a lot more space in the womb than you. Surprised—'

'Actually, I was half a pound heavier.' Jen clapped them both on the shoulder. 'How about we do this in here.' She led them into a room that was more a cupboard than an office, despite the chair and computer wedged between the shelving units stacked with off-brand cleaning products. 'I'm guessing you're here about Wendy Malcolm?'

Marshall nodded. 'How is she?'

'Badly dehydrated. We've administered saline to try and bring her back up. She's sedated too.' Jen leaned against a shelving unit. 'But Wendy is in a bad, bad way. I know you two are both going to ask to see her, but that's not going to happen.'

Marshall nodded again. 'Wouldn't dream of guilting you into letting us see her so we could catch—'

'*Rob...*' Jen sighed. 'There's a reason we don't let cops like you two in. You upset our patients! Wendy needs time to recover!'

Marshall held up his hands. He wasn't a stranger to being hit by her. She might be small, but she was fierce. 'I'm joking.'

'It's not funny. If Wendy's going to make a full recovery, it's because you've left her to us. The doctor is with her just now, so just let us do our job. Okay?'

'Your brother saved her, Jen. Some sick bastard held her in a garage. But he was killed. We need to find who did it.'

'Aye, but not now.' Jen stared at Marshall. 'So that case *is* why you're back home then?'

'Right. I'm here for two things. One, why was he killed. Second, recovering Wendy.'

'You did the important one. Fifty percent isn't bad, Rob. But you being you, you want to try for both, right?'

'Right. Has she said anything?'

'I'm not letting you in there. Wendy's just not in any fit state to talk.'

'That's not what I asked.'

Jen slapped a hand off her forehead. 'Okay, when the paramedics brought her in, we were able to bring her round to ask some questions. Allergies, that kind of thing.'

'Were you there?'

'No. But the nurse who dealt with it said Wendy was speaking. She muttered something about Callum speaking to someone before he left.'

Elliot's eyes widened. 'There was someone with him?'

'On the phone, I think.'

Elliot sucked in a deep breath. 'Say anything else?'

'Girl's out of her box, Andi. Delirious. Could've been imagining it.'

Elliot did a slow three-sixty. Not easy in such a cramped space. 'But it could be a lead on who killed Cameron. Talking to someone just before he died makes me think it's his killer.'

Marshall could follow her logic to a certain extent, but it didn't lead that much further forward.

Or did it?

'We've got the call records, right?'

Elliot was staring at her phone. 'For Wendy?'

'No, Derek Cameron.'

'Right, right. Shunty has them.'

'For his phone? Not a burner?'

Elliot scowled. 'Of course.'

'Andrea, can you call him?'

'That clown's probably lost them, mind.' She shot a glare at Marshall then stalked away, stabbing her finger off her phone screen.

Marshall watched her go. 'Thanks, Jen.'

'You think this might help?'

'We didn't know about it, so aye. Anything like that could prove useful. Thank you for telling us.'

'Not a problem.' For a moment, he saw his sister instead of the fierce nurse. Her doubts, shames, fears. She looked over at him. 'Oh, was going to ask you something. Mum's picking Thea up from her father's tomorrow. Wondered if you wanted to do it instead? Spend the day with her?'

Marshall smiled at her. 'I'd love to.'

'Okay. Cool, I'll tell her. Take her to the zoo, maybe?'

'Isn't she too old?'

'Never too old. She's into biology and zoology and stuff. She can thank you for that thing with the computer.'

'Did it work?'

'Did what?'

'Her friend lost their essay.'

'Oh that lying little madam... It's her essay, isn't it?' She grabbed her phone from a charging cable, hit dial and put it to her ear. 'Thea, it's Mum. Have you lost your essay?'

'I'll see you around, Jen.'

But she wasn't paying any attention to him. 'I can only help if you tell me!' She scrunched up her face. 'Where are you? Come right here. Now! Don't you dare!' Her mouth hung open. 'She hung up on me!'

Marshall slipped out into the corridor.

Elliot pressed her phone to her blouse. 'Shunty's checking for me.'

Marshall leaned against the wall opposite her. 'You know you shouldn't call him that, right?'

'What? Shunty? Everyone's got a nickname, Marshall. It's all part of the fun.'

'What's mine?'

'You're not a member of the team.'

'Charming.'

Elliot put the phone back to her ear. 'Hi Rakesh.' She winked at Marshall, then a frown formed, deepening the longer she listened. 'Okay. Keep on it.' She held a hand over the phone. 'Okay, so Cameron received a call not long before he died.'

'That looks a lot like someone lured him there, Andrea.' Marshall motioned for her to hand the phone over. 'Rakesh, it's Rob. Talk to me about that number.'

'Hey, Rob. Kirsten thinks it's a burner.'

'Okay. That checks out. How many calls did it make?'

'Seven.'

Marshall shared Elliot's glower. 'Unusual for a burner.'

'Cameron's is on a pay-as-you-go contract with GoMobile.'

'Can you get names of who he's spoken to?'

'Sure.'

'Oh, and locations of that phone whenever that phone's made a call, please?'

'Can do. Why?'

'I want to run a geographical profile on them. See if we can pin down who's making the calls. I worked with cops in Durham to use that trick on a case ten years ago. Built up a list of locations I could profile. Sounds fancy, but it's just a map. But when you combine it with the psychological profile, it can lead you places. In that case, it gave us the picture that let us identify a suspect, who confessed.'

To most of his crimes, but not all...

'Will do.'

'Thanks, Rakesh. This is great.' Marshall handed the phone back to Elliot. 'We've got a set of leads here.'

'Just a sec, Shunty.' She tapped the mute button. 'Let's hope that clown doesn't make an arse of this.'

'You shouldn't be so hard on him.'

Her lip twisted into a snarl.

Marshall's phone chimed. An email to his Met account from Siyal. He opened it:

See attached.

Thanks,

DS Rakesh Siyal

Marshall opened the spreadsheet and started scanning the list of names.

'Is that your reminder to update your Fantasy Football team?'

'Hardly.' Marshall didn't rise to it, just kept reading through. 'All the calls that burner made.' Oh, hang on. 'One name sticks out.'

'Go on?'

'Tam MacDougall. The guy renting the space to Cameron. Refused to let us in there until I gave him no option.'

'I know him, Marshall. He's a bloody idiot, but he's not a killer.'

'Are you certain? Seems shady as hell to me.'

'Really? Why would Tam MacDougall kill him? And why now?'

There was another suspect, one Marshall didn't want to think about. So he just shrugged at her.

'Besides, why's Shunty sending that to you and not me?'

'Because I asked nicely?'

'There's nicely and there's rank.' Elliot put the phone back to her ear and nibbled at her lip. 'Okay, Rakesh, can you send it me as—' She paused. 'Oh. I haven't got it yet. Interesting.' She looked over at Marshall. 'He's running it through cell site analysis and that call to Cameron was made from somewhere in Melrose.'

Marshall could picture it. 'Okay, so Cameron's called out, leaving Wendy at his garage. He thinks he'll return. But he met his killer and he got attacked, resulting in his death.'

She turned to talk, then turned back and put the phone on speaker. 'Rakesh, you're on with DI Marshall.'

'Hiya, Rob.' Siyal sighed. 'Gone through the other six calls. I'm doing what you asked and sticking pins in to Google Maps. Looks to me like it's all near Gala.'

That checked out. And gave them bugger all.

Marshall let air out slowly.

Elliot snorted at him. 'You thinking that was going to give us a smoking gun?'

'Hope is important, Andrea.'

Siyal's voice rattled out of the speaker. 'Rob, have just sent you another spreadsheet. Suggest you look at it.'

Marshall got out his phone and sure enough, there it was. 'What's this?'

'The car spotted outside Phoebe's house. Cars matching that description starting NB. White, grey, silver.'

'That's going to be a lot of legwork, Rakesh. Can you just get on with it?'

'Aye, sure, but there's a name on there flagged on the case.'

CHAPTER FORTY-NINE

...

The laptop's in my bag, tugging at my shoulder.

A shiver up my spine, down my arms. Tingling everywhere. Awful.

Those assholes at school, Clare and Sara, they love all that ASMR bullshit. Those videos of people whispering or popping bubble wrap. Made their skin do that freaky thing. Didn't work on me, but being in a dumb-ass spooky church does.

Couldn't *get* any more spooky than here. Creepy as hell, even during the day. All the windows are covered over with massive boards. Not even sure there's any glass left.

Why here?

This isn't where Wendy is.

Had he lied to me?

This is a mistake.

Go to the police.

Now.

My uncle. He'd know what to do.

That's it. I turn heel and storm back over to the front door. Reach into my pocket for my phone, ready to turn it back on.

Wait.

Something creaks behind me.

I turn around. Nobody there. Just my imagination.

Stupid. So stupid.

I've got to get out of here.

A hand grips my shoulder, tight. A voice in my ear, whispering 'Hello, Thea.'

CHAPTER FIFTY
MARSHALL

If Siyal was the slowest driver in the world, Elliot was the fastest. Hitting a hundred on the dual carriageway between Carlisle and Newcastle, the road passing in such a blur that Marshall didn't even catch the name – he suspected it was the A69, but couldn't be sure.

Supposed to take two and a half hours, but she'd done it in one and three quarters.

She pulled out to overtake a coach and looked over at him, taking her eyes off the road for another chunk of time to check her phone.

'Andrea.' Marshall pointed ahead of them. 'Road?'

'Right.' Elliot shifted her gaze back. 'You're awfully quiet over there.'

'Just mulling it over, that's all.'

'A lot of mulling.' She shook her head, nostrils flaring, then sucked in a deep breath. She was staring at him again, but his pointed finger got her to look straight ahead again. She reached over and yanked the radio up.

Pringle's voice.

'—not often we can take credit for saving a victim of a serial killer before they become one, but that's what's happened here. Thanks to the diligent efforts of my team, we—'

Elliot snapped the radio off. 'Clown.'

Marshall grabbed the door handle as they swerved around three cars, then weaved in to undertake a slow driver in the fast lane. 'You want to find his killer too, don't you?'

'That's why I'm doing this with you, Marshall.' Elliot huffed out a long sigh. 'Elephant in the room time. You really think it might be John Hulse?'

Marshall felt that stabbing in his gut again. 'My old boss was shocked when I told her. She can't believe I'd even think it was him.'

'But you do.'

'I think it's possible, yes.' Marshall didn't want to shut his eyes for even a second. 'John could be Cameron's killer. I met him on my way up from London. He's in a bad way. Retired from the Met. His lung injury leaves him breathless. He's working as a cabbie.'

'Being a cabbie gives him an excuse to be driving around southern Scotland.' Despite closing on the exit for Hexham, Elliot pulled out to overtake a Volvo. 'Take a fare up to Edinburgh airport, great cover for calling someone in Melrose and meeting them up on a viaduct. Not wanting to channel Pringle too much, but using a Taser fits. If he's infirm like you say, the exertion of strangulation would be too much for him. Easy to get hold of a Taser with an ex-cop's contacts. Stunning Cameron means he could do what he needed. Like chucking him off a bridge.'

'But a Taser wouldn't make it look like a suicide.'

'Right. It was clearly a murder.' Without indicating, Elliot pulled into the exit slip road, getting a blast of horn from a lorry. 'Cameron's a wanted man. All your pal Hulse would have to do is track him down and hand him over to the cops. Right?'

'Go on?'

'But maybe he was going to take him to us, but he fell over?'

'I've thought about that. John doesn't trust anyone, least of all the cops. Least of all me.' Marshall shut his eyes now. 'And he called me the other night, asking a few questions about the case, about my profile.' He paused, reopening his eyes to see them hurtling past a long lorry on the slip road. 'And that now feels incredibly suspicious.'

'It could just be a coincidence, right?'

'What couldn't?' Marshall watched the countryside shoot past. A sign for somewhere called Anick, which he was sure was on the east coast and spelled Alnwick. 'It could just be the obvious outcome of me turning up and telling him Cameron's dead. All that trauma resurfacing. I thought I was giving him closure, but all I've done is let him know that I'm working on the case, that I'm closing in on Cameron's killer.'

'He's monitoring an active police investigation into himself?'

'Right. Exactly.'

'Let's see what he's got to say.' Elliot pulled onto a long single-track lane, following it around until it ran parallel to the dual carriageway. Ancient trees on both sides, like they were driving into a country estate that had been butchered by the construction of the main road. A tall wall on the left, marking out the limits of a country estate.

Then they pulled out into a field, surrounded by tall walls on all sides. Must've been a walled garden at some point, but all that remained was two containers sitting in an L-shape. Navy, metal-sided, the kind you'd see on the back of a lorry. Steps led up to doors cut into the sides.

No signs of life, but a Skoda was parked there.

Marshall got out and clocked the NB plates on it. Not a Volvo or a Vauxhall or whatever. A Skoda. Just like what Siyal had unearthed. The car he'd met him in.

Shite, this was looking bad. Really bad.

Elliot nodded slowly, scanning around the space. 'Let's—'

The left door clattered open and Hulse stepped out, then limped down a set of steps, carrying a mug. Liquid sloshed out either side. He didn't look up, just kept his focus on each step. Looked like he could go down at any moment. He lowered himself onto a lawn chair and sipped from his cup. His expression soured when he saw Marshall.

'I'm leading.' Marshall didn't wait for a response, just charged over to Hulse. 'Afternoon, John.'

He got a raised cup and a harsh cough. 'What brings you here?'

'Need a word.'

'Could've called.'

'Could've, aye.' Marshall stayed standing, but kept a distance. 'Thought you were staying in your mum's cottage?'

'Rent that out. Why you here?'

'Need to know your movements on Sunday night.'

Another sip, then a grimace. Acrid coffee breath wafted over. 'Why?'

'I think you could hazard a guess John.'

'What?' Hulse rested his cup on the upturned beer crate and stood up, fists clenched. 'Think I killed Cameron?'

'An innocent man wouldn't get angry, John, he'd be able to explain.'

'Should trust me.'

'Trust, sure, but it's important we verify too.' Marshall stuffed his hands in his pockets. A defensive gesture, one that he hoped would de-escalate the situation. 'On Sunday night, someone called Cameron's mobile not long before he was killed. Thing is, the number's a burner. And a car matching your description was spotted outside his home.'

'So?' Hulse laughed. 'Oh, so it's me? You just assumed. Well, you can piss off.' He stormed towards the steps, then pulled up with a grunt. 'Bastard.' He bent low to grab his thigh. 'Don't have a warrant. Please go.'

Elliot pursed her lips. 'You know it'll look better if you come voluntarily.'

'No.'

'John, I hate doing this, but if you killed Derek Cameron, you deserve everything that's coming your way.'

'And if not?'

'Then I'll apologise.'

'Apologise, then.'

'Only if I'm wrong.'

'Bullshit.' Hulse limped over to Marshall, nostrils flaring. 'Leave!'

'John, cooperation looks more like the actions of an innocent man.'

Hulse sighed. He looked around, forward again, then lashed out with an elbow. Whatever else he'd lost over the previous two years, his speed was a big part of it.

Marshall had seconds to twist his head out of the way and double down, pushing Hulse forward until he toppled onto the lawn chair. He grabbed Hulse by the wrist and twisted his arm up his back. 'Stay right where you are, okay?'

The cup flipped over and sprayed coffee over the loose hardcore, knitted together with grass.

'I did nothing!'

'Have you been meeting Cameron?'

'What?'

'At his flat.'

Hulse snarled at him. 'Course not!'

Elliot snatched the cuffs from Marshall then snapped them onto Hulse's wrists. 'John Hulse, I am arresting you for the murder of Derek Cameron.' She gestured with her head towards the trailer.

'On it.' Marshall walked over to the steps and climbed up. He stopped and peered inside as he put on his nitrile gloves.

Dark and gloomy. Two windows cut from the metal, more hatches than anything else, and both shut. He got out his phone and switched on the torch, then stepped inside.

A laptop slept on a table made from more beer crates and planks of wood. A living area with rudimentary facilities: a small tabletop fridge; a gas camping fire; portable TV; leads ran outside towards solar panels. Probably had a generator for winter. Quite a pathetic existence, but no signs of a Taser.

Marshall walked over and opened the door.

A bedroom. Hand-made bed, sleeping bag on top. Clothes hung from a free-standing rack. A drum kit against the far wall with some recording equipment.

That was it.

Marshall didn't want to think where Hulse went to the toilet.

No sign of the Taser. Nowhere even to hide one. Thing was probably at the bottom of the Tweed, where he'd killed Derek Cameron, or in the Tyne, a few hundred metres away from here.

Marshall stepped back outside and saw the blue lights coming towards them. Local uniform back-up, way too late.

Hulse was standing now, letting Elliot put the cuffs on from behind. 'Taking me to the local station?'

'That's the only thing you're going to say?' Elliot laughed. 'Not about how you pushed Derek Cameron off the viaduct?'

Hulse dipped his head and let Elliot lead him over to the pool car.

Marshall let his breath out just as the first drops of rain hit him.

Such a bloody waste of a life.

CHAPTER FIFTY-ONE

Hawick's police station was the old divisional HQ, now reduced to a backwater outpost under Police Scotland. Curious how Pringle based himself down here, rather than up in Melrose or Gala.

The whole area was tough to police because of how spread out it was, but surely there were better locations than here. Only Newcastleton and Langholm further south of here were even settlements and the area was virtually crime free, with most of the action centring around Galashiels and the towns to the north along the Tweed.

A bit grander than Melrose's station, but not much. Same boxy look, but big enough to be a high school.

Elliot pulled into a visitor's space, though it seemed like they were the only ones here. She turned around to look at Hulse on the back seat. 'Let's get you inside, then, shall we?' She opened her door, glancing at Marshall. 'See you upstairs, okay?'

'Sure.' Marshall got out into the howling rain. July and it

felt like February. He was missing London's brutal heat, with that stifling lack of air in the summer.

He watched Elliot lead Hulse into the building's rear entrance.

He'd murdered Cameron rather than picking up the phone.

The whole thing rattled around in his stomach like the cheese and chutney sourdough from lunchtime.

A deep breath, then he walked over to the front door, infested with TV crews and journalists. Teeth gritted, checking his own phone as he walked, to see if that trick worked. He needn't have bothered – none of them paid him any attention.

A cameraman was filming the back door. The rest were too busy to pay Marshall any heed. Might as well be a cleaner.

He walked up to the pair of uniforms guarding the place and flashed his warrant card. They let him through and he tried to ignore the calls now coming from the rabble.

The reception area was an oasis of calm, or the eye of a storm. Someone's budget had stretched to freshening it up so it looked like a hairdresser's salon.

Crap, Marshall still hadn't got that hundred quid back from evidence.

Nobody behind the counter, but his card actually worked here. The reader beeped and gave him a green light. He pocketed it and climbed the stairs, looking out on the crowd in the car park.

His phone rumbled in his pocket, but he kept walking. The submarine warning sound coming from his mobile made him stop. He knew what it was – a text from his mother:

Robert,

I just wondered if you were free for a coffee or something a wee bit stronger maybe? If you are returning to London, please could I request you would call in before you leave?

Regards,

Your mother

So formal. Made him chuckle.

He stopped and tapped out a reply:

I'll be around for another night, but I'll set off early tomorrow. I'll pop around later.

He sent it and felt like a wave of revulsion wash over him.

Graham Thorburn hadn't meant any malice by his words the previous night, but he'd unlocked all the guilt over Kate Pierce.

Hard to be angry with him. He was just an old guy, his best days behind him. Someone his mum couldn't say no to.

Sod it, they deserved their happiness.

Marshall opened the door onto a long, dark corridor. Someone had blasted half a can of Lynx here and very recently. It hung on the air like dust motes after shaking out bedding.

DCI James Pringle

First door. Brass plate, the text below scratched out. Might be a modern building, but that was straight out of a Victorian-era bank.

Marshall knocked on the door and stepped in without waiting for a reply.

Pringle sat at a round meeting table in the window. He glowered at Marshall and it softened into a grin. 'Ah, Sir

Marshall of Melrose. I'll tap a sword off your shoulders later, but have a seat at the round table.'

Marshall sat opposite him. 'I'll take that as a thank you, sir.'

'This sword is double-edged. I'm not happy that you went off with Elliot. You're too close to the suspect.' Pringle unmuted the conference phone. 'Tina, you still there?'

'Sure am.'

'Okay, well, DI Marshall has joined us.'

'Hey, Rob. Well done.'

'Thanks, boss.' Marshall sat back, arms folded. He knew it was projecting hostility, but he couldn't help it. He felt hostile.

Pringle leaned forward, and Marshall caught a strong blast of deodorant. 'Sorry, Tina, you were saying?'

She clicked her tongue. 'Thing is, do you actually have anything connecting John Hulse to Cameron?'

'That's an excrement question.' Pringle grinned at his own joke. Jesus, he was exhausting. 'Kirsten Weir, we're all counting on you.'

The line crackled. 'My team are working away in the garage, cataloguing and...' She exhaled deeply. 'We've found a gym bag full of sexual torture devices. Cameron was a real sadist. But a very clean one. The workshop is virtually forensically dead.'

'Virtually schmirtually.' Pringle rolled his eyes. 'Tell me. What have you actually got?'

'Two sets of hair and skin flakes. The latter will be a while, but some of the hairs match Wendy's colour. There are some fibres that might match Cameron's clothing. But I think that'll be the sum of it. We'll just find Cameron and Wendy there.'

Pringle stifled a yawn. 'Just like the flat, the car and all the other crime scenes?'

'Aye, but in our favour, he probably hadn't got the chance

to finish cleaning that garage. So we're still processing it and have a lot of analysis left to complete. We might get something else.'

'Fingers crossed.' Pringle held them up like a boy scout. 'Everything crossed. Toes. Eyes. Vas Deferens.' He grabbed his crotch.

Rickards snorted down the line.

Marshall couldn't tell if it was humour or disgust. 'But you've got nothing on John Hulse?'

'No, we don't.' Kirsten, sounding tired. 'I'm driving down to meet colleagues in Northumbria Police at his home. Again, that's going to take time to process.'

'Hardly.' Marshall smiled. 'He lives in two trailers and doesn't seem to own anything.'

'Let's hope we get the answers soon.' Pringle sprang to his feet. 'Thanks for the time, gang. I've got another press conference to beast. I'll be in touch.' He reached over and stabbed the end-call button. 'I much preferred policing when it was all done locally.' He swung his suit jacket over his shoulders, then marched off. He stopped in the doorway and turned to face Marshall. 'Thank you.' He smiled, then charged off out of the room.

That was it?

What was the point in asking him to come up here just to bugger off?

Marshall heard voices out in the corridor.

John Hulse...

Hard to think he was capable of this. Of killing Cameron. In time, he knew he'd process this. But Marshall understood perfectly well why he'd done it.

Being able to execute on it was another thing entirely.

Could he really blame him?

Of course he could. He should have come forward and spoken to the police. Not Marshall, just anyone.

He didn't trust them anymore – they'd failed him, left him with a limp and a wheeze – but he should still have come forward.

Dickhead.

Fucking dickhead.

Pringle dashed into the room and started rummaging around in his drawers. 'Forgot my sodding phone.' He held up an old-fashioned Samsung and frowned at Marshall. 'You okay there, big guy?'

Marshall ran a hand down his face then hauled himself to his feet. 'I'm okay, sir.'

'Must be tough. Someone you trusted let you down.'

'Murdering someone's a bit stronger than letting me down.'

'I'm sorry to hear that.' Pringle walked over and held out his hand. More second-hand deodorant splashed across Marshall. 'Thank you for the help.'

Marshall shook it and smiled at him. 'Thank *you* for letting me do my job again.'

Pringle flashed up his eyebrows but didn't say anything.

'This… I forgot I was good at being a cop. And how much I enjoyed it.'

'It's like coming home, eh? And we've got this from now. You can mosey on down the "frog and toad".' Pringle did the air quotes with his fingers.

'I'll be leaving first thing tomorrow.' Marshall walked over to the doorway, still blocked by Pringle. 'I'll just walk down the apples and pears now, sir.'

Pringle barked out a laugh. But he placed an arm in the way, blocking Marshall's exit. 'But last time I told you to leave, you got involved in the case again. This time I mean it. No malarkey. You and DI Elliot were right to investigate that lead but you know you can't take a direct lead in the prosecution, given your previous with Mr Hulse. Get yourself a nice meal, see some friends, then get back to London. It's over for you, Inspector. Take a win as a win.'

'Sure thing, sir. But I'm due a hundred quid from the operation at the hairdresser.'

'Didn't DI Elliot return it?'

CHAPTER FIFTY-TWO

Back in Melrose, Marshall walked along the short corridor towards Elliot's office for the last time. He knocked and listened. Sunny again outside now. What a day. No sounds, so he opened the door and entered.

DS Siyal wasn't there. He owed the big lump a goodbye. Maybe he'd done enough of the encouragement, of the words to the wise, but he wanted him to know he had, if not a friend, then someone to talk to about the shit of being a direct-entry cop.

An envelope sat in the middle of Elliot's desk, marked for him. One too few Ls in his surname and one lower rank. He hoped it was a joke and opened it. There was his money, all hundred quid of it. He put it in his wallet and a note tumbled to the floor. He crouched down to read it:

> You've got Shunty to thank for this. He vouched for you.
>
> Love,
>
> Weirdo

Kirsten. And she'd left her phone number.

Marshall got out his phone and tapped it in, then sent a text:

Thank you for the cash. Rob x

He stuffed her note into his wallet with the cash.

She seemed like a good laugh and they'd hit it off when they had the glass of wine. But when he got close to people, they left him. He couldn't face the inevitable rejection. He'd just have to leave it.

Everything was foggy, like he was in a smoky room, like he had covid again.

He could call Rickards and moan about being taken off the case. But it wasn't his, it was theirs.

And it was over.

He'd been able to help, to solve the case that had broken him.

It wasn't just Marshall who'd been broken by that case. Hulse had taken two bullets and they hadn't even caught Cameron. Somehow he'd tracked him down, then decided to kill him.

Let it go. Hulse made his choice.

Head back to London, investigate the car crash. This was over.

Marshall left the room and shut the door. Aye, he'd done a good thing here. Saved a victim, caught a killer.

He strolled down the corridor, hands in his pockets. He should call Kirsten and correct the x.

God no. No. Just leave it.

He passed a meeting room and stopped dead.

Siyal was sitting in there. A female DC next to him. Phoebe Thompson between them, shaking her head.

Cameron's neighbour.

Marshall knocked on the door.

Siyal looked over and frowned. He got up, said something, then joined Marshall out in the corridor. 'Hey.'

'Just wanted a word before—'

'I know I should've checked those plates.'

'It's not that. I just wanted to say goodbye.'

'Oh. Okay.' Siyal grabbed his hand and shook it. 'Well done, Rob. Well done.'

'Thank you, Rakesh.'

Rather than letting go, Siyal tightened his grip. 'I mean it, Rob. Elliot's been calling me my actual name.'

'Great to hear.' Marshall freed his hand and smiled, but his eyes were drawn to Phoebe Thomson.

Not your case.

Not your case.

Not your case.

'What's happened?'

'Nothing's happened. Why would you think that?'

Marshall tilted his head towards the room. 'Why's she here, then?'

'Oh, right. Elliot wanted me to show her Hulse's photo.'

Marshall raised his eyebrows. 'You don't have a VIPER suite?'

'Have to go up to Edinburgh for that.'

Small-town policing. Got to love it. 'Anyway. Has she identified John?'

'She clammed up.' Siyal got out his mobile and checked the screen. 'I'm getting nowhere, and Elliot keeps bouncing my calls. Only person she doesn't answer the phone to.' He clenched his jaw, hard enough to stretch the skin.

Not your case.

Not your case.

Not your case.

Marshall waved at the room. 'Need a hand?'

'Me and Kelly have got it, sir. It's cool.'

'Phoebe's just sitting there, saying nothing. That doesn't seem to me like you've got it in hand.' Marshall raised both of his. 'I'm happy to back off, okay, but I can help. One thing I am good at is interviewing people.'

'Okay, on you go.' Siyal stepped aside. Didn't look too pleased about it.

Marshall felt a stab of guilt as he entered the room and took Siyal's seat. Still warm. He focused on Phoebe, trying to get a measure of her. Her long hair shrouded her face. Whatever was going on inside her skull, she was hiding. He could just leave her, but women like Wendy Malcolm and Caroline Reynolds needed closure.

Pinning Cameron's murder on Hulse would help them.

Who was he kidding? It was nothing to do with the victims, so much as him.

Marshall smiled at her. 'Hi Phoebe, do you remember me?'

She looked at him through her wall of hair. 'Detective Mackay, isn't it?'

'Marshall. Rob Marshall.' He gave her a few seconds. 'Do you recognise the man in the photo?'

'Keep saying to these two.' She waved a hand at Siyal and Kelly. 'I don't know him.'

'It's okay. Nothing more's going to happen to you.'

She tugged her hair out of the way and showed the aubergine skin around her eye. 'You didn't stop *this*, did you?'

'Phoebe, what's happened to you is sickening. It's a sad fact of the modern world that it's not an isolated incident. Far from it. And all you did was suffer in silence, while your husband was away for an extended period. You were lonely. So bloody lonely and you had nobody to confide in. Nobody to talk to. So you spoke to Declan. Your neighbour. It's okay. You did nothing wrong.'

She loosened her hair back in front of her bruised eye. 'That wanker's saying...' She waved a hand over to Siyal by the door. 'Saying how Dec raped and killed all those lassies...'

'It's true, Phoebe.' And I told you, but you didn't listen last time. 'Only two of them survived.'

'Christ.'

In Marshall's mind's eye, he saw Wendy Malcolm lying on the table. Saw her saying 'help'.

He used to see Kate Pierce's dead body.

Progress.

'Phoebe, thanks to you, we've managed to save another. She's in hospital. Thanks to your help earlier, we saved her.'

'Okay.' Phoebe sat back, snorted, then leaned forward again. Whatever was going through her bloodstream – drugs or just caffeine – she was a ball of energy. 'Okay, so I do recognise the man in that photo, aye. He was in that car.'

'You're sure of that?'

'Sure.'

'You know his name?'

'Nope. Dec never mentioned it.'

'Did you speak to him?'

She nodded. 'About Dec.'

Marshall felt the thrumming of his phone in his pocket. No ringtone, so he let it play out. He focused on Phoebe and tapped the photo again. 'Is this the man you told us about earlier? The one on the stairs?'

'Nope. I never saw this guy with Dec.' She shook her head again, each swish revealing a flash of the bruise again. 'He knocked on the door, asked a few questions. Said he was looking for Dec.'

'Did he name him?'

She stared deep into Marshall's eyes. 'Now you mention it, he might not have. Could be he was just being nosy. Asking me questions about him.'

She wasn't far off.

Sounded like Hulse was mining her for info on Derek Cameron. 'He was definitely sitting in the car?'

'That's what I said, aye.'

'Was there definitely another man?'

'Aye. Older than him.' She tapped the photo. 'Never spoke to him, but Cal was definitely with him.'

The door opened. 'Marshall, can I have a word?' Elliot was in the doorway, hands on hips.

Marshall smiled at Phoebe. 'Thank you, this has been helpful.' He got up and followed Elliot out of the room.

She slammed the door behind him and scowled at him. 'You're supposed to be off this case.'

'Sorry, I just wanted to say goodbye to DS Siyal.'

'And you just so happened to accidentally interview someone. Clown...' She sighed. 'Marshall, I can't order you to go, but you need to listen to Pringle. He'll drop a nuclear bomb on you if you don't stop arsing around.'

'I can handle him.' That tough guy talk was the bullshit he hated about the police force. 'Sorry. I shouldn't have done that.' He thumbed at the door behind him. 'I should've let DS Siyal get on with it.'

'You're totally right. But it seems like you got her talking, so we'll say nothing more about it.' She pointed along the corridor. 'Now, *get*.'

He didn't need to take another telling. 'Goodbye, Andrea. It's been an interesting experience.'

'So it has.' She smiled. 'Now, I hope to hell that I never see your face again.' She waved behind him. 'Bugger off!'

He laughed, then walked away from her. The interview

room door shut and he glanced behind him to see he was alone in the corridor.

He hoped Phoebe Thomson got some closure on her life, hoped she moved on and didn't become another statistic of a pathetic man's jealousy and insecurity.

He pushed out into the stairwell and checked his phone. The missed call was from Jen. She'd left a voicemail.

'Hey, bro. Word on the street is you're buggering off back to London? Wondered if you fancied a catch-up. My shift finishes soon, so come and meet me at work, then we can go and get something to eat.'

CHAPTER FIFTY-THREE

Marshall rested the tubs of baked goods on the counter and smiled at the nurse behind reception. 'Got these for you and your team.'

She frowned at him, but it didn't stop her taking them. 'Flapjacks, millionaire shortbread and brownies. Mmm.' She looked way too young to be working anywhere, let alone in a hospital. 'What's this for?'

'For bringing Wendy Malcolm back from the dead. And for just doing your job. I wanted you to know how much I appreciate the work you lot do. It's not been an easy time for you.'

'Thank you.' She smiled at him. 'I'll pass them on. We've got a break coming up.'

'Is Jen Armstrong here?'

'First left, second right.' She cupped a hand around her mouth and whispered, 'Warn you now, she's doing her expenses. She'll be grumpy as fudge.'

'Oh, I know how grumpy my sister can get.' Marshall gave her a smile and walked off, following her instructions.

First left, second right.

Wasn't it?

First right, second left?

He couldn't remember, so he tried the first way round.

Sure enough, he could hear Jen's voice booming out of an open door. 'Paul! Shut up!'

He didn't want to go in while she was shouting at her ex, but she sometimes needed harnessing like a wild horse.

Marshall eased it wider open and stepped in, trying to get his sister's attention.

She was leaning over the phone, clutching the edge of her desk. 'Paul, you've been letting Thea slack off. It's your fault her grades have slipped!'

A long pause. 'How do you know, Jen?' The phone was on speaker.

Marshall waved at her, then thumbed outside.

She shook her head rapidly, then pointed at the spot he was standing on and mouthed, 'Stay.'

So he stayed.

Jen turned back to the phone. 'I know because she got her exam results this morning, you daft sod. They're not good.'

Paul sighed down the line. 'Not everyone can be a brainbox like you, Jen.'

'A brainbox. Christ, I wish. Maybe she'll be just like her dad, eh? A total waster.'

'Charming.' Paul sighed again. 'Listen, the reason I called is to let you know that I can't have Thea over to stay tonight.'

Jen slumped back in her seat, eyes shut. 'Again?'

'Aye, sorry about it. You'll need to pick Thea up from her mate's house.'

'And why can't you?'

'Something's come up at work, sorry. I'll make it up to her.'

'Will you fuck.' Jen picked the phone from the cradle and

slammed it down. 'Dickhead.' She swung around. 'Why the fuck did I marry that arsehole?'

Marshall shrugged. 'Search me. Your taste in men's always been—'

'He's *such* a dickhead. Letting me down's one thing, but he's letting our daughter down.'

'What's happened?'

'Her grades have really slipped this year. She'll have to resit two Highers next year to get into uni.'

'That'll be why she's doing a dissertation in July?'

'That's a whole other thing. She missed a couple of months with covid.' She rubbed the stress out of her eyes but left a load in there. 'She's a bright kid, Rob. I just don't know what's happened.'

Marshall could've pussyfooted around it, but it was his sister. She deserved the truth, straight. 'Could it be anything to do with the divorce?'

'Probably.' Jen let her hair down, then set about retying it. 'I had no choice. Paul's a total dick. You heard him, right?'

'I did and I don't believe him.'

'What?'

'People who lie use vague terms like "something's come up". If it was genuine, he'd have details. He'd apologise for blowing up your evening.'

Jen blew air up her face. 'I'm on the early shift today, so I can see my divorce lawyer—' She checked her watch. '—in like two hours. I wanted to get a coffee with you first, but now I've got to pick up my bloody daughter from Innerleithen.'

'Jen, I'd offer to collect her, but I don't really know Thea and it'd be awkward.'

'Good chance to get to know her. But I get it.' Jen picked up the phone and hammered the keypad. 'I'll have to ask Mum *again*.' She put the handset to her ear. 'Was our info useful?'

'Earlier? It was. We just arrested the man who killed Derek Cameron. My ex-partner.'

'John?'

Marshall nodded.

Jen exhaled slowly. 'Wow. I'm shocked. He seemed okay when I met him. That time Thea and I stayed at your flat for a London trip.'

'Christ, that's right. You kind of hit it off with him, didn't you?'

Jen blushed. 'No. No way.'

'See what I mean about your taste in men?'

'Ha bloody ha.' She frowned. 'But I saw him recently.'

'What?'

'Bumped into him downstairs. Had a coffee with him. Said he was waiting on— Mum? Hello, it's Jen.'

Hulse being here could be a coincidence easily explained by the fact he's a taxi driver, up here fairly often.

Still...

The fact Cameron had been killed so close to home, to where—

Marshall swallowed back angry tears, tasting them deep in his throat.

Something still didn't stack up about it.

'Mum, please. Just pick Thea up from Innerleithen.' Pause. 'Got a lot on tonight. Paul can't take her and I've got to— Lawyer, right. Fine. Thanks, Mum. I owe you.' Jen put the phone down again. 'You're off the hook, champ. Mum's going to do it.' She sat back and got out her mobile phone, then hit dial. She dug her knuckle into her eye socket. 'I'm worried I'm messing it all up.'

'Jen, I know how tough it is raising kids. It's part of the reason why I haven't had any.'

'Aye, and our father just upping and leaving when we were

six, that would be the main part of why we're both so screwed up.'

Her bad taste in men was common-or-garden daddy issues. Left her open to manipulation.

Not that he was innocent of that himself.

She stared at him. 'It's not far off, though. Is it?'

'It's not that simple, Jen. Important you don't beat yourself up.'

She stabbed a finger off her phone then again and put it to her ear. 'Thea's bored. School holidays are so long and, while he's a *total* prick, Thea misses her dad. And her pals at school. We don't live that far away, but it's far enough, you know? Sitting on her own all day with Mum, which is enough to rot anyone's brain.' She killed the call. 'Nobody answers the bloody phone anymore.' She tapped out a text and tossed her mobile onto the desk. 'Thea's starting at Gala Academy next month. Of course, she wants to keep going to Peebles with her pals, but I can't drive her over there every day with my shifts. Can't afford to live in a decent place there either. And I have to keep relying on Mum.'

Marshall smiled. 'I'd offer to drive her if I lived locally.'

'You living in London gets you off so many things.'

Maybe once Marshall had left the police, his next chapter could be closer to home. He doubted he could ever live back in the Borders again, but he should be much more present in Thea's life.

Jen shot to her feet. 'I've managed to get an earlier appointment with my lawyer, so let's get that drink and catch up properly. Fancy getting shit-faced.'

'Sounds great.' Marshall winced. 'Crap. I'm meeting Dean Taylor.'

'Dean.' Jen grunted. 'Another example of my taste in men

right there. At least I don't pick gay ones anymore. He's still an arsehole, isn't he?'

'I'll see. Text me when you're done with the lawyer and I'll come meet you.'

'Sure.' Jen stood up again. 'You want to speak to Wendy Malcolm?'

Marshall shook his head. 'I wasn't asking.'

'No, but she was asking to speak to you.'

'Jen, I'm not on the case anymore. They've made that very clear.'

Jen gave a flash of her eyebrows. 'Do you want me to rescind my offer? Or do you want to let another woman down?'

'Woah, that's below the belt and my balls are stinging.'

'Come on, Rob. She asked to see you.'

He didn't have a choice, did he?

She led him out into the corridor, then skipped around the cleaning machine like she was still doing ballet, then opened a door. 'Here you go.'

Wendy Malcolm lay on the bed. Eyes closed, breathing slowly. Skin hanging off her like she needed to shed it.

Looked like she'd died.

Then her chest moved.

Marshall took the seat next to her and waited. He knew he shouldn't be here. Should've passed this to Siyal or Elliot.

'You saved me.'

He looked over just in time to see her eyes close. 'Hi, Wendy.'

'You found me.'

'We all did, Wendy. It was a team effort.'

'Your sister... She said it... was you.'

Marshall smiled at her. 'I was the one who managed to get into that room where you were.'

'Cal's dead?'

'That's right, Wendy. Callum's dead.'

'Good.' She shut her eyes like it happened to someone else. 'Took my car to the garage. Dad couldn't do it... At the rugby club... Someone came to collect it. Callum. He seemed nice, so I... I dropped my guard. Met him a few times. Cinema in Gala. Food. Hotel in Clovenfords. Melrose. Nice place in Hawick. A gentleman. Seemed like it. Don't know... what happened... that night.'

'The night he took you?'

'Right. Supposed to pick me up. Was it someone else?'

'No, Wendy. We know it was him. We've got video of ... what happened.' He cupped her cold hand in his. 'He's dead, Wendy, he can't hurt you anymore.'

'How?'

'Someone killed him. We have a suspect in custody. You told the nurse about the phone call and that was helpful, Wendy. More than you can realise. We found the killer because of that.'

She pushed her head back into the pillow. 'You keep saying killer.'

'Right. And?'

'Two men there.'

Ants crawled up Marshall's spine. 'What?'

'Not just Callum. I was abused by two men.'

CHAPTER FIFTY-FOUR

The machines in the room throbbed and thrummed. Marshall was going to be sick. 'Two men?' His mouth was dry. 'Are you sure?'

She tilted her head – as close as she could get to a nod. 'Talking to each other and to me as they did it.'

'Wendy...' Marshall didn't know what to think about it.

She was in a very bad way. Damaged, broken by her ordeal. It could be her imagination.

But...

If it was two attackers, if Cameron had an accomplice?

Shit.

Hulse had been...

Marshall tried not to extrapolate – he needed to get more information.

'You were delirious, Wendy. Is it possible you could've imagined it?'

'No! I wasn't. When I woke up, I think I'd been drugged? I wasn't sure if it was a dream. But there were definitely two men there. When they were... When they...'

'You said you heard him on the phone, could it have been that?'

'No. This was Saturday night, when he took me. I think he moved me. After someone called him. I sort of remember being drugged again and taken somewhere else. The first place was near the road, the second further away. But I woke up and there were two people there. They...' She gritted her teeth. 'They took turns.'

'Can you describe them?'

The slightest tilt of her head. 'One had a scar on his hip. Like, a really bad scratch.'

Cameron, where he'd tried to remove his birthmark.

'The other definitely didn't. He was much hairier.' She choked up with tears. 'I'm... What they put me through. I can't... I... I feel so stupid for falling for it. And...'

Marshall tightened his grip on her hand. He couldn't process it. Two attackers would change things. 'Is there anything else that could identify your second attacker?'

'I can't remember.'

'Thank you, Wendy.' Marshall got up and walked over to the door. The nurse from earlier was waiting there, her hand in a bucket of brownies.

He waved at her, getting her attention, then kept his voice low, 'Have you run a rape kit?'

'Came back negative.'

'Negative? Seriously? DNA's viable for up to seventy-two hours after the last attack. That was Sunday night. And she couldn't clean herself because she's tied to a table.'

'Can I ask you to keep your voice down?' She put her brownie down on the lid. 'There were signs of repeated sexual assault but no DNA was present. We detected signs of a harsh chemical being used upon her, both externally and otherwise.

It's burned her skin. She'd been cleaned up, like a pro had done it.'

And Marshall had a good idea what kind of person would be that particular professional.

An ex-cop.

John Hulse.

CHAPTER FIFTY-FIVE

Marshall pulled up at Melrose police station and hit dial on his phone as he got out.

Elliot bounced the call again.

Bloody hell, he was trying to help her out!

A blast of hailstones scattered across the tarmac. In July. It was freezing. He ran over to the entrance and hauled the door open. His suit was dotted with tiny white balls of ice, like he was a groom on a wedding cake.

A few people were in there, and they seemed to know each other. Husband and wife huddled together at the seats, his arm around her shoulders.

Son at the desk, panting for some indiscernible reason. 'I swear it happened, so don't try to say to me it didn't. Bright lights in the sky, in the hills just south of Traquair.'

Elliot's husband was standing behind reception, arms folded. 'And what do you expect me to do? Call Fox Mulder?'

'I expect you to do something! My mother was missing on a UFO for hours!'

'They call them UAPs nowadays. Unidentified Aerial Phenomena.'

Don't get involved...

Marshall swiped through and took the stairs two at a time, then burst into the corridor. Elliot's office door was standing ajar at the end. The window on the left was getting pelted by hailstones, stacking up against the sills.

Marshall nudged her office door open and peered in.

Elliot was sitting at her desk, resting on her elbows, her long fringe dangling in front of her face.

'You okay?'

'Jesus Christ!' She lurched to her feet and turned to face away from him. She swept her hair back and rubbed at her temples.

'Andrea? What's the matter?'

She wouldn't look at him. 'The TV appeal.' She pointed at the box on the wall. 'Pringle made me lead it.'

'Right.' Par for the course with a DI. 'And?'

She turned back around to face him, her bloodshot eyes like tomatoes. 'I've had four calls from sex pests complimenting me on my looks.'

'Oh shit, I'm really sorry.'

'Unless it was you peeling bananas down the phone, you shouldn't say sorry.'

'Peeling bananas?' He got it. 'Oh. There are a lot of sick bastards out there.'

'Right. Bet you don't get it, do you?'

'Not that, but I've had stalkers. Two men and a woman. Lot of disturbed individuals out there. Our society's sick.'

'Keeps us in a job, eh?'

'I'd rather be on the dole than live this life.' Marshall walked closer to her, but kept enough of a distance. 'Few years back, I was on TV in similar circumstances to you, appealing for witnesses for all of Cameron's murders. Trouble was, it made him familiar with members of the team. It's how I thought he knew me by name. How he could recognise me. Though maybe he'd been staking us out. But it was John Hulse.'

'Thanks, but I can handle myself.' She blinked hard a few times then put her hands on her hips. 'I'm pretty sure Pringle ordered you to bugger off, Marshall, and yet you're still here. Making a habit of not listening, aren't you?'

'I wouldn't be here if you answered your phone.'

She crossed the room to her desk and picked up her mobile. 'Jesus, *six* missed calls? Talk about being a sex pest.'

'We've got a problem.' Marshall ran a hand down his face. 'I visited my sister at the hospital and Wendy asked to see me. To thank me.'

'Oh Christ, no. Tell me you didn't...'

'I did.'

'Marshall, you are such a bloody cliché. Always the hero.'

He let it wash over him. 'Wendy's identified a second attacker.'

'Just when I think it's over...' Elliot collapsed into her chair. 'A second attacker?'

'She says she was raped by two men. One had a patch on his hip. Cameron. The other, she doesn't know.'

'So you think it's Hulse?'

The idea that his partner could be a rapist burnt away at the pit of his stomach. 'I don't want to think it, no, but I'm open to the possibility he might be connected to this. For starters, Phoebe Thomson identified Hulse as Cameron's visitor.'

'Aye, but it's the other guy we're interested in now.'

'That could be someone getting a squash racket restrung or something trivial.'

'I've got Shunty and his team going door-to-door again in Cameron's block of flats to confirm if it was Hulse or not.'

'Take it you've got nothing so far?'

'Not a sausage.' She was shaking her head. 'The hard truth is, Phoebe saw Hulse there. We thought he wanted to confront Cameron, but I'm thinking they were in cahoots.'

Marshall swallowed hard. 'Andrea, Cameron shot him. Why would he be co-raping women with the guy who shot him?'

'You saw where he was living, Marshall. It's possible your pal Hulse has gone completely insane. And it's not just Wendy, is it? Caroline and Audrey were local-ish to Hexham.'

Elliot was right. Close enough to Carlisle and Longtown. 'What's the plan?'

'We've got Hulse in custody.' Elliot unlocked her computer and scanned down the screen. 'The Procurator Fiscal and superintendent in Edinburgh have requested a charge tonight, so they're piling pressure on Pringle. But Hulse isn't speaking.'

'Figures. Ex-cop like him. Knows all the tricks. And how to avoid them. And he's pretty taciturn at the best of times.'

'I was expecting you to offer to do it.'

'Despite what you might think, Andrea, I'm nobody's hero. This is your case.'

'Damn right it is.' Elliot put her phone to her ear. 'Bastard just bounced my call.' She scowled. 'Sir, it's Andrea. Call me ASAP.' She ended it and hammered out a text. 'Wanker.'

'Now you know how it feels.'

'Aye, aye.' But she was lost to her texting. Whatever she was typing, it was longer than a book of the Bible.

All the way down from the hospital, Marshall had flipped between two possibilities. Hulse wasn't involved, Hulse was involved. Nothing could determine which one was right.

Sod it.

He walked over to the whiteboard and scrubbed it clear.

Elliot was on her feet, her arms windmilling. 'That was important!'

'Secret Santa 2019?'

'Right.' She evaded his gaze. 'What are you doing?'

'Thinking out loud.' He wrote Hulse on the top left and circled it. 'Is he really a killer?'

'You're the profiler.' She walked over and joined him staring at the blank space. 'Does he fit your profile?'

Marshall didn't know. But it felt like there was something he wasn't quite grasping. 'Two men abusing Wendy is *not* in my profile. I had Cameron as a loner. Which he is.'

'Just takes one raping friend, doesn't it? The only person in his life, leading him down a very dark path.'

'But is it Hulse?'

'Assume it's not.' She snatched the pen out of his grip and wrote 'AN Other'. 'Maybe Cameron met that special someone up here. Or on a sex club's anonymous website.'

'Okay, both are plausible.'

She tapped on Hulse. 'Back in the day, you told me you were worried there were leaks from your case. Right?'

'It's more wondering how Cameron recognised us. How he knew to clear out of London.'

'Okay, that's what you said earlier about him monitoring your press conferences. He knew you. Could he know John?'

'I don't think so. Just me and Rickards did the appeals.'

She wrote "Cameron", then drew a line connecting it to Hulse. 'What if Hulse was in cahoots back then? What if that's how Cameron managed to escape back in the day?'

'Like you said, he shot Hulse! Surely he'd shoot me instead?'

'Maybe that was the plan, but Cameron wanted to take him out. Kill the evidence. But Hulse survived because of you.

And maybe they've patched it up since. Or it could've been planned that way all along. I mean, it's good cover. Right?'

'Maybe.'

'Even if it all points to Hulse being the second rapist, he just won't speak.' Elliot got her phone out again, then put it on speaker. 'Sir, did you get my text?'

'In the middle of a—' Whistle. '—briefing with the brass in Edinburgh.'

She rolled her eyes at Marshall. 'Does my message make sense, Jim?'

'It's a bit convoluted, but you honestly think this Hulse character is a conspirator?'

'We don't know, sir.' Marshall stepped closer so he'd be heard. 'Wendy Malcolm iden—'

'Inspector, I thought I told you to clear off?'

'You did, but I keep getting dragged back in.'

A sigh. 'A likely tale.'

'Sir, Wendy Malcolm identified two rapists. Derek Cameron was one, but we don't know who the other one is. I think it's possible that John Hulse is one of them. We should keep having him in custody until we eliminate him. But if it's not Hulse? It could happen again. The whole cycle.'

The line went silent. 'Inspector. Listen, I want to thank you for your diligence and passion. You're a shining light, a real beacon, but you need to step away. This isn't your case anymore. And you sure as shinola can't speak to Hulse – any defence lawyer worth their pink Himalayan salt could tear our case apart. Our hands are tied here. You of all people must know the lay of the land.'

'Right, sir.' Marshall recapped the pen and set it down on the ledge under the whiteboard. The room stank of toxic ink now. 'I'll leave it with you, then.'

'Thank you. And I do mean it.' *Beep*, and he was gone.

Marshall didn't know if it was the phone making the beep or Pringle's mouth.

Elliot looked like she was going to chuck the mobile through the window. Outside, the sun was shining again – looked like it hadn't hailed in months. 'Right, so where the hell does that leave us?'

'Leave *you*, you mean? Pringle's right. John's a friend and ex-colleague of mine. I can't be on this anymore. Besides, I've got an appointment or two. And I need an early night before I hit the road tomorrow.'

'You're just going to walk away?'

Marshall shrugged. 'I can take a telling.'

Elliot stared at him as she twisted her fringe around her finger. 'I'm going to get in touch with Caroline Reynolds again. The only other survivor. See if she had two attackers.'

'She didn't mention it to me.'

'No. But maybe you didn't ask the right question.'

CHAPTER FIFTY-SIX

'Sure I can't get you a menu, sir?' The barman brandished one like a Wembley street kid would a knife.

'I'm just here for a drink.' Marshall checked his watch. Dean was running late. And he was bloody starving. 'What do I call you?'

'Whatever you like, sweetheart, but it'll cost you double.' He bellowed with laughter. 'Carlos is what everybody calls me.'

'Okay, Carlos. Is Dean around?'

'Not in tonight.' The barman walked off.

'Excuse me?'

The barman went behind the bar and yanked down his towel to dry the glasses. 'At a thing in Edinburgh.'

'A thing?'

'Corporate job. Some French wine supplier trying to pimp stuff on him for the shop.'

Bloody hell.

He could've warned Marshall.

He could've gone to pick up Thea, for instance. Taken her to that ice cream place in Innerleithen. If it was still there.

He stared into the glass of red he hadn't touched, then got to his feet. 'Can you make sure this glass is charged to him instead of my room?'

'Already on the house, sir.'

Sod it.

What did he have to lose?

Marshall sat back down and took a drink of it. Decent stuff. Suppose it paid to run a hotel when you ran the quality off-license just along the street.

Still, why had Dean just buggered off?

Expect Delays played through the speakers. *Cops and Robbers*.

Blast from the past.

Marshall sat back, shut his eyes and listened. Hulse's favourite band. Got into some controversy a few years back, hadn't released anything since. Hulse was a man who didn't like much, but loved them.

What was it about friends letting Marshall down? Was it something in him? Or were people just shit?

Could Hulse really have done that?

Really?

The Hulse he'd worked with? Absolutely not.

But the Hulse Marshall had met in that car park near Newcastle? The one he'd arrested? There was a darkness in his eyes now. Living with chronic illness for so long could do things to people. Change them. Some lived with it, some were paralysed by it, but some...

What Hulse went through was a brutal experience. The acute shock of being shot, twice, bleeding out in a grotty pool car in Hammersmith.

Then the chronic pain after the recovery. Every breath like he was underwater. No longer able to run five miles before his shift, now struggling to walk five metres.

But could he really rape women?

With Cameron?

That was still a bit too much to believe.

Surely his troubles hadn't pushed him that far.

Surely.

But killing Cameron? Marshall could buy that.

Not that Hulse would speak to anyone, not even him.

Marshall got out his phone and texted Jen:

> I'm in the hotel bar. See you when you're finished.

He took another sip of wine as the stereo shifted to Dire Straits. Now it was time to get out of here.

'Supposed to be meeting Dean for a drink.'

Marshall looked over at the bar.

The barman was showing Kirsten to Marshall's table. 'Here you go.'

She stood there, smiling, then stopped the barman getting away. 'No. Dean Taylor. Not him?'

'Aye, sorry. You'll have to put up with this sack of joy.' Carlos trudged off to the bar, then turned up the music so they were drowning in *Sultans of Swing*.

Kirsten let her bag fall to the floor. 'I'm thinking this has been forced on us.'

'Dean's matchmaking us.'

'We were doing well ourselves, weren't we?'

Heat burnt up Marshall's face. 'Were we?'

'I thought we were. Aren't we cool?'

'Right, sorry. Aye, we're cool. Cool and the gang. Oh. Em. Thanks for getting my cash out of evidence.'

'Thanks for the text. I was going to reply, but the day kind of got away from me.'

Marshall took a sip of his wine. 'You look like you could do with some company.'

'Don't let me keep you.'

'I've got ages. Don't sweat it.'

'Fun and games today. Supervising the arsehats in Northumbria. Listening to Elliot moan about everything.'

The barman put a glass in front of her. 'On the house, madam.'

'Thanks, Carlos.' She watched him go. 'Bloody Dean. How did he lure you here?'

'Just a general catch up. Haven't seen him since—' Marshall swallowed hard. 'For a while. A long time. Half my life.'

'Wow. You've not seen him in twenty-five years?'

'Hang on, I'm not *fifty*. Told you that last night. I might not look it, but I'm thirty-six. So it's eighteen years, give or take, since I left this town.'

She leaned over the table. 'The lure he used on me was needing to talk about a friend he hadn't seen in a long time.'

'What a twat.'

She sucked in the aroma from her wine. 'Dean told me this friend has history with the Leaderfoot Viaduct.'

'Did he?'

'That why being up there on Monday spooked you, right?'

Sod it, she deserved the truth.

The depths of his trauma.

Marshall took a deep breath. It stuck in his throat.

'It's something I don't talk about and it was ages ago, but being back here with what happened on the viaduct, it brings back bad memories. The summer before university, my girlfriend jumped off that bridge.'

'Shit.' Kirsten's mouth hung open. 'Sorry, I didn't know.'

'Dean does.' Marshall couldn't figure out what he was trying to achieve here, but he'd made a pact with himself to stop hiding things from people. 'Thing is, Anna didn't kill herself. Didn't try to. She fell from the viaduct after... Someone abducted her. She got away. I've lived with that ever since. I blame myself.' He took a sip of wine. Barely tasted it. 'We think she was groomed and abused. Anna didn't speak about what happened because she couldn't – she was in a coma for two years. Never told anyone, me or Jen, my twin sister. They were best mates at school.'

'Jesus, Rob. That's awful.' She reached across the table and took his hand. 'I'm so sorry.'

'It's why the place is all locked away up there behind those big gates.'

'That must be... The whole thing is... Impossible.'

'Right. That's the word for it.'

'Shit. I can't even imagine. Losing someone like that.' Kirsten grabbed his hand again and squeezed.

'Being back here reminds me a lot of what happened with Anna.' Marshall waved around the room. 'We drank in this bar. Under new management now and under-age boozers aren't a thing anymore, but this was one. Bent the law, probably had a local cop or two turning a blind eye. We were in here the night she was taken. Jen and I lived around the corner, up the hill, but Anna lived in Gattonside, over the bridge. I wanted to walk her home, but she wouldn't let me. Insisted on it. I don't know why. But she never showed up there, then a few days later, someone saw her running down that road from Newstead to the viaduct. Passed her in their car, but they didn't stop... And then she just jumped off the bridge. Landed on the road. Someone found her, rushed her to the hospital, but her injuries were too bad.' Marshall took a deep drink of wine. 'The thing I tried to figure out is why. If we'd known about the abuse, we could've saved her. If we'd known who was doing it. We were at her cousin Doug's house in Gala, looking for her there, but she'd gone in the completely opposite direction. If we'd known her dad was abusing her, it'd be a different story.'

'How did you find out?'

'A few weeks later, I found a journal she'd stashed in my bedroom, under the mattress. She wrote about her suffering, about the things he'd do to her. "This all happened when I was nine and I forgave Dad. But now it's happening again." He got charged. Had an alibi, but it was weak. He died on remand. Massive heart attack. Never confessed. Swore he was innocent. Her mum blamed us.'

'That's who was here the other night?'

Marshall nodded. 'Jen stayed in the area to fight it, to be strong.'

'And you fled?'

Marshall couldn't look at her. 'I couldn't handle it, Kirsten. The whole thing. Her lying on a ventilator in hospital. I was down in Durham and I drove back every weekend until the end... And Jen... She *works there*. Every day, she goes to the place where Anna lived her last two years.' He grimaced. 'Kirsten, I've spent my life trying to help people avoid what we went through. What Anna went through, sure, but knowing for certain who did that to her has plagued my life. I should've known what was going on. I should've been there for her. To let her confide in me. But she never did.'

'You can't blame yourself, Rob. You were just a kid.'

'Aye, maybe now I'd be different. But back then, I *was* a kid. I did blame myself. It's what drove me to study psychology and criminology. When I didn't find any answers there, I did a PhD at Durham and trained as a criminal profiler, working with Jacob Goldberg. If anyone could figure it out, it'd be him. He helped me try to figure it out, but we didn't get any answers. But we worked with Northumbria police, investigating crimes in the north-east.

And I loved it. I really fucking loved it. I became a profiler, like in the FBI, and we caught some real pieces of work. But it didn't help me here.' Marshall patted his heart. 'It was all too abstract. Too theoretical. Reactive, reflective. And that's why I joined the Met. There, I could focus on action. On stopping people before they'd killed. Saving victims before they even knew they were at threat.'

'You're a direct entry as a DI?'

'Right. They do things differently down there. They respect psychologists. Sure, the Met's got its dark corners, but there are some very forward-looking areas.'

Kirsten took a sip of her wine. 'Elliot said you're leaving the force?'

'Handed in. After what happened to John and... Kate Pierce.'

She nodded like she knew exactly who she was.

'I couldn't face it anymore and I somehow ended up investigating serious car crashes. Of all things.'

The giant grandfather clock ticked to the hour, then started its cycle of chimes. The barman turned up the music again, The Eagles drowning it out.

'You can talk to me anytime. Okay? Day or night. You've got my number.'

'Thanks, but I've paid a shrink a lot of money.' He raised his hand. 'Sorry, I don't mean to be so flippant.'

'No, I get it. We barely know each other. But you need a friend, Rob.'

'Aye, look how the last one turned out.'

'Who?'

'Never mind. Just a bad joke.'

Kirsten put her glass back down. The whole outside was covered in her fingerprints. 'You don't seem to stick to things.'

'What?'

'You were a PhD, then a profiler, but that wasn't enough. So you became a cop, but you moved on from that when stuff went down. And you don't go back home. You can't commit to anything because you're worried you'll let people down. You sacrifice yourself for the needs of others, but you don't look after what's right for you.'

He wanted to stand up, to run away.

Because she was right.

All that money he'd spent on therapy, just to sit in that dark room with a wee clock between him and his therapist, who'd never got to the answers like Kirsten had, and certainly not as quickly.

'That's pretty deep for a crime scene investigator.'

'Not just you who's got a degree in psychology. And I got a fast-track when I joined. Sure, I'll never be a chief constable, but one day I'll be at Gartcosh leading things and shaping strategy across Police Scotland.'

'You're right. I haven't focused on me. I'm thirty-six and all I've tried to do with my life is exorcise her ghost. Those victims of Derek Cameron's in London, each one was Anna. With Kate Pierce, I thought I'd find her alive. It'd be like stopping Anna killing herself. And the reason I'm leaving the police... When I was tracking down Derek Cameron, I fucked up. Spooked Cameron and he fled London. Huge mistake. The whole thing was a huge mistake.'

'Rob, you just have to accept what happened and move on with your life.'

He rubbed tears out of his eyes before they formed. 'Not a night when I don't dream about it. Now, I know what happened to Anna. I believe Jen. I believe that Anna's father was abusing her. Dying like that means he got off with it. And I don't have closure on my girlfriend's death.'

Kirsten smiled at him, a kind smile, then took a sip of wine. 'It's a lot to carry all your life, you know that, right?'

'I know. But what else can I do?'

'Start living? Would Anna want you to be obsessed?'

Marshall took a drink of wine. 'Part of me knows I need to put it all behind me, so I can move on. Or so my shrink says. It's that, or I can spend another twenty years searching for answers and still finding none because they're all in the distant past.'

Kirsten looked like she was going to add something.

Footsteps thundered behind him, coming towards him like a herd of bullocks. Jen appeared, arms folded, forehead creased. He knew when his sister was pissed off and she looked like she was going to punch someone or something. That Elliot and Pringle would be investigating who she'd murdered.

Kirsten tilted her head to the side. 'You okay, Jen?'

She grinned at Kirsten. 'Hey, not seen you in a while.'

'Haven't broken my arm in a while.'

Jen didn't smile. 'This is very cosy. The pair of you.'

'Both staying here and... it's all a long story.'

'Robert "Long Story" Marshall.' Jen checked her watch.

Marshall pulled up a chair from the next table. 'Here. Can I get you a drink?'

'A prolapse.'

Kirsten grimaced. 'A what?'

Marshall winced. 'Think of a jäger bomb, but the Jägermeister's not sitting in Red Bull, it's in white wine.'

'Jesus!'

'Okay, a glass of white wine.' Jen took the chair, finally smiling. 'And a shot of Jägermeister.'

'Two ticks.' Marshall walked over and the barman was pouring already. 'You don't know what I want?'

'Got cracking hearing.' The barman tapped at his ears. 'Prolapse, glass of grenache and two more of chateauneuf-du-pape.'

Marshall stood there, feeling about ten stone lighter. Kirsten was the first person in years he'd been able to unburden himself on. He looked over at them and she was looking at him, smiling. He returned it then gave the barman a coy smile. 'A prolapse is a thing?'

'Aye, but she's getting a murder weapon instead. White wine with a chaser of jaeger, instead of it all being in the same glass. They're on the house too.'

'Thank God I'm not paying for it.'

'Dean's a generous guy. Good boss. I'll bring them over.'

Marshall walked back over and got that tingling feeling that they were talking about him.

'He's world class at beating himself up.' Jen had her arms folded. 'But Anna was my friend, as much as his girlfriend. We've both been traumatised by it.' She looked over at him. 'Why are you still beating yourself up, dickhead?'

Marshall was close to getting up and walking off. Felt that desperate need to run away.

'Oh aye, Rob, just leave again. Well done.' Jen took her drink from the barman, shaking her head. 'I'm sympathetic about what happened to you, but you buggering off like that... That was something I had to go through alone. You went to Durham, I stayed here. I'd lost my best friend and, worse, I lost my twin brother. We'd spent pretty much every second of our lives together from the thirty minutes we were all waiting on you in the operating theatre. Then you drifted away.'

Marshall felt tears prickling at his nostrils. All the emotion that was wrapped up inside was about to come pouring out. Either she was going to get it both barrels or he was going to cry himself into a dried-out husk.

Jen's phone blasted out. 'Christ, perfect timing.' She got up to take the call.

Kirsten looked shocked, trapped between two siblings. Two warring twins. 'Are you okay?'

Marshall was beyond language. Or a million miles away from it, untethered and floating in space.

'It's okay, Rob. Alright? I'm sure she didn't mean to be so brutal.'

'Oh, she did. It's... Fuck. I deserve it, to be honest. And she deserves to hear my side of it.'

'You're quite a pair.'

Footsteps ran back.

Jen, out of breath, eyes wild. 'Rob, Mum can't find Thea. Can you help me?'

CHAPTER FIFTY-SEVEN

The day's weird weather had outfoxed the station's central heating. Like a confused plant flowering in a mild January, the boiler seemed to have turned to its winter settings in the middle of summer, shoving the temperature into the high twenties.

Marshall was already sweating as he made his way along the corridor. The hailstones had long since melted from the windowsills outside, leaving dry brick.

'Thea's a bloody nightmare, Rob.' Jen was following him along the corridor. The place smelled of her rose perfume. 'Absolute bloody nightmare. Just like her bloody father.'

'She's probably fine, Jen.' Marshall stopped at the end and knocked on Elliot's office door.

Nothing.

He opened it and peered in. No sign of her.

Great.

'Wait in here.'

She went inside, but didn't sit. 'You think I'm overreacting?'

'God no. If she was my kid, I'd... Better to overreact and regret than to feel there was something you could've done.'

'Like with Anna?'

'Jesus, Jen.'

'I'm serious, Rob. I don't know why you were talking to Kirsten of all people, but I'm glad you were finally opening up to someone about what happened. It was brutal, Rob. It broke us all. Not just you.'

'I'm sorry I didn't talk to you about it. I couldn't talk to anyone. It's taken a lot of therapy to be able to open up.' Marshall stared up at the ceiling. 'Hard not to replay it all and think what happened was my fault.'

'You did have that big argument with Anna that night.'

'What argument?'

'She stormed off.'

'We didn't have an argument. Is that what you think?'

'Deny it all you like, Rob, it's—'

'Jen. We didn't argue. We never argued. Anna had an early start at the Co-op and just wanted to walk home alone. It was Dean's birthday, remember? She said we should make sure he lost a lot of braincells that night.'

'Christ, that's when I invented the prolapse.' She looked over at him, frowning. 'Seriously, you didn't have an argument?'

'Seriously. That's what happened. You could ask her mother. If she answered the door to us.'

'She still blames me, but her husband was touching up his own kid, so he deserved everything he got. He paid the price for it. And I'm glad. But we could've saved Anna.'

Marshall was buzzing. He needed to get away from her and this conversation. 'Jen, this isn't helping with Thea. She's only been gone a few hours. She'll turn up. But I'll see what I can do.'

She looked over at Marshall. Her fierce exterior had given way to the vulnerable side.

'She's a teen, Jen. Probably didn't charge her phone and it's run out of juice.'

'Right. Little minx turns it off all the time.'

'Who was she with today?'

'Old school friends from Peebles High.' Jen picked up her phone and checked the screen. 'Mum's through there now, but she can't find her at any of her usual haunts. Graham's due back home soon, so if she goes back there, he'll call Mum.'

'That's covered.' Marshall held up his hands. 'Has she done this before?'

'Once, just after I split from Paul.'

'Okay, well, I'll see what I can do. Stay here.' Marshall shut the door and walked back along the corridor. He got out his phone but Elliot hadn't responded to his text or his call and voicemail.

Great, great, great.

Marshall charged back towards the tiny incident room through the toasted air, the hot radiators burning the accumulated stoor.

Needn't have bothered.

The place was empty.

Not quite; one cop was sitting at the desk by the window.

Siyal's nemesis, Acting DS Jolene...

Marshall didn't even know her surname.

Sod it.

He marched over to her. 'Sergeant.' He needed to treat her like she wanted to be. 'Have you seen DI Elliot?'

Jolene looked up from her laptop, gave him a withering glare, then went back to it. 'Who are you?'

'DI Rob Marshall.'

She turned around again. 'Oh, sorry, sir. Didn't recognise you. Aren't you off the case?'

'I am, but I need to speak to Andrea about another matter. So, have you seen her?'

'Think she's down in Hawick. Or up in Edinburgh.'

'Which?'

'I don't know, sir. Sorry.'

'That doesn't help.'

'Sorry, sir. She's got me pulling together evidence for the charge sheet, so I need to get on with it.' She switched her focus back to her laptop.

'On you go, Sergeant.' Marshall stood up tall again.

'Thanks, sir.' She went back to hunching over her laptop.

Marshall took the seat two behind her. Gave him a view of what she was up to and meant she couldn't see what he was doing. He shook the mouse and – bloody hell – the machine was locked to Police Scotland. His Met login wouldn't work here.

He tried it and proved his theory. Brilliant.

He looked up and now Jolene was on the phone to someone.

Jen was understandably overreacting and Marshall wanted to help. After what they'd both been through, a teenage girl going missing in the summer didn't leave the best feeling. He needed to nip this in the bud. Track Thea's phone location and find her.

But to do that, he needed help.

Marshall waited until she put her phone back down. 'Sergeant, is DS Siyal still on?'

'Shunty? Why do you want that clown?'

'He's a good officer.'

She rolled her eyes and went back to her laptop. 'Sure.'

'Listen, if you want some advice, parroting DI Elliot's

name-calling isn't going to get you far. Treat him like a human being and you'll earn respect.'

'I'm sorry, sir. He's a good guy, just needs toughening up. That's all it is.'

'Make sure you toughen him and don't break him, okay?'

'Of course. But you've got the wrong end of the stick when it comes to Andi. She's a great cop. Really helped my career. Really good friend too.'

'Glad to hear it. Do you know where he is?'

'Downstairs, interviewing the suspect. Gather he's saying nothing, mind.'

Marshall wouldn't be able to get Siyal to leave that interview, not with all the pressure from above. He had to hope Jolene had a better nature he could appeal to, so he walked over and sat next to her. 'Listen, I need a favour. My niece, Thea, has gone missing. It's probably nothing, but... I need to find her. Can you run her phone records for me?'

'Are you serious?'

'A hundred percent. Please. I'm desperate here.'

'Have you got a warrant?'

Marshall stared hard at her. 'Sergeant, this is a small favour.'

'She's your niece, though. This sounds like bollocks. I can't just do that.'

'If it is bollocks, then great. I'll have found her and you'll be due a favour from me. But if it's not, you were ordered to by me. None of it's going to stick to you.'

Even Marshall didn't believe it.

'What's her number?'

Aye, either she was daft or she could see a favour owed by a senior officer was a good thing.

Marshall scribbled it down on a Post-It and stuck it to the top of her screen.

'Thank you.' She typed it into a box and it disappeared, replaced with a warning that Marshall couldn't quite read. 'Must be tough for you, sir. An ex-colleague going rogue like that? Doesn't feel good, does it?'

'You got experience of it?'

'A bit.' She sniffed but didn't seem to want to get any further into it. Might explain her attitude if someone had stretched things a bit far in the past. 'Your niece's phone is off. And has been since lunchtime.'

'What's her last-known location?'

'Innerleithen. Last activity is two texts to her parents, sent just before it was turned off. Could've sent any number of WhatsApps, mind. They're encrypted and we can't get at the content. Getting the metadata needs a warrant.'

Still, that stacked up.

But didn't give him any way of finding her, save for scouring the area around Innerleithen. The Tweed valley, filled with cyclists nowadays.

So someone would've seen her.

But that's all he had on it.

'Where's her last location?'

'Looks like it's on the high street.' Jolene clicked on her laptop and the screen filled with a map of the town, overlaid with a blue circle. 'That's where the cell site places her.'

A big area.

She could get a bus to Gala or Peebles.

Peebles would be her school, where her friends were. Besides, his mother was out that way – she was like a bloodhound when it came to errant teenagers.

'Have you got access to the CCTV inside the bus station in Galashiels?'

Jolene raised her eyebrows. 'Are you kidding me?'

'I'm serious. It should've been done as part of the investigation.'

'It has been, aye. But this is really stretching things, sir.'

'Humour me. It'll get me out of your hair.'

She shook her head, but worked away at her machine. 'It'll take me a minute or two to find.'

'Thank you.'

'She could've got off at Walkerburn, Clovenfords or Wood Street on the way there.'

'Let's see if she's there.'

'You're the boss.'

Onscreen, the bus arrived and Thea was first off.

Marshall felt a jolt of— Something. Not relief, but hope.

She walked across to another stance and got on a waiting bus.

Jolene tapped a finger off the screen. 'That's going to Jedburgh.'

And Marshall wouldn't get any resource to hunt her down. Just him and Jen.

Marshall had no idea what she was doing going to Jedburgh. He hauled himself up to standing. 'Okay, thank you for this. Let's call it two favours.'

A dialogue box popped up and Jolene frowned at it. 'Weird.'

'What's up?'

'I've just run that number and, at one o'clock, your niece called a phone number that's flagged on the system. The burner used to call Derek Cameron on Saturday night.'

CHAPTER FIFTY-EIGHT

Marshall stood in the tiny observation suite, his mouth dry. The place stank of Pot Noodle and regret.

Jolene might've been a help with the telephony, but she had no idea where her boss was. Not in Hawick or in Edinburgh, but in the interview room downstairs, sitting next to Siyal.

Opposite John Hulse.

Elliot's voice boomed out of the speakers. 'Caroline Reynolds.'

'Who?'

'Come on, John, you can't keep playing it that way.'

'No idea. Sorry.'

'You might be surprised to learn that she survived her ordeal. She lived through it. We've spoken to her. She identified *two* men. One was Derek Cameron, but the other... Bit of a mystery on that score. It was you, wasn't it?'

Hulse shook his head.

Marshall needed to get out of the room, knock on the door and speak to Elliot.

Tell her what he'd just found, beg for her help.

Thea hadn't run off.

Hulse had taken her.

He felt sick, his stomach churning as though he'd drank some off milk.

Marshall loosened his shirt's top button, but kept the clip-on tie in place. Did up his suit jacket, even though it was melting in here.

He got it now – the heating wasn't failing automatically; Elliot had pumped it up to get Hulse to sweat.

It wouldn't work – Marshall had sat in baking London afternoons with him and he'd put on layers rather than taken them off.

Marshall left the obs suite and hurried along the corridor. He knocked on the glass and waited, fidgeting with his cufflinks.

The interview room door opened and Elliot squinted out. 'What?' Then she focused on him. 'Marshall? What are you still doing here?'

'Just wanted to know how it's going with him.'

Elliot shut the door behind her and stepped down the corridor, away from the interview. 'Trouble with interviewing ex-cops is they know how to keep quiet.'

'So you're getting nowhere?'

'Aye, and very fast.' She licked her lips. 'Why are you still lurking around?'

'My niece is missing. Thea Armstrong.'

'And you thought you'd—'

'Turns out she called... Well, the burner that rang Derek Cameron on Sunday night. Lured him to his death. Thea called it just after one.'

'We picked Hulse up at half three down near Hexham.'

'Plenty of time to meet her, abduct her and take her somewhere on the way, then get back home.'

Elliot's forehead pulsed with shock. 'Does he know her because of you?'

'Andrea, I've got no explanation for why Thea would be calling him.'

'Jesus Christ.' Elliot ran her hand through her hair, slicked with sweat. 'Hulse was working with Cameron. If there were two of them... Christ. Another victim. We thought it was over, but...' She fixed him with a hard stare. 'How sure are you about this?'

'Thea fits the victim profile.' Marshall tried to physically distance himself from her, to get some objectivity. 'Vulnerable because her parents are divorcing and she's going to a new school, living miles away from her pals. Lots of opportunities there.'

Elliot paced down the corridor, then swung back to Marshall, arms folded. 'How did he find her?'

'I don't know. John was my partner and... Christ, he met her a few years ago, down in London.'

'Okay, that's one thing. But how did he find Thea? Social media?'

'Could've done, aye. Kirsten and Jolene are going through it all for me now. Thing is, he's been lurking around the Borders. We've got a few sightings of him in Melrose and Gala.' Felt like the snake was climbing up his throat. 'My sister bumped into him at the hospital. Met him for a coffee.'

'Jesus.'

'Andrea. Let me speak to him.'

Elliot looked at him, eyes narrower than ever. 'I can't.'

'I worked with John for years. I know him. How he ticks. How to get him to open up, so his grunts become syllables.

I'm an advanced interviewer. I can get inside his mind. Please. It's not because she's my niece, it's the fact there's another victim out there. She could be anywhere. And only he knows where.'

Elliot looked down the corridor, like that could give her answers. A bead of sweat slid down her forehead. Then she stared back at Marshall, hard. 'Okay.' She grabbed his shoulder. 'I'll cover you interviewing him, but do it by the book. Okay?'

'Don't know how else to do it. Thank you, Andrea.' A final nod and he entered the room.

Like going into a sauna. Tiny, with no windows. Stifling heat – he could feel the radiator blasting out from the doorway.

Siyal was scribbling in his notebook.

The lawyer was doing the same. An old guy in brown tweed who looked like he'd given up on life.

Marshall turned back to Elliot. 'Can you turn the heating off, please?'

'Sure.' She shut the door and he heard her footsteps thudding away down the hall.

Siyal looked over at Marshall. Then restarted the recorder. 'DI Rob Marshall has entered the room.'

Hulse was focused on a fixed space on the wall, arms folded, mouth closed. Barely breathing, like a hibernating bear.

Marshall sat down opposite and tried to make eye contact, but Hulse wasn't playing ball. Like he was staring through Marshall.

'John, John, John.' Marshall shook his head. 'We've been friends for a few years. Colleagues for as long.' He left a pause. No reaction. 'And I trusted you, John. Thought you were a good man and a better cop. Honest. Dependable. Reliable. I've dealt with more than my fair share of stuff, as you know, but I've never been so let down by anyone in my life as I have been by you, right now.'

Hulse blinked.

'Not for one second did I think you were capable of abduction, rape and murder.'

Nothing.

'All the time we were hunting for Derek Cameron, you were working *with* him.'

Nothing, not even a blink.

'You knew Kate Pierce was alive, didn't you?'

Hulse's forehead twitched.

'You knew she was inside that garage. You'd visited there to rape her with Derek Cameron. But you didn't lead us there afterwards. I mean, sure, you were in a hospital bed, but you were able to talk. Instead of passing on her location, John, you let her die because you were worried she'd identify you.'

Hulse still said nothing. But he was blinking more frequently now.

'John, you're going to prison for your part in this. There's no escaping that. We've got a *ton* of evidence on you.'

'Nope.'

Speaking was good. 'That burner's yours, isn't it?'

'What burner?'

'You used it to set up the meeting with Cameron.' Marshall left a long pause, the only sound the brushing of Siyal's pen against the notebook. 'And now I find my niece called you?'

Hulse looked at him. 'What?'

'That burner had a call from Thea. One minute and seventeen seconds. It's yours, John. What were you doing?'

'No idea what you're talking about.'

'You can deny it all you want, John, but we all know you're lying. All of us. Even your lawyer here. Maybe you deny it to yourself, but on some level you must feel guilty for helping

Derek Cameron, for working with him, for covering up for him, for *raping* and *killing* all those women.'

Hulse shut his eyes.

'You cope with it by denying it to yourself. It never happened. Nope. "Not me, guv." But it did, John. You worked with Cameron. And I should've known Cameron had an accomplice. Abducting and dumping all those victims without getting caught is too complex for one man to pull off. He needed an inside man, someone who knew the operational procedures, who could fudge evidence trails, knew how to scrub a crime scene and who could warn him. You were leaking the investigation to him!'

Hulse opened his eyes again, but he looked like a lost child. He was close to breaking. Close to confessing.

Marshall leaned forward. 'John, speak to me.'

Hulse sat back, arms folded. 'Saying nothing.'

So close...

Needed another way to crack his shell.

'John, it's much better for you to get this off your chest.'

'I haven't done anything! I was working all morning.'

'Up here in the Borders.'

'No!'

'Come on, John. She called you. The location was just south of Galashiels.'

'Not me. At home. Reading.'

'Can you prove that?'

Hulse looked up, then scanned the corners of the room. 'I...'

'John, you met her two years ago. Jen and Thea stayed at my flat in London. They were going to that West End play, then getting the train to Paris. It was just before the incident with Cameron... Is that when you started planning on abusing her?'

'No.'

'She was fourteen then.' Marshall left another gap.

Looked like Hulse was going to fill it, going to say something, but he just shut his eyes again.

'An ex-cop grooming a *child*.'

Hulse shifted his focus to the tabletop. Scratching at the wood with his fingernail.

'She was *fourteen*, John. *Fourteen!*'

Hulse clenched his fists.

'And then you met Jen for a coffee recently. Was that to find out about Thea's life? To repeat what Cameron did in London? Building up that picture, where you knew precisely when you could take her?'

Hulse shook his head.

'How did you start with him?'

'Who?'

'Derek Cameron. How did you get involved with him?'

Hulse shook his head again.

'The man who shot you. Who got you retired from the force. Who made you limp. Made you struggle to breathe. What I really don't get is why you'd rape women with him. Why? Why, John? Just tell me.'

'Jesus, Rob, it's not me.'

'John, I'd love to believe you, but why does all the evidence point to you?'

Hulse banged his fists off the table.

A crack in the shell.

Humour him.

'Okay, so why was your phone on in Melrose on Sunday night to call him?'

'It's not mine!'

'You met Cameron, didn't you? Killed him, didn't you?'

Silence.

'John, Wendy Malcolm was blindfolded and forced to have

sex with two men. We know Cameron was one of them. Were you the other?'

More shaking of his head.

'You were in league with him back in London, weren't you? Leaking information to him, right? How many women did you rape in that garage in Surbiton, eh? You could've saved Kate Pierce! We found her body, John. *I* found it! You could've saved her. John, you could've saved her!'

Hulse sat back, arms folded, eyes clamped shut.

Keeping quiet. Still denying it. His training kicking in.

If Marshall didn't smash his shell open soon, the crack would heal up. 'John, Derek Cameron left Wendy tied up in his garage in Galashiels. She would've died if we hadn't found her. Help me. Where is Thea?'

Hulse looked right into his eyes. 'I don't know.'

Marshall almost believed him. 'You've got her, John! Where is she?'

'I don't know where she is! I've never met her!'

'I need to save her, John. You can help me. Otherwise, Thea will die, John, a brutal and slow death. Tell me where she is, John. I'm begging you, man. She's my *niece*. I've not been the best uncle, not recently, but please, for the love of goodness, tell me where she is.'

Hulse slumped forward, his elbows cracking off the table. 'I've groomed nobody. I don't even remember meeting Thea at your flat. Was I even there?'

'You drove them to King's Cross to get the train home.'

'I don't remember it.'

'Do you remember meeting my sister for a coffee?'

'No.'

'You didn't meet anyone for a coffee at the hospital?'

'No. I... Maybe. I don't know.'

Marshall stood up. 'I give up. You're talking shite, John. I've tried, but you're going to rot away in prison.' He walked over to the door. Then stopped and slowly turned back around. 'I'll ask you one. Last. Time. Where is Thea?'

'I don't know. And that's the truth.'

Marshall could tell Hulse believed it. Trouble is, he didn't. Not yet. 'John, where is she?'

'No.'

'You can save Thea, John. Just talk to us, okay?'

'I don't know where she is.'

Marshall walked back over to him, standing over him. 'None of this stacks up, okay? Please. Just tell me what's going on.'

'I can't.'

'John, your car was seen outside Cameron's house. Saturday night until Sunday. You've been identified.'

Hulse swallowed hard.

'Talk to me.'

'I want to, but... Only you.'

'Because you think you can get it kicked out of court if you talk only to me?'

'No, because you're the only person I can trust.'

Either he was appealing to Marshall's seemingly notorious ego, or he meant it.

Marshall sat down again. 'So talk to me.'

Hulse sat there, shaking his head.

'John, you're in deep trouble here. You need to talk to me. It's your only way out.'

Hulse looked at his lawyer. 'Give us a minute.'

'But I don't—'

'Get. Out.'

The lawyer stood up, then grabbed his stuff and left the room.

Hulse shifted his focus from the door to Siyal. 'You too.'

Siyal checked with Marshall, got a nod, then followed the lawyer out of the room.

Marshall waited for the door to click, then smiled at Hulse. 'Now are you going to talk?'

Hulse reached over and stopped the recorder.

'Just you and me, eh?'

Hulse was looking right at him.

Marshall got a jolt of fear. He wasn't the most physical of cops, whereas Hulse was. Or used to be. Right now, it'd be a reasonably equal match. He'd just have to hold out. And keeping him talking was the best way of doing that. 'Where were you this afternoon, John?'

'At home. You came and arrested me.'

'Before that.'

'Fare. Hexham to Edinburgh airport. First thing. One way.'

'Why didn't they fly from Newcastle?'

'Funeral in Reykjavik in Iceland. Two flights a week from Edinburgh, one from Newcastle. Didn't get much choice.'

'Sounds convoluted. And you said you were reading.'

'I was before that.'

'Okay, after your fare, you were free and in this area.' Marshall made a circle around them with his fingers. 'Got a call from my niece. Abducted her. Have you raped her yet?'

Hulse clenched his jaw so tight his teeth crunched. 'Went straight home. Then you came. Then all this bullshit.'

'John, we have a ton of evidence against you. Cameron's neighbour has identified you. You spoke to her. She saw you knocking on his door. What am I supposed to think?'

'You want the truth?'

'No, John, I'd rather you kept on lying through your teeth about this.'

Hulse leaned back, stretched out then rested his elbows on the table edge. 'Been hunting for Cameron. What he did to those women, partly, but mostly because of what he did to me. Can't breathe some days. And I'm in so much pain. I just wanted to find him. Catch him. Stop him.'

'How did you know he was up here?'

'I didn't. Then I read about Karla Ewing. Matched the MO, more or less. Did some digging. Found Caroline Reynolds. She survived. I approached her, but she wouldn't speak to me. Then I lucked out. Did a deep dive on their social media. Caroline had posted a photo on Facebook. At a barbecue in a friend's garden. Cameron was in the background.'

'You're sure it was him?'

'Two days before she was abducted. Nine before she was found, barely alive. It was a lead.'

'Why didn't you go to the cops?'

'This was only Thursday last week, Rob. I'm not a vigilante. I was going to report it. I just wasn't *sure* it was him. Needed to make sure.'

'So prove it to me.'

Hulse rubbed his fingers off his palms, looking around the room. 'I posted the photo of him on a dummy account and Facebook did that facial recognition thing, pinning Cameron's face to a couple of accounts. Declan Connolly. Callum Davidson. Both lived in Galashiels. He had accounts on there so his victims could check them out. See him with his dog or as a member of some art groups or at a wedding or whatever. He was so thorough, but that's where his MO fell apart, because I knew it was him. So I catfished one of the accounts. When that didn't work, I tried the other. I pretended to be Taylor McKay, a girl who matched his victimology. Made up some stuff, got a photo off a website. Taylor joined this online art group Declan Connolly was in. And Taylor got him interested. Exchanged a few messages. Taylor suggested they meet. Cameron insisted we speak on the phone first.'

'You called him on that burner?'

'That's not mine, Rob.'

'But you arranged to meet him on the viaduct?'

'No.'

'Come on, John. You were doing so well. Why start lying again?'

'Because I'm telling you the truth here.'

'Okay, continue.'

'I didn't call it because I thought it was a burner. Didn't want him to smell a rat until I knew it was.' Hulse grinned wide, pleased with his detective work. 'An old Met contact who owed me one tracked his number. Gave me everything I needed. Wasn't even a burner. A contract job. Cell sites, texts, calls, you name it. All were in Galashiels. Langlee. Trouble is, you don't get a specific location, you get a circle. It could've been any number of flats in three blocks, or a few other houses around there. So I pretended I had fares up to the Borders and staked out the area.'

'Sounds like bullshit to me, John.'

'It's not. Cameron came home on Saturday night. I knew where he lived. But I didn't strike. Saw him talking to this woman. I waited. So I spoke to her. Phoebe, her name is. Said she's friends with Dec. One of the Facebook profiles. Anyway, I pretended to be his long-lost friend. Wanted to surprise Dec for his fortieth birthday. Swore her to secrecy.' He was scratching at the table again. 'Cameron was doing it again, wasn't he? I needed to stop it. So I followed him in his van.'

'Where did he go?'

'I don't know. His van was turbo charged. He disappeared. I followed the A7 all the way up to Gorebridge, but I must've lost him on any number of back roads.'

Marshall swallowed down his gasp. 'This was Saturday?'

'Sunday. I'd sat outside all night, toying over whether to

call the cops. Decided to. But he didn't come back. Thought he'd run. Again.'

'Wendy Malcolm was inside a garage. Wendy was inside that van.'

'Shit.' Hulse stood and yelped with pain. 'Jesus Christ.'

'If you'd called, the police would've saved her a lot earlier. Her chances of pulling through would be a lot higher. As it was, we could've never found her.' Marshall raised a hand. 'You'd done all this clandestine investigation, beat the cops at their own game. Well done.' He clapped.

Hulse snorted.

'But forget about that. What did you do?'

'Nothing.'

'Nothing?'

'Nothing. I was going to return, but you called. Told me Cameron was dead. Felt relieved.'

Marshall's breath was stuck in his throat. 'Cameron was there to meet someone. Was that you, John?'

Hulse locked eyes with him. 'No.'

Marshall sat back in his chair. Arms folded. He had no idea what to think. John Hulse wasn't one to lie, but it all seemed so—

No.

It felt true. All of it. The clandestine investigation. The regret over not calling it in. It fitted with the person he knew.

But it still left questions.

Who was Cameron meeting up there?

Who had Thea?

Hulse must've been telling the truth about the burner. The timings didn't quite work.

So who had Thea been calling? Was it the same person?

Marshall leaned forward. 'John, this is all good stuff. Nicely worded, a well-crafted story. I'm willing to believe it, but I need proof. Is there anything to back this up?'

'No.'

'You know how this all looks. The Procurator Fiscal and the SIO want to charge you.'

'Rob. I'm asking you to prove it wasn't me.'

CHAPTER FIFTY-NINE

Kirsten sat behind Elliot's desk, her fingers dancing across the keyboard of her laptop. 'Fingers crossed.'

Marshall held up his hands, crossing the index and middle fingers on both.

Elliot's office was back down to a human temperature. The window hung almost horizontal, letting in both the evening's cold and the shouts of drunk teens in the park.

Where Thea should be.

Not should. She shouldn't be drunk, but she should be free to hang out with her friends. Not be stuck somewhere, at the whims of—

Who?

If it wasn't Hulse, who was it?

Elliot nudged the door open and handed Marshall a coffee, the steam billowing up between them. 'I know we shouldn't have caffeine this late, but hey ho. I have a feeling this is going to be a long one.'

Marshall took his cup and sipped the acidic instant. Beggars can't be choosers. 'Thanks.'

'Thank Shunty, not me.' She drank hers like it wasn't boiling. 'Do you think your lying, raping, killing pal's on the level?'

'Andrea, I need to know if Hulse is telling the truth. Trouble is, Hulse's story checks out, to a certain extent. Nothing against it, but it's not conclusive either.' Marshall took another sip and grimaced. 'But John's always been a loose cannon. Had a reputation before I took over. I tamed him, but he's still a wild horse at heart.'

'There are loose cannons and then there's what he is.' But he could tell from her grimace that she wasn't going to change her mind. Or she wouldn't admit it if she did. The way she said it backed up what he'd heard from Jolene. Something went down here – something changed a lot of people. 'You got some previous with this kind of thing?'

Elliot sipped coffee instead of answering. Now wasn't the time, clearly.

'Uncross those fingers, boys and girls.' Kirsten clicked both of hers. 'We're in.'

Elliot set her coffee down on a stack of paperwork. *My other mug is a vase*. 'In what?'

'Luck.' Her screen was filled with an image. Caroline Reynolds held a greasy burger with both hands, ketchup and mustard smeared all over her face. A summery scene. As summery as it got in Scotland. Friends behind her on the lawn, clutching bottles of beer or glasses of wine.

Derek Cameron was right there.

Not aware he was being photographed. Jeans, trainers, Arsenal T-shirt. Dark blue with cyan writing. 1886. The one he was found wearing.

Marshall tapped the screen. 'What's that mean?'

'In relation to Arsenal?' Kirsten googled Arsenal+1886 and the screen filled with information.

In 1886, Dial Square FC were founded by munitions

workers at the Woolwich Arsenal in south-east London, which they soon changed their name to. They became Arsenal when they moved to north London later on.

Which got Marshall thinking...

'Kirsten, is that USB drive still here?'

'You're lucky.' Kirsten leaned forward to focus on her computer. 'It was imaged this afternoon.'

'Still encrypted?'

'Correct.'

'Can you try that as a code?'

'What? 1886?'

'Aye.'

'Okay...' She messed about with her keyboard then got in. 'Holy shit, that worked.'

'What?' Elliot clattered her coffee down on the table, spilling it everywhere. 'You're into his drive?'

'Just looking through it now.' Her screen was filled with a single directory. 'It's... Photos and video files.' She swallowed hard. 'Oh god. The names. Erin, Caroline, Karla, Deanna.'

Despite the cool room, a bead of sweat ran down Marshall's spine. Names he recognised from London, some from the trail north, and others he didn't.

Becky was timestamped in the gap between Surbiton and Northwich.

Marshall looked at Elliot. 'We need to cross-match Becky against missing persons from the south of England, the Midlands, around Manchester. Anywhere in England, basically.'

'I'll get Jolene on it.' Elliot got out her phone. 'Can you open them?'

Kirsten took a deep breath. 'You sure about this? Because this feels too easy. The number on a T-shirt he was wearing in a photo unlocks all of this?'

Elliot shrugged. 'It was what he was wearing when we found him.'

'Those sticks weren't for him, they were for us.' Marshall could see it all now. 'He wants to confess. He wants us to know who, why. All of it. He couldn't open up to us, but he knew he was dying. This is his way of telling us.'

'Okay, then.' Kirsten double clicked on Caroline1.jpg and the screen filled with a scene from hell.

Caroline Reynolds, the surviving Longtown victim, was resting on a workbench, tied up and gagged. Looked like the same place as Wendy Malcolm.

Marshall tapped the screen. 'That's the garage in Galashiels.'

Elliot leaned forward, squinting. 'Think you could be right on that score. Not that long a drive from Longtown to Gala. And he did it both ways. Abduction then... dropping her off after he thought he'd killed her.' She pointed at the screen. 'There's an arch there, isn't there?'

Marshall could see it. 'So this isn't where we found Wendy. He had access to more than one garage.'

Kirsten opened up the next image.

A different angle of Caroline, but a man's naked hip was in the foreground. His hip was a mess, all bloody and raw.

Elliot winced. 'That's our guy.'

Derek Cameron.

Marshall crouched next to Kirsten. Something caught his eye. 'Can you zoom in?' He circled the area on the far side of the image.

'Here you go.'

The section of the image blew up, but it didn't help any. There was maybe a figure there, but it was too dark to make anyone out. Kirsten fiddled with the colour levels but it didn't help much.

Elliot picked up her coffee again. 'Could be Hulse.'

'Could be anyone.' Marshall stood up again. 'Could be a goblin up from his subterranean lair. Could be a vampire.' He caught Kirsten's grin. 'Can you go through them quickly?'

'Sure.' Kirsten opened another scene of hellish depravity, then another, then another. Again, again, again and again until it was a flipbook from Hell. All similar angles, focusing on the victim. 'He isn't showing up again.' Again, again, again.

Marshall felt sick.

The image changed and Caroline was liberated from her bonds. She looked dead, her head tilted to an angle. She was dead enough to fool Cameron. Not long after, she'd be dumped back near her workplace.

But hours later, she'd be recovering in hospital in Carlisle.

The next photo was Wendy Malcolm. Clothed, tied up. Out of it.

In the next one, she was naked, her bonds doubled and tightened. A rag stuffed in her mouth. Eyes open, but barely.

Next, a close-up of her face.

Then a portrait of Derek Cameron, his nose obscured by the giant play triangle.

A video.

Kirsten looked at them in turn, then clicked on it.

Cameron looked up, then down, then deep into the camera. 'This is one of those "if you're watching this, then I'm dead" videos. I bloody hope it is, otherwise you've caught me, figured it all out, got into my stash and I'm right in the stinking doo doo. But well done, whoever you are. You're probably a cop and you got the code off my T-shirt.'

He rubbed at the stubble on his chin, then snorted, hard like he had really bad hay fever or his septum was about to burst all over his hand. 'Here's the thing, I saw this criminal profile of the Chameleon in the papers. The cops think he's me, right? About how I have all these fantasies because of my upbringing. Tough relationship with Mum. Dad never on the scene. But they were barely right. The Met cops thought it was just me doing this, but it ain't. How wrong can you be?'

He laughed again. 'I was just following orders. Following the leader. I can see how it was now. How he made me do it. He was controlling me, manipulating me. Want to know how I know?'

He paused, like he was expecting an answer. 'I began stalking girls and playing mind games with them. Nothing too bad, really. I stopped it before it became physical. It's a power thing, knowing I can do it. Then it became physical. I became part of their lives, knew them better than they did themselves. Knowing where and when I could strike. But I stopped short, didn't I? Because I knew I'd get caught. So I stopped.'

He smirked. 'I had a difficult time growing up. Mum tried her best, but the odds were stacked against her. And my old man... And I wanted to kill him for what he'd put us through. Problem was, I was beaten to it by a heart attack. I went to his funeral, pretended I was some distant relative, and just sat there. Soaking it all in. I'm good at that. And it's amazing what people let slip when they're grieving, even if they don't mean to.'

He looked away from the camera. 'But I got chatting to this geezer. My old man's best mate. Would've been his best man if he'd married Mum. And we hit it off, actually. He was a good guy. Helped me forgive my old man for what he'd put me through. I learnt how tough his own life had been, and what my mum had put *him* through. You never know everything about a situation, do you? When they heard my dad had knocked up my old mum, her brothers kicked the shit out of him. Said he wasn't good enough for her.'

He banged his fist on the desk. 'Who the bloody hell do

they think they are, eh? Two pricks from Wembley who'd never worked an honest day in their life. And Dad was a bloody Dean at the college. Sure, my mum was a student and he shouldn't have done what he did with her, but he tried to do the right thing when she got in trouble.'

His mouth twisted up. 'So I could finally understand why Dad couldn't be in my life. Still angry with him for not taking me with him, but it wasn't his fault. Angry with him for not fighting it. And I could see why Mum was such a fuck up. Weren't her fault, neither. But...'

He sighed. 'My old man's mate, though, he's... I don't know how it happened, to be honest, but I started seeing him like he was my therapist. Talked to him about it. Why I did it. Obviously I told him it was just fantasies, but... but we soon discovered our mutual taste for certain things sexually. I don't mean in each other, right? We ain't bent. But what we like in ladies. Like I said, controlling them. I'm not stupid enough to deny any of that, but... The truth was, I wanted to see them suffer. He reckons it's me transferring some of my anger at my mum onto someone else.'

He folded his arms. 'Sharing that kind of thing doesn't just happen overnight, does it? No, you need to do it by inches. Over a few months, we'd meet up, go to the casino, chat up birds. Get into a few scrapes with them. And this one time, I saw this bird over in the corner, past the blackjack tables. She was paralytic with drink, but the bouncers didn't seem interested. I joked, saying I could do things to her. So he... He just went and did it. Acted the knight in shining armour, took her into a cab, took her to a hotel. And he... made me watch. And the things he did to her, they'd sicken you.'

Cameron ran a hand down his face. 'But that was it. I was hooked. My previous experiences had all been about following them. I mean, I was good at identifying victims, seeking out women I could get at, who I could isolate and do what I wanted to. That was what I got off on. The thrill of the chase, building this picture of their lives. But he got off on the act itself. The torture. The rape. The murder. I could list their names now, but where would be the fun in that? It's on this drive. Photos of them. My little note files on their lives.'

He smiled like he'd made a joke. 'Thing is, the cops should've caught us. We were stupid. Clueless, really. That girl in the casino was a bit naughty. We could've easily got caught for it. But we didn't. She was pumped full of so many drugs and pills that when we dumped her in a back street, she couldn't remember fuck all.'

He grimaced. 'Poor Erin was the first real one. I mean, I knew her. And the cops, those stupid sods, they interviewed me and let me go. Could never understand why, but my accomplice also seemed to have an ability to know where the police would be at any time. So he gave me an alibi and I got away. Gave them some cock and bull story that'd throw them off the scent. Cushty.'

He shook his head. 'Found Deanna on the bus. Bloody hell, she started talking to me and wouldn't shut up. Just gave me everything. And I kept on finding them. Girls like that.' He paused. 'Until the cops found me. They knew all about the buses. Just happened to be there. I was unprepared. Spooked me and I panicked. Shot that copper, didn't I? Meant to kill both of you, but I only had two bullets. Never fired a gun before. Fuck me, the noise and the kickback are... Only, he didn't bloody die. He was the first one I tried to kill myself.'

Elliot reached over and paused it. 'He's saying it wasn't Hulse?'

Marshall was staring at the frozen face on the screen.

Intentionally leaving a witness had screwed with Marshall's brain, thinking he was being toyed with. But it was just a mistake, a combination of his inexperience, Marshall's profile and his quick thinking with the seat release that saved his life..

And Cameron wasn't a killer yet then...

Was that true?

He looked over at Elliot. 'Could be he's trying to protect him.'

'Hmm.' Elliot hit play again.

'And now they knew who I was, so fuck me, I was on the run. Couldn't stay in London.' Cameron stared into the middle distance. 'So I moved to Birmingham. Easy to slip in there. But I still had the hunger. I found Becky. Took her, held her, but I couldn't end her life.'

Kirsten hit pause and looked up at Elliot. 'You want to update your search?'

'Please.' Elliot tapped out a message. 'That change anything in your profile, Rob?'

'My profile is all over the floor, Andrea.' Marshall reached over and pressed play again.

'Then I just did it. Killed her. Too easily, really.'

Marshall hit pause again. 'Cancel that update to the information request.'

Elliot hammered out another message. Queen of the texting. 'Play, please.'

Kirsten complied.

'I could feel the walls closing in, so I moved to a place near Manchester. And the bloodlust was strong again. Seems to ebb and flow. Moved to Kirkby Lonsdale. Same. Then Carlisle. Same.'

Marshall had to walk around the room. Couldn't face looking at him anymore. 'He's stepped out of his master's shadow. He's taking the lead now.'

'So he's not working with Hulse?'

Marshall shrugged. 'Maybe. His partner was the killer, he's now able to do it all himself. Stands to reason.'

Kirsten clicked the mouse again – Marshall hadn't seen her press play.

He reopened his eyes. 'I thought moving to Scotland would help. See, that's where my old man's from. Ross Cameron from Selkirk. But it didn't stop it. Trouble is, wherever you run, there you still are.'

He tugged at his septum. 'I was working this job on the roofs down in Longtown. Same thing happened as everywhere else. Found a girl, kidnapped her. Called him up and asked if he wanted to get the band back together, as it were. He couldn't resist. Turns out I'm not as good as I used to be because she's still alive. That's when I found out about my cancer. Trouble is, there was a problem with my NHS records. The bogus name I was using at the time didn't include anything medical and the hospital kept pushing me for my GP's information. So I had two options. Give them Derek Cameron's records and get dobbed in, or accept my fate. Rather live free.' He laughed. 'Rather die free. Accept death as a free man, rather than the rest of my life in prison.'

He shook his head. 'The diagnosis, though, made me reflect on my life. The things I've done. The crimes I've committed. I joined this church and it made it clear to me. I'm dying of cancer because I'm being punished for what I've done. I know I have to stop if I'm going to find redemption. I can't stand the pain anymore, so I know my time's coming. She has to be the last one.'

Cameron was actually crying. 'I need to repent for my sins and pay for what I've done. And he... He still wants to keep doing this. I need to stop him. He called me back and we're meeting up. We need to sort this out.'

Outside the office, rain battered off the open window.

Marshall walked over to nudge it.

'Thing is, he told me he's got another prospect. Some girl called Thea.'

Marshall froze. It all clicked into place, like gears in a clock.

After Surbiton, they'd split apart. Cameron had learnt his master's ways, learnt how to kill. And had done, a trail of dead through the northwest into southern Scotland, then they'd reconnected to inflict their torment on Caroline Reynolds.

Cameron jutted his chin out. 'So this is it, I'm going to meet him, try to persuade him that it's over. If he stops, great. Let's call it even, yeah? When I get back, I'll let Wendy go. I'll go to the cops. Confess it all. But if this goes south, then you've got this recording. Maybe you can put Graham Thorburn in prison.'

CHAPTER SIXTY

Marshall sat in the passenger seat, rocked by the car, numb to all physical sensations.

Graham Thorburn was Cameron's accomplice.

The words rattled around his skull.

It made sense – Derek Cameron's father had been a lecturer.

Must've been how he knew Thorburn, working in that same world.

The chance meeting at his funeral, the sharing of a predilection.

Jesus Christ.

Rain hammered off the windscreen.

Elliot's wipers couldn't keep up with it. She glanced over at him. 'You okay there?'

'Would've been much quicker walking.'

'Aye, sure. But if he's not there, then what? Walk back? Take the bus?' Elliot pulled in, just down the hill from Mum's house. 'How do you propose we play this?'

Marshall didn't have to think much. 'You wait outside with DS Siyal and uniform. I'll go in.'

'Not going to happen.'

'Please, I need to—'

'You can't, Rob. Because I can see what's going through your mind. You want to tear his limbs from his torso, then make him eat them. Or something worse. And you're family. Remember – you're here as an advisor. So stay out here, okay?'

'Fine.' Marshall sat back and folded his arms.

The car door clicked then slammed.

A few seconds, then Elliot passed over his line of sight. Knocking on the door. Flash of warrant card. Mum stepped out into the rain. Asked something, probably if they'd found Thea yet.

Marshall's phone blasted out.

DCI Tina Rickards calling...

He answered it. 'Boss?'

Sounded like she was in Piccadilly at rush hour, but it was probably just a busy incident room. 'You okay?'

'You really want to know, or do you just want an update?'

'Time and a place for feelings, I suppose.' She sighed. 'Listen, I've got the team here going through Cameron and Thorburn's backgrounds. Their friends and family, looking for anyone at that funeral. Don't have a record of a Ross Cameron ever working with Thorburn, but there is a Richard Cromarty, who changed his name from Ross Cameron by deed poll.'

'That figures. Cameron senior was on the run from Cameron's mother's brothers. And it maybe gave Cameron the idea to switch names.' Marshall felt a flaring of heat in his throat. 'Or Thorburn.'

'You're the expert. Not sure what it gives us.'

'Corroboration. What about finding anyone who would leak to them?'

Sounded like Rickards had stepped into a broom cupboard. Probably her office. 'I don't know, Rob. Could be anyone, despite how much trust I have in the team.'

But Marshall knew precisely who it was who'd leaked. 'It was me.'

'What was?'

'I leaked.'

'You what?'

'Accidentally. Thorburn helped update my profile. He knew it all because I'd told him.'

'I suppose you had approval from the Commissioner.'

'That's it?'

'What, do you want me to haul you over burning coals or something?'

Marshall didn't have anything. He was expecting to be fired. Maybe that would still happen. Right now, he was useful to them.

'Hold on a sec.' Sounded like the door opened and someone spoke. 'Thank you. Rob, we've connected Graham Thorburn to Deanna Casey.' Victim two. 'He taught at her university.'

Christ.

'Cameron said on his video he found her on the bus.'

'I suggest that Mr Thorburn put him up to it.'

Marshall looked over at the house, fire burning in his veins. Didn't look like Thorburn was in, though. Or that Mum was playing ball.

Marshall needed to help. 'Thank you, boss. That's... That's a lot to take in. I'll call you when we know more.'

'Likewise.' And she was gone.

Marshall sat back. He needed to get in there. Tear the house apart. He'd grown up there, lived with his sister, his mother and his grandparents until he left the town. He knew all the nooks and crannies in there. Where to hide *anything*. And where to find it.

Like Anna's journal...

He opened the door and rain splashed his leg.

His phone blasted out again.

Kirsten calling...

He answered it straight away. 'You okay?'

'Are *you* okay?'

'Not really.'

'You can talk to me about it.'

'I will. Just... You know?'

'Aye.' She paused. 'Listen, I'm going through the files on the stick and I've found some other information. There's a text file. A history of their victims, with dates and all the rest. Goes back twenty-five years.'

'That's too long, isn't it?' Marshall thought it through. 'Scratch that. Thorburn's sixty-two. He's been doing this for a long time.'

'Exactly. Anyway, the first victim... There's a document which goes into pornographic detail about how Graham Thorburn abused her over four years.'

'What's the name?'

Kirsten paused. 'I'm so sorry, Rob.'

The words couldn't come out.

'I am so, so sorry.'

Anna.

Anna was Thorburn's initial victim.

The pattern of exploiting vulnerable women began with her.

Her grief over her brother, who died in a motorbike accident, and the family moving from Kelso to Gattonside.

The abuse she'd suffered at the hands of her father.

And of course Thorburn had to kill her to shut her up.

'Thank you.' Marshall ended that call and pushed the door open wide. He stormed up the hill and went right up to his mother. 'Where is he?'

'I keep telling her, Robert, Graham's not home from work yet.'

'Let me in, Mum.'

'Oh, so *now* you want to come in?'

Sod it. She was getting the truth. Unvarnished.

'Mum, Graham has been abusing and killing women over a number of years, in London and elsewhere. He's a serial groomer of vulnerable young women. Then abducting. Raping. And killing them.'

'This isn't—'

'He started with Anna!'

Mum stopped her hysterics. Arms hung at her side. Mouth open.

'And I used to meet up with him when I worked in London. He was helping me build a profile on Anna's death. The profile was on himself! And he was gleaning information about the case against him.' Marshall felt like he was going to throw up all over the doorstep. Not for the first time, but right now he was stone-cold sober. 'And now Graham's been grooming Thea.'

'That's nonsense!'

'Mum, it's not. We've got evidence. Please. Do the right thing here. Tell us where he is before it's too late for Thea.'

'Can't.'

'I'm begging you. Tell us where he is.'

'I can't tell you because I don't know!'

'Mum, he's a monster, the monster who abducted, raped and killed Anna. Another six in London. Others. And he's kidnapped your granddaughter. Where is he?'

'I don't know.'

'Does he have a phone?'

'Of course he does. He's just not answering it.'

'Give me the number.'

'I wish you'd say please once in a while.' She held out her phone.

Marshall snatched it out of her grasp. 'Thank you.' He got his own out and called Kirsten, rain running down his face. 'Need you to run a number. Last known location would be ideal.'

CHAPTER SIXTY-ONE

The trouble with tracking phones by the cell towers they connected to was you invariably got a large search area. Some could track to three metres, but never when you needed them to.

This one was hard to cut down quickly, despite the manpower Elliot was throwing at it – must be half of the local cops out.

Other end of Melrose from Marshall's home, big posh houses that used to house mill owners or their professionals.

Part of the team spread out down towards the houses on the path overlooking the Tweed.

Others were going door-to-door on the road. Canvassing. Getting witnesses. The kind of work Marshall hadn't really done himself as a cop, but had come to value both as a profiler and a senior officer. Sometimes the smallest sighting blew everything wide open.

Elliot held a brolly up, keeping herself dry. Didn't seem to want to offer it to Marshall. 'Getting nothing here, Rob.'

Marshall scanned the area again. A ridiculous number of

churches of all flavours. No idea what they used to do around here, but it took a lot of repenting for the sins the locals incurred. 'Have you got people inside the churches?'

'The ones on High Cross, aye.'

The fork in the road that wound round to Darnick, the very slow way out of town.

The big church on the other side was older than the others and swaddled in scaffolding, climbing up almost to the top of the spire. The graves must've been shifted from the grounds as there was a lot of housing going up around it. From the photo-realistic illustrations, the church was going to become executive apartments.

'What about that one?'

She held up her phone. 'Can't get hold of him.'

'Hold of who?'

'Tam MacDougall.'

'He owns it?'

'He manages it on behalf of the owners.'

'Andrea, he owned Cameron's garage in Gala.' Cogs whirred in Marshall's head, slotting pieces into place. 'This is how he got the derelict buildings for Cameron.' He marched over the road towards it. 'Are Methods of Entry on shift?'

'On call, aye. But we can't just—'

'We need in there now.'

'We don't know if—'

'Come on, we've got reasonable cause. Your pal Tam must be connected to Graham Thorburn somehow.'

'Bloody hell.' Elliot got out her police radio and spoke into it. She scowled. 'They'll be an hour.'

'We don't have an hour. We don't really have minutes.'

Elliot turned and waved. 'Over here!'

Two big men ran over. One was lithe and strong, with a hard look to him. The other was DS Siyal.

'One thing that clown's good at is getting into buildings.' Elliot waited for them to join them, then clicked a finger and pointed at the church. 'In, now.'

Siyal frowned. 'Ma'am, that should be Methods of Entry's—'

'They're on their way, but it's going to take too long. I need that door open. If she's not in there, I'll take the heat. Okay?'

'Okay.' Siyal walked over to a squad car and got out a red battering ram, then lugged it up the path towards the church, clinking like a bag of work tools.

The other big lump hit upon the genius idea of trying the door.

It opened to a crack.

'Christ, Craig.' Siyal dropped the battering ram onto the flagstones. 'Could've tried that before I went to get this.'

Craig laughed. 'Shunty, man, you'll be the death of me.'

Siyal got into position by the door. He held up his gloved hand and counted down on his fingers.

Five.

Four.

Three.

Two.

One.

He hauled the door back and let Craig enter first, then slipped inside himself.

Seconds later, Siyal stepped back out and was waving at them.

Elliot and Marshall hurried over and Marshall got inside first.

The old church was dark and empty, the pews long since removed. Streetlights shone in from the left side, dowsing a table in red and white light from the stained glass.

Siyal and Craig stood either side of it, obscuring the view.

Marshall stepped forward until he was just behind them.

Someone was tied to a chair, not moving. Way too old and way too male to be Thea.

His head lifted up.

Graham Thorburn.

What the hell?

Marshall raced forward, but Siyal stopped him with his hand.

Something glinted to the side. A figure stepped forward. A serrated knife glinted.

Siyal clicked on a torch and caught Thea's face.

Marshall felt a stabbing in his throat.

He'd rushed here expecting her to be a damsel in distress, but here she was, abducting the abductor.

She dropped the knife with a clatter that rattled around the large space, then rushed over to Marshall, burying herself in his arms.

He wrapped them around her, half to comfort her, half to make sure she didn't have second thoughts.

Big Craig and Siyal jerked into action, working away at Thorburn's bonds.

Marshall held Thea by the wrists. 'You did the right thing.'

'I'm sorry, I…' She twisted to look back over at Thorburn, then nodded at Marshall. 'Thank God you're here.'

'Thea, it's okay.'

She collapsed into his arms again. 'You don't know what he's done!'

'No, I do know. We know everything he's done.'

'He took Wendy!'

'Thea, we know.' Marshall tilted his head to the side. 'You knew her?'

Thea nodded. 'In my year at school.'

'You were at Peebles, right?'

'So was she. Moved to Selkirk after her mum died, but stayed at the same school. Unlike my mum, her dad *could* be arsed to drive her there every day. She left last year.' Thea broke off and looked at Thorburn, as Siyal undid his bonds. 'I saw him speaking to Wendy at the school gates when he collected me a couple of times. Flirty. Seedy. I tried to talk to Mum about it, but she brushed it off – he's just a friendly man. I mean, sure, he's creepy AF, but he's Granny's boyfriend, right?'

'Thea, I totally agree. And we know what he's done. Thea, we've got evidence linking him to—'

'I've got evidence myself! You have no idea what I've seen!'

'What have you seen?'

She shifted her focus to him. 'Brutal stuff. Sick stuff. I...' She stared at Marshall again. 'You know how I got his old computer to help with schoolwork? He thought he'd cleared it out. Deleted everything from it... When I lost my essay, I did what you asked. I tried to recover my files, but I undeleted... I... I found his trove of depravity.' She glared at her uncle. 'Do you know what he does?'

'I do, Thea. We do. We've seen the images ourselves. He's sick. He'll be going to prison for a very long time. Probably never be released. He's killed at least six women, possibly another five before Wendy Malcolm.'

'He killed her?'

'You don't know she's still alive?'

Thorburn was looking at them, mouth wide. 'What happened?'

'Don't lie to me, Graham. You know.'

'I swear I don't. I tried to get Derek to stop but he wouldn't listen. I... And then I found out about Wendy and I was trying to find her!'

Thea swept her gaze between them, finally settling on Marshall. 'What's he talking about?'

'He didn't do this alone, Thea, but we have a witness saying he killed his partner in crime. He will go to prison.'

Her lip curled up. 'My God.'

'What happened here, Thea?'

'I wanted to find Wendy. I thought... I'd seen a show on Netflix where someone didn't speak and this missing guy died. I needed to get him talking. So I called him and met him and thought I could get him to confess. But he... He had a knife and he held me. Asked me what I knew. Then... I kicked him in the balls. Tied him up to get the truth out of him. But my phone battery died and... I didn't want him to get away. I couldn't leave him. He said he didn't know where Wendy was.'

'We'll go over this all later. Okay? Don't beat yourself up. It'll all be fine.'

The door thudded as Elliot and Kirsten entered the church.

Marshall beckoned Kirsten over and leaned in to Thea. 'Kirsten here's my friend. We need to get those files you found. Can you go with her and show her the laptop?'

'Okay.' Thea led Kirsten over to a backpack. Kirsten attached a tag to it, then took a series of photos of her taking a laptop out. 'Come on, then. I might need a bit of help finding the files once I've taken a copy of this machine, okay?' She left the place with Thea. 'You look like you need a cup of tea.'

'Coffee, please.'

'Sure thing.' Kirsten led her out of there. In a few minutes they'd be back in the station.

'Christ, what did she tie these with?' Big Craig was trying to cut the cable ties with a Stanley knife. 'He must've got these from Guantanamo.' He wasn't getting anywhere. 'Shunty, go back to the motor and get the bolt cutters?'

'You do it.' Siyal seemed to stand that little bit taller. 'I'm the sergeant. Not you.'

'Fine.' Craig strolled off outside, shaking his head.

Elliot raised her eyebrows at Siyal. 'Can you escort Kirsten back to the station, please?'

'But I—'

'She's a civilian. Need you to supervise it.'

'Fine.'

Elliot watched Siyal go. 'How do we release these?'

Thorburn sucked in a deep breath. 'In, then out, then in again.'

'Sounds like rubbish to me...' Elliot set about working at his wrist.

Thorburn looked at Marshall. 'Robert, it's all a lie. I swear I'm innocent.'

Marshall walked over to him. 'I know you're not.' He leaned over him. 'I know you killed Anna.'

'Anna? What?'

'Don't play that game with me.' Marshall pulled him up to his feet. 'This isn't your first rodeo, is it? After our father upped and left, you moved in on Mum. Young single mother. Two kids. Boy, girl. You were grooming Jen, weren't you? But she was too close, so you homed in on Anna. Her friend. My girlfriend. You kidnapped her. She got away and ran, but you found her and you killed her.' Marshall could barely hear his own words.

'That wasn't me!'

'I know it was you. We've got the document.'

'What document.'

'Derek Cameron kept a copy.'

'What? How?'

'Don't play games with me!'

Elliot stood up, scowling. 'That trick worked.'

Marshall snapped a cuff on Thorburn's wrist. He wasn't getting anywhere now.

Thorburn lashed forward and smashed his skull into Marshall's forehead.

A flower of pain exploded in the middle of his nose.

Hands grabbed his shirt, pushing his chest back.

He stumbled, then landed on someone.

Something metal clattered to the floor.

He could only watch as Thorburn picked up Thea's knife and plunged it into Elliot's stomach.

She gasped. A deep cut, too deep for the pain to register.

Thorburn tripped her and she fell back onto the floor. Then he cut across the nave and disappeared through a door.

Marshall was kneeling now. Couldn't breathe. He stood up.

Elliot lay on the floor, blood spilling out of her abdomen.

He had to get him. Had to stop him getting away.

But he couldn't leave her like that.

She coughed hard. She stared at him. 'Go! Get him!'

'Andrea, he stabbed you—'

'I'll be fine! Don't let him get away.'

Marshall looked back at Craig over by the door. 'Get an ambulance! Stay with her!' He grabbed his baton, then ran through the side door into a small anteroom.

Two doors and a spiral staircase leading up.

One was wide open. Would've been the minister's office from when this place was a church. Empty, just an old boiler in the corner.

The other door was locked. Bigger and heavier, probably led outside.

How had Thorburn got out and locked it?

A creak came from up the staircase.

Marshall stopped dead, stopped breathing. He listened hard, through the darkness.

Faint steps. Bare feet on wooden boards. Another creak.

Thorburn hadn't got out.

Marshall followed him up the stairs, one at a time, snapping out his baton as he went. He rounded the second turning, his breath coming harder and harder, tried swallowing it, catching it.

All that scaffolding outside...

Thorburn could climb down. He could get away.

Marshall staggered, drowning under the weight of dizziness from the head butt.

Heavy breathing like his lungs couldn't replenish.

He got up to the final spiral.

Giant bells hung up there. Two stained glass windows opposite each other, looking across the town. One had a door next to it.

Thorburn had to be out there. Just had to be.

Marshall took it slow, each step as heavy as his breathing. Fire burnt up his legs, up his spine. He pushed through the door out onto a stone platform, lined with a low wall. The church spire still towered above his head, wrapped in sheeting, though he was now a long way from the ground. The wind blew right through him, making his coat flap.

Sure enough, Thorburn was clambering over the wall onto the scaffolding, already half over.

Marshall took a swing at him. Caught his arse. The jolt reverberated up his arm.

Thorburn tumbled over the wall.

Marshall leaned over.

Thorburn lay on scaffolding boards on his back, wheezing hard. He rolled over and got up onto all fours, then grabbed the ladder leading down.

Marshall vaulted over the wall and landed with a crunch.

Thorburn spotted him and backed up against the wall. 'I'll jump!'

'Suit yourself.' Marshall lowered his baton. 'Jump.' He waved down at the building site below. Stacks of bricks and timber covered in flapping sheeting. 'One less raping, murdering scumbag is fine by me.'

No way was Thorburn going to jump. He was just going to try and wheedle his way out of things. Like he always did.

'You're better than I expected, Robert.'

'Not good enough to spot you earlier. Like in London. Can't believe I got you to help me.' Marshall stepped forward, inching closer to him. 'Do you feel guilty for what you did to Anna?'

Thorburn shook his head. 'Robert... I'm...'

Marshall gripped the baton tight. So easy just to lash out, let the metal clonk off his skull, send him flying to his death. Or better, to a broken back and his remaining life spent in misery.

'Kill me, Robert.' The cuff dangled from his wrist, the other side still open.

'No. Kill yourself.'

'I can't, Robert. Please. It's just your word against mine. They'll believe I killed myself.'

So fucking easy to comply.

Just one gentle push.

Then it'd be all over.

Anna could rest in peace.

Marshall could.

But Marshall lowered the baton. 'If you're going to jump, jump. Don't bring me into it.'

Thorburn turned around and took one tentative step towards the edge, looking down at the ground. 'Robert, I don't know what to say.'

'You've fucked up my life. Killed my girlfriend. Killed all

those women. You fucked up the investigation. You deserve to die.'

'I can't kill myself, you'll have to—'

Marshall swept the baton around Thorburn's throat.

He could do it.

Right now.

Push him.

Send him flying down to the ground.

Make sure he didn't spin so he landed headfirst, so his spine shot through his brain. So he died.

He *should* do it.

End his life.

End all the misery.

Make up for all the trauma he'd inflicted on so many people.

To finally pay for what he'd done to Anna.

It would be so easy.

Just push him, send him flying to the ground. Kill him. For all he'd done. He deserved it. All of it for this.

Marshall jerked him back away from the edge and leaned against the wall.

Choking him.

Kill him. Stop him breathing.

CHAPTER SIXTY-TWO

Marshall shouldn't have had that coffee earlier. He was exhausted, physically and mentally, but he couldn't sleep. And he really needed to. He sat there, eyes shut, but his brain was still on full power, whirring through everything.

Maybe it wasn't the coffee that did it.

Could have something to do with finding out who'd been responsible for what happened to Anna.

When he'd opened up to Kirsten about it, he'd felt so exposed. Laying everything bare like that was a difficult thing.

But if he hadn't, she wouldn't have known, wouldn't have been able to connect the dots when she saw the answer to the biggest question of his life.

To the proof of it.

The lie that had tormented him for almost twenty years. Over half his life.

He clicked the loose handcuff onto the scaffolding.

'What? You're arresting me?'

Marshall shook his head. 'Stopping myself from pushing you over the edge myself.'

He opened his eyes to the dim glow of the hospital's after-hours half-life.

Should have pushed him.

Should have made him pay.

Dark outside the windows, but blue crested the hills – it was starting to get light even this early. Rain thudded off the glass, streaking down it like snakes racing to the sill.

A cleaner tried to tame his giant machine, tried to guide it around the corner, but it was a tough one to get around.

Mum walked past it, clutching two beige plastic cups, then squelched over to him. 'Robert, I got you a hot chocolate.'

'Thanks.' Marshall took it from her with a genuine smile. 'How are you holding up?'

She didn't sit, instead walking around like she'd been plugged into the mains rather than running on batteries. She sipped her coffee and gave a little gasp. 'I don't know, Robert. I don't know what to do with myself.'

'I'm not sure a coffee will calm your nerves.'

'No, but it'll make the time pass quicker.' She sat in the chair next to him, toes planted on the floor, right leg jigging up and down. 'I don't know how I can live with myself. I let a monster into her life...'

'It's not just Thea. You let him into mine and Jen's life a long time ago.'

'Aye, but...' She leaned forward and became still for once. 'I'm so sorry, Robert. For what he did.'

Marshall looked away, tears blooming. 'Did Thea ever speak to you about him?'

'What? No. Why?'

'Just wondered.'

'Come on, son. I know when you're lying.'

He brushed at his cheeks, then looked around at her. 'After we found her, she told me she had a suspicion about him. She was going to talk to you or Jen about it, but I don't think she got around to it. But the reason she met him there, in that church, was that she... she'd found all these video files on his old laptop.'

Mum's turn to look away. Feet dancing. 'Should never have insisted he give her that infernal machine.'

'Be thankful you did. Now we've got two sources of evidence for his involvement. Graham's going to spend a lot of time behind bars. The rest of his life.'

'And the next one.' Mum slurped coffee. 'Thea's the one good thing I've got in my life just now, Robert. She's been a godsend to me. I've been so lonely and she's filled the time.'

'I'm sure she's grateful to spend the time with you.'

Mum laughed. 'Oh, she must think I'm a right cow.' Her look darkened. 'Robert, I am sorry – truly sorry – for what happened to Anna. I had no idea.'

He looked right at her, into her soul. Saw the truth, that she was as much of a victim as anyone. He nodded. 'I know, Mum. Nobody knew. Her diary... Jen and I thought it was Anna's dad...' He swallowed down a bitter taste. 'He didn't take her. He'd abused her when she was younger. We just assumed it was him who took her. Everyone thought he was a child killer. He'd been abusing her, he just...'

'Listen, Anna was a troubled girl. Whatever happened to her, she wasn't right.'

'Wasn't *right*?'

'I know you thought you loved her, Robert, but she was difficult.'

'How can you say that?'

She pinched her nose. 'I'm not being clear.' She let go and exhaled slowly. 'What I'm trying to say is it could be both things are right. I think she had been abused by him. All the signs were there.'

Marshall nodded, but it didn't give him any consolation.

'Okay...' Jen squeaked out into the hallway and tore at her gloves, getting them off with a loud snap. Her gaze shot between them. 'Got one for me?'

Marshall held up his hot chocolate. 'You can have this, if you want.'

'Have you spat in it?'

'Charming. Haven't even touched it.'

'Thanks.' Jen took it and sniffed at it. 'Budge up.' She wedged in between them. 'The good news is Thea's going to be fine. More therapy than anything and she's a tough kid.'

'Well.' Mum stood up again. 'I'm going to spend a penny.' She rested her cup on the table and scurried off down the hallway.

Jen watched her go, a long sigh escaping her lips, then looked at her brother, over the lip of the cup. 'Thank you, Rob. You stopped Thea from... Well...'

He took her hand in his. 'It's okay.'

'No, it's not. This is fucked up. Totally fucked up. I feel guilty as hell.'

'You? Why?'

'Thea didn't tell anyone about Wendy. She tried to go it alone. She was lucky.'

He could tell her about the warning, but beating herself up wasn't going to get her anywhere.

Marshall wrapped his arm around her shoulder. 'Jen, I've had to learn that whatever happened, happened. Nothing I can do will change the past. I can only change the future by controlling the present as I walk through it. That's it. The pain of the past, of what happened to Anna, of all that... It's in the past. I can't stop her dying, I can't stop whatever she went through. But I can do stuff in the here and now. I got Wendy back alive. And Thea... I made sure she didn't kill him.'

'You didn't kill him, either.'

'No, exactly. I could've done. Easily. *Should've* done, maybe. He deserved it. But I didn't because I've learnt from the past. Graham Thorburn needs to pay for what he's done to people. Anna probably wasn't the first and Wendy won't be the last he tried it on. But there are at least eleven dead women whose families can start to recover from their ordeal. Or at least know they've got the answers to what happened. That knowledge can let them begin healing. And they know it can't happen again to anyone else.'

Jen slumped back, bashing her head against the wall. She took a sip of hot chocolate. 'You can see her, you know?'

'Thea?'

'No, you daft sausage. Andrea. She's just in there.'

'Right. Okay.' Marshall stood up but his legs were like someone had stuck pins all the way up. And sent them to sleep. Took a few strides before he got any feeling below his waist. He stopped outside the room and looked in.

Elliot lay on her bed, eyes wide open. A saline drip in her arm, wires from electrodes all over her. She looked up at him with bloodshot eyes. 'Marshall. Hey. How are you?' She smiled the smile of someone who'd just had a shitload of morphine.

He shrugged. 'I'm okay. Had better, anyway.'

'Tell me about it.' She tried to shift forward, but stopped. Took a deep breath, grunted, then twisted her head to the side. 'Word of advice. Never get stabbed, especially not there.'

'Heard the surgery was a success?'

'Right, aye. Doc says I'll have another big scar down there. As if my caesarean wasn't sexy enough.'

'Scars add character.'

She laughed, but her wince showed it was painful.

'Sorry, I'll try to be less funny.'

'You're not funny in the slightest.' She was smiling, though. 'Thank you for—' She coughed. 'Thank you for catching him. You're probably the only cop on the force who wouldn't have pushed him off that church.'

'I came close to it.' Marshall took the seat next to her. 'Listen, I wanted to thank you for encouraging me to go after him. After last time, I would've stayed with you. Made sure you were okay.'

'But you wouldn't have caught him. I was fine. Siyal drove me here, bless his socks.'

'You should be less hard on him. He's a good guy.'

'He's just not a cop.'

'Let's see how that pans out. But thank you, Andrea. You helped me make the right decision.'

'You might be a smug dick, Marshall, but you're my kind of smug dick. It's been good working with you.'

He looked away from her. 'And you.'

'What's your plan now?'

Marshall exhaled slowly. 'Got leave until Monday, so I'll lurk around here, making sure Thea's okay. Help Jen. Mum. Whole lot of stuff. Then I'll drive back to London on Sunday. Hopefully I'll still be recognised by my cat.'

'You have a cat?'

'Big boy called Zlatan. Does that surprise you?'

'Actually, no. Cats are sneaky buggers too. Just like you.'

Marshall got up and yawned. 'It's nice to see you're okay.'

'I'm pretty far from okay, Marshall, but I'm not dead.'

CHAPTER SIXTY-THREE

Yesterday's freak weather was now a distant memory. Marshall stood in glorious sunshine. Wairds Cemetery was a long strip of manicured grass on the lower slopes of the Eildons. Above, some mature trees dotted the lush fields climbing the trio of conjoined hills.

Time had weathered the sharp granite edges, but the etched writing was still as clear as the day it had been carved.

Here lies
Anna Jane Kelso
1986-2003
Much loved, much missed
Taken too soon

Taken way too fucking soon.

Marshall crouched and brushed away the bouquet of perfumed flowers to see the photo of her set onto the grave-stone. A shot he'd taken on his first digital camera. A hike up the hills nearby on a day like this, and they didn't reach any of the tops. He'd lost almost twenty years of days like that, had it snatched away from him.

Shit, how arrogant was that?

They might've broken up a week later. Uni would've been tough, her at Glasgow and him at Durham.

But he'd give anything to have her alive.

His own life, if necessary.

She deserved to have those missing years back, to live her life.

The last few hours of her life, when she'd been at Graham Thorburn's mercy, he couldn't begin to imagine how much she'd suffered. The rush of hope at escaping, dashed by her death falling from the viaduct.

Deemed suicide, but now he knew the truth.

Murder.

He looked north but couldn't quite see Leaderfoot Viaduct from up here.

Still, Thorburn had known precisely what he was doing. He had killed Cameron right here to get Marshall on the case. Probably thought he could keep an eye on him, get some insight into the investigation. Get some more leaks, overtly or inadvertently.

It all made sense.

Apart from why he'd taken Anna from him.

Thorburn was a monster with no feelings. A psychopath, dead to any emotions but his own needs. Everyone was a pawn to him, a bit-part player in the story of his life.

To be manipulated.

Exploited.

Used.

Killed.

He'd got away with it so many times. Marshall didn't know

how many, but Kirsten would have as good an idea as anyone now.

He took one last look at the grave and just let it all go. The tears flowed down his cheeks and, for once, he just let them come. Let them slide down, dropping onto the grass.

Jen wrapped her arm around him and leaned in. 'Hey, hey, it's okay.'

He hugged her tight, drinking in her strong perfume. Smelled like the sea, somewhere exotic. 'No. It's not. It's not okay.'

'No, but you've put her ghost to rest, Rob. If there's any part of her soul or spirit still around, it's at peace now.'

Despite the hippy crystal slant to her words, she was right. If she'd suffered in the afterlife because of what happened, then she wasn't suffering anymore. She was ready to move on.

'I'm angry at myself, Jen. I wasn't there for her when she needed me most.'

'You're the one who was talking about whatever happens, happens.'

'Aye, doesn't make this any easier.'

'You should focus on the fact that she has justice for what happened to her.'

Anna's mother stood next to them, dabbing her cheeks with a tissue. She looked up from the gravestone towards Marshall, her cheek flickering and pulsing. 'I heard you were here.'

Marshall didn't care about how. 'I'm so sorry, Mrs Kelso, I don't know—'

She reached in for a big hug and clung on to him.

Marshall held her there for a long time. No words passed between them, but he felt a closure to it all.

This was her forgiving him for accusing her husband.

This was her thanking him for catching her daughter's killer.

She broke off then knelt in front of her daughter's grave. 'I'm so sorry this happened to you, my love. I'm so sorry.'

Marshall walked away from her, giving her peace and space. He looked at his sister, following him. 'I was thinking I should go and see Mum.'

'Thea wants to see you. She wants to spend time with her favourite uncle.'

'Only uncle.' He sighed. 'Okay, let's go and see that niece of mine.' He took her hand and led her back to his car.

He opened his door and felt lighter than he had done in years.

Jen got in and he took in the view, across the Tweed and Leader valleys to the rolling hills beyond, lush and green. Hardly any houses. Hardly any people.

Aye, it wasn't a bad place to live.

His phone chimed with a text message.

Kirsten:

You've forgotten something.

CHAPTER SIXTY-FOUR

Marshall found Kirsten in the forensics office. 'Hey, got your message.'

She wouldn't look at him, instead focusing on the machine she was attending to. 'Oh. Hey there.'

'What have I forgotten?'

'The rest of that bottle of wine.'

'Oh. Right.' Marshall collapsed into the chair next to her. 'That's your present.'

'And I liked sharing it with you.' She looked over at him with a piercing stare. 'When are you going back to London?'

'Sunday. Mum's not in a great way. Thea too. My family needs me.'

'The offer's there.'

'Might be a forty quid bottle, but I don't think that means it'll last any longer. Especially in this heat.'

'Oh.' She looked back at her machine.

'Kirsten, I'm bad news. I think I like you or might like to get to know you. But... Me and relationships don't get on.'

'It's twenty years since you tried.'

'With good reason.'

'Rob, if you want my opinion... You spend too much time in your own head, trying to figure out what's going on inside other people's without inviting anyone else into your life.'

'Pretty much. Trust me, it's better that way. Just me and my cat. In a flat in London.'

'Okay. That's pretty unequivocal.'

'Come on, Kirsten. You can do a lot better than me.'

'A man who opens up about his feelings, who admits to his traumas, who tells the truth all the time? Hard to beat that.'

'I...' Marshall felt the thickness in the back of his throat. 'Long-distance relationships can be difficult, right?'

She looked over at him. 'It's okay. Forget I said anything.'

'Kirsten, it's not that—'

'Inspector.'

Marshall twisted around.

Pringle was in the doorway, arms folded. 'Little birdie or two told me you'd be here. Got a minute?'

Kirsten barged past and left them.

Marshall stood up. 'What's up, sir?'

Pringle whistled, hands in pockets. 'You doing okay, champ?'

'No, sir, I've just visited my dead girlfriend's grave and...' And really blew it with Kirsten. 'What do you think?'

'I deserved that.' Pringle winced. 'If you want to know what I think, then I believe you're finally beginning to process a lot of the trauma you've been through over the last twenty years. Coming to terms with what happened back then will mean you're ready to move on with your life.'

Marshall couldn't even look at him. 'That's a lot of supposition.'

'I know it sounds a lot. But I know a thing or two about

grief. How it eats away at you. Corrodes you. Does funny things to your thoughts. Like to your pal.'

Marshall looked around at him. 'John Hulse?'

Pringle nodded.

'He's no friend of mine. A lot of this pain could've been avoided if he'd just talked to me.'

'Very true.'

'Is he still here?'

'After a long interrogation consisting mostly of grunts and "Didn't fucking do anything. Told you I'm innocent." I had to let him go.'

'Why?'

'Not against the law to conduct an investigation yourself, is it?'

'No, but...' Marshall swallowed. He just wanted to speak to him. Maybe he should visit on his way back south.

'You saved your niece from doing a very bad thing. Thea won't face charges for any of it. Graham Thorburn will.'

Marshall stared hard at him. 'Just do me one favour and put him away.'

'We will do our best. The evidence is stacking up nicely against him. No matter who he brings in to defend him, we've got him.'

'Thank you, sir.'

Pringle didn't seem to be at any risk of shifting his arse from that doorway anytime soon. 'I gather you're on the way out?'

'Rickards told you?'

'Yes, she did. Yes she did, did, did. And we had a little—' Pringle whistled. 'Put our heads together with a crack and... Would you like to stay here?'

Marshall frowned. 'Excuse me?'

'How's about it, darling? You and me. You a DI in Police

Scotland. Me your boss. Be part of the MIT, like myself and DI Elliot. Way I can sell it to—' He whistled and pointed at the sky. '—them upstairs is that you'll be a strategic asset. Criminal profiling across the East division. West and North too, if we need it.'

Marshall scanned his eyes for any sign of a wind-up, but couldn't see any. 'Is this on the level?'

'The big bad wolf signed off the budget this morning.'

Christ, this was a big thing. Staying on as a cop. Working up here, back home, doing what he wanted to do all along.

It'd let him see what was between him and Kirsten.

How could Marshall say no?

AFTERWORD

Thank you for reading this book.

It means a lot to me to be able to write and publish book one in a new series. I could bore you with some "inside baseball" stuff about book publishing, but a series is usually as strong as its first book. I think I've spent a few years writing what I think are good books but they're fifth, ninth or fourteenth in a series, so it becomes law of diminishing returns. This book is the culmination of almost nine years of writing full time and I thank you all for the support in letting me live out that dream.

As for Mr Marshall, well he'll be back in a few months in WHERE THE BODIES LIE. As I write this, I'm about halfway through it and I'm really enjoying where I'm taking the characters – I hope you enjoy it when it comes. I have current plans for another two in the series and then we'll see what I do after that.

As ever, massive thanks to James Mackay for the editing work at outline stage and after the first draft, it fixed a lot of howlers, especially around Rob's backstory.

As usual, huge thanks to John Rickards for his copy editing, one day I'll remember some of the things you point out in comments. And last but not least to Mare Bate for proofing it. If you notice any errors, which are all my fault, then please email ed@edjames.co.uk and I'll fix them.

If you could leave a review on Amazon, that'd be a huge help, cheers.

Finally, if you sign up to my mailing list (link at the end) you'll get a free ebook prequel to this, called FALSE START, starring not Rob but Shunty, AKA DS Rakesh Siyal. A whole short novel devoted to him, covering how he earned that nickname. I'm really pleased with how it's been received and have big plans for him. Let me know how you get on with this or that book.

https://geni.us/EJM1FS

Cheers,

Ed James

Scottish Borders, December 2022

ABOUT THE AUTHOR

Ed James writes crime-fiction novels, primarily the DI Simon Fenchurch series, set on the gritty streets of East London featuring a detective with little to lose. His Scott Cullen series features a young Edinburgh detective constable investigating crimes from the bottom rung of the career ladder he's desperate to climb.

Formerly an IT project manager, Ed began writing on planes, trains and automobiles to fill his weekly commute to London. He now writes full-time and lives in the Scottish Borders, with his girlfriend and a menagerie of rescued animals.

If you would like to be kept up to date with new releases from Ed James, please join the Ed James Readers Club.

Connect with Ed online:

Amazon Author page

Website

facebook.com/edjamesauthor

twitter.com/edjamesauthor

instagram.com/edjamesauthor

OTHER BOOKS BY ED JAMES

DI ROB MARSHALL SCOTT BORDERS MYSTERIES

Ed's first new police procedural series in six years, focusing on DI Rob Marshall, a criminal profiler turned detective. London-based, an old case brings him back home to the Scottish Borders and the dark past he fled as a teenager.

1. THE TURNING OF OUR BONES
2. WHERE THE BODIES LIE (May 2023)

Also available is FALSE START, a prequel novella starring DS Rakesh Siyal, is available for **free** to subscribers of Ed's newsletter or on Amazon. Sign up at https://geni.us/EJM1FS

SCOTT CULLEN MYSTERIES

Eight novels featuring a detective eager to climb the career ladder, covering Edinburgh and its surrounding counties, and further across Scotland.

1. GHOST IN THE MACHINE
2. DEVIL IN THE DETAIL
3. FIRE IN THE BLOOD
4. STAB IN THE DARK
5. COPS & ROBBERS
6. LIARS & THIEVES
7. COWBOYS & INDIANS
8. HEROES & VILLAINS

CULLEN & BAIN SERIES

Six novellas spinning off from the main Cullen series covering the events of the global pandemic in 2020.

1. CITY OF THE DEAD
2. WORLD'S END
3. HELL'S KITCHEN
4. GORE GLEN
5. DEAD IN THE WATER
6. THE LAST DROP

CRAIG HUNTER SERIES

A spin-off series from the Cullen series, with Hunter first featuring in the fifth book, starring an ex-squaddie cop struggling with PTSD, investigating crimes in Scotland and further afield.

1. MISSING
2. HUNTED
3. THE BLACK ISLE

DS VICKY DODDS SERIES

Gritty crime novels set in Dundee and Tayside, featuring a DS juggling being a cop and a single mother.

1. BLOOD & GUTS
2. TOOTH & CLAW
3. FLESH & BLOOD
4. SKIN & BONE
5. GUILT TRIP

DI SIMON FENCHURCH SERIES

Set in East London, will Fenchurch ever find what happened to his daughter, missing for the last ten years?

1. THE HOPE THAT KILLS
2. WORTH KILLING FOR
3. WHAT DOESN'T KILL YOU
4. IN FOR THE KILL
5. KILL WITH KINDNESS
6. KILL THE MESSENGER
7. DEAD MAN'S SHOES
8. A HILL TO DIE ON
9. THE LAST THING TO DIE

Other Books

Other crime novels, with Lost Cause set in Scotland and Senseless set in southern England, and the other three set in Seattle, Washington.

- LOST CAUSE
- SENSELESS
- TELL ME LIES
- GONE IN SECONDS
- BEFORE SHE WAKES

MARSHALL WILL RETURN IN

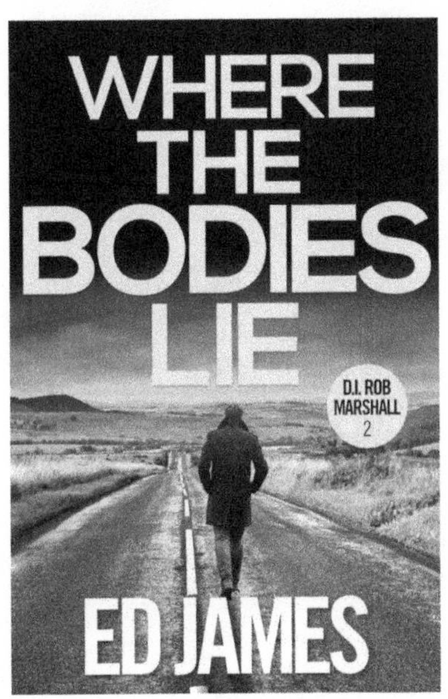

Where the Bodies Lie

1st May 2023

Preorder now:

https://geni.us/EJM02

ED JAMES READERS CLUB

Available now for members of my Readers Club is FALSE START, a prequel ebook to my first new series in six years.

Sign up for FREE and get access to exclusive content and keep up-to-speed with all of my releases on a monthly basis.

https://geni.us/EJM1FS